A WHITE LACE

A TAINTED TINSELTOWN BOOK

MILENA MCKAY

Copyright © 2022 by Milena McKay

This is a work of fiction.

Any similarities with real life events are coincidental and unintentional.

All rights reserved.

No part of this book may be reproduced in any form or by any electronic or mechanical means, including information storage and retrieval systems, without written permission from the author, except for the use of brief quotations in a book review.

For permission, contact mckay.undercover@gmail.com

Cover and art design by Em @onewritergirl

PRAISE FOR "THE HEADMISTRESS"

This is a book you're going to want to have on your bookshelf, both digital and physical, and read again and again for many years. I know I will.

— JUDE SILBERFELD, WWW. JUDEINTHESTARS.COM

The writing is gorgeous. It's lush and descriptive on an emotional level. I highlighted so many passages simply because I enjoyed rereading them to savor each word. McKay executes fantastic world building in The Headmistress turning Three Dragons Academy into a character as important as Sam and Magdalene.

— VICTORIA THOMAS, WWW. THELESBIANREVIEW.COM

If you are looking for an exquisitely written book with beautiful metaphors, well-fleshed characters, a little action/intrigue, and a beautiful romance, look no further. The Headmistress is one of a kind.

— GABY MAURINO, WWW. LEZREVIEWBOOKS.COM

*To those who take the first step,
and to the therapists who hold their hands on this long journey...*

"You may not control all the events that happen to you, but you can decide not to be reduced by them."

— MAYA ANGELOU

PART I
WHISPER

Whisper

part 1

1

NEVE'S SILENCE AND EMPTY SPACES

"*I*'ve been fucking my studio's spokesperson for the past four months. I cannot seem to quit her. I'm here for you to make sure I do."

She had strolled into this session with a well-formed plan of how things would go. Having done her research, she did not expect her words to shock the sphinx-like therapist. And yet, while the silver-haired woman with more letters after her name than the alphabet contained, did not blink an eye, the gold-tipped fountain pen in her hand stopped its movement. Good. Professional, but there was a tell that what she'd heard gave her pause.

It boded well for Neve Blackthorne, who, in turn, gave nothing away. Instead, she sat down in a comfortable chair opposite the older woman and thought that the sole shock-and-awe of her appearance, not to mention the trademark low, quiet timbre of her voice, always accomplished their desired effect.

Neve had selected Helena Moore after thorough research of the top Los Angeles psychologists. A search she had, for once, not delegated to her trusted assistant. Barnaby would have asked questions, but even if he would not have dared–out of self-preservation if nothing else–he would have still wondered. And needing a shrink meant showing weakness. Barnaby wouldn't judge her–he was enraptured by her–but all the people standing in line with bated breath, waiting for her to slip up, detesting her very existence, surely would.

Neve knew she was easy to hate. Many did, in fact. She had money, she had connections, but most importantly, she had the kind of power that made or broke not just individuals, but entire companies. And she did all of that. Routinely, in fact. She was ruthless and her armor knew no chinks. Neve flicked a tiny piece of lint off her pencil skirt and crossed her legs. The most powerful woman, nay person, in the movie industry did not show weakness. If she did, the sharks would come circling right away.

So Neve had taken up the search herself. And all the roads had led to this distinguished, hardly perturbable woman who was now regarding her out of watery, gray eyes. Perhaps they'd once been a lively charcoal. If charcoal was even ever lively.

Neve bit the inside of her cheek, centering herself. She was rambling inside her own head. No matter how much of a show she was putting on, the sheer idea of being here, of talking about things she kept secret, this whole wretched situation she found herself in, was appalling. Her skin crawled, goosebumps running up and down her arms from the utter invasion of privacy she was about to embark upon. And all these thoughts running wild, seemingly unstoppable, were shaking her focus.

Helena Moore tapped the Montblanc against her notepad. Despite her earlier surprise at Neve's opening salvo, her face seemed to have lost some of its trepidation.

"I am not an addiction specialist, and you speak about her as if she was..." The soothing voice did nothing to actually calm Neve's frayed nerves. She knew her face did not show her disquiet. Years of practice to not give an inch in this high-stakes game of poker that was her life had taught her as much. Neve deliberately uncrossed her legs. The fact that this woman still saw enough to make such a pinpoint assertion grated on her.

"As if she was a drug. She is." The truth behind the words sent a chill down her spine. Her words were quiet, and she permeated their usual cadence with impatience to avoid this very line of inquiry. Or was it to hide the pool of dread in her stomach? No, that was absolutely not it. Neve dismissed the thought right away.

The reason why she was here was no longer important. It was how to move forward—to escape this vicious cycle she rode—that was paramount.

Yet Dr. Moore seemed hellbent on thwarting her with useless questions. Neve waved a hand, effectively ending this particular avenue of conversation. "None of it matters. I have chosen you." She allowed cutting coldness to dominate her voice and smiled. A sharp, lethal smile, showing fangs. If she was to have to drag herself through shards of broken glass, she would do her best to scare the living daylights out of this unflappable woman in the process. At least something to look forward to as she flayed herself alive. Or 'opened up', as the therapist would surely call it. Neve almost sneered at the ridiculous concept.

This time, the highly esteemed and world-renowned Dr. Moore did blink, and then, drawing a deep breath, she set her notebook aside, steepling her hands to either give herself time to recover from essentially being put in a very uncomfortable place, or to simply regroup. Neve didn't care about the good doctor's feelings. She was here to rid herself of this horrendous, unexplainable weakness and to move forward. If it gave this woman pause, or if it disgusted her, Neve cared very little.

As time dragged and silence reigned, Neve observed the steepled hands. They bore the signs of age, but also showed a tremendous, likely decades-long level of care from what she guessed were high-class manicurists and expensive moisturizers. Graceful, attractive, capable hands. Like Audrey's. Except Audrey's were only twenty-eight years old and bore neither the signs of age, nor of expensive care. Yet they were beautiful. Neve swallowed.

A discreet cough of the owner of the older pair of hands penetrated her daydreaming, embarrassing her at being caught. Dr. Moore gave her a long, assessing look and seemed to have come to a decision of sorts. "Tell me about her then, this drug of yours."

Neve smiled again, and she knew it looked fake. It was the kind of expression you'd paint on when you were backed into a corner and tried to put a pretty face on a difficult situation. But it was also the smile of a chess player who understood she had met a worthy adversary for the first time in a long time. Helena Moore would be an unpalatable experience, simply by virtue of what she was—a therapist Neve was forcing herself to see—but she would also prove a challenge. And Neve Blackthorne never once shrunk from those.

"As I said before," she replied as she ran her thumbs over her fingernails, feigning supreme interest in her own immaculate manicure. "She is a spokesperson for the studio. My Vice President of Communication's protégée, in fact. He calls her 'the brightest new star on the scene.'"

Dr. Moore's gray eyes were sharp and knowing. "And what would you call her?"

Danger, punishment, penance. Pleasure, temptation, escape. Neve had many choice appellations for one Audrey Clare Avens. Yet she stilled her heart, looked Dr. Moore straight in those knowing eyes, and lied.

"I don't call her anything at all."

They were going to get caught, Neve thought as she panted her orgasm through her clenched teeth, back pressed hard against the door of her ground floor office. They were going to get caught, and it would be a disaster. The Wicked Queen of Tinseltown, the CEO of Gannon McMillan Pictures, one of the Big Six studios in Hollywood and hence the world, was going to be found with her tongue down her Junior Communications Executive's throat, with skilled fingers–the same ones Neve could not help but think about during her earlier session with the therapist–three knuckles deep inside her, and that maddening thumb rubbing circles over her clit.

They were going to get caught, and it would all be her own doing. Because it simply wasn't enough for her. Nothing was when it came to Audrey Avens. Audrey Avens who had fucked her in the executive bathroom just this morning and who looked so deeply irresistible, Neve had orchestrated this complete sham of, 'I am going home with a migraine and someone please deliver this speech to me, because I have to be at this useless event that I, for some reason, simply cannot miss. Oh, and bring it over ASAP, meaning you Gustavo can't do it since you're otherwise engaged, and let me send Barnaby on a fake assignment to Anaheim, which may as well be the Yukon in this traffic.'

So of course, Audrey, who could read her and her whims like an open book, volunteered to drop off the papers, hence here they both were, Neve with her head thrown back, breath coming in the long exhalations of someone who'd just survived a near heart attack, and Audrey studying her with that possessive gleam an artist usually gives a well-made creation. Well, she did this to Neve, left her breathless and shaking and disheveled, and still so hungry for more.

The knowing expression did not falter when Neve met it head-on with her less than steady gaze. How many people looked her in the eyes these days? Gustavo? On occasion. Morag? Her stylist knew better. In fact, absolutely everyone in Hollywood knew better. You never looked Neve Blackthorne in the eye. And yes, she had cultivated the affectation herself. After all, one never stared directly at a cobra either.

And yet, here was this twenty-something girl who went to battle with Neve and for Neve every day and never once wavered, never once cowered before her. Like an equal. Utterly fearless. Or utterly foolish. Maybe both. Even now she looked at Neve with an expression of sly fondness, even a little triumph, and just as Neve was about to say something, Audrey slowly licked her fingers, one by one pulling them between those delectable lips, and all thoughts simply vanished from Neve's mind.

"I'll take a shower before I go. Gustavo and his hound nose are bound to smell you on me, and where would that lead us?"

And then, like she hadn't rocked Neve's world in more ways than one in the past five minutes, Audrey gave her a lingering wet kiss, making sure Neve tasted herself, her own ruin. One more touch of lips and Audrey was gone from the room. The taste of ruination lingered.

Neve had come very close to said destruction several times in her life. Her divorce had been bad. It was public and humiliating, and Neve had felt like a complete failure. Despite everything, she had once been fond of that good-for-nothing cheater who'd thrown her over for a younger model. Having affection for him had not been enough, and she'd been unable to give him anything else, no matter how hard she'd made herself try. And so he'd done something that, in her eyes, was both anathema and the greatest of insults. He'd left.

Armand Melgren was a French-American millionaire from a distinguished family whose lineage and stock portfolio were unimpeachable. He was well read, well traveled, and well versed in the art of playing the games rich and famous people played.

And unlike with most people, Neve could stand spending time with him, both vertically, at various parties and professional outings they were obligated to attend, and occasionally horizontally, on their California King bed, where she was just as happy to lose sight of him as she was to have him reach for her. It was a high testament to how well she had taught herself to tolerate him.

If there was one thing Neve Blackthorne had learned early,

it was that if it's not so bad, if you could stand it, no matter what *it* actually was, then you could successfully power through. If you could just endure it.

Life wasn't meant to be roses. It was mostly thorns. And so, with Armand, she had never expected overwhelming happiness and instead settled for quiet, inauspicious contentment. Boring dinners and boring sex. Boring togetherness amidst long periods of living their own busy, fulfilling lives as high-powered executives. She'd silently and gratefully tolerated that.

Apparently Armand could not. And in the process of being caught by the ever-hungry-for-a-scandal paparazzi–with his pants down on top of his secretary–he'd made a spectacle of Neve.

Unsurprisingly, the media and the world had taken his side. She was too cold. Too distant. Too unlikeable. All his former girlfriends were on DMZ TV with gossip about their relationship and how Armand was an angel incarnate, and that surely Neve had driven him to cheat. He even believed as much himself.

"If you would've been as enthusiastic about sex with me as you are about corporate takeovers or the new movie rights you seem to acquire like handbags these days, maybe I wouldn't need someone else to sleep with me!"

Neve had chosen not to rise to the bait, which only infuriated both Armand and his media-hungry hordes–or should she say attention *whores*?–even more. Still, it hadn't been so bad. Neve could stand it, and she did.

Very soon her success in rebuilding a floundering movie studio and returning it to the Olympic Pantheon of Hollywood had become the dominant story.

Gannon McMillan Studios' revival took precedence, even over sex scandals, as the old, stuffy Hollywood institution that was on its way out and circling the bankruptcy drain made its grand entrance back into the limelight. New movies filmed, new rights acquired, new stars, new directors, a brand-new executive office. Neve Blackthorne took Hollywood by storm.

With a well-written column here, a strategically placed photograph there, and, of course, the rapturous success of Gannon McMillan, the world had moved on, and she was once again triumphant.

You should have known better. Nothing is ever easy for you. The other shoe will drop.

The voice in her head sounded suspiciously like one from a past she dared not revisit. A past she *could not* stand. A past that she had to hug herself against with chilled and trembling hands as she tried to push it away.

Still, she should have known better. She should have expected that the voice would be right. For the other shoe had dropped.

The protracted custody battle had been worse. It was even more public than the divorce. Fuming and hurt over losing that battle and having to pay through the nose for breaching the terms of their prenup, Armand was speaking to the press at every turn. He was going to have his way and hurt Neve where it mattered most. He was going to take away her child and further embarrass her in the court of public opinion.

And so the monikers, the horrible little stories of her tantrums and irascibility, her demanding nature, and her alleged disregard for labor laws—or any laws when it came to her precious studio—started trickling down to the media. DMZ was having a blast assigning her a new nickname every other day. You name it, she was called it.

The Wicked Queen. The Demon. The Frigid Bitch.

Well, perhaps she warmed up to the first two much more than to the last one.

She had endured that storm as well. After all, it was bearable, because she had hope that in the end, she'd prevail in court, and that allowed her to be able to still stand it all. Barely, but she could. The thought of only having supervised visits once in a blue moon with her precious boy was the first thing in a long time that had made her afraid.

Still, with her toddler by her side, she appeared dignified and stoic, if aloof and indeed cold in all photos. Armand's vindictiveness and dirty tactics ended up costing him. The court disregarded all innuendo and gossip and gave the couple joint physical custody of the minor Harlan Melgren Blackthorne, age four. She also got her son for all the holidays in what she suspected was an attempt by the judge to stick it to her ex-husband for being a smarmy idiot.

However, despite a horrible divorce, an awful custody battle, and countless other scandals and public flagellations of her character, nothing could come close to the potential threat of getting caught having a sordid little affair with a girl twenty years her junior and her subordinate.

"You'll be ruined. Worse than nothing. Finished. Just like I told—"

Her limbs went numb, and she shook her head, attempting to clear it. With difficulty, she rid her thoughts of the memories. They were just that, memories. And everything had happened so long ago, perhaps it was all in her mind? Time had the horrible ability to distort reality.

"Don't tell... Don't tell..."

On the heels of the loud hiss came a whisper, and Neve closed her eyes. *Not real. None of it was real.*

She had to focus because none of her previous brushes with ruin could even attempt to come close to how horrible being caught would be. In fact, it would be the absolute worst thing that could happen to her. It would destroy her. And that she could not stand. For the first time in her 48 years, Neve Blackthorne had reached a level where the things occurring around her and to her were ones she would not be able to survive. And yet, for all her fear, she could not help herself. Drug of choice indeed.

Lost in thought, standing on the back deck of her sprawling Malibu mansion overlooking her private section of beach, Neve missed Audrey coming out of the shower. Over her shoulder, she could see the girl making her way through the debris they'd left strewn around the office, gingerly picking up her clothes. Wrapped in just her towel, Audrey turned her head and caught Neve staring. A warm, adoring, cheeky grin and the towel was dropped. Utterly fearless. Was it a wonder she couldn't help herself?

Neve turned away so sharply, the vertebrae in her neck popped. She didn't know why, only that the moment was becoming too much. Too intimate. Too affectionate. Too hungry. She pretended that she was giving Audrey her privacy to get dressed and not that she was terrified by what was happening between them. The juxtaposition of the two states, hers and Audrey's, did not escape her. Naked and bold, fully dressed and petrified.

A low vibration from Audrey's phone, thrown hastily on the desk, jerked Neve back from her musings. She flinched, and the fear stung her again. Par for the course, her breath became shallow as she listened to every word.

Caught, caught, caught... They would get caught.

But Audrey's voice was calm, nonchalant even, as she answered.

"...no, no, boss, I'll be back in the office in about an hour." Gustavo, Gannon McMillan's Vice President For Communications. Audrey called him that. Ironically, not even on her first day had Audrey referred to Neve as anything remotely similar. Granted, absolutely nobody addressed Neve as anything but Neve, but the point was well made. Gustavo was Audrey's boss, Neve was Gustavo's boss, and everything that was happening here was so completely inappropriate it was horrifying. "Yes, I delivered..." Oh, did Audrey ever deliver. She delivered each and every time.

"Neve? Well, you know what Neve always says. So more of the same..." *Yes, yes, harder, more, more, more...* "I'll see you soon, and we'll talk about the early screenings for Unity. I have questions and I think others will, too."

Neve tuned out the business talk. Neve had never tuned out business talk in her life. Yet, here she was, turning away again and stepping onto the warm sand. Bracketed by two sets of cliffs, the mansion was the only way to access the ocean shore.

As always, the sand beneath her bare feet centered her somewhat. And the continuous whisper of the ocean, its foamy fingers trying to catch her ankles, calmed her. She stood still, inhaling the salty air, the peace of it, the permanence. These were two redeeming qualities this place had held for her–the true scent that only the Pacific Ocean held–and the silence. No, LA was never silent–neither was NY, the city of her past that she cherished above others–but here, on her own slice of beach and facing her own piece of ocean, it was quiet.

She had traveled all over the world, seen and experienced things that other people only dreamed of. She had resigned herself to never really having a home. Splitting her work life between LA, NY, and Europe wasn't conducive to much stability. Neve still remembered the conversation she'd had with Gustavo after she'd bought the Malibu mansion.

"It's beautiful here." He'd sipped his brandy gingerly, savoring both the liquid and the sunset over the ocean. But she knew him too well, and she knew he was hiding behind compliments.

"Say what you mean to say." Her voice was rough even to her own ears.

"Nothing really. With Harlan at boarding school weekdays, this place is... Well, it's a big, empty space, Neve. Just like that penthouse of yours in Manhattan."

He was, at times, with one or two exceptions, her only friend, and so she allowed him the horrible presumptuousness by simply shrugging off his concern or whatever it was he was trying to convey.

"I like empty. And I like this." She had inhaled the ocean scent. The unique blend of salt and wind and all the possibilities.

The scent enveloped her now still, years later, and so did the silence. The mansion was more lived-in, but no less empty. And the ocean still called to her like nothing else. Well, perhaps there was someone else who called to her like the ocean...

And tonight, the two combined. The salt and the wind were infused with the subtle scent of Chanel N°5, a perfume that Audrey favored. On her skin, the tender notes of peach and vanilla came through most prominently, and they were the ones Neve could still sense on her own skin and hands.

"I have to head back, Neve." Audrey's voice managed to sneak up on her, sounding now right next to her shoulder. They were of a height, and it was at once refreshing and disturbing not to be looking up into her partner's eyes. Granted, she did so enjoy looking up at Audrey when she knelt in front of her, and when those eyes unfocused in pleasure.

"Neve?" The voice was gentle, never rising, even in inquiry. Not a single high tone. Not a decibel out of place. Audrey was a fast learner in more things than just how to please The Wicked Queen of Tinseltown.

"I heard you."

Audrey finally came into focus and stood close to Neve, shoulder to shoulder, watching the sunset. Despite an hour-long–if she was lucky–drive back to Gannon, Audrey seemed in no hurry at all.

"Gustavo has thoughts on Unity."

Unity was their grand, new production touching on the

#metoo movement. Neve should care more about this. It was a script she personally appreciated. Hand-selected. Right now, it seemed somehow unimportant, despite being her one big awards contender this season.

"I have mine," Audrey continued. "You know I stay out of the production details, but some issues will complicate the marketing strategy, and this is why I'd like to be in on every single early strategy meeting…"

Smart, thoughtful, brave. Everything Neve had ever wanted. Everything Neve could never have.

"Is there a reason I need to know all this? Are there issues with the strategy I am not aware of?"

Anyone else would cower instantly. A raised eyebrow from Neve was a sure signal of impending doom. Audrey just smiled, a corner of her mouth lifting first before the full dazzling grin revealed itself.

"No issues. Yet. But all things considered, I'd like it to stay that way. And I'd like to consult with Jameson Walker. Her book raised the bar for any #metoo productions. Shame she wasn't brought in as a consultant. Still, I'll take what I can."

Yes, very smart indeed.

"Audrey, if there are no issues, the details do not interest me." But she nodded slightly, because the suggestions were great. Sure, absolutely not Audrey's job, not even close, but a consultation with the leading expert in the field didn't hurt anybody, even if they were doing it for PR's sake.

Audrey extended her hand, and it took all of Neve's strength to neither flinch nor lean into the touch, but the girl simply tucked a strand of Neve's hair behind her ear.

"I'll see you tomorrow for the staff meeting." A kiss on her cheek, as gentle as the voice that said the goodbyes, and the girl was gone, leaving behind just the scent, Chanel N°5 disintegrating into its sweet variables.

"Tomorrow," Neve whispered, so quietly, she wasn't sure

whether she'd said it or wished it. She wanted so much to see Audrey tomorrow and for everything to be as it was tonight. But fear was pulsing strong and heavy in her chest and she knew that tonight was the night when something had to give. Give in, give out, or give up, though, she wasn't entirely certain which.

Somehow in her ruminations about ruin, the past, present, and future, an absolute certain divorce from her current husband hadn't even registered as another casualty of Audrey and her getting caught. But a divorce would absolutely follow.

Hers and Dmitriy's marriage was a business merger. God knew, there were few things worse in mergers than embarrassing dalliances made horribly public. She knew Dmitriy wasn't faithful to her. She did not expect him to be. His affairs were acceptable, since he limited them to high society and kept them quiet. Neve's extensive network of informants had apprised her of the news of his occasional night with a widowed baroness Von Something-or-Other every time he was in London. He was being discreet and rather *posh*, all things considered.

But Neve's affair with an underling would rock their carefully staged arrangement like an earthquake. He would divorce her in an instant, and, the humiliating public scrutiny aside, she would get stuck with alimony payments this time around, footing the bill for atrocious habits like cigars, golf, and rum. Who in their right mind thought drinking rum was acceptable anywhere but on a tropical island? *So gauche.*

She still remembered how he had finally accepted that she'd never again need him for anything other than the public eye.

"I appreciate the honesty, Neve, I truly do. It's very Russian of you, cold, detached, calculated. No emotion. I can deal with that."

Very Russian had almost made her flinch, but only for a second. Close, but no cigar for him on that one. And she dared not think of how close he had come to figuring out the truth. She'd extended her hand, and he'd shaken it, sealing the deal.

But Russian or not, he wouldn't be by her side if she and Audrey were caught. And they would be and soon. Neve could feel it in her bones that were still thoroughly melted from the mind-blowing series of orgasms that beautiful mouth and those graceful fingers had given her.

"I have to end this."

How many times had she told herself this? In fact, she had taken to talking to herself out loud, which was embarrassing enough on a whole new level. And mostly, all she was telling herself was that one sentence.

"I have to end this."

This... whatever the hell this was that had her pouncing on Audrey the moment she crossed the threshold of whatever clandestine space they found themselves in. Whatever the hell this was that had her locking them in the small office on the ground floor of her Malibu mansion and fucking Audrey within an inch of her life, three fingers pumping furiously until she clutched and bit her lips to muffle her cry.

Whatever the hell this was that had Neve swiftly kneeling at Audrey's feet to taste her essence off her still quivering thighs and lips and clit and make Audrey come again, simply because Neve could. Simply because, for some utterly maddening reason, nothing in the world felt like having this girl come for her, around her fingers, in her mouth, fall apart with her name on her plump, reddened lips, pouty from all the kissing, biting and sucking Neve had bestowed on them.

And in the past four months, Neve had bestowed a lot and often and so damn hungrily, because she simply could not get enough. She was half crazy with this reckless need. She played it fast and loose and selfishly risked them both for a few moments of the dazzling heat of Audrey taking her in the CEO's private bathroom or sticking her hand under Neve's skirt in the back of the company limo before some award ceremony.

Her days and her nights were filled with memories of Audrey's skin, with the sounds she made, with the shy smiles she gave her as she was trying to pick her panties off the floor, only to discover them soaked and ripped, because Neve hadn't been able to wait. She never could, anyway. Not for new scripts, not for the final cut of a movie, and not for her black coffee. So why should she wait to suck on Audrey's clit when she could smell her arousal the moment their lips touched as she pushed her against the office door?

Her own arousal would spike even higher, since Audrey's wetness meant she was thinking about Neve on her way to the mansion on the ocean shore, no doubt imagining all the things Neve would do to her and she would do to Neve.

"And my God, did Audrey ever *do* to you!" Neve shook her head even as the words left her mouth in a breathy whisper. In fact, she did to Neve better than anyone, better than Dmitriy, back when they still pretended the marriage wasn't what it really was, and better than Armand with his ardor. Neve had always tried to dodge those bruise-inflicting aberrations, pretending to throw her head back in the throes of passion.

"Throes of passion..."

Turns out she had not known what that phrase meant until Audrey took her at her desk, kneeling before her and spreading her legs, pulling her thong to the side and silently proceeding to turn her brain to mush, her body into fire, and her world into bedlam. And if that wasn't passionate enough, Audrey had continued by taking her forcefully, from behind, on her knees, in her office after hours.

Neve walked closer to the ocean, the crush of the waves against the cliffs soothing as much as the solitude. Another clandestine encounter she'd gotten out of unscathed. Dmitriy would be home later tonight. Or he would not. Either was fine by her. Her son was at his boarding school. She was alone, and she was safe. Again. This time.

Yet the grip of fear didn't leave her as she settled into the deck chair and closed her eyes. With her mind in upheaval and her heart rate spiking, Neve clutched her jacket tightly in her hands, her fingers coming across a pin with the studio logo on it. The metal glinted in the fairy lights strung on the deck, a tangible representation of everything she stood to lose if their little interludes were to be discovered.

She was still throbbing between her thighs, but she chose to ignore that sensation. Tonight, more than on any other night, she felt reckless, too careless in her actions, and it scared her. Dmitriy could have walked in at any moment. The lengths she went to, to be with this girl. The lengths she went to, to be taken by this girl. It was too much, and it was time to stop.

She had been selfish in allowing this affair to begin, and she was selfish to end it simply because her own fear was choking her.

"It was nothing. Nothing at all." She said it out loud, if only to hear the words spoken. She remembered saying them ages ago, trying to find a way out of having been caught with something or another.

Neve sighed, and images of bright green eyes invaded her mind. Guilt flooded right on the heels of all that brightness. To be touched... To be seen... To simply feel something among the dead and decayed silk and velvet and glossy photographs of high and drunk actors and perverted producers and directors.

They all left her cold, encased in ice. But for those fleeting minutes, Audrey made her feel alive. Made her feel unfettered joy, perhaps for the first time since Harlan's birth. But all this feeling alive be damned when she was hyperventilating on a beach at midnight in agony. After four months of living and breathing said sheer unrestrained joy, Neve was ending it.

Decision made, she gave the ocean one last look. It frothed

back at her, always in motion, always there for her brooding and her tempestuous isolation. She walked through the quiet mansion, the soft snores of her son's dog in his crate accompanying her as she switched off the lights along the way.

Neve supposed it was a fitting comparison, her turning off the light in the spaces still permeated with the subtle scent of peaches and vanilla, and her extinguishing the life out of her affair with Audrey while walking through the eerie darkness of her home. She knew that what she had to do next would hurt her to some extent, but it would hurt the girl more and both would be plunged into darkness for a while. But it had to be done.

Ironically, she wasn't thinking about how she would break it to Audrey. This time it was the 'how' that was irrelevant after all, since the result would be equally devastating. While Neve could chalk her own attraction to the girl up to a midlife crisis or to pure indulgence and selfishness, she was old enough and experienced enough to know that there was love in Audrey's eyes when she looked at her, true love and all-consuming trust and adoration. Audrey loved her, and Neve, continuing the pattern of being selfish and self-indulgent, was about to destroy that love.

They were going to get caught. It would be an unacceptable ending to an otherwise most satisfactory entanglement. So Neve braced herself to do what must be done. If her heart ached just a little in the process, she would write it off as penance for acting so out of character.

2

NEVE'S PREROGATIVE

"*H*ypothetically, what would happen?" At Neve's slight head tilt, Dr. Moore elaborated. "Indulge my curiosity. If you were caught, what would happen?"

The therapist's face betrayed none of the curiosity she professed. It held a neutral expression, but Neve could see that something was lurking underneath the poised veneer. They were evenly matched then, both cat and mouse in this game.

"Juno Buchanan would fire me posthaste since a 'morals clause' is written into my otherwise ironclad contract. No matter how valued I am by the studio's board, no matter how much money I make them. And believe me, I make a lot of money."

That was all true, but Juno, as the board's chairwoman, would take one look at the morning papers and sign Neve's fate before she took the first sip of whatever convoluted soy chai spice concoction she passed off as drinkable these days.

Dr. Moore made a note, which, for some reason, grated on Neve's nerves more than her previous lack of note-taking. She chose to ignore her own irritation.

"Armand would challenge the current custody decision, arguing that someone who was fired for sexual harassment at the workplace simply could not continue to raise and educate an impressionable nine-year-old."

Dr. Moore nodded, and Neve closed her eyes at the onslaught of unpleasant thoughts.

"The press would go berserk and paint me as a sexual predator in the throes of a midlife crisis, seducing a naive ingenue who is under my supervision. A lesbian sexual predator, of all things."

The thought of the potential fallout of being outed and othered yet again made her want to vomit. She'd be eviscerated, trampled by the press and in the court of public opinion. No, coming out wasn't an option.

"So either way, you'd be finished in the world of high-flying executives, despite the movie industry being tremendously liberal and tending to protect its own. Is that what you're saying?" Dr. Moore's pen made a couple more notes. Neve gritted her teeth.

"It is liberal, and it is protective, but you have to be male to qualify for either of those benefits. If I was a man, nobody would bat an eye if I was banging my own employee. They'd even overlook the homosexual aspect of it. But Hollywood, like any other industry in the world, is unforgiving to women. You have to be perfect. And there better not be any scandal attached to you if you are the CEO of one of the most important studios in Tinseltown."

Neve shook her head, and she and Dr. Moore looked at each other in complete understanding, for perhaps the first time. Yes, every woman understood Neve's point. Then Neve lowered her gaze. Because there was more to this. There was always more.

"That said, I am not blind to my reputation, to my history, or to who my enemies are."

Surprisingly, Dr. Moore smiled.

"Oh, the industry would pounce on you, no question. The ensuing cabal would be legendary. There would be dancing and singing, and declarations that 'the Wicked Queen is dead! Long live another Queen!' Allison Summers would be licking her chops at the prospect."

Neve actually shuddered. What a horrible visual that was. Allison Summers was the only other woman CEO in town, helming Laurner Studios, and she fancied herself worthy competition for Neve and Gannon. A most horrid, tasteless woman.

The look on Dr. Moore's face was now one of complete and utter enjoyment. "Are you familiar with the Ice Queen trope?"

Neve blinked. She wasn't sure what exactly she'd expected from her sessions with Dr. Moore, but discussing literary and cinematic cliches was definitely not it.

"Are you actually saying...?" How incredibly ridiculous could this conversation become?

"Prominent characteristics of an Ice Queen, aside from power, intelligence, and beauty, are decisiveness, detachment, and at times cruelty. In fact, they are some of the most defining ones. Today, you have displayed all of them. I'm frankly looking forward to what other traits you'll exhibit. And if it will be fear driving them, as it often does for the famed Ice Queens. Self-preservation is a powerful incentive, after all."

"Tropes? Cliche characters? What method of treatment is this?" Neve's voice slipped into one of her coldest tonalities. She also quieted, and Dr. Moore was forced to still her breathing to hear her speak. As tactics went, this one always paid off. If she wasn't so confused, Neve would be pleased.

"It's not. In fact, it has nothing to do with treatment of any kind. You didn't come here to be treated, Neve. You're here to speak your mind in a safe environment and to have a mostly mute sounding board to bounce your own thoughts off. I guide those thoughts, ask you questions, but you generally spend our hour entirely in your own head."

Dr. Moore's smile faded somewhat as Neve simply stared at her.

"Ah-ah," a raised finger stopped Neve's words. "I'm not saying you don't need treatment. I'm not saying I can't help you. I'm saying you are screwing around on more than just your husband. You are sitting here and wasting my time. But since you are dead-set on keeping up these pretenses, I thought I might as well inject some themes into our mostly one-sided conversations."

"What are you saying?" Neve still thought that this session was beyond surreal and even more insulting.

"Since I'm not treating you, we could talk about other things. But I have to say the similarities, the whole Ice Queen concept, it's fascinating."

"You see me as a character and I fascinate you?" Two could play this game, Neve decided.

"I imagine you, the not-so-real you—or the Neve Blackthorne that you project into the world—fascinates an inordinate amount of people. I also imagine you are well aware of that. The persona is too well practiced, she doesn't miss, she lands every blow she delivers, from the eyebrow-raise to the curl of your mouth. But what is fascinating to me is what makes you, what makes that persona, what it has become."

Dr. Moore took the pen that she had been toying with and pointed it squarely at Neve.

"You came in here today and declared that you are ridding yourself of your 'silly infatuation' with Audrey. Then you proceeded to detail how you'll do it. And you also told me you've already started by asking your assistant to arrange a lunch with your—by your own account—in-name-only husband, while your lover was standing right there." The pencil ticked off Dr. Moore's perfectly manicured fingers one by one.

Neve suppressed the sudden urge to slap the woman. The gall! The sheer insufferable courage of talking to her this way. Nobody else dared. Maybe Audrey. Maybe that was the undefinable thing that attracted Neve to her. Neither Audrey Avens nor Helena Moore gave a damn about who Neve Blackthorne was. They talked to her any way they wanted and said what they meant. And wasn't that the one refreshing quality that drew Neve like no other?

And so she laughed. A genuine laugh, to which Dr. Moore's answering smile blossomed fully.

"Alright, I'll play, Dr. Moore."

After all, Helena Moore and her damn pen were right about one thing. She did land every blow she delivered. She'd had plenty of time to practice her aim. Life had taught her well.

"You're chipper this morning," Morag's voice, dripping with sarcasm, jarred Neve out of her uncharacteristic stupor.

Her stylist's gumption, however, wasn't out of character. But her own apathy certainly was. Several sleepless nights meant that, by the time Morag had rolled into the Malibu mansion for the daily session of transforming Neve into the Hollywood icon she was, Neve had a well-defined plan of action with only one objective. She had to end her affair with Audrey, and she had to end it on such terms that this little weakness Neve had for her would never again have the opportunity to be indulged. She had to remove Audrey from her life in order to preserve said life.

If Audrey hated her just a little when all was said and done, it was a price Neve was willing to pay. This whole affair, she'd decided, was down to boredom and self-indulgence, after all. She'd handle it. The alternative was unthinkable, and this particular course of action she could tolerate. Or so she'd told herself throughout the night.

"It's 6 AM, McKinley." Even as she said it, she knew she wasn't fooling anybody, least of all her stylist of more than twenty years. At times, Neve thought of Morag as a friend. And wasn't it a kick in the ass to acknowledge that there were precious few in her life whom she could call that? Morag, Gustavo if she squinted, because they worked together, and sometimes some lines were not to be blurred, and Neve was above all his boss. She examined her face in the large mirror, where Morag was busy with her hair.

A memory from the previous week intruded. Audrey had sat on the couch in the downstairs office, with Neve slumped, straddling her lap, having just come almost out of her mind, the strength of the orgasm surprising her. The maddening fingers were still inside her. And then Audrey reached up with her other hand and slowly traced her cheekbone. The fingertips were gentle as they followed the hollow of her cheek before sliding to her mouth and tracing the lower lip.

"You have the most fascinating face." The voice had been quiet, and for some reason, tears had welled behind Neve's eyes. "Well, everything about you is fascinating. The hair, rich, full, iconic, the cut Morag gives you is unsurpassed. The Lady In Black. Black hair, black silk dresses and skirts, red lips, black heels with red soles. An icon." Audrey's voice sounded hollow, like she was simply making a detached observation.

"But it's your face. When all the trappings are gone, when you're naked with me like this. Wanton, hungry, free. Skin, bone, muscles, tendons. This is the best you. It's still your face that draws me most. The sharp planes of the cheekbones are too prominent, the lower lip too full, and the jaw... God, your jaw... I keep fantasizing about touching this very line, where it meets the neck." Audrey's fingers followed the words, and then the cool lips placed a single chaste kiss right below the ear before the fingers moved lower. Neve swallowed and felt her neck move against the faint touch.

"And your eyes. Your violent, violet eyes." The fingers now wrapped themselves gently around the base of her neck, not applying any pressure, but their sheer presence made Neve even wetter. Audrey was looking her straight in the eyes, violet-blue meeting bright green, and when the hand that had remained between Neve's legs finally moved, the palm pressing firmly into her clit, Neve thought she'd pass out.

The words, the hand on her neck, the pressure on her clit... But it had been the unblinking stare, the complete focus those eyes held in them. Full of purpose, full of love, Neve had not been able to face them any longer, so she'd closed her own, giving herself up to the moment, cursing her own weakness, cursing Audrey's power, and craving more, always craving more. Always fearing more.

But now her own eyes looked back at her, the mirror reflecting the same emotion she knew Audrey had been able to see in her that day. Fear. Audrey hadn't said anything, but she was too gentle, too accommodating, too much afterwards. And Neve feared even more.

Belatedly, she noticed that the practiced, if slightly jerky movements of a different pair of talented hands had stopped, and Morag was looking right back at her, their gazes meeting in the mirror.

"Now you have got me concerned." The thick Scottish brogue was untamed after decades in LA, and it gave Neve comfort that some things, no matter how ephemeral the world was, simply never changed.

"I'm just tired." It wasn't a deflection, not that much of a lie. She *was* tired, and the sleepless night had nothing to do with it. Despite the long shower she'd taken before going to bed, she could still feel Audrey's touch on her skin, could still smell those tantalizing remnants of peaches and vanilla. Wasn't it strange that, out of the dozen or so ingredients that particular perfume was composed of, the two most basic notes—the sweet and fruity and thoroughly dependable ones—were the ones that Audrey's skin held and safeguarded and that clung to her, and hence to Neve, through a full day and then through an evening of rather strenuous activities.

"I guess you *are* tired. That's not like you at all. And you just confessing to it like this is even more disconcerting." Morag took up the brush again, the long strokes pleasantly massaging Neve's scalp. "You'd normally be asking me twenty different questions at once, whom I saw, what's new, and what the word on the street is."

Neve gave a sly smile at that, the corners of her as yet uncoated lips lifting a fraction.

"I don't have to prompt you, McKinley. If there's anything I need to know, you'll tell me, and if there's anything juicy enough that I don't need to know, you'll still tell me, since you can't help yourself. Gossip and this," she gestured towards the array of makeup scattered on the vanity, "is something you are simply amazing at."

"Ha, flattery will get you everywhere, but it will not make me less concerned about your current state. Fine, lass, I'll drop this and since you're asking nicely—"

"I haven't asked at all, but you are clearly chomping at the bit to tell me something massive, so out with it before you choke on it."

Their eyes locked in the mirror again. "Grace Bishop is having an affair with her PA."

Neve twisted her mouth in a show of disappointment. "Really. Groundbreaking news, McKinley." The sarcasm-infused drawl did not deter Morag.

"Her very young, very female PA."

Oh... That stopped Neve short. The bile rose in her throat, and she gripped her chair's armrests until her knuckles turned white. Morag was prattling on, and Neve forced her fists to unclench very slowly and very deliberately, as not to attract attention to her moment of abject horror. She blinked once, twice, and tried to focus on what her stylist was saying.

Bishop had been a constant presence on big and small screens throughout the years, her focus on the stability of long-term TV dramas that guaranteed a steady income and constant exposure. Still, her occasional appearances in artsy movies were always memorable and usually garnered her attention and awards. In fact, a year ago she'd starred in one of Gannon's critically acclaimed melodramas and was nominated for a slew of things, winning a Golden Globe. These movies that Neve green-lit weren't profitable. Not in the least. But they were art, and Neve would get her investment back on the blockbusters Gannon churned out like clockwork. And that money would pay for her true passion. Well-made, classic cinema.

Neve liked her choices, in as much as she could appreciate the art of them, the creativity of the acting, and the master at work that Grace Bishop clearly was. But what made Bishop even more extraordinary was her daring, take-no-prisoners approach to life. Her social media was a fascinating carousel of emotions. She was interesting and engaging, fun and charismatic. She was also very married. To some C-list actor. And Neve wasn't aware the marriage was a sham. Come to think of it…

"Her husband is threatening a public scandal." As if reading her thoughts, Morag spoke with uncharacteristic rancor. "I heard he's been blackmailing her for a couple of months now, and she is draining her bank accounts to keep him quiet. The girl she's involved with had a breakdown, and Grace put her up in some clinic. From what I heard, Grace had real feelings, and it was a love story, nothing dirty or reprehensible. That's all I know."

"They will crucify Bishop." Neve had to shake her head at her own outburst.

Morag tsked at her unexpected movement. "Hold still, will 'ya? What's gotten into you today?" Neve chose to ignore the rhetorical question, and Morag went on. "Yes, yes, that they will. You know how it goes in this town. And she's got some projects lined up…"

Neve tuned Morag out again. Yes, she knew how it went in this town. The C-lister husband would eventually no longer be satisfied with whatever blackmail money he was getting from Grace and sell his story to the highest bidder. Bishop would be publicly eviscerated, not simply outed, but outed as an adulterer as well. The power dynamics of that relationship, in the age of #metoo, would play a major role as well. Neve suppressed a shudder.

"You will be next... You know it... All secrets and all lies come out..."

"Don't tell... Don't tell..."

The voices appeared again, sharp and loud, overwhelming her. Her ears were ringing as she tried to return her focus to the present and to Grace Bishop. Her career would be effectively over. A shiver ran down Neve's spine. Minus the blackmail, which really was the last thing she needed, she could be Grace Bishop. She *was* Grace Bishop. All that was left was the public exposure and her life, too, would be virtually over.

Morag's steady tug on her hair made her raise her eyes.

"Now, tell me what's going on with you, lass. You have got this look as if you've seen a ghost, and it wasn't friendly."

Neve forced a smile, calling all her acting prowess into action. "Are ghosts ever friendly?"

Another "tsk" followed from her stylist, this time one that smacked of exasperation.

"I'm thinking about going to New York at the end of the week." She observed carefully as her stylist tried and failed to school her facial expressions. Then, abandoning all pretense, Morag sighed and put her hands on her hips.

"New York? You're supposed to go a month from now. I know your every move, Blackthorne. I have your schedule memorized better than mine."

"I have business." Neve raised the telling eyebrow, which Morag chose to ignore. Neve should really know better.

"Business my arse! Tired, spacing out, now going to New York four weeks before you're due there!"

"You're forgetting yourself." Her quiet words sobered Morag in a second.

"Ay, apologies. I'll clear my schedule. There's just a museum opening and a couple of premieres in the coming days. I only have four or five clients. I'll send someone else in my stead."

Neve watched carefully as Morag performed the mental gymnastics of laying waste to what she knew was an overflowing calendar full of appointments. Neve made sure of this in fact - that Morag was one of the most, if not *the* most successful stylist in LA. One word from the *Wicked Queen* opened all doors in this town, after all.

Plus, Morag was sensationally talented, so garnering the reputation of being able to please her, the ever-impossible-to-please Neve Blackthorne, was just an added bonus. But as unpredictable as she could be, she'd leave Morag behind on this one. If she was strategically retreating from LA and from Audrey, there was no need to upend Morag's life in the process.

"I'm going alone."

Morag actually gasped and clutched the brush to her chest.

"Nobody touches your face but me. And if more people knew I do your hair as well, I'd never ever sleep in this town and be booked 'till the Rapture. So the same goes for this beauty." Morag actually ran her fingers almost reverently through the now perfect coif.

"I'm sure I'll survive on my own for a couple of days, because yes, nobody touches me but you."

She'd missed the double entendre in her implication until Morag barked a laugh before sobering.

"More's the shame that. Married to a prince you are, handsome as the devil himself. And yet he touches that titled bitch in London more than he touches you."

Having Morag know everyone and be sought after by the whole town had its perks, since she was Neve's chief informant. But sometimes, just sometimes, Neve wished Morag would have a little less information and would tell her even less of what she knew. Not that Dmitriy having an affair bothered her.

He was a healthy man with obvious needs, as much as this excuse disgusted her. But it was the implication evident in Morag's voice, that Neve was somehow the victim in this arrangement of theirs, that rankled her.

"Be that as it may. After tomorrow's premiere, you can have a week off from our early mornings."

The hands returned to her hair, and the brush carefully made its way through the dark tresses, with Morag huffing a breath, then going to work on her face. And Neve returned to her brooding and her planning.

"Barnaby, coffee." Her modulated tones obviously disturbed the atmosphere at Gannon McMillan, since several heads shot up from behind computer monitors and from the waiting room in front of her office. Normally, Barnaby, as her assistant, oversaw supplying Neve with liquid gold. But lately, Audrey had taken to bringing her the mouthwatering brew on Tuesdays, since the day started with a briefing by the comms team, with Gustavo's people delivering the latest on how the studio's projects were faring in the news. Although de facto, it was Audrey who was running the show.

Neve shaking up the new normal caused Audrey to stare at her and Barnaby to squeak and stutter.

"But, but... Audrey just... on your desk..." Oh, if he only knew what Audrey had done on that desk. Shaking her head to indicate displeasure with him for daring to question her and to clear it of the lascivious thoughts, Neve raised an eyebrow and Barnaby scurried away.

"Somebody, please arrange for an hour of free time today for lunch. Gustavo, I don't care what nonsense you want to rope me into this afternoon, or who you want me to see or be seen with, clear my schedule. I want to have a moment to just enjoy myself from time to time. My husband will be joining me."

Even as she said it, Neve was aware that Audrey's eyes went from bright with excitement to startled and hurt. "I think the Providence would be perfect for a nice meal. Michael Cimarusti and Dmitriy are good friends. We love going there."

She deliberately used plural pronouns and affected an air of genteel enthusiasm. It was important not to overplay her hand, to not dive in too deep too soon. Despite her youth, which vexed Neve daily, Audrey's intelligence impressed Neve just as often. She'd never believe a rushed attempt at deceit.

"Neve—," Audrey was obviously not going to question Neve's sudden eagerness at spending any amount of time with her husband outside of official functions. They didn't discuss personal matters a whole lot or, in fact, matters of any kind, because fucking really consumed all their encounters. But Audrey, being as observant as she was, must have figured that Neve and Dmitriy had a relationship that, while professionally beneficial to both, was mostly window dressing. Still, Neve did not care to hear what Audrey had to say.

Thankfully, Barnaby's arrival with her coffee ended any line of inquiry, and the morning passed in a flurry of meetings. In a lull, she remembered her earlier conversation with Morag.

"Barnaby, get me Grace Bishop's agent. Whoever that may be–"

"I'll look into it." At her glare at his interruption, he closed his mouth with a resounding snap.

"That would be Jude Caulfield." Audrey's voice sounded competent as ever. Neve inclined her head.

"Well then, Barnaby, get me Caulfield and arrange for Gustavo and Audrey to have a very visible lunch with Bishop herself."

"Is something about to go down? Are we averting a disaster? Should I keep my ear to the ground?" Barnaby, who on a good day read the room like a pro, was not doing a great job of it today. Still, he was one of her best spies, along with Morag.

"Yes, yes, and yes. And if there's ever a need to remind people that I happen to appreciate the talent of Grace Bishop, today might be that day, Barnaby."

As he busied himself writing down the latest directive, Neve caught Audrey's nod. It was apparent she was also in the loop, and somehow, that nod of approval brightened Neve's day. Which was clearly absurd, and something she wanted to avoid at all costs. Brightened? Nonsense! She did not care at all about esteem in general, and Audrey's in particular. In fact, it was one of the big reasons she was trying to extricate herself from Audrey by going to this cursed lunch with her husband.

"Is that all?" Neve gathered her papers. All these maudlin thoughts were getting to her. She had a studio to run.

"A situation involving the two male leads of *Stay*." Audrey's voice had that resolute, no-nonsense tone to it. She had Neve's full attention. *Stay* was one of Gannon's most profitable and well-viewed shows, acclaimed by both critics and audiences alike.

Suddenly, an unfamiliar voice interjected.

"Oh, nothing really. The guys were joking with the fans. Twitter is making more of it than it warrants because of the fannish obsession with that one actress."

Neve turned her head slightly in the direction of the underling speaking. *Donald Zayn. Donny* to his friends. Assistant Vice President for Talent. Well-connected, supposedly a mean poker face. Plays Thursday nights with Juno and her cabal. Hence the position at Gannon. High enough to make a ton of money, not significant enough to get in Neve's way. Which may have been a smart plan by Juno when she'd foisted this poker buddy of hers on the Studio. Shame really... The actual Vice President, Samira Khan, was on vacation, Neve registered vaguely. Well, Samira would have to return much sooner than planned.

"An obsession with an actress?" In the reigning silence, her quiet tone sounded carefully neutral. Knowing that tone led only to one thing and one thing alone, Gustavo suddenly found the windows interesting, and Barnaby busied himself with writing something in his notebook. Probably a reminder that Gannon would be hiring a new Assistant Vice President for Talent.

Finally, Donny spoke again, "Well, yeah, the length the fans go to make this one couple–*ship* or whatever those goofs call these things–happen is kind of embarrassing. We have been firm that this is a family show, and no gay relationships will exist on it. Still, they keep pushing. Twitter, Instagram, polls. It's unhealthy. So the guys, the actors, rightfully laughed it off. Nothing serious, really. All in good fun." He took a long swig from his glass and wiped his sweaty brow. But his smile was wide, and he seemed rather proud of his assessment of the situation.

Neve thought if this guy was able to fool Juno, she was either bad at poker or Donny was slipping, because he reeked of fear and of self-importance and she could read him like an open book. Not a particularly interesting one. A DNF from her.

"Audrey?" Neve did not take her eyes off Donny. He gulped and tried to regroup. Under Neve's scrutiny, his hand trembled slightly when he re-filled his glass from the pitcher. Barnaby lowered his head, almost burying it in the notebook. Gustavo was now looking at the opposite wall. Audrey's eyes were locked on Neve.

"On an Instagram live, the two actors in question mocked a group of fans that attend most of the show related events and have a podcast dedicated to it. The group has been actively trying to lobby for a potential relationship between the two female main characters. The video is all over twitter, and by afternoon will surely be featured in most of the fandom-related outlets."

Donny's brow was now drenched, and the tissue he was trying to use to save his dignity was not helping. Neve had not taken her eyes off him as Audrey spoke.

"So let me make sure I understand, Donny." She drawled out his name with particular distaste and lowered her voice further. His eyes grew huge listening to her, unable to look away. "A show that is the flagship for this age group dedicated lineup, teases–practically queerbaits–a relationship between two women. It sells like hotcakes. Fans set up sites, polls, and get the ship in question to trend on Twitter every so often, thus encouraging us to make this happen. And instead of supporting the fandom that creates a constant stream of free publicity and promoting our show, its stars mock said fans, losing the studio all these free content creators, resulting in a PR disaster? Am I getting all this right?"

Audrey nodded, Gustavo coughed, and Barnaby hid entirely behind his notebook, his shoulders shaking ever so slightly.

"Looks like I am. So Donny here is also of the opinion that all of the above is not serious. And in good fun. Was 'locker room joke' going to be your next argument to dismiss misogyny?" He swallowed audibly, but remained silent. Neve ran her fingers over the rim of her glass, making it sing. In the quiet of the conference room, for a second, it was the only sound that could be heard. "So, this good fun has cost my studio money and generated quite a lot of bad publicity, Donny."

Neve closed her laptop with a quiet snap. Her staff flinched as if she'd fired a gun. Everyone knew the next words would lower the boom. And who was she to deny them the satisfaction?

"Have those actors fired from my show. And Barnaby, have security escort Donny from the building."

Her assistant, it seems, had known what was coming before she even spoke, because he simply opened the doors to the conference room and several uniformed men materialized like magic.

"What? You can't! Juno will have your ass. You frigid bitch." Donny's screams echoed loudly as he was being escorted from the room. Neve almost winced before grinding her teeth and moving on.

"Oh, and Barnaby, get me the agents for those actresses. Let's see how inclined everyone is toward LGBTQIA representation."

Audrey folded her hands over her laptop's keyboard. "I am certain that they will be very amenable. And that would also be Jude Caulfield. For both of them. I looked it up while you were giving that asshole all the rope in the world to hang himself."

"Is Caulfield suddenly the agent for everyone? Bishop, now these two?" Neve tipped her chin up in inquiry.

"Just for gay Hollywood." Audrey's whisper made Neve smile. Of course, Audrey would know.

Neve surveyed the table. "Opinion?" Gustavo just waved his hand at Audrey, and she took a deep breath before speaking.

"Well, if you go forward with the LGBTQIA rep on this show, it will cause some waves. We will have to be ready for considerable pushback. It is a flagship for a reason. But there's also a rather large LGBTQIA fanbase that can swing our way, with Laurner canceling their one queer rep show."

Neve made a mental note to look into the cancellation issue. There was always something she could pick up from other people's trash. There was a certain irony in that thought, one she did not wish to revisit just now. An irony that, if she had any say, she'd never think about at all, along with everything else from her past.

Dragging herself back to the present, she did not miss the way Audrey had navigated the complex waters in front of her. It made Neve proud. It also made Neve wet. She wanted to roll her eyes at herself in disgust.

"And you have the problem of having Juno and the Board." Audrey's quiet but decisive voice went on. "We are progressive, thanks primarily to your ability to blunt the more conservative elements of the business by virtue of how profitable we are. But this is a two-pronged issue. You just fired and humiliated her man, and are you saying you are swinging radically left with a family values show? And then there's Grace Bishop..." Yes, Audrey made her very wet. Too bad Neve's decision was firm.

"Leave Juno to me. As for family values... Where is Samira?"

"Bahamas." Gustavo's expression was one of longing. His love for the islands was no secret. "Her first vacation in three years–"

"Too bad for Samira. Get her back ASAP. She should know better than to leave that empty suit in charge of her department."

As she paused, Barnaby raised his hand.

"Ah, Neve... That LGBTQIA rep? What should I tell Jude Caulfield?"

"There is a script circulating that would be perfect for her clients. A small-budget artsy thing but with a lot of potential. Maybe not Academy Award potential, but festival-circuit-worthy. I think the fans will be pacified if we put the two actresses in question as lovers in a movie and give them tons of lesbian content while leaving the show to enjoy its high 'family values' rating."

Neve grimaced in disgust and made the air quotes gesture. Still, she knew her overall resolution to the situation was underhanded and exploitative. Which made her no better than Donny. But this was business. And she saved the show and some acrimony with the Board while also giving the fans what they wanted.

"And Gustavo? The sheer distance of how far beneath me this issue is, is rather astounding. You all should be doing your jobs, and I hope to never hear about this again. Also, make sure the showrunners don't just kill off or write off those mouthy idiots. Recast. The characters continue. The actors do not. Am I clear? Dismissed."

Gustavo whistled and left, smirking. She could hear him mumbling, "Fuck around and find out, I guess," to Barnaby, who replied with an awed, enamored murmur of, "I love her when she's like that," as they exited.

As the staff filed out of the conference room, Neve did not miss Audrey's hot, lingering gaze. It appeared that her being ruthless and a little vindictive was doing it for more than just Barnaby. Maybe she hadn't lost her touch at all. That executive bathroom was looking very appealing to her right about now. Too bad she had a lunch to go to.

Sitting across the table from Dmitriy, after being greeted and air-kissed by Chef Cimarusti himself, Neve started having second thoughts about her plan. Not so much about ending things with Audrey. That had to be done, if only to spare herself the persistent panic attacks and visions of being drawn and quartered in the court of public opinion after being dragged naked through Beverly Hills.

This indulgence of her whim had gone on for far too long. She was jumping at her own shadow. Every meeting with Juno was agony, trying to decipher her usual pontificating monologues and wondering whether she knew and when the hammer would fall. And now she had fired Donny, and Juno would be in her hair about him soon enough.

God, Neve just wanted her life back, and it was past time to send Audrey along to finally start her own. If only she wasn't so damn appealing. And if she wasn't as infatuated with Neve. The conversation with Dr. Moore about the godforsaken Ice Queens came to mind, and Neve pushed it away ruthlessly. Her therapist knew nothing. And she was right about nothing.

The sudden barrage of thoughts intruding on her mind made her head spin. She could feel the cold sweat pooling at the base of her spine. Her breathing was becoming shallow, and she closed her eyes to take a second.

Not now, not now, God, not now...

She was sitting in the middle of a beautiful restaurant, prominently enough that there would be DMZ pictures of them by the end of the hour. She was doing so while eating delicious food and ordering a lovely Zinfandel.... She took careful, deliberate breaths, flexing her fingertips around her glass, the cold condensation soothing her. When her hands stopped shaking, she lifted the glass and took a sip, then another. The room stopped spinning.

Her thoughts returned to the luxuries surrounding her. All of those beautiful, grounding things were being squashed into absurd boredom by having to share them with Dmitriy. He was neither arid nor sniveling. But for the life of her she couldn't figure out what in the world she had ever seen in him.

He gave her that absolutely gorgeous smile of a man who knew how dramatically handsome he was. And handsome he was indeed. He was also talented and on a fast track to being one of the most sought-after directors in Hollywood, after establishing himself as a jury favorite in Cannes, Venice, and Berlin for years. His intellectual cinema had paved the way for him to make the jump across the Atlantic, straight into the embrace of pretty much all six of the studio greats. His project queue was massive, and strictly speaking, Neve wasn't entirely certain if he really needed her as much as she needed an intelligent, in-demand, never-home, beautiful husband to show the world.

She could hear Dr. Moore in her ear. *Stop avoiding the truth.* Yes, he was handsome. He was talented. He was interesting. Just not to her.

Yes, Dr. Moore, he is all of these things, and all I want is for bright green eyes to look at me and those soft hands to run up and down my neck.

And thus Dmitriy, for all his brilliant mind and wonderful talent, was rather insipid in comparison. And wasn't that a kick in the teeth?

Neve was taken aback by the realization that four months of affecting extreme professional preoccupation while getting her spokesperson out of her various designer clothes could open one's eyes to the total lacking in one's own husband.

She knew exactly what she'd been thinking two years ago when she chose him, and the proof of how correct her thinking was, was reflected in the number of paparazzi who were lined up outside to get a glimpse of them. Was it really his fault that Neve found Audrey so delightful, in or out of attire? That even an hour with Dmitriy felt wasted? And yet, for her plan of self-reclamation to succeed, she would have to be convincing enough in her attempts to make it look like she had a quasi-normal marriage with him.

Audrey, her bright and insightful Audrey, would never believe that Neve was suddenly in love with him. She knew too well that Neve didn't spare much thought for her husband. But Audrey also knew that some things were just too precious for Neve to lose. Her son, her career, and her public image always came first. So all Neve had to "sell" Audrey on was an honest effort to preserve either or all three of her treasures, her trifecta.

And to top it all off, Neve was well-aware that Audrey—who knew Neve was faking it for publicity and respectability to absolve herself of her crimes—would likely not jump until she was pushed. And so Neve had to push. Hard. Hard enough that Audrey would never look back.

As their lunch ended, Neve made it a point to kiss Dmitriy squarely on the lips in front of the paparazzi. His distinct surprise at an unexpected display of affection, as well as his not-at-all-subtle lascivious glance down her Marc Jacobs blouse, spelled that she would likely have some explaining to do sometime soon. It didn't matter. She had one purpose today: making a statement. Since one could always count on there being photographers in front of the Providence, one could also be sure the picture of the kiss would make its way online before her driver delivered her to the office.

If Neve was curious whether her plan of feeding the lens-carrying sharks had worked, all she had to do to confirm her success was to see Audrey parked outside her office with a thunderous face.

"Good thing you're here," Neve took her time to put her sunglasses in their case, instantly dismissing Audrey who was standing at attention, vibrating like a tight string. Yes, Neve knew well enough what Audrey wanted to tell her. But she was in no mood for recriminations, and Audrey really should know better than to even attempt any such thing here at the office.

"I want you to work with David and Stephen. They're messing up their respective media presence in the worst way. You were right during the morning briefing, I believe they could benefit from your guiding hand in devising their publicity strategy. Their project is already a failure, I don't want the size of the failure to be known outside my walls. Oh, and let Gustavo know how it went afterwards." Neve glided into her office, thus forestalling any attempt by Audrey to press Neve for answers.

She clenched her jaw as she watched Audrey walk away. *Petty, petty, petty.* She closed her eyes and wanted to lay her head on the cool surface of her glass desk. Giving Audrey a job that any lackey in the communications department could and usually did handle, was petty. Telling her to then report to Gustavo instead of herself was cruel. And highly effective, since Audrey knew well enough that Neve would always, always, *always* manipulate her time and her obligations in such a way that they'd end up alone together.

"Well, some things need to be blunt and obvious, so there will be no doubts afterwards."

"You said something, Neve?" Barnaby's uncertain voice sounded from outside her door. Neve rolled her eyes at her own foolishness of speaking out loud.

"Yes, how hard is it to pick the phone up when it's ringing, Barnaby?"

Since the phones were not, in fact, ringing, Neve could see her assistant's pretty face contort into a mask of utter incomprehension, then concern. Well, at least he was the highest-paid PA in Hollywood.

Neve shook her head. Her little misdirection with Audrey had ensured that she would be too busy to unload on her the number of questions Neve knew her little production was generating. It also guaranteed Audrey's absence from her sight for a while.

Her quiet, dark house kept all her dirty secrets of temptation and satiation. Not only did she not want to answer questions, but she also didn't trust herself to be alone with Audrey.

With both her and Audrey focusing more on other types of pursuits and letting some of the more mundane professional responsibilities slide by in the past four months, Neve had enough things to assign to Audrey to keep her occupied for a couple of weeks at least.

While Audrey was busy and very obviously quietly stewing at Neve for evading her and brushing her off, Neve herself was reminiscing about those aforementioned pursuits that she was now missing. Such activities as sneaking into the CEO's private bathroom for a quick afternoon fuck, with Audrey bending her over the sink and taking her from behind, her skirt hastily pulled up and her ass cheek stinging with a red imprint from several slaps delivered by a sure hand, while long fingers stroked her into a quick, hard climax. Those memories made her forget why she was sending Audrey to join some godforsaken crew in Vancouver tomorrow.

After two weeks of subterfuge, Neve was getting closer to the edge. Her trip to New York had come and gone. And so had Audrey's dispatch to Vancouver. After tossing and turning in bed for what seemed like forever, she finally relented and climbed down to the study to curl up on the couch. She loved this room. Every single surface here held memories of her and Audrey.

One particular memory came unbidden. It had been a night just like this, just over four months ago, a week after Audrey had knelt in front of her for the very first time. They'd still been shy with one another, still tentative. If their office trysts and after-work-quickies were fast and furious, this one evening had been tender and filled with some tentative emotion that Neve was afraid to analyze in-depth.

Dmitriy was on a trip, and Neve had been pacing the ground floor ready to ravish Audrey on sight, burning up with hunger and desire. However, the storm outside had Audrey arriving late and soaked to the bone. So when Audrey's cold, trembling lips had touched hers, Neve had quieted her ardor and unconsciously set to warm Audrey up instead of setting her on fire, as appeared to be their normal.

The memory was so vivid, perhaps enhanced by the same sounds of rain coming down and the same darkness of the room. These memories, the good ones and the bad, were a complete sensory overload. Neve had almost been able to taste the droplets on Audrey's skin as she'd uncovered her body and slowly traced the translucent skin with her lips and fingertips, every so often returning to that generous mouth that welcomed her with warming lips and an agile tongue that seemed to understand the need to soothe instead of inflame. She couldn't get enough of those gentle kisses, the slide of supple lips over hers, the sweet taste of Audrey permeating her conscience, burrowing into her very soul.

She couldn't taste enough either, yet her mouth was tender, savoring every second and every touch and every shared breath. Those lips with their Cupid's bow that she traced with the tip of her tongue causing Audrey to shiver, sigh contentedly, and try to catch Neve's tongue with her own.

Neve playfully withdrew her mouth just out of reach, and Audrey smiled at the surprising mischievousness. That smile was so bright, so genuine in its happiness and tenderness, that Neve was momentarily struck speechless. It was too much. There had been too much emotion on Audrey's beautiful face, too much sincerity and guilelessness, and so Neve had to kiss that smile, feeling it grow even more under her mouth.

That night she'd undressed Audrey for the very first time. The sight of all that flawless, pale skin, the curving lines of full breasts, her sculpted waist, and the flare of her hips, had Neve's hands trembling. They stood so close, their mouths seemingly unable to part for more than mere seconds to draw breath, Audrey naked and Neve fully clothed.

Neve thought she had never experienced anything more

erotic in her life. Her fingers moved of their own accord, tracing lines and curves until finding wetness and heat. They both moaned loudly at the touch, and even though they'd been doing this for a week, Neve felt like she was touching Audrey for the first time. Perhaps she was. And so her fingers were feather-soft, teasing, light, and tender, playing in the wet folds, making Audrey tremble with want, making her plead quietly—for what she perhaps didn't know herself.

Just when she had Audrey on the very edge, Neve had slipped two fingers inside, gently bringing her to a shuddering orgasm.

On that rainy night, with the sound of the storm outside cocooning them in this room and separating them from the rest of the world and from their lives, Neve had been gentle and unhurried. Maybe for the first and only time since their affair had commenced, she'd also been unafraid. Unafraid of the emotion behind the touch of her fingertips and of the feeling behind the caress of her lips.

She had never again allowed herself to be this unafraid, and the enormity of all she had to lose had firmed her hands and rushed her mouth afterwards.

Neve had also never indulged in thinking of that night, yet now that she was ending all of it, the taste of Audrey as Neve had licked her off her fingers in the afterglow, was returning to her just like the memory, its vividness transcendent.

Lying on the couch, Neve was feeling decidedly out of sorts. With the past haunting her at every corner, she was disoriented and yearning.

She was also totally disgusted with herself for acting in a way that would have appalled her younger self. *Younger self?* Her current self was appalled as well. Appalled at her cowardice, at her indecisiveness, at her weakness when it came to Audrey.

The Queen who ran an Empire with an iron fist was playing

childish games to rid herself of a problem of her own making. Heavens, Audrey wasn't a problem. She was a beautiful girl who'd had the misfortune of falling for her. But she was also the temptress who consumed Neve's days and nights and drove her out of her mind with fear. Fear for her and, if Neve was entirely honest with herself, fear of her. Audrey scared her, scared her breathless.

The power she unknowingly wielded over Neve was unprecedented. Audrey could equally elate and destroy her with one word, and Neve never felt more alive than when she was under that power. It was intoxicating, it was terrifying, and it had Neve behaving like a scheming high-schooler, playing games and creating stratagems to drive her away.

She should just tell her, should just confess that she hadn't slept normally in weeks, that her mind was tearing itself apart with panic and desire, and that this situation was completely unsustainable. But confessing her fear to Audrey was even more ludicrous to her than playing these silly games. No, Neve couldn't confess a weakness to anyone. After all, the Wicked Queen had no weaknesses.

Still, the games had to stop, because as much as panic was choking her, Neve had her dignity, and this whole situation had devolved into something unbecoming of her. The games would stop tomorrow, she decided. And Dr. Moore would be right once again. Cruelty for the sake of self-preservation would reign as the Ice Queen's signature trait yet again.

3

NEVE SINGES WINGS

"*Do you play chess?*" Dr. Moore stood up and gracefully walked toward a side cabinet. Neve watched her move, eyes narrowing. She was up to something, but this particular session was on the heels of many a sleepless night, and her mind and heart were just not in it.

"*I don't, no. Games are for children.*" Neve shook her head, and her rain-straight hair caressed her jaw, the action serving as a distraction and a circuit breaker for her, preventing a mental short. The advantage of sensory stimulation without having to bite the inside of her cheek. "*I do know the rules, if that's what you're asking.*"

"*You are something, you know that?*" The doctor was grinning at her.

"*I am not sure you mean that as a good thing, but I do, in fact, know that.*"

Dr. Moore actually chuckled before she placed a beautiful white wooden chess board between them on the coffee table. She took out a tall, slim figurine, setting the piece on the board.

"*This is you.*" Neve watched as the marble Queen occupied her place on a square. A Pawn followed, "*This is your marriage to Dmitriy.*"

"You're not subtle at all, Doctor. Sure, I married him for a purpose and he is useful, but a Pawn?"

"Pawns are expendable. There are many of them." Dr. Moore's voice did not show any particular emotion. She drew another figure out of the satchel and placed it to the left of the Queen. "The Bishop is your job." Before Neve could say anything, a Knight found his place next to the Bishop. "This is Harlan."

And finally, a Rook stood next to the Knight. "Your outing as such."

Neve actually wanted to yawn. "If this was a book or a movie, people in the reviews would be griping that your metaphors lack not just subtlety but originality. And they would be right on the money. Rook, castle walls, how droll..."

Finally, when Dr. Moore raised her eyes, she was holding a King in her hands. But she didn't place him on the board.

"All these pieces? They're the lines of defense. Whether a Queen, the most powerful figure on the whole board, needs them or not, is beside the point. You told me about all the lines that you would never cross. I think it is more than that. All those lines are your defenses. Against whatever it is you are protecting yourself from."

Neve felt herself stiffen and swallowed hard, then narrowed her eyes to study Dr. Moore's. They showed something that was short of genuine interest. Neve was yet to put her finger on the exact emotion that was projected at her. So she just nodded, awaiting further commentary from the therapist.

"These pieces, they simultaneously protect you and you protect them. To attain the latter, you have put your plan in motion." Again, the words were spoken with no inflection, no question.

She reached out and carefully—avoiding touching Dr. Moore's fingers, dreading any additional sensory stimulation—took the King out of her hand and then placed him back in the satchel. "There's no King in this story. And let me indulge your preposterous metaphorical farce here, Doctor. The Queen needs her life back." She felt like her own words were bubbling to the surface and she was unable to stop them. "I need my life back." If her voice sounded unconvincing to her own ears, she chose to ignore it.

"So you've been saying since you darkened my doorstep the first time. Are you trying to convince me or yourself? And does it even matter, Neve? We're in Hollywood, after all, it's all an illusion."

"I'm convinced. In fact, I have been convinced since I realized the girl imagines herself to have some sort of feelings for me." She knew she'd almost spat out the word 'feelings' and saw the infinitesimal change in Dr. Moore's face. Now Neve could tell exactly what she was confronted with. Deep disapproval. Well, she had seen worse. She had been subjected to worse.

"Decisiveness. Doing what has to be done. What needs to be done, despite peril, or at times despite rhyme or reason. That's another Ice Queen trait, you know."

Neve rolled her eyes. "We are back at this again."

"In books, the character in question always makes the hard and often harsh decision, obviously for the greater good, or for her own good."

"Obviously." Neve mocked.

Dr. Moore's eyes crinkled now, but there was no mirth in them, and she continued speaking as if Neve's sarcastic retort did not register.

"You believe you're doing the right thing. Despite how many lies you tell yourself, or me, or her."

"I am empowering her to move forward!" The impassive woman did not flinch at Neve's outburst, and her expression of deep disapproval didn't change. "And it's like ripping off a bandaid. Quick and done."

Dr. Moore watched her thoughtfully before lowering her gaze. Yet there was nothing demure about her words when they came.

"You are hurting her. But then you do have a reputation for it…"

Neve raised an imperious eyebrow and was satisfied that Dr. Moore's remark seemed to hang in the air, the good doctor apprehensive enough, seeming to calculate whether to continue.

"Speaking of reputation..." Dr. Moore's careful tone made Neve's hackles rise. "I've done some research. Discreetly, of course. You do have one in this town. The epithets vary, but there's a red line. You've been called 'the sun' quite often. I think it started with a particularly ass-kissing journalist trying to depict you as Louis the Fourteenth, and how the French king was influential in the arts flourishing under him. But then the myth of you as the sun took off. Did you know this?"

Neve turned away in utter disgust. Not this old chestnut.

"I'm familiar with the article." The man never worked on the West Coast again. For all the gauche metaphors.

"Ha!" Dr. Moore actually laughed, and Neve flinched, the loud noise jarring in its unexpectedness. She gripped the armrests tighter, her knuckles going white.

"He's not the only one who's referred to you this way, Neve. I found it particularly telling that it's used both in a very flattering light, pun intended—the power you have, the way you elevate projects from total obscurity and turn seemingly dead and buried things into living breathing masterpieces..."

This time Neve did not turn away nor scoff. A compliment was a compliment, and this one happened to be absolutely true. She was the best at what she did.

Dr. Moore went on, "All things in Hollywood revolve around you—but then there's also the other side of that power and how most things that come too close to you, well, die for lack of a better word."

Neve sat quietly, her heart pounding in her ears. Perhaps her lack of outward reaction emboldened Dr. Moore.

"All this talk about you being the sun made me think of Icarus. Are you familiar with the myth?"

"I am."

"Don't you think that Audrey is your Icarus and you are singeing her wings for getting too close to you?"

Neve gritted her teeth, trying to tamper down a sudden wave of nausea. Dr. Moore went on, her pen ticking off one more finger on her hand. "While perfectly fitting, the Icarus myth only applies so far."

Bile in her mouth, Neve raised her chin, ready for the punch. The therapist delivered. "The sun didn't hurt itself when Icarus died. And you are hurting yourself."

Before Neve could reply, Dr. Moore's voice full of derision added, "As for the band-aid... I don't know. It feels very much like for both of you, the band-aid has been there for quite some time and might even have become a second skin. So you're flaying her and yourself. Is that what you're saying?"

"Don't tell... Don't tell..." The hushed whisper seemed to paralyze her for a second before she turned away, knowing that her silence spoke volumes.

If Dr. Moore noticed her reaction, she did not show it. Her follow-up was disarming. "Well, at least in the fashion of the best Ice Queens, you're being decisive about it."

There was even less to say after that, and Neve sat in her chair, fingers steepled in front of her, thinking of the decision and the plan that she was about to unleash on Audrey. On herself.

Damn Dr. Moore and her insightfulness.

―――――

With so many of her recent actions being so unlike her, Neve thought ruefully that she might as well do one last thing that was uncharacteristic for the Wicked Queen of Hollywood. If it really took the cake in her cockamamie plan to end her affair with Audrey, all the better. She never did things by half measure, anyway.

"I need you to go to the Mancini reception with me tonight."

Raising his yet unshaven face from his morning coffee, Dmitriy gave her a long look.

"The Providence a week ago, the *Love Affair* premiere the

very day you came back from New York. Now the Mancini thing. Are we having a love affair of our own here, dorogaya?"

The Russian word cut sharply. Far sharper than he ever could fathom, even though he was aware she was fluent. She sidestepped the past and focused on the present. He was being suspicious and facetious, bringing up a long forgotten endearment. Neve knew she was no longer dear to him. But she needed him for this. And if his attitude and crass jokes were what she had to tolerate to get the job done, she'd do it. It wasn't that bad. She could stand this.

"Spare me, dear."

He gave her a long look and put his cup down carefully.

"I may need you to tell me what exactly is going on here, but you know I'll do whatever you need."

Yes, he wasn't the issue in their relationship. Neve sighed deeply and sat down to explain in detail what had to happen at the reception. She was certain Dmitriy was glad he wasn't drinking his coffee anymore. He might have choked on it otherwise.

———

So here she was in all her splendor, wearing an off-the-shoulder, gold McQueen gown and dancing with a thoroughly bored and just a touch tipsy Dmitriy. Did he really need all that liquid courage to do what needed to be done? It was so hard to get good help these days. Neve almost shook her head in disdain. But any show of displeasure would be caught by Audrey who, Neve had noticed, had been watching their display as a ridiculously happy couple like a hawk from the moment Neve and Dmitriy had made their way into the Ritz's crowded ballroom.

And Neve knew that Audrey was watching, because Neve, in turn, was watching Audrey. In fact, her whole evening, the insipid greetings and endless ass-kissing that she had to endure from famous and not-so-famous actors, directors, producers and executives alike, was made marginally better because Audrey was in the same space. Breathing the same perfume-saturated air. Gliding on her red-soled Louboutins among the rich and famous, as if she belonged. Well, she looked like she very much belonged. A gorgeous backless dress with slits so high, they made those beautiful legs go for miles.

Everyone needed to speak to Neve. She was just that important. But everyone *wanted* to speak to Audrey. She was just that beautiful and attractive. And Neve's eyes followed her every move across the room, from one group of ridiculous, classless people to the next. Audrey's smile, which she displayed openly and often, seemed genuine in a place where absolutely nothing else was. Not the teeth, not the hair, and not the breasts. Everything was for sale in their world, it was a matter of paying the price.

As Dmitriy led her back to their table, Neve closed her eyes. No, not everything was for sale. Not everything could be bought, even in Hollywood. She opened her eyes just in time to see Audrey politely decline a glass of champagne from one of the sons of an oil magnate. He was all burnished gold skin, muscles and money. But Audrey did not want him. As she managed to gently extricate herself from his clumsy clutches, her eyes unerringly found Neve as she sat down in her spot at the central table. But Audrey did not approach.

How ridiculous to want to talk to her, to know that she wanted to talk to Neve, too. Yet being forced to spend her time plotting an utterly insane charade that would make sure they never spoke again.

"Neve..." Ah, and here was one person in particular with whom Neve really did not want to speak. Juno made her way over and unceremoniously plopped down in Dmitriy's chair, who understood that he was not immediately needed and made his escape, carrying away his plate of food.

"My assistant kept trying to find you all day. Is 'unavailable' the new 'I made a big boo-boo and am avoiding my boss?'" A slightly trembling hand reached for Neve's untouched wineglass and dragged it closer. So the old hag was already in her cups. Perfect.

"You aren't my boss, Juno. I work for the Board."

"You always loved your semantics. We both know who runs that Board–"

"And we both know who runs Gannon McMillan and who makes said Board very, very happy." Juno drained the glass and opened her mouth, but Neve had enough. And Audrey was looking more and more tempting by the second, watching her with concern from across the room, clearly aware of what was happening between the two women.

"Juno, I made a business decision. I make them daily. Hourly. *Stay* is making us a lot of money, mostly—if not only— due to the chemistry between the two leads. These things happen. I will not kill the golden goose. And do not send me any more of your poker buddies."

Juno snapped her fingers, and a server appeared behind her shoulder.

"Another." She raised an empty glass towards him. He vanished just as quietly as he'd appeared. Neve braced herself for an argument. For an onslaught of bitchery. No, Juno couldn't technically stop her, but she could make things very difficult for her if she really wanted to. And she was famous for her conservatism.

Yet the older woman tipped back in her chair and lazily stretched her legs in front of herself.

"Donny was a dick anyway. And honestly, this is so small. So insignificant. Do your thing, Blackthorne. And don't disappoint me." With that, she pretty much snatched the wine glass from the approaching server and was gone.

Neve blinked once, then pushed away the plate in front of her, if only to give her hands something to do. Juno didn't care. How... odd?

However, someone else in the room cared very much, and Neve could feel Audrey's gaze on her again, their eyes meeting as Neve raised her own. But she just shook her head at Audrey's silent question and looked around for Dmitriy. It was time to get the show on the road.

She signaled her husband, and while he nodded in her direction, she could tell he was barely keeping himself from rolling his eyes at her. In fact, just that morning when she'd told him that she needed a very public and very inappropriate show of spousal affection, he'd done just that.

He'd rolled his eyes at her and said, "Dorogaya, honestly, you are the smartest woman I know, but occasionally you make decisions that completely contradict my previous statement. You really need me to do that? In public? To ensure that said public is convinced that we are as idyllic as we appeared in our recent outings? Who the fuck cares, Neve? It's Hollywood, nothing is real."

His words echoing Dr. Moore's took the cake. She was so tired of it all.

"Dear..." She drew out the word at him to the point that her tone was pure venom. "In this town, particularly in this town, someone always cares." Before she deigned to explain herself further, he gave her a leer.

"Aha, so it's like that..." But he'd just waved away any explanation she was or wasn't willing to give him. "Fine, Neve, let Barnaby give my assistant the details. I'll be there and I'll do... Well, you."

And so Dmitriy was playing his part well enough tonight. He was a brilliant director after all, and not a half-bad actor, if his hands and his face were anything to go by. The look of desire was almost genuine, Neve thought. And his hands, gliding closer and closer to her ass as he pulled her towards him, told a story of their own. And even as her husband was guiding her in the direction of the spurious bathroom in the back, Audrey's eyes met hers, and for a second Neve thought Audrey could read her thoughts, her fear and apprehension, because she took several steps forward and was getting close enough, close enough to reach out to. But Neve did no such thing.

And then, just as Dmitriy opened the door for her, the music changed, and the slow dances were over, with the new beat thrumming agony in her blood. The reality of what was about to happen dawned on her, and she felt cold sweat at the base of her spine.

Neve was about to have Dmitriy fuck her in the bathroom in the middle of a reception. As ghastly as that sounded, and as little appeal as it held for her, she was also about to add even more humiliation to her already rather painful evening and make Audrey stand guard by the bathroom door.

Predictably, upon being issued an order to "mind the door" from Neve, Audrey's eyes widened in comprehension, and then the look of shock was surpassed by an expression of hurt so pronounced that Neve almost reconsidered. It was beyond cruel how much she was hurting her. To make her live through the sounds of Neve being taken just behind the closed door, not even two feet away.

Except Dmitriy smiled at her and just stood there, inches away from her in the empty bathroom without touching her.

"Wha—" A finger to her lips and a heavy grunt was his response, and then he did push her back with an exaggerated bang. His smile never left his face as he acted out a nearly brilliant sex scene against the bathroom door, with people in close proximity certainly hearing his performance. And he did it all without so much as laying a finger on her or mussing her hair.

And the Oscar goes to...

With her thoughts racing from astonishment to relief, Neve finally stepped up her own end of the bargain and threw her head back with a loud moan. If she sounded fake to her own ears, well, nobody but her needed to know that.

It was over rather quickly, Dmitriy clearly having no desire to prolong the farce, and with a low growl and a sharp, painful bite on her naked shoulder that was sure to mark, he drew away from her.

She raised her eyebrow at him but he just laughed before leaning in close to her again and whispering in her ear, "I'll do many things, dorogaya, but I won't be used quite like that. Our arrangement was never ugly. Let's not stoop that low now." He gave her a surprisingly gentle peck on the lips, one that was sure to transfer some of her lipstick onto him, and stepped out of the bathroom.

Looking in the mirror, trying to assess the damage to her appearance, Neve reasoned that the pain in her shoulder was penance and just part of the price she would be paying very soon.

"For the better, for the better, this is for the better." The whispered chant did nothing to prepare her to face the music.

Unable to stomach the look on her own face, Neve swept out of the bathroom. One glance at Audrey, and the seething rage on her face was enough to tell Neve the shot she'd taken had more than hit its mark.

"Audrey, good. Since you're still here, bring me my wrap and get Barnaby to call for the car." Even as she spoke, she knew it would not be a successful forestalling tactic. Audrey's face was undergoing a number of transformations reflecting the emotions that ran rampant through her. Hurt, anger, rage, and then, at the mention of the wrap—her eyes finally landing on the bruised shoulder, showing the teeth imprints by now—Audrey's face shut down. It was as if something had broken inside her, and she just stopped responding.

For all the strength of the emotion, Audrey seemed to recover quickly, and her fingers flew, tapping on her phone, no doubt telling the missing-in-action Barnaby that he needed to let Neve's driver know he was needed immediately.

After finishing with her phone and getting the wrap, Audrey gently deposited the silk on Neve's shoulder, careful both of the crowded room and prying eyes, as well as of the painful bruise. Neve could tell how much it bothered her, a slight catching of breath betraying her distaste for the mark.

While something had definitely broken in Audrey at the sounds, sight, and at the sheer cruelty of what Neve had done, she knew she would not escape unscathed from this situation, and a conversation would be forthcoming. Audrey would want to be heard, to spew all the venom that Neve had been building in her these past two weeks. She just hoped it wasn't tonight, when she was so battered, sore, and emotionally drained from this humiliating little spectacle she herself had enacted.

In making her escape from the ogling crowd, but mostly from Audrey, Neve ducked into the car without a backward glance. She barely blinked anymore at the cameras, but the screaming of the paparazzi still made something inside her flinch. Hence it took her a moment to realize that karma was paying her for all her sins tonight, because just as her driver was about to close the door, Audrey slipped in right behind her, eyes sparkling with unshed tears.

"To the office, Mitch, please."

Even as her eyebrow rose in question, Neve took the time to be amazed at Audrey's courage. So she would be confronted in her own office, in the place where it had all started, where Audrey felt in control enough to have taken the first step and to have initiated this ridiculous dalliance between them.

Perhaps it was for the best, the whole affair coming full circle. So Neve just nodded and kept her silence throughout the ride until they entered the darkened building.

"What do you think you're trying to accomplish?" Audrey whirled on her the moment the door to the elevator closed. "This isn't a bad romance trope that you're reenacting here, is it? The total failure to communicate that leads to the main characters' painful separation? It's considered inelegant and outdated, Neve. Nobody wants to read or watch that anymore!"

What was it about her life recently that everyone around her just had to mention absurdities like outdated literary or cinematic tropes? First Dr. Moore, now Audrey. Hadn't her own life pretty much proven once and for all that people would consume content that is good, bad, or mediocre as long as it was en vogue?

In this town, she was the one setting the trends. And Audrey of all people should know better than to rely on any kind of permanence in Hollywood. People, like fads, were never permanent here. Because nothing was real, nothing you could touch, feel, smell–and even then, it was usually yanked out of your reach, so you should never, ever believe in its perpetuity. Neve would know all about that. And, she thought, Audrey was about to.

Audrey, who was standing there, holding her ground, so fearless yet again, and Neve wanted to cry for reasons that she did not care to examine. Sure, pushing Audrey away was a bad trope, just like a boss having an affair with an employee was one, and a middle-aged, lonely woman having an affair with a girl almost half her age was the trope to top all others. Neve was close to becoming one massive walking cliché. In her profession, that spelled death. Nobody could do this to her, she would never allow it.

Even under these ghastly circumstances, Neve appreciated Audrey's sarcasm and her perceptiveness. God, she was going to miss her, her intelligence, her wit. The show must go on, though. She had to finish her role to regain her peace of mind.

"It would have to be a romance first for this to be a romantic trope, bad or otherwise." Her tone was deceptively cool, even though Audrey's capability to see right through her with ease had rattled her considerably.

Audrey recoiled as if Neve's words had hit her like a slap across the cheek. She started, then seemed not to know how to follow the opening salvo.

Neve swept out of the elevator, and without looking back, entered her office. The enormous studio complex was mostly empty, and the darkness outside the windows contrasted sharply with the glaring lights in the hallways. Her empire didn't look as impressive as it did during the day, when the bustle and activity of hundreds of worker bees drowned out the loneliness of their queen.

"You're forgetting yourself, Audrey. I will not allow this presumptuous behavior." Trying to regain the upper hand, Neve chose attack as the best defense. "Commandeering Mitchell, hijacking my plans, speaking to me this way... Romance? I think not."

Audrey's eyes were no longer tear-filled. They brimmed with hurt and resolution.

"I see what you're doing, Neve. Romance tropes be damned. You're breaking up with me in the most despicable way you could think of. Funny how you pride yourself on all that courage and all that groundbreaking bravery in this world of glitter and velvet ropes, yet you have to screw your husband in the Ritz's bathroom to try to hurt me enough to leave you!"

The sheer amount of truth that was contained in a handful

of sentences was uncomfortable for Neve to swallow. Yes, everything around them was fake. From the scenery to the people. Nothing was real except Audrey, and Neve knew exactly why she was so attracted to her. The honesty of who she was and, more importantly, what she did to Neve were essential. She touched Neve like nobody else. Neve felt her. And she would absolutely never allow herself to feel again. Look at what it was making her do.

And the perceptiveness that Audrey had to see right through her foolishness, through her absolutely idiotic attempt... Well, that was nothing new, Audrey's intelligence was part of that attractive parcel. But she didn't expect to be read as easily, no matter how out-of-character and ridiculous she was acting. So she leaned in slightly, opening her stance, and looked Audrey right in the eye. And when she spoke, her voice was infused with mockery.

"You're being delusional. Breaking up? We would have had to have been together in some grotesque fashion for something like that to even occur. We had a fling. You must be out of your mind to believe it was anything other than that. I have my family and my marriage. I've been neglecting both. I don't explain myself to my employees. Yet here I am."

"I see." Audrey moved closer to her, and it took all of Neve's experience and her vaunted courage not to take a step back. But something inside her fractured as she stood her ground, something broke into two sharp pieces, one desperate to reach out to Audrey, and one just as desperate to escape. Neve wanted to reach in and take those fragments out, because they were tearing her to shreds.

Clearly oblivious to the battle that wrought and bludgeoned Neve, Audrey continued, "You've had enough of us, and you're moving on. Would it have dented your crown to climb down from your throne of lies and talk to me? Just fucking talk to me. Not around me, not over me, but talk to me. Something changed and you're done with me, but surely you could have just told me?"

Audrey's voice rose slightly with the questioning inflection at the end of the sentence, but she kept it low, and Neve felt like crying again. Audrey clearly wanted to scream. To hurl things and words at Neve. But she deliberately did not. How could she be this gentle, this careful with Neve when Neve was being anything but?

Neve was slipping into emotion, into guilt. So she desperately wanted to get out of this conversation, out of this office, and out of this mess of her own creation. But she knew she had to keep pushing, had to keep hurting Audrey in order for her to leave and never come back. Because for all her resolute actions and cruel words, Neve knew deep down that her own legendary willpower was no match for the havoc Audrey was wreaking inside her.

And there was one more thing. Neve knew Audrey had to be far outside her reach, because if the shards in her chest were any indication, she herself would never be able to truly stay away. That was the crux of it all and the reason for her cruelty and the spectacle. She could keep lying to Dr. Moore and to Audrey. But it was time to be honest with herself. Neve would not be able to stay away. Audrey had to be made to hate her. She simply would not be able to stand knowing Audrey was close by. And so she pressed on.

"I'm surprised by you, Audrey. I thought you had enough sophistication to understand that this little arrangement was for our mutual physical satisfaction. I guess this level of sophistication was too much to expect." She prayed that the desperation in her voice could pass for indifference, because she couldn't even swallow past the lump in her throat. If this failed, if Audrey didn't take the bait, Neve would never be able to do this again. How had Dr. Moore put it? *Flaying?* Indeed. So she kept hammering.

"What did you think was happening here, Audrey? What did you think we were doing? We were fucking! I'll admit it was satisfactory, but I'm surprised that someone who regularly pontificated to me and to everyone else who'd listen about the strength of her ambition, would settle for being a cheap version of *the other woman*."

If anyone knew when her own words would deliver a fatal blow, it was Neve. She had perfected and honed that sense of accuracy to cut to the quick. It was part of her charm. Nobody cut people at the knees or the heart, as accurately as Neve Blackthorne. And so she could tell that she had just delivered that killer blow.

While Audrey had been trying to gather steam into her arguments and was certainly delivering some painful truths of her own, Neve ended the battle before it even had a chance to fully begin.

Audrey flinched and turned away from her, obviously hiding her tears. Neve vividly remembered the imagery of cutting one's own leg off while trying to escape a bear trap. You were gaining freedom while losing a limb, the pain and the cost excruciating.

"God, Neve. Why are you doing this? This... all of this? It's so unnecessary. One word from you and I would have surrendered my life, my future, for you. I thought..."

So she was right, Neve thought. She had guessed Audrey loved her, but to have the confirmation now, amidst all this carnage... She'd think about it tomorrow, she'd think about it tomorrow. She threw her shoulders back, looked down her nose, and lowered the boom.

"You thought what? You thought it was love? Don't be an idiot! I thought I could count on your maturity to understand these things. Others did, so I just assumed..." Neve trailed off strategically, the dangling end of the declaration not giving Audrey any respite.

If this conversation was opening her eyes to anything, it was how young and naive Audrey still was. Perhaps the realization was even fortifying and justifying Neve's actions a bit. Maybe not the way she was going about it—she knew her cruelty was still over the top—but she could see that Audrey's naiveté and her feelings had taken a pretty firm hold on her brilliant mind. *Surrender her life?*

"*Others?*" Somehow it was possible for Audrey to have turned even paler, her tear-brimmed, green eyes huge and the only splash of color on her bloodless face. Her pale lips were moving without a sound passing through them.

Neve chose not to dignify the question with an explanation. After all, she was good, but some lies were better left unexplained to avoid getting lost in the details. So she turned away, facing the darkness of the sky and the myriad of lights, her eyes jumping from one to the next, to the next, seeking purchase, seeking refuge from the heart she was breaking just a few feet away from her.

"We seem to have a situation here, Audrey. I cannot continue to work with you if you're operating under some misplaced impression that what has been happening in the past couple of months meant anything at all."

"Four months! Almost five. Stop pretending you don't remember!" Audrey clasped her shoulder and turned her around violently, pushing her against the floor-to-ceiling window. "Do you want me to make you remember?"

Neve was too experienced not to see the kiss coming from a mile away. Perhaps she was even hoping it would come, baiting Audrey the way she had. Still, when it arrived, it was brutal and sweet at the same time.

Audrey's mouth was bruising, and her hands were gripping just a touch harder than they needed to. Neve knew her arms would be sporting the evidence of this farewell. She took more of the penance she had accepted earlier would be coming her way, and she took it with equanimity, refusing to struggle against the crushing embrace.

For the second time in one evening, she welcomed the pain, knowing too well that once it was all over, she would miss even this. She knew that this ache would feel insignificant in the emptiness that awaited her.

She even allowed herself the small, selfish weakness of tentatively answering the kiss, licking into Audrey's mouth, savoring one last time. Audrey's mouth was all pain and tears underneath the sweetness that always brought longing and want to Neve. The taste of that elusive solace, of remembrance of all the nights they'd helped each other drive the darkness from the door.

Neve indulged for just a moment before going completely still, trusting that, despite her anger, Audrey would never truly hurt her. It struck her that, although she was treating her despicably, Audrey loved her and would never cross that line with her.

As expected, Neve's stillness must have penetrated Audrey's anger, and when she raised her face from Neve's mouth, it was etched with shame.

"I'm sor–"

"Save it, Audrey. It was fun while it lasted. While I'm not averse to some rough play, I'm just not in the mood tonight." Her tone was mocking again, knowing it would only amplify Audrey's shame but also smooth out the rough edge of guilt the girl was feeling for bruising Neve. She really didn't want Audrey's guilt on her conscience as well. Her heart, her feelings, her hurt—it seemed inevitable that all of those would land squarely in Neve's court—but she did not want Audrey to flog herself for something Neve had provoked in her search for escape.

"So, it all meant nothing to you, then?" The voice was quiet, and now the tears were falling unchecked, as if Audrey wasn't aware of them and hence wasn't trying to wipe them away. Neve almost whimpered under the onslaught of tenderness for her. Almost reached out...

"I enjoyed myself. I enjoyed you. However, I was unaware you were operating under some foolish pretense that this was more than it is. I thought you knew that certain things are what they are, nothing more."

"You enjoyed me." It seemed to be a statement, so Neve remained silent. Audrey's eyes burned so bright, so much feeling concentrated in all that green. So much beauty breaking in front of Neve. "My father used to tune pianos. He used to take me with him sometimes. I remember he'd start with one note, and would move slowly to another, then another. Once he'd have a middle A, he'd then tune the lower A..."

Audrey stood utterly still, her lips barely moving, her big teary eyes emotionless at last.

"Strange how I'm thinking about this now, and I have no idea why I'm even telling you this. Maybe to say that, to me, for the longest time, you appeared as a priceless musical instrument. One crafted by hands of centuries-past maestros. Beautiful and majestic. Just slightly out of tune. As if you moved through life with just a small variation of sound, and all you needed was to find that one note to correct the rest to. You know, they adjust full octaves to that one note. A whole piano is tuned to essentially one sound..."

She was sure Audrey hadn't envisioned this as an uppercut. But it very much was one. *A small variation.* Well, here she was being *othered* yet again. *Deficient.* And so she was. Had always been. Neve bit the inside of her cheek. For once, the metallic taste of blood did nothing to ground her.

"How very patronizing of you to think I'm somehow broken. And how very, very naive. With this little speech, you're simply proving that my decision was perfectly justified. Naive, immature and unsophisticated. Did you imagine yourself to be that one note? My savior." She heard the bitter sarcasm in her own voice, but with the girl getting closer to the truth with every sentence uttered, Neve just wanted it all to stop. "There are over 200 strings on a piano, Audrey. Don't strain yourself."

"At least I'd have done my best. I do have a perfect musical ear. It seems what I lack is time. And you lack courage. Or maybe I was just fanciful. And your heart isn't out of tune at all. Maybe it simply wasn't ever in this concerto."

Audrey looked at her for a moment, the bright eyes drying under Neve's scrutiny. Then her shoulders straightened, and she seemed to regain her composure.

"Consider this my resignation, Neve. Thanks for everything. Or is it thanks for nothing?"

Neve watched Audrey as she turned on her heel and exited the office. She stared silently as Audrey briskly walked out of the reception area, out of Gannon McMillan, and out of her life. If all of the above got suddenly dimmer, Neve chose to ignore any and all references about Icarus and the sun that appeared in her mind.

4

NEVE AND THE 21 BLOCKS

"*And now?*"

Neve was getting better at reading the normally impassive therapist, but the sleepless nights and the amounts of whiskey still lingering in her system were making it difficult. Disdain? Disappointment? Or simply a lack of interest, since the question was asked in a tone that did not particularly invite an answer.

"Now nothing. I'm not thinking about her anymore. She's..." Saying it out loud was what had driven Neve to the bottle in the first place, and it had not become easier despite the passage of days. "She's gone."

"Are you cured, then? Since you're not thinking about her anymore?"

Yes, definitely disappointment.

"I'm only asking because, when you came to me all those months ago, you had a game plan. You had your four untouchables–your son, your job, the way the world saw you and your sexuality, your husband even..." Dr. Moore pointed her Montblanc at the sparsely populated chessboard that stood between them on the coffee table. The Queen, surrounded by her defenses. "You had to remove Audrey *from your life in order to keep them. By hook, crook, or whatever it all ended up transforming into. Your plan has succeeded. You have managed to free yourself from Audrey."*

Each word was like a slap.

"I have."

"Then why are you still here?"

"What, me coming to you doesn't conform to your vision of an Ice Queen? Showing weakness, or whatever totally asinine theory you have been spouting for months?" Neve's voice was barely above a whisper, but each word was a lash.

"I'll let you know when you lose your crown, Neve. Why are you still here?"

"Because it seems that I'm still not free." The truth hurt in ways she could not yet allow herself to fathom.

"And so, have we come full circle?" Dr. Moore took a deep sip from her mug.

"Is this you telling me 'I told you so'? Isn't this abusing whatever deontological ethics you pretend to follow?"

Neve's snarl was met with a smile. "Ah, but I'm not treating you. Merely keeping your secrets." Another sip. "You haven't answered my question."

Neve looked behind the pale halo of her therapist's hair and struggled to keep her voice even. Lying was becoming harder with each day. Or maybe just here, in this office, to this woman who seemed to see through her like Audrey used to. Except Audrey was no longer looking at her. At all.

"I am not thinking about her. I'm not." Shockingly, a sob threatened to escape. God, Neve Blackthorne breaking down like a common person in therapy. She wasn't even undergoing any therapy, for crying out loud. She clamped down on the emotion and reached for what little honesty she could muster. "I am not thinking about her, and I can't stop thinking that there are exactly twenty-one blocks between where I am and where she is."

"Twenty-one blocks?"

"Yes, right now, there are exactly twenty-one blocks between us. Me, here in your office, and her, hopefully still asleep in her bed in her shabby apartment. It's 7 AM. She's not a morning person, more of a night owl. But if she is awake right now, her hair is disheveled, and she is staring blearily into her coffee, those squinting eyes shadowed by sleep, slightly dulled by it, as she tries to clear the cobwebs from her mind."

In the ensuing silence of the room, the steady stream of early traffic was barely audible. The luxury of quiet in the threatening onslaught of noise outside.

"You know, I rarely speak about my own life to my patients, but since we established that this isn't what you're paying me for, I will tell you this. Only once in my life, many years ago, was there a person who knew exactly how I woke up, what I'd do, and what my eyes looked like in the morning light. And I regret very much that I did not follow them to the ends of the world."

The words were warm, tinged with something Neve had not heard yet in this office, and the previous disappointment was gone. Winning affection by being pathetic. What a concept.

"Therein lies our problem though, Doctor. She was willing to go to those ends. And I could not let her. Because unlike yours, her regret would have come had she actually gone the distance."

A huff was all she got as her answer.

"In any case, I am not thinking about her anymore. No, I'm not. And whiskey helps me to continue to not think about her if it becomes too much. If I can't stand it anymore." She hoped the stone-cold resolution in her voice would spill over into her waking hours and into her sparse dreams.

"Mom?"

Harlan and the ever faithful Sheppard scrambled into the room, the dog enjoying the full-time presence of his boy during his school break. She scrambled to shove the glass under the table, hearing it break in the process, and then simply closed her eyes at the thought of the mess and Harlan still seeing it, no matter how much she tried to hide it from him. At almost ten, he was quite astute. Surely her genes had won whatever battle they had wrought with Armand's.

She opened her eyes to catch the tail end of concern in her son's, who rushed into the office, his dog—a rescue mutt, completely unsuitable and thoroughly undignified, yet much beloved—on his heels.

"Mom, can I come to the studio with you today? I'll even leave Shep at home, just so he doesn't inconvenience anyone there."

"May I..." The correction came automatically, and she saw Harlan's expression relax a little as a cheeky smile replaced the concern. Had he said it on purpose? To see if she cared enough? If she was sober enough? No, no, no, he didn't know about any of that, about checking on your parents' inebriation or anger levels. Would they lash out? Would they... No, Harlan was a happy, well-adjusted child. He didn't have to try to find out if his mother really cared.

"You may, if that's what you want to do on your few days off school. You may even take Sheppard. I never tire of hearing Gustavo squeal at the dog's excessive, if unrequited, love for him." She smiled, and Harlan's grin turned mischievous. They shared a glance that co-conspirators normally do. Poor Gustavo.

Still, she was his mother, and she could read him like an open book.

"Why the buttering up, sweetheart?"

The blue eyes widened, then dropped. Caught. "I wanted to see some people over at HQ, is all."

Ah, an ulterior motive.

"*Some people?*" She stood up and walked towards him on

legs that were only a little unsteady. He was getting tall, his silky dark mop of hair—perpetually in need of a haircut—reaching her sternum. Soft and feathery like her own. Disheveled unlike hers. At the touch of her hand to his chin, he raised his face to hers, and mother and son watched each other, suddenly wary. Her lifelong instincts of self-preservation knew a blow was coming. His guileless expression never wavered as he delivered it.

"It's been a while since I've seen Audrey, mom. Last time, she said she'd show me some things around the pavilions."

The words were so innocent. The bluest of eyes so pure. So unlike her violet ones. She was happy, perhaps for once, that among so many similarities in their faces, she wasn't looking into her own eyes right now, as his tentative voice was filled with longing for Audrey. Yes, she had left a mark on more than Neve. How very predictable of her. Too bright not to touch the light-starved around her. And Harlan seemed to be even more like his mother than she'd thought he was. Just as captivated by that light.

Perhaps she'd have shielded Harlan from Audrey, had their affair begun earlier. After all, one never introduces one's mistress to one's child. But Harlan had met Audrey well before Neve succumbed to temptation. And Audrey had been much too irresistible a friend for the then eight-year-old boy. She didn't even have to try. She was herself, kind, funny, interesting. Harlan was enraptured. Like mother, like son.

Her silence must have stretched for too long because he reached over and linked his smaller fingers with the ones still caressing his face.

"Mom?"

Neve was terrified that, if he called for her again, if he said *Mom* again, the walls would come down, and she simply would fall apart. She had just enough whiskey in her to keep herself together, but the flood was building inside her, and if she broke in front of her son, she would not be able to stand it. She was barely holding on as it was.

"Audrey doesn't work for me anymore, sweetheart." Did she just end the sentence on a sob? She knew she must have shocked Harlan because, in the next second, his thin arms encircled her waist, and he buried his face in her chest.

She could stand this, she could stand, she could stand this, rang like a mantra in her mind as she ran her fingers through his silky hair.

The morning after Audrey had resigned, Neve made Barnaby get her coffee from a different place than usual and did not think about Audrey. She had fired the first three spokespeople Gustavo brought in without an explanation, demanded her assistant change her schedule ten times, and smirked all the way to lunch with Angelina because Barnaby and Gustavo just might walk into traffic from panic and exasperation alone. She did not think about Audrey.

She'd worked in silence with Gustavo on a strategy for their new project and ignored his sideways glances and quiet sighs. After the fourth sigh, she threw him out of her office and followed that up by tossing the printed copy of their game plan in the trash. Quentin would have to hawk his project to someone else. What was he thinking, casting all these willowy, brunette knockoffs, anyway? Of course, her anger had nothing to do with Audrey.

When she happened to overhear Gustavo mention to Barnaby that the LA Tribune was checking the references of one Audrey Avens, applying for a position as Senior Entertainment Columnist, Neve pretended not to hear it. She really didn't have time to think about nonsense. If she subscribed to the Tribune a couple of weeks afterwards, it was simply because she continued to not think about Audrey.

When she couldn't stand it anymore, she did what she'd told Dr. Moore she would. Her determination to not think about Audrey was becoming too much. She needed some help. Just to make sure she succeeded, that is. Because Audrey and journalism seemed to be a match made in heaven, and in mere months, it had become very hard to ignore the rising star in LA entertainment journalism.

In her eagerness to get said help, she called Elinor Moncrief. They went way back. Elinor had always been very bright, so Neve didn't need to say very much.

"Darling, in case you have not been paying attention, a new reporter at the LA Tribune is doing some satisfactory reporting on the local scene. Perhaps New York Times International might take a look at her? If her work might lead to said reporter being recruited to any of their European offices, that might be satisfactory as well. "

Laughter at the other end of the line wasn't quite what Neve had expected.

"You don't call for years, and when you do, instead of saying 'Hello love, how have you been?' you insinuate that you're doing me a favor, when in fact I suspect I'd be taking a problem off your hands."

Yes, Elinor had always been exceptionally bright, like someone else Neve knew, and was absolutely not thinking about. So when the Editor-in-Chief of New York Times International did not mince words and went straight for the jugular, Neve was not surprised.

The thought of Elinor's intelligence and unerring ability to ferret out her weaknesses in obviously knowing exactly what Neve was asking for made her think of Elinor's bright, eager brown eyes looking up at her from her knees. They went way back indeed. Neve had thought that part of her life over and done with, a mindless indulgence, reckless abandon. *Reckless... Indulgence...* No, of course, none of that made her think of Audrey. At all.

Neve needed distance if she was to continue on her quest. Perhaps an ocean between them would prove to be enough. Distance, that's all there was to it.

Maybe Dr. Moore was right? And maybe Neve herself was wrong? But it was too late now. She had hurt Audrey. She'd pushed her away as hard and as cruelly as she knew how, making damn sure she would never come back. She'd ended the ridiculous affair, and yet here she was, months later, wandering through her quiet Malibu mansion in the middle of the night, dragging her fingertips over the surfaces that still held memories of them together.

She was pathetic, and she felt utterly disgusted with her own displays of such maudlin behavior. She felt untethered and lost and in desperate need of a distraction while waiting for Elinor to help with putting the necessary distance between her and her drug of choice.

The universe was sadly proving to her that she had to be mindful of her wishes. Because the much wished-for distraction materialized unexpectedly one morning soon thereafter as she walked into the reception area of Gannon McMillan, and it was very unpleasant indeed. She was aware that normally her appearance in the offices was announced well before the elevator doors opened onto the third floor, security alerting her assistant to her imminent arrival, resulting in everyone within sight scrambling to attention or to imitate a flurry of activity.

On that particular day, neither her assistant nor any other lackeys were jumping to attention, nor were they greeting her. In fact as she strode closer, she saw Barnaby and the new girl, one of the numerous recent hires in Gustavo's department with whom he was still unsuccessfully trying to replace Audrey. The girl, whose name Neve still had not bothered to learn, huddled close to Barnaby's computer.

"Oh fuck me, this is just ridiculous!" Barnaby's predictable exclamation sounded both exasperated and impressed at the same time. "A hundred thousand subscribers? In 6 months? And what the hell are they even subscribing to? It looks like a bunch of ragtag stories about your neighborhood lesbians. A hundred thousand subscribers! Are there even that many sapphics in the whole of California? I mean, sure, she was 'exceptionally bright'..." Neve could tell that Barnaby was trying to imitate her by quieting his voice and affecting a rather snooty accent. "But to land on her feet like this?"

The appellation of 'exceptionally bright' could only be referring to one person, since Neve had heard it—or rather said it herself—many times during Audrey's tenure at Gannon. Her attention immediately piqued, she slowed her pace, stopping just out of sight of her wayward employees.

"From all these gushing comments, it looks like she has not only landed on her feet, but also in a lot of laps. And rumor has it, it's not just the comments that were gushing either." The girl's snicker was positively obscene.

"Don't be disgusting. It's more than enough that these fans of hers are gross as can be. Fawning over her like... like groupies. It's positively indecent how they throw themselves at her in these comments. 'Oh Audrey, step on my neck! Oh, I'd give anything for her to choke me.' It's filthy." Barnaby was making gagging noises.

"I don't know, Barnaby..." The voice of the new girl was suddenly shy and unsure, but there was a breathless quality to it that Neve immediately disliked. "I saw her last Friday night at the Infinity Club opening. I mean, she's like a celebrity now, you know. My friend and I spent an hour in line waiting to be admitted, and the guard on the door just flung the velvet rope open for her, like she was an actress or something. And she does so look like her namesake. That Old Hollywood charm and adorably nice. The whole gay scene knows her. That blog of hers is so popular, and she's just so uh, beautiful and approachable, so yeah, all the women there were all over her. It wasn't indecent or anything, she was just so nice and uh, hot and well..."

The girl trailed off and took a deep breath. Neve got an unpleasant foreboding.

"I introduced myself, and she was really sweet. I mean, we danced and yes, she's so popular but so cute about it, totally unassuming and uh, well, one thing led to another..."

At this point, Neve understood exactly why the breathlessness in the voice had bothered her. The worthless wench was lusting after *her* Audrey! It was preposterous. Her mouth went dry. How dare this... this... Neve closed her eyes. How dare she put her hands on something that was Neve's?

And on the heels of the rage came shock. Her stomach filled with ice. It had been weeks. Months! This was finished, over. Why was she still reacting with this intensity? She'd gotten what she wanted. She'd rid herself of the distraction that was Audrey. This was beyond enough.

While the power of her rage astounded her, it also sobered her like a summer thunderstorm sweeping through. She was being irrational. She needed to calm down. This wasn't like her at all.

But her nascent and absolutely unjustified possessiveness aside, Neve was also curious, and she wanted to find out more about Audrey. So she reached deep for her control and took a cleansing breath, trying to steady herself as she listened for more.

"What do you mean, one thing led to another? You fiend. You slept with Audrey? *Our* Audrey?" Barnaby's outrage and proprietary inflection would have been amusing under other circumstances, but Neve just closed her eyes and held her breath, desperately trying to catch the answer to the question. She swayed just a bit.

"Neve! Good morning!" Gustavo, who was rounding the corner towards the reception area, jerked her from eavesdropping on her gossiping employees. Belatedly, she remembered that he was her nine o'clock appointment, and it was precisely a quarter to. As naturally as possible, as if she had not just spent five minutes desperately trying to hear whether her former spokesperson fucked her current spokesperson, Neve favored Gustavo with a glare and a nod before striding into her office and ignoring the pair huddled behind Barnaby's desk.

It would have been highly entertaining, the way the two of them scattered like mice at the light, except she still hadn't gotten her answer and by the look of sheer panic on their faces, it was unlikely she ever would. Was she above asking? She really wasn't, but Gustavo's long, speculative look told her he was assessing her for more than just whether she'd overheard the latest gossip. Gustavo, damn him, had always been too perceptive for his own good and knew her way too well.

So a discreet inquiry was out of the question, because Gustavo would know exactly why she was asking right away. Not knowing left jealousy burning like acid in her stomach. One of her more noble reasons—at least the ones she'd been telling herself—in pushing Audrey away, had been to set her free, to live a new life, to pursue other things. Apparently, Neve had not factored in what Audrey's freedom would mean for her. Wasn't she supposed to be done with all this by now?

Sitting down at her desk and opening her laptop, it didn't take her very long to find out that, apparently, Audrey had pursued a great many things. And a great many women. Many *unsuitable* things, and many unsuitable women, by the looks of it. So many unseemly, unsuitable, totally unacceptable women with long legs and big breasts, and why was Neve torturing herself this way? Her breasts were perfectly acceptable, if on the smaller side. Audrey used to adore them... Spend hours on them... God, she was losing her mind, wasn't she?

Already captivated by the flood of information Google was providing about her former spokesperson's pursuits, Neve canceled her nine o'clock meeting, despite her cheeks flaming. Gustavo and his perceptiveness would have to wait. Plus, she couldn't deal with him right now, anyway. How was she supposed to focus when it turned out Audrey Avens was an internet sensation? Audrey Avens–the living lesbian legend, judging by the rave reviews and drooling comments from all corners of the internet. Neve ended up canceling her whole morning.

Vanity Fair had a short blurb about the LA Tribune entertainment columnist who was 'setting the blogosphere alight' with funny, insightful stories, pictures, and little articles about being gay and single in LA. There was nothing remotely *little* about it. Audrey had put her Gannon contacts to good use, was a welcome guest at every party or nightclub, and was using her access and connections to write about the scene and the people around her.

Every post and every picture told a story, a captivating snapshot of a life being well lived, interspersed with humor, warmth and compassion. Even in writing about her burgeoning love life, Audrey managed to find humility and humanity in essentially one-night stands that did not degrade or disrespect her partners. Her many, many, many partners. Reading about each encounter was painful. Neve chose not to analyze this pain. There had been enough thoughts and brooding. It was time to do something.

She called Elinor.

"Darling, this blog of hers reads like a book full of adventures; captivating and titillating, witty and salacious, showing off a gift for writing that I've rarely encountered. Audrey is very talented," Elinor gushed.

"Her subject matter is puerile, definitely obscene, and occasionally profane." Neve couldn't help herself, seething about her friend not leaving well enough alone and continuing to discuss the one topic she herself did not want to even touch. Or maybe she still wanted to touch too much.

"Be that as it may, she manages to maintain a focus on humanity and humor. Her voice is strong and genuine, her style is fresh and distinct, her topics authentic in their unabashed honesty of her pursuits, ranging from sexual gratification to happily ever after." Elinor sounded positively smitten.

"Are you charmed, then?" Neve spat out. She couldn't help herself. Venom was almost choking her. She had to spew it somewhere. She herself was charmed, despite feelings of possessiveness eating her alive. Elinor just chuckled at her angry outburst and hung up on her.

At work, she tried to reign in her vitriol as much as possible, which was easier said than done since she rarely denied herself a good outburst when one was warranted, but even for someone who rarely regretted the unfairness of her own behavior, things were getting more and more out of hand. So out of hand, in fact, that she found herself sitting face to face with Juno Buchanan over overpriced canapés in some new, hip, and truly horrible place that the chairwoman sadly favored.

"Neve..." The affected way Juno said her name always grated. A little scolding, a little affectionate, prolonging the 'e' to where it was tortured to near exhaustion. Juno perhaps thought it made Neve feel special–the fact that she had her own way of pronouncing the two syllables of the name. Instead, Neve resented every single patronizing sound that came out of Juno's mouth.

"Neve, I hear you are on a rampage." Despite the grotesque

accusation—and talk about the pot calling the kettle black, since Juno was notorious for her own eccentricities when she was in a bad mood and certainly for going on firing tears. But despite the admonishing, something told Neve the older woman was not really angry with her.

Before she could answer, Juno waved her away. "I'm not here to give you a sermon on staff morale. If they wanted morale, they'd never work another day in the entertainment industry."

Neve glanced outside at the paparazzi who were chasing some poor starlet to her car that was waiting curbside as she exited the restaurant.

"I hate this town." At Neve's surprised, raised eyebrow, Juno laughed. "Pish, you hate it, too. It sucks you dry. The tainted misery of Tinseltown. Nothing is free, and everyone has an agenda."

They looked at each other for a long moment before her interlocutor reached for the horrible concoction she was drinking. Something frothy. Neve held her silence.

"Gah, you are utterly impossible. I'm not here to lecture you because people are finding you more irascible than usual. You are on course to make Gannon more money than in any other year, so why would I care? I am just here so when those board members ask me why Neve Blackthorne is firing people by the dozen and canceling projects left and right, I'll be able to say we had a delightful lunch, and our financial projections are double the previous year. So answering my own earlier question, I don't care, Neve. I don't care."

As the older woman dug into something that looked like cat food, Neve once again looked out the restaurant window where the photographers were now no doubt intent on their next victim—whoever that might be—coming out of the establishment. When the flashes went off, Neve turned to her carbonated water and ignored the emptiness in her chest. She just wanted to go home, lie on the sofa where Audrey had held her close, and scroll through the wretched blog, which brought her more emotion than anything else these days.

———

Occasionally, among the blog posts about the trivial and the mundane, Audrey discussed things that Neve did not want to be reminded of. The latest one was about movies, Audrey's love for them as she attended some premiere or another. She quoted a classic, the 'here's looking at you kid' being nicely incorporated into the essay's narrative.

Neve was instantly transported back to a rainy evening they'd spent simply sitting on her back deck. The promise—or threat—of perimenopause seemed to have eluded her and she was regular like clockwork, so when she'd gotten her period that evening, it had not surprised her. What did surprise her was that for some reason, when she'd noticed blood on the underwear that Audrey gently slid off her thighs, she hadn't canceled the evening tryst and simply sent her lover on her way. Perhaps that fact should have given her pause. But it hadn't.

She shoved away the thoughts of why, but when Audrey still reached for her, Neve demurred and sidestepped the embrace. She wasn't a prude by any stretch of imagination, but despite Audrey's blushing willingness to still go forward with their lovemaking, Neve for once took charge of how the evening would go. After a quick shower, she simply poured them whiskey. She just wanted to be in Audrey's presence. God, Neve should have run for the hills then and there. How did she not see that they were in too deep?

They sat and looked at the ocean and traded little trivia tidbits about the Golden Era of Hollywood.

"We had a class at my boarding school. An elective. The

History of American Cinema. I was fascinated. Then they had to cut that. The school went through a massive reform and a major downsize. And then it just burned down." Audrey did not seem torn up about it.

"Excuse me? Your school burned down? And you went to a boarding school?"

"Yeah, back home in Massachusetts. I have to say, I only caught the tail end of its glory days before it was almost bankrupted, but it was gorgeous. A small island off the coast. Picturesque. The scent of jasmine everywhere." Audrey kicked off her heels and stretched her long legs.

"And does it surprise you that my folks had the kind of money to send me to a private school? They did. Well, while dad was still alive. Then he died, the school burned down, and mom brought me back home. I went to a public school for my high school years. But that History of Cinema class stayed with me. I knew I was hooked. What about you?"

Her eyes were alight with curiosity, and Neve was reluctant to extinguish it. She should have known then and there that she was in over her head. Not even her husbands were allowed to ask her those kinds of questions. They all knew better.

"Wouldn't you like to know?" So she smiled slyly instead and reached out to Audrey, combing her fingers through the long, luscious, mahogany tresses.

"Fine then, keep your secrets." Audrey caught her hand and kissed her knuckles one by one before her mouth moved lower to tease the sensitive skin on the inside of her wrist.

"Ah…" Neve could not suppress a moan and also a smile. How easy some things were with this girl. How utterly joyful in the dullness of the everyday drudgery and treachery in this town. "No need to bring up the hobbits…"

"I knew I could count on you to know the nerdy references. Now come here," Audrey patted her lap. "I know you said no sex, but indulge my make-out desires."

Neve had tried for an imperious eyebrow raise. She really wasn't a lap-straddling kind of person, but they fit so well, and Audrey had looked so delicious. So Neve had not protested that being able to recognize a quote from a trilogy with seventeen Academy Awards wasn't nerdy. It was professional. Or something.

Neve couldn't seem to help herself. She read the blog posts and tortured herself with the memories they evoked. And there was one more thing. The pictures on the blog stood out just as much as the writing, some random, some mundane, some breathtaking in their simplicity and clean lines. Capturing everyday life, Audrey was giving it a unique perspective.

Among the images of LA and its many women were wonderfully candid pictures of Audrey herself. Neve's critical eye could detect flaws in the photographer's technique but not in the model, smiling blindingly at the camera, holding a Starbucks go-cup, or looking pensively at the rose-tinted dawn sky.

Audrey was perfection in every shot, the long waves of silken hair falling over her shoulders, the big, wondrous eyes dominating a flawless face, the high chiseled cheekbones, denoting a recent loss of weight, and the jutting collarbones telling a similar story and tugging at Neve's already tender and abused heartstrings.

Even more heart-rending and bringing a sting to Neve's eyes were the funny, touching selfies of Audrey looking rumpled and sleep-creased, adorably hamming it up for the shot, all tangled hair and beloved eyes. *Beloved*? What was this madness?

"Well, you wanted her to have a life. Beware what you wish for, because you might just have it all." Except it didn't feel like she had it all. It felt like she'd lost everything.

"I'm sorry, Neve, I didn't catch that." Neve flinched, not realizing she had spoken out loud, until Gustavo appeared in front of her with a concerned look on his face.

"Why are you here, Gustavo?" For the life of her, she couldn't remember them having a meeting of any kind, and his expression didn't bode well at all. He looked slightly subdued and a bit apprehensive, which meant he wanted to talk to her about the one thing she really did not want to talk to him about.

Neve had a vague suspicion that, while she and Audrey had fooled many people, they hadn't been successful in deceiving those closest to them. While she kept Barnaby too overworked and too enraptured by the Neve Blackthorne public persona to see much else around him, Gustavo had not been as easily swayed by her attempts to disguise her recent affair.

If he had an inkling of how she spent her mornings instead of attending meeting after excruciating meeting filled with talentless hacks, then he was here now to offer sympathy, or worse, advice. He had probably imbibed some alcoholic fortifier to get his gumption up. Astute he might be, but at least she was glad she still scared him somewhat.

Still, Neve wanted none of his input or, god forbid, compassion or whatever it was that had taken him all this time to get the courage to say. Her resulting glare seemed to scorch him, and he faltered in his response.

"Ah… I guess I can always come by later, if you're busy." He was giving her both a way out and a way into the conversation, but Neve was having none of that.

"Immensely busy. Barnaby, get me Elinor Moncrief." Belatedly, she realized that her avoidance tactic had backfired massively, Gustavo's face turning from sympathy to downright pity as he turned and left her office. Of course, Gustavo knew who Elinor was now, and he must have some idea of who Elinor had been to her twenty years ago.

He was her right-hand man even then, as she'd plucked him from the obscurity of working for a second-rate production company on Broadway and dragged him along for the ride of both their lifetimes when she was hired for Gannon–first as a lowly executive, and then appointed as the youngest CEO of a US movie studio ever. As her eyes and ears, Gustavo naturally saw not just what was out there, but also what was next to her. Or who was next to her, in the case of Elinor, or damn it, Audrey.

It mattered little, though. At the end of the day, Gustavo would keep his counsel. What was most important right now was that Neve was not getting any distance from her addiction. She continued to consume every bit of information she could get, whether it was through the LA Tribune bylines—which were getting better and longer every day—through the office gossip that still occasionally spilled over details about the former spokesperson, and now via the accursed blog, that kept her up at night, because she inhaled every word and gazed at every picture.

She still needed her distance though, because that way lay her only salvation, and so she was supremely displeased that it had been three months since she'd called Elinor to cash in on the favor, and no such favor had materialized.

"Neve, even I know better than to require a reminder from you!" Elinor's businesslike voice and aggressive approach did little to put a hitch in Neve's stride.

"If no reminder is required, Elinor, then why haven't things progressed?" Neve clutched the phone, her white knuckles standing in sharp relief to the blue veins running the length of her narrow, long-fingered hand.

As ridiculous as she felt, as humiliating as it was, asking her former paramour for help in dealing with her current obsession, knowing she was very close to surrendering to her utmost desire was worse. It wasn't a matter of *whether* Neve would, but *when* she would not be able to stop herself from making the trip to Silver Lake and knocking on Audrey's door. Distance was sorely required.

"Things have not progressed, dearest, because your girl is very good at negotiating." There was no salaciousness or innuendo in Elinor's tone - neither in the endearment Elinor had started to use twenty years ago and had maintained ever since outside of public settings, nor in the assumption that Audrey was hers. Because whether the girl lived a rich and busy life as the hippest entertainment reporter and 'celesbian' about town in Hollywood, Neve knew that her own heart would never accept calling her anything other than 'her Audrey.'

"She is negotiating everything, from her position, to her portfolio, to her legal rights to that fantastic blog of hers, since —as you know—the Times is normally very circumspect in what our reporters blog about and how they do it. So, there are a lot of conditions on both sides. In the meantime, she remains in LA. However, I'm quite pleased to tell you I like her a lot, and if all goes well, I'll be even more pleased to welcome her here in my offices. By the way, dearest, how's her French?"

And now there was both mocking salaciousness and innuendo in Elinor's voice, each one sadly perfectly justified, since Neve could feel the heat rising in her cheeks at the memory of Audrey's French.

5

NEVE'S EPIPHANY

"*It's been a year, Neve."* Dr. Moore leaned over and took the pencil from the coffee table in front of her, fingers brushing off imaginary dust. The office was too pristine for such things as dust to even attempt to appear here. God, she was ascribing animate thought to dust now.

"I am capable of reading the calendar, you know."

Neve was stalling and did not care that her therapist knew it. She'd done nothing but stall and drag time by its sumptuous collar ever since Audrey had left for France. Still, she was here, in this spotless office in front of this unflappable woman who had listened to her for the sum total of 52 hours, and perhaps she owed her just a little bit of honesty.

Like clockwork, the hissing voice reared its head.

Don't tell...

But Neve dug her nails into her palms and pushed through the fear. Small victories. But these days, she was ready to take the small ones.

"If there is one thing that I do not regret about this..." She stumbled over the words, trying to find one that fit and did not reveal too much at the same time, "... estrangement, it is the obvious growth that Audrey has undergone since then."

"Do you believe you've done her a kindness?" The pen stopped its slow scroll in the notebook.

"There is nothing kind about what I've done."

"And what have you done?"

Neve chose to ignore the obvious bait.

"You aren't expecting me to answer that, are you? Elinor was right. The girl is growing by leaps and bounds, her work getting better and better, her writing and her photography getting a distinctive quality and style that is unmistakable for anyone else." Neve took a moment to collect herself. Her eyes trailed toward the window and the palm trees in the distance. She really hated this town. The oppressive heat, the traffic. What was she doing here?

When she turned back, Dr. Moore was waiting patiently for her to continue.

"All I mean is that her voice stands out whether she is writing about the plight of Sudanese migrants or about alternative uses for scarves she's been taking off French women in an effort to try to prove another preconceived notion of hers that all French women wear them. I love that voice."

"Just the voice?" The pencil started its slow, torturous beat again, even as Neve's heart stopped.

———

Cannes Film Festival began as an unmitigated disaster. Every new screening was a waste of time and seemingly a ton of money. Not even the latest Gannon-produced take on the #metoo movement, which was received with modest acclaim and thoroughly unenthusiastic platitudes. They weren't booing, but Neve felt it was only a matter of time. She was starting to have serious doubts that she would have anything of note to show for this year when all was said and done.

It was worrying her, because she had never, ever, in all her years with the studio, walked away empty-handed during an awards season. But at this rate, she would have nothing to put in her glass display come February.

Neve could blame herself. After all, she'd seen all three cuts before approving them into distribution to festivals and private screenings. She could practically hear the litany of 'awards don't make you worthy of love, Neve' and 'you will not lose everything you have simply because a movie will fail' in a voice that was remarkably similar to Dr. Moore's.

It did quiet the other voice in her head that was screaming. *There will always be someone better, always. It's not that hard, since you're defective!* But the fake Dr. Moore, who had not said any of the above since she was not treating Neve, was currently winning by the skin of her teeth, and Neve chose to call it a victory and listen to that voice instead.

A few moments later, she shook her head and tried to focus on the task at hand. Fixing what she must have messed up while she was moping like a complete fool over… Nobody, she'd been moping over nobody at all.

Gustavo's grim face and periodic *tsking* unsettled her further. It was a sign that her current torpor was not simply because of her persistent dark mood. Neve's irascibility of the last year was easily explained and had nothing to do with the new trends in moviemaking, but Gustavo's gloom was certainly due to the quality of the films being screened in front of them during the first two days of the festival. It was a bad omen, since Gustavo usually reserved judgment until at least day three.

Sure, the fact that all the movies were bad was bittersweet, since their rivals were having just as dismal of a showing, but that their three flagships of this year were not garnering standing ovations, was not something either Neve or Gustavo liked to see.

"I don't remember things being this glum when we watched

Unity back last month. Should we consider re-cutting it?" Gustavo's lips pursed, either at the situation or at the wine he was gulping. Neve drank hers without tasting it.

As was becoming their little tradition on these European jaunts, most nights—after attending the various after-parties—they shared a nightcap in the form of a bottle of red wine at the bar of whichever hotel they were residing in. While at the Cannes festival, it was the lounge at Hotel du Cap-Eden-Roc, where the Gannon contingent was staying.

The luxurious surroundings, all caramel leathers and soft carpets, did nothing to soothe the mood. After two glasses and more discussion about tentatively reshooting or re-cutting some of the scenes in at least two of the movies with content they could successfully film in LA instead of incurring sky-high expenses by returning to locations in Iceland or Ireland, Gustavo excused himself to make a call.

As she waved him away and drained her glass, her mind spun. She could already see both the amount of work, if done right, and the expenses spreadsheets. None were things she liked to even entertain, but if organized properly, they could be accomplished. Scenes reshot, budgets expanded to pay for it all. She'd make it work, and Gustavo's PR would put lipstick on the very pretty pig. Neve closed her eyes and massaged her temples. She should have paid closer attention. Her flagship movie of the season...

You will never amount to anything!

Stop, stop, stop...

"Are you okay?" Gustavo's sudden appearance by her elbow startled her and his voice, particularly the note of concern in it, made her slowly take her fingers off her face and give him a disgusted look.

"Order more wine, Gustavo..."

"...and mind your own business." He finished for her, but signaled for the bartender.

She really should go up to her suite and get a plan in place for what could and would be changed in *Unity*. She had won two Academy Awards years ago for directing, and her eye was as impeccable as ever. Well, when she was not being a total fool. But she had no desire to return to her rooms. As sumptuous and comfortable as they were, and as much work as she had, her suite also held a set of papers that had been waiting for her ever since she'd checked in on Sunday night.

Dmitriy had followed through and filed for divorce, his attorney sending the paperwork to Cannes to avoid any further delays and proceed with the dissolution of marriage. Even though Neve was the one who had broached the subject of separation to Dmitriy, it grated on her that he'd proceeded with the course of action quite this efficiently.

Two months ago, as New York Times International Edition published its first article under Audrey Avens' byline, Neve had drunk herself into a near stupor and told Dmitriy, who'd found her slumped on the couch in the ground floor study, that their arrangement was no longer working for her.

"I guess it hasn't been working for either of us, Neve. And for some time now." Dmitriy's hands had been sure and gentle as he helped her up. As if she was fragile, as if he was trying to avoid the big, messy, bleeding wound dead center of her chest, he'd handled her with such care. He also watched her with the expression of someone who knew not doing so would be fatal. She turned her face away from him.

"I hope you don't think I'll apologize..." Her head was spinning, and she wished he had just left her in the study, the room still bringing her solace when not much else could.

"I'd accept it if you did. I'd even apologize right back. I wish I could say we had a good run, but..." Dmitriy trailed off as he helped her navigate the stairs to the second floor.

"Except we had no run to speak of." Neve extricated herself from his arms when they reached the top and slumped against the doorway to her bedroom. She was apprehensive about going inside, the space holding no memories and none of that solace, since Audrey had never crossed its threshold.

"Not much of a run, no. Do you want me to draw up the paperwork?" They'd watched each other like rival soldiers across enemy lines. His gaze had held so much pity that Neve wanted to slap him across his handsome face.

"Do what you wish, Dmitriy."

Looking back now, sitting on a high leather stool ensconced in the corner of the Bellini Bar inside the Cap-Eden-Roc, Neve thought that he actually could be efficient on occasion. Too bad said efficiency was occurring at the end of their relationship. Perhaps things could have gone differently between them if he'd shown such diligence and zeal before.

You're not being fair to him, a voice that was suspiciously similar to Dr. Moore sounded in her ear. Funny how Neve's conscience now had a face and a name. Dr. Moore would have a field day if she knew.

She shook her head and laughed mirthlessly at the absurdity of her thoughts. Even if Dmitriy had been Mr. Efficiency himself, there was no chance in heaven or hell he could have stopped Hurricane Audrey from causing the sheer destruction she'd unleashed on Neve's life. *Continued to unleash,* Neve corrected herself.

A year after Audrey had walked out of the Gannon offices, she still consumed Neve's thoughts. And despite the time and distance, the feeling of desolation was as acute as it had been six months ago, when the emotions had cut her to ribbons every night, and she'd drowned herself in whiskey and self-pity. She couldn't even say that, in the time that had passed, she'd found a better coping mechanism than alcohol.

Audrey was no longer just a cab ride away, but at regular intervals, she still unwittingly prompted reminders of herself, and Neve found herself utterly powerless to avoid them. She still read Audrey's blog about the exploits of a young journalist trying to find her place under the sun. She smiled, and for the first time in a long time, she felt like it was a genuine, if regretful one. Neve had been that sun once. And Audrey was her Icarus.

The months following Audrey's move to France were a fascinating series of stories about French cafes, French croissants, and the unadulterated joy that apparently were French women. Oh, so many beautiful, available, and chic French women.

When she'd arrived in Paris, Audrey had sheepishly admitted that she'd moved to France with some deeply ingrained cliches about them and had set out to either prove or disprove them all, one blog post at a time.

Months later, she was on cliche number eight, after covering French kissing and the perpetual impression of all foreigners that French women are particularly sexually liberated. The last article's cliche pertained to their preferences for shaving or waxing their body hair. The 3,000 word post was funny and interspersed with anecdotes about cultural grooming practices, and Neve could easily draw her conclusion that Audrey had done quite "thorough research" for the article.

Peripherally, Neve was aware that Audrey was becoming as much of a staple of the nightlife in Paris as she had been in LA following their breakup. Her connections from Gannon and the Tribune, augmented by her own 'star power' and current employment at Times, were opening a lot of doors for her.

In the preceding months, Neve had also become aware that Elinor decided to use Audrey quite differently than her Tribune editor had, moving her away from entertainment and into human interest stories covering migration and human trafficking across Europe.

"She is utterly wasted reporting on those ridiculous posers, dearest. With her empathy, her heart, and her open mind for a good story, she's perfect for covering the most gut-wrenching beats there are. She really brings out the best and the worst in both her subjects and the stories. She has such a talent for the tearjerker, Neve. Not to sound over-the-top, but really, she's done some amazing things with stories nobody at my Editorials or Features wanted to touch for months!"

The Times editor had all but gushed during their short lunch a month ago when she had visited LA for some conference or another. If Elinor's eyes were glinting just a touch too bright when she spoke of Audrey, Neve tried not to dwell on it.

Occasionally Neve saw Audrey's photographs accompany her reporting, and the work would reflect such empathy and poignancy, it would take her breath away.

"She's really diving deep with her photography these days, dearest. If I didn't know her and her thirst for storytelling and writing, I might be afraid that I could lose her to some fashion magazine down the road or, you know, a film studio!" Elinor had smiled, and there'd been just a touch of rebuke in that gesture that had not quite reached the eyes.

As Gustavo bid her good night, Neve reached for her glass again. It had been a couple of days since her latest therapy session, where Dr. Moore had casually upended her world to the beat of a Montblanc pen against the smooth surface of her palm.

Neve remembered how sitting upright in that comfortable chair in front of her therapist—her skin flushed and struggling to draw breath as her chest was being constricted by some unseen vise—she had realized she loved more than that voice, that through all the fear, all the terror and pain, she loved Audrey.

What had she done? She had gone and fallen in love, amidst panic attacks and tears, with a girl who haunted her dreams. And under the dim light of a bar in Cannes, nauseous and numb, Neve realized just how deep her feelings ran. Surely it was the worst time to recognize how hopelessly, senselessly she was in love with someone she'd pushed away in a fit of cruelty and fear.

She shook her head at herself. Neve Blackthorne was known for her perfect timing, yet here she was, in the midst of an impending divorce that was about to go very public, having earth-shattering revelations about love.

"Dr. Moore, I'm fairly certain my heart is incapable of such gauche banalities as love," she'd told her therapist before she'd escaped the wretched session twenty minutes early.

And wasn't she supposed to be above such a lack of sophistication? The irony wasn't entirely lost on her, since that had been one of the many targeted accusations she had thrown Audrey's way when she had told her she had feelings for Neve. Such foolishness.

Yet no doubt about it, her heart was beating double-time, and she was on the verge of hyperventilating. Oh, what had she done?

The rhythmic clicking of high heels on marble broke through her reverie, and the effect of the interruption stopped her impending anxiety attack dead in its tracks. She had to wonder about what deity was ironically turning the tables on her. Here she was, confessing to herself that she had feelings for Audrey, whom she had treated horribly to save her own skin —and said deity laughed in her face by sending this particular girl to this particular bar in the heart of Cannes right at that moment.

She would have recognized that gait anywhere. God knows she'd waited for Audrey to walk into a room often enough to know the cadence of her steps. Despite her training and her attempts at grace, Audrey was innately just a tiny bit clumsy. It was so endearing how her stride would occasionally falter. It did not waver this time though, and once the heels were muffled by the lush carpet that surrounded the bar, Neve knew her time to collect herself and her wayward feelings was up. The girl was standing right behind her.

In her mind it was like one of the classic Hollywood movies. She was almost tempted to turn around with a retort of, 'of all the gin joints in all the world,' but Neve was never trite or given to cliches. *Roll camera. Action.*

The scene unfolded in slow motion as Neve turned, and her eyes met Audrey's. The sight hit her square in the chest with the power of a defibrillator. No girl. Not anymore. A tall, slim woman was standing in front of her. The luscious, brunette locks were gone, replaced by a short, boyish pixie cut, with longer bangs falling teasingly over her eyes. "So very French".

She must have said it out loud, because the otherwise inscrutable features softened, and a mirthless smile blossomed on the pouty lips.

"When in France... Good evening, Neve."

The generous mouth moved, and distantly Neve registered the words, but her mind was busy, engaged in cataloging all the changes in the face and body she thought she had known as well as her own.

The short hair revealed a narrower face, the remnants of the youthful fullness it had still held last year gone. The change, in turn, unveiled stunning sharp cheekbones that were offset by eyes that seemed to dominate the beloved face. *Beloved. Not madness anymore.*

The cut also uncovered the long expanse of Audrey's graceful neck, all alabaster skin and translucent veins. A pulse was beating somewhat erratically just beneath the delectable angle of the jaw, and to Neve's surprise she understood that her slow appraisal of the changes in Audrey was unnerving the woman and making her uncomfortable, perhaps even angry.

As their eyes met, the anger became apparent. Anger and something else, something hiding in those wide green depths. Something that looked remarkably like desire.

Words were escaping Neve. How could she be expected to speak when all her senses were alight with a terrible, unfathomable longing that had been unknown to her until now? If she thought she'd been missing Audrey while not seeing her for a year, well, she was certainly dying for her now that she was standing right in front of her, glaring at her like someone might at one's mortal enemy. But even that forceful glare was doing things to Neve's insides. The strength of that gaze was making her wet, was making her crave, made her want to beg to be bent over this very bar stool, rich patrons of the Hotel du Cap-Eden-Roc be damned.

She wanted to say, "An entire year has passed and I still want you, want you with the heat of a supernova. But I'm so afraid, dear heart, I'm so afraid..." But Neve held her tongue and bit her lip. Nothing had changed.

"I see little has changed, Neve." Audrey's words startled her out of her reverie. God, was she this transparent? "I see you still don't deign to offer me the common courtesy of simple human communication. Answering greetings is still beneath you?"

Ah, the brash boldness was new too, but blessedly Audrey was still not a mind-reader. Neve grappled to find her infamous dismissive tone of voice.

"You've grown daring in your exile in France."

Audrey sputtered at the words, and it was gratifying to see that, despite Audrey's newly gained otherworldly quality to her husky tone and mature posture, Neve still had the power to easily provoke this woman.

Not bothering to hide her wry smile at the realization, Neve waved her hand carelessly. "No, no, that wasn't intended as a question. But this next one is. I assume you're disturbing my evening for a reason?"

"I need to speak to you."

"Well, you've spoken to me. Clearly, your objective has been accomplished. Now run along." She made a production of dismissing Audrey with a tilt of her head and returned her attention to her fourth glass of wine. It tasted bitter on her tongue. *Please, please, leave. I cannot stand that. I cannot stand that at all.*

"Don't be rude, Neve. Invite me up to your room." Audrey's assertiveness had always been so attractive, so very tantalizing, but Neve refused to give in, even when fighting this feeling was torture.

"I think not, Audrey. I'm not sure what you wanted to achieve by showing up here, but for old times' sake or not, I'm not in the mood."

To her surprise, Audrey laughed and, just like Pavlov's dog, ingrained, habitual emotions were unleashed in Neve again. Audrey's laughter had always brought elation, trepidation, and arousal. As if Neve needed any more of that. The scent of Audrey, Chanel, and that unique fragrance that was all woman had had her on edge since the moment Audrey had stepped close enough for Neve to sense it.

"God, what the fuck am I even doing here?" Audrey rolled her eyes but did not move away. "Invite me up to your room, Neve. You'll want to hear me out. I don't think you want me to spill the details of how your boss is trying to sell the studio out from under you right here in the middle of one of the most popular lounges of the festival. God knows who in here is even now wondering what the hell it is you're doing talking to the Gannon pariah."

The short monologue stopped Neve's glass halfway to her mouth and made her take a furtive look around. Seeing some vaguely familiar faces in the shadows of the lounge, Neve signaled the bartender to charge her room for the drinks she'd consumed this evening, stood up, and wordlessly exited the Bellini, Audrey's heels clicking an almost uniform rhythm behind her.

The elevator ride took forever and did nothing to quell her desire or her memories of being ravished in similar elevators in other hotels, only without the state-of-the-art discreet cameras that were now recording their every move.

Her hand, however, was steady as she keyed open her suite. Audrey's low whistle at the surrounding luxury made Neve bristle.

"Why are you here, Audrey? Are you so desperate that you have to make up some story about Juno to get into my room?" Fear and irritation at herself for *being* afraid were making her angry, and she was desperately trying to summon her vaunted control. She mostly succeeded, judging by Audrey gritting her teeth at not being able to visibly discomfit Neve.

"IV&X will make the announcement some time this week, right in the middle of the festival, that they're acquiring the majority stake in Gannon McMillan. While I'm not sure what the short-term plan is regarding your future, in the long-term, Danilo Rosilianni has been tapped to take over. The Gannon and McMillan families might be happy with the studio's performance, but IV&X is a business first, and Rosilianni is known for making quick money. The contract isn't signed yet, but they have all their plans in place. Rosilianni has been working on recruitment, especially since this will be a dual power grab. IV&X is also purchasing Miramar, which they'll announce tomorrow."

Audrey made her way closer to the bank of windows overlooking the stormy Mediterranean. Foamy waves crashed into the rocks below them, the tension heightened by the darkness of the room. Neve had not bothered to switch on the lights.

They'd dealt in the shadows before. They seemed to be destined for them again.

"A good friend of mine handled some parts of the potential future merger. With this acquisition, the Hollywood landscape is going from Major 6 to Major 4, and that's big news. Several of my former sources from the Tribune and other media outlets have either helped make this happen by working with Juno Buchanan or signed on as various future executives."

Shell-shocked, reeling, Neve turned on the small lamp and poured herself a glass from the first bottle that was closest to her. At her raised eyebrow, Audrey shook her head and went on.

"The Gannon McMillan board will be forced to accept the transaction as a fait accompli, since it would be beyond embarrassing for the studio to reverse a very public announcement. The vultures would start circling right away. The drop in shares alone would spell disaster. Rosilianni, for all his messy entanglements with various D-list actors, is still entirely too well-respected in London and LA. Gannon isn't in trouble, but he can make it rain. And IV&X wants it to rain hard."

Audrey shook her head, and her face, even in the shadows, reflected disgust. "And they're notorious for promoting that homophobic douche canoe, Peter Cross. Pardon my French. Actually, I'm not sorry, as he doesn't deserve to have eloquence wasted on him. Miramar already has him booked for three of their flagship productions. He isn't even that good of an actor. He keeps denying his bigotry, but is still seen with the same crowd that funds anti-trans organizations and legislation."

Neve stopped her pacing and turned sharply to see Audrey's disapproval.

"And I've noticed you've given him quite the juicy role in *Unity*. Yes, it's literally three scenes, but you made *him* the voice of reason and collective conscience? Talk about putting the fox in the henhouse, a bigot in a movie about victims of bigotry?"

With her mind still reeling from the revelations and rocked to the core, Neve glanced around herself, eyes unseeing, before finally turning away from Audrey, and focusing on the tempestuous waters. She felt adrenaline flood her veins and her survival instinct kicked in. Oh yes, she could totally see Buchanan maneuvering the Board this way.

The old, crotchety, yet remarkably malleable representatives of the two families had been arguing for years that the studio could make more money if they either sold half the shares or agreed to produce more profitable content. As if Neve hadn't been delivering record revenue for years. Yes, she could see how Buchanan would easily bend them to her will.

"Juno always did prefer to ask for forgiveness rather than for permission. Is there anything else, Audrey?"

"Wow, so much for that, then. You're welcome, Neve. I guess I should have known better than to expect that you would actually appreciate my help." Audrey took a couple of steps away from the window, and her eyes landed on the divorce papers spread on the coffee table. Unbidden, she sat down on the couch and slowly perused them, the small lamp providing poor light, making Audrey squint at the text. Neve wanted to be outraged at the presumption, but her mind was already in overdrive.

"Would you look at that? All those attempts to save that pathetic marriage of yours, and he still dumped you... well, well, well."

Oh, so Audrey had developed a cruel streak along with that brashness. Unlike the latter, the former did not suit her. Neve did not recoil, but it was a close call.

"What do you want, Audrey? A thank you? I'm appropriately grateful for your efforts to warn me. Is that enough to mollify your nascent ego?" Spiteful words were falling from her mouth, and she knew she was powerless to stop them. She was in fight-or-flight mode, and Neve Blackthorne never ran away from anything.

"I learned from the best, Neve. No bigger bitch out there than you." Audrey was now lounging comfortably on the couch, having thrown the paperwork back onto the coffee table. "Still, this is rather sad when all is said and done." She stretched, Neve's eyes tracking every move of those legs in the dusk. The lithe muscles distracted her enough that the next question surprised her, since it was such a non sequitur and said in such a gentle tone.

"Is Harlan alright with this? I know he cares for Dmitriy."

Dichotomy in action. From cruel to kind. From pain to longing. Perhaps these were all just sides of the same coin. Neve's coin.

Audrey's kindness was predictable, no matter what had transpired between them. Yet Neve still despised how weak it made her, how tears threatened at the decency and purity of this woman.

You make me weak, dear heart...

But she said nothing, unsure of her own voice, just nodded and turned away again.

Behind her, the leather of the couch betrayed Audrey stretching again. When the low voice sounded once more, it carried none of the earlier kindness.

"*Irreconcilable differences*, huh? Did he mean, 'my wife prefers eating out her spokesperson on her desk'? Because those are rather difficult *differences* to reconcile." Audrey's laughter was brittle and did nothing to smooth the jagged edge off the memory of spreading Audrey's pale thighs and leaning in to greedily lick all that wetness that always awaited her there.

"Or are we talking about the *irreconcilable differences* of taking four fingers from said spokesperson and being fucked out of your mind against the front door of the mansion you share with your husband, coming so many times you couldn't walk up two flights of stairs?"

Audrey's hand stroked the leather of the couch, fingers tracing the seam, but her eyes never left Neve's as she continued.

"Or maybe you couldn't reconcile having your ass spanked in the executive bathroom until it was red and tender, and you could barely sit in your chair during meetings, squirming through your dinner with him, knowing that your employee would arrive in a couple of hours and you would beg her to kiss it all better and then to eat you out on the carpet in the study? Oh, I loved it when you begged, Neve. I sincerely doubt he's ever heard you do that though, and I think therein lie those *irreconcilable differences*, don't they?"

The effort it took to fight the blush and not tremble at the deliciously provocative words Audrey was hurling at her was gigantic indeed. Neve thought she managed to maintain her equanimity, but it was a close call. The things Audrey did to her. She was wet and throbbing.

"Your point, Audrey?" Neve marveled at the coolness of her own voice. She turned around and almost laughed at how, despite the movement, the vista in front of her didn't really change. A stormy sea contained by rock and sand and shore. Audrey at her most volatile, keeping it together for the sake of gaining the upper hand. Either way, she couldn't help but notice the parallels.

Sighing, Audrey lithely uncoiled from the couch and walked up to her. Easily crossing the room in three long strides, she invaded Neve's personal space, gently placing her palm on her cheek, bringing their faces just inches apart. Neve could feel the hot breath on her temple.

"No point, Neve. I said what I came here to say." Audrey's mouth was moving just a breath away from hers, so close Neve could almost taste it. She wanted to scream from impotence, unable to escape the spell Audrey had her under.

"I guess I was also wondering if we could reenact some of the scenes that caused those *irreconcilable differences* between you and your soon-to-be ex-husband, you know, for old times' sake. Now that you're a free woman and all." Audrey's lips burned a trail from Neve's temple to the corner of her mouth, stopping at the very last moment. That moment was enough though, for Neve to marshal the last of her defenses. She wanted to submit, to surrender, but not like this. God help her, not like this.

"Go to hell." She took a step back, out of Audrey's sphere, and the cool hand cradling her cheek fell away. She felt the loss to her very core.

"I'm already there," Audrey spat before turning for the door. As parting shots went, Neve thought it was a worthy effort.

6
NEVE GETS HURT

"Well, that's your Pawn gone." Dr. Moore, with an unfathomable expression, toppled the piece in question off the board where the remaining three figurines flanked a rather lonely-looking Queen. "How has Dmitriy leaving made you feel?"

"Oh, so now you're acting as my therapist? Suddenly, after an entire year?"

Dr. Moore sighed and pursed her lips.

"Yes, yes, fine. You'd have treated me a long time ago if I wanted to be treated." Neve threw her head back, long diamond earrings soothingly swaying along her neck.

"You're stalling."

Well, when she put it like that. Yes, Neve was stalling. How to explain years of fear? Years of loneliness and everything that came with that.

"It's not that he left, Dr. Moore. It's that he left me."

"Ah, so you'd much rather be the one doing the leaving?"

Neve shook her head again. The light playing off the diamonds was glinting on the office walls, giving it a slightly whimsical feel.

"I don't appreciate things being taken from me. I'd rather discard them myself."

"Rather cold, since he is a person. Though also accurate, since you did discard Audrey."

The glint of diamonds on the walls stopped dead as Neve felt herself freeze in shock. As hits went, that one hit its target.

"But I hear you, especially since Juno Buchanan was taking Gannon from you. And that wasn't something you'd ever allow."

"Juno and I dealt well with each other for almost twenty years. Her attempt to sell the studio out from under the families and under me was a betrayal that went too far. Dmitriy was never mine. Audrey had no business being with me. But Gannon? Gannon was mine. And I simply couldn't allow anyone to take it away from me."

"Have you had any more panic attacks?"

Neve deliberately crossed her legs that were suddenly leaden and checked her manicure. Inside, her stomach was doing flips, and she could feel the telltale pressure in her chest. The words were thrown out there nonchalantly, as if Dr. Moore wasn't shooting in the dark, trying to catch Neve in the truth. So she tried to push through the numbness, hoping to reach for her vaunted calmness.

"No." She was pleased that her voice sounded clear with finality.

"I'm only asking because a person with as much talent as you as a creator and director should have no issue with visualization and using that to carry you through an anxious episode. Our happy places often do."

Sneaky bitch, putting coping mechanisms in Neve's mind.

"Is this how you're not treating me, Dr. Moore?"

The good doctor did not have the grace to act caught.

"No, that is simply how I sustain a conversation with you and occasionally look out for you, Neve. You're still not ready for treatment."

"And why is that?"

"You're still determined to punish yourself instead of dealing with *what happened. And getting hurt instead of getting better is your preferred method."*

It only took one call to Gustavo's room to get this show on the road. With Audrey's perfume still hanging in the air, Neve was shoving her savior out of her mind and getting to work. Juno thought she could go and sneak behind Neve's back in the middle of the night and assumed the Board would have to swallow it, because nobody would want the embarrassment of opposing a done deal with IV&X.

The stock alone would take a considerable beating. Not to mention Gannon McMillan's reputation would be in tatters, a complete and utter laughingstock. And if one thing was unbearable, both in entertainment and business, it was making a public spectacle of yourself. A show, sure, but not a circus. Your reputation was all you had and once gone, it was gone forever. Some things were never forgotten, no matter how many news cycles passed.

So she had to fight a war on two fronts. First, she had to ensure that, even if the deal went through, there was absolutely nobody who'd be able to replace her, chief among them Danilo Rosilliani. Otherwise, there'd be no way back from this. With everything she had lost in her life, one thing was a constant. Gannon had been her rock when she got divorced from Armand, when he'd almost taken her child away from her, when she was all alone, and when she recklessly dove into the deep waters of her love affair with Audrey and almost drowned in them. Gannon was always with her. She could not lose Gannon. She *would* not lose Gannon.

And the biggest battle that would absolutely ensure a complete victory in the war itself was stopping the sale of the studio to IV&X.

The plan came together quite simply. Thirty minutes ago, Gustavo had stormed into her suite, made himself comfortable on the couch, arranged his robe demurely, taken one look at her face, surreptitiously sniffed the air, raised his eyebrow and pointed to the papers on the coffee table.

"I guess I don't have to ask how you found out about this whole mess. Put away those divorce papers before Barnaby hurts himself when he tries to contort his body into a pretzel of happiness and sexual exuberance because his idol is newly single."

"Gustavo, don't be gross!"

"If I can't make a joke at the expense of your recently acquired, future double-divorcee status, then I'll want a lot of coffee. And yes, I realize it's ironic that you're going to order *me* coffee."

"Gustavo... The drama..." Neve's voice was no longer affronted, her exhaustion bleeding into it. She really had no time for his jokes.

"Neve, I'm trying to cope in my own way here. Unfunny jokes and silly drama at your expense are all that's sustaining me. The sale of the studio aside, if you're going to take out Rosilliani, you have to either buy him off or scare him off. And while you are quite scary in your own way, I think you and I both know that it would be easier to make him an offer he can't refuse."

Neve raised a finger as she ordered room service and Gustavo took a breath, his chest rising and falling rapidly. She could always count on him to be angry on her behalf. She could also count on him to offer her solutions. When she hung up the phone, he went on.

"Offer him something else, something more enticing to him than the intrigue and fatigue of Gannon. He's been at Miramar for two years. We've both heard the rumors that he's not a fan of, you know, the actual grind, but his ego demands that he gets to make a dignified exit."

"So you're saying IV&X offering him Gannon is that 'dignified exit?'" Neve bit her lip as she considered the possibilities. Contours of a plan were taking shape in her mind. But the price of some parts of the plan was exceedingly high. She looked at Gustavo, who seemed to be eyeing her in return.

"He was never into actually running a studio. He's a man of leisure. He loves to be the center of attention, but he doesn't have the nous for movies. His tenure at Miramar wasn't the success anyone had hoped it would be, hence the studio is being sold to IV&X. And I mean, I guess he facilitated the sale?"

Neve leaned against the window, the glass cooling her shoulder through the silk of the blouse.

"That would make sense. Help Ivor Nowak and IV&X get Miramar on the cheap, and we will give you a much bigger and better job? Sounds like something IV&X would do. They have been pretty ruthless and cutthroat, not to mention underhanded, since Ivor took over ten years ago. They are unquestionably a business empire, but they don't know movies."

Gustavo opened the door to room service and smiled at the sleepy and slightly spooked young server. Before he could scare the boy further, Neve pulled out a hundred euro bill from her purse and handed it to the fresh-faced youth who still stood in the doorway gaping at the two of them. They probably presented quite the picture. Her in her evening finery and Gustavo in nothing but a bathrobe. She took the cart from the server and pulled it further into the room, turning back around in time to see Gustavo wink at the kid.

When the door closed, she tsked at him.

"You are incorrigible."

"Ah, but I'm harmless and even he knew that." As Neve poured him coffee, he gave her a strange look. "Let's circle back here for a second, Neve. Hiring Danilo makes little sense for Gannon."

She stepped back to the bay of windows, and a sense of déjà vu enveloped her. Just an hour earlier, it had been Audrey standing at her shoulder. If she tried hard enough, she could still smell her.

"But it does, Gustavo." Before he could ask useless questions, she simply went on. "Danilo finished what the previous owners of Miramar started. He ran that studio into the ground. Now IV&X will buy it for peanuts."

Coffee burned her tongue, and she hissed. Her next words burned her mouth just as much as the coffee had.

"Can't quite do that with Gannon. Right now, under the present Board, I am not expendable, the studio is profitable. The families cannot simply fire me. The litigation I'd bring for unlawful termination would be insanely costly, not to mention just bad. But a new owner can fire anyone they want. The whole staff, including the CEO. The way my contract is structured, I'm tied to the ownership, as are you, as is everyone else in the executive suite."

Now the wheels were turning in earnest in Neve's mind. Gustavo clattered with some china behind her, but she grit her teeth and ignored the sudden noise.

"So the plot is to replace you?"

"As much as I'd love for the world to revolve around me, Gustavo, it unfortunately does not. I'm certainly disappointed that this is not the case." He grinned at her sarcasm as she went on. "The motive isn't murky, though. If you were to preserve the profitability of your investment and maintain Gannon at its peak, wouldn't you want the best for the job? Why would you then hire the worst? Why fire Blackthorne and install Rossilianni?"

Gustavo's eyes lit up, going huge.

"Because they don't want to preserve Gannon at its peak!"

Neve took a sip, scrunching her nose at the substandard, bitter aftertaste.

"Indeed. Gannon has the biggest—bar none—library of films and cinematic rights in the world. No other studio can compare. We have been buying left and right, after all…" She let the end of her thought dangle, and Gustavo picked it up seamlessly.

"Because we're launching the Gannon McMillan streaming service that would rival any others on the market."

"IV&X doesn't want Gannon. Nor Miramar, for that matter. IV&X have invested billions in their floundering Flix Stream. Acquiring Gannon and Miramar would ensure Flix soars. And it doesn't matter if the studios themselves die a quiet death, their catalogs would ensure longevity for Flix."

"Fuck." Gustavo sat down.

"Very much so. Ivor has done this to many of his properties. Newspapers, magazines, multimedia companies. Buy, gut, move on. It's nothing new under the sun, I'm afraid, Gustavo."

"But Danilo… He knows that corporations focused on profit only and not on product will fail in Hollywood. Everyone knows—you, me, Danilo—that true art and corporations do not mesh. Movies are too much work, too much ephemeral shit like creation and trends, and about which way the wind blows. Too much work, too much juggling." Gustavo's theatrical recitation almost made Neve smile.

"Danilo's willingness to be part of this is a surprise to me though. He's not evil or cynical. But he is vain…" Neve took another sip of coffee, the plan coming together in her mind. She turned to look at Gustavo, only to find him looking at her, his eyes suddenly sad, yet determined.

"So get him a top dog position in a major *something,* and he will stab Juno and the suits at IV&X in the back quicker than you can say *action!*"

"Gustavo, other than my own—and forgive me if I don't

surrender it lightly—there's only one corporate executive position I can offer him." Even as she spoke, she could tell Gustavo knew what was coming. In fact, all his horsing around was his way of shrugging it off, of trying to tell her he knew and accepted her decision.

"Yes, you can only swing one new exciting endeavor his way. Perhaps if you had more time, you'd convince some other corporation to take him on, but we only have until the deal becomes common knowledge. And considering Audrey already knows, that's not much time at all. If *she* doesn't publish the story, someone else will, and you know it."

She started to speak, but he raised his hand, effectively stopping her.

"You and I go back decades, Neve. Yes, you planned on making me head of Gannon Streaming. And I was very much looking forward to making it into what you and I envisioned. 'World domination,' wasn't that what we called it? And now you have to give it to him. The role is separated from the studio per se, so he is your peer rather than an underling. It's not a creative job, and it's very much a camera-forward one, he'll love it. He will also be perfect for it. Not that I wouldn't have been."

He smiled, but his eyes did not crinkle, and Neve could tell he was being brave for her sake as he continued. "And for me? You will think of something, Neve. I have faith. Just like I had faith in the girl who left without saying goodbye a year ago. The one who showed up tonight—she left an unmistakable Chanel trace in her wake—to warn you. To help you. Also, Barnaby was right. She is rather predictable in playing it safe with that particular perfume. It's classic, but a safe choice. She should be more daring."

And now his smile was honest and heartfelt, its warmth touching Neve. "But I guess developing a bad habit such as Neve Blackthorne is as daring as one could ever get."

Neve had no problem with secrecy. She lived her life

surrounded by a relative shroud of mystery. After all, that was her allure. But Gustavo's breezy attitude towards her entanglement with Audrey and his unflinching support with the IV&X and Rosilianni affair were giving her strength, propping her up in a way she was unaccustomed to.

"I guess I see why you got so sleepy earlier tonight, scampering out of the bar in such a hurry. Tell me, do the two of you have secret signs or something?"

Having some of her suspicions about her friend being involved in the events that transpired earlier confirmed, Neve was surprised to feel lighter, freer. Her shoulders relaxed a bit, and she unclenched her jaw. A weight she'd had no idea she'd been carrying had lifted.

"No secret signs, but I might get t-shirts made? Maybe... If only plain cotton wasn't so ghastly!"

"Last time you wore a t-shirt, we were in New York, you had a ponytail, and were living with that beautiful boy who was dancing on Broadway." She stopped abruptly and bit her lip at her own lack of tact. To her horror, Gustavo's eyes welled up.

"Yes, he was a beautiful boy. He's been gone for over twenty years now, and..." He waved his hands at her, taking a deep ragged breath. "No, no, it has been twenty years, after all. And I did have a wonderfully luscious head of hair, and he really loved that ponytail." He turned away from her, trying to wipe his eyes.

He still did have great hair. It fell just short of his collar in salt and pepper waves—a bit more salt than pepper these days—and it showed no signs of thinning. But he never put it in a ponytail anymore. Neve thought she now knew why. When he turned to her and cleared his throat, his eyes were dry.

"Barnaby will be here any moment, and if he sees me in tears and you with that totally uncharacteristic apologetic expression on your face, he might think we are, God forbid, human. Let's stop this maudlin nonsense and get to work. You will need more than a place for Rosilliani. And you will need some form of insurance against the deal going through as well."

Feeling that the somber moment had ended, it was time to take charge. The knock on the door jarred both of them out of the emotional scene. As Gustavo turned to open it, Neve straightened her shoulders and hardened her voice, shaking her hair out of her eyes and the melancholy out of her mind.

"I'm Neve Blackthorne, Gustavo. I've made half the people in this industry household names, and those who were not made by my hand still owe me their mere presence among the stars on Hollywood Boulevard. I won't cower behind anyone. Attack has always been my preferred defense. I don't need insurance. I need a weapon."

She heard the door open and turned around to see Barnaby and Morag standing in the doorway with varying degrees of awe on their faces.

Gustavo laughed and nodded at Neve with an 'I told you so' smirk before ushering both of them into the room. "Barnaby, wipe the drool off your mouth. Let's get to work here, people! The fate of Hollywood as we know it rests on our shoulders." Barnaby actually shuddered, and Neve wanted to laugh.

But laughter was not the predominant emotion once she brought both him and Morag up to speed.

"You might think that's an exaggeration, this whole 'fate of Hollywood' thing." Morag's voice was calm, but Neve could hear the underlying chill. "But how is this possible? If this goes through, if these two sales move forward, Hollywood as we know it, will be decimated. Buying studios to destroy them and drain their catalogs for online content? What will happen to movie theaters? To US movie production, for Christ's sake? A lot of filming already takes place in Vancouver and Eastern Europe and other places. The cast can go there, but the crews most certainly cannot. So it's cheap contractors, hourly wages…" Her face betrayed deep concern.

"Do you think the crews' union might have something to say about all of this?" Neve could feel the smile uncharacteristically stretching her lips. Yes, unwittingly Morag had offered her part of the solution, but this also pushed her towards the crux of the issue.

"And you are right, it is absolutely not possible, or should not be possible. After buying Miramar, IV&X will own one of five. If they acquire one more—especially one as big as Gannon McMillan—they will own over one-third of the market. I think the DOJ Antitrust Division might have a lot of thoughts on that issue, don't you?"

Then something that Audrey had said tugged at her memory, and she added, "Oh, and Gustavo, while we're at it, let the Unity team know we are going to need re-shoots for parts of the film. I want Peter Cross' role recast."

Three pairs of eyes watched her with something akin to shock.

"But Cross is the best part. His role is small, yes—three scenes and reshooting them won't involve much cost—but it is one of the most powerful portrayals in the movie. Everyone said so yesterday during the screening." Barnaby's hand actually shook when he pushed his glasses up his nose. "He's a sure thing, one of the most exciting rising stars. Gannon has him slated for at least four more projects."

"And now he will no longer rise. And tell J.J. if he does cast him in that ridiculous reboot of his, I may find myself unavailable for any future collaborations."

"Neve—"

"I want the *Unity* role gender-flipped. Don't you think Grace Bishop would be exquisite as God? God's much too clever and has too much subtlety and wit to be a man, anyway. And a middle-aged, cold, aloof woman has more gravitas in her pinky than Peter Cross does in his whole, steroid-filled body. Can you imagine Miranda Priestly playing God in a movie? We can't get

Meryl, so I want Bishop." She continued as if Barnaby had not spoken.

When he opened his mouth again, she simply stared him down, and for a whole minute the suite was silent. *Better.* "I wasn't aware I needed to explain my decisions, but since we're about to get rather close over the course of this night and the following days, let me tell you this... Gannon will not empower homophobia under the guise of religious piety."

"So you're afraid of the fallout that comes with him being associated with the radical right and how it will reflect on Gannon?" Barnaby's voice trembled just a little, clearly at his own audacity to keep questioning her motives.

Gustavo though was clearly not fooled by the assumption that Neve cared about public outcry. Moreover, his shrewd expression and the long look he was giving her told her he knew very well where her information had come from and why she was blacklisting one of the most popular new talents in Hollywood.

"Something like that." She took a long sip from her whiskey and relished its burn down her throat.

"You know, she's just a little bit scary when she's like this." Barnaby's whisper to Morag was barely audible, but it was unmistakably infused with utter awe. She did not grace him with an answer. Picking up her phone, she was already doing the mental gymnastics of converting the time zone from midnight in France to DC and wondering if the Attorney General would remember that he owed her a favor or ten.

They drank coffee and strategized, drank whiskey and made more plans. Then Gustavo or Morag would make a suggestion, Neve would make the call, and Barnaby would write everything down. It didn't seem to matter that they were waking directors, producers, union leaders, or DOJ attorneys in the middle of the night. When Neve Blackthorne called, everyone in the business picked up the phone.

By the time morning peeked through the forgotten drapes, the number of people actively working on their side was extensive, and the Hollywood Crews Union leader had been talked down from marching on Gannon McMillan to, as he put it, "smite the imbeciles who were about to destroy the entertainment world!" *Smite!* Some people really did think themselves to be God. Or they were just massive divas.

Still, his words touched Neve deeply. "We stood by the first time, when Miramar was bought, and then it was ground into dust within two years. Corporate culture and the world of Hollywood are not a match made in heaven. It's been proven time and again. They want to make money, other costs be damned. And the crews are the first to face the hardship of those cuts. The safety on the sets plummets. Those expenses are the first ones to go. The superstars will always make their millions. You've been making money, Ms. Blackthorne, but you have never been unfair to my people, so it's always been a pleasure dealing with you."

The growing list of names and the voices on the phone all calmed Neve down and reinforced her faith in herself, her belief in her own professional immortality and immovability. Dozens and dozens of the most influential people showed their unflinching, unwavering support of her. She hadn't been kind to all of them at all times. She certainly hadn't *made* all of them, but she had been instrumental in their continuous success and their prosperity.

Neve knew loyalty was a commodity, and that theirs would likely only last for so long, but she also understood that—despite her unbending nature and her sometimes unreasonable demands on them—they respected her professionalism, her perfectionist nature, and her relentless strive for quality films. For art. For the freedom to create and deliver the audience-craved illusions.

They knew her, and that was perhaps key. She was a known quantity. Her ideals and ideas often matched their own. When dealing with the most unpredictable of industries, it was easier to navigate the fickle waters with a captain that would steady the ship instead of capsizing it for the sake of money and personal glory.

They all knew Neve would guide them, as she had done through many crises, market crashes, financial cuts, and budget constraints. She would find new avenues of investment, China or Singapore or God herself, and they looked to Neve for leadership in moments of hardship. Hence they were standing by her now, when her own crisis was ravaging her life and threatening her livelihood.

After that night, the rest of the week passed in a blur of premieres and very public lunches, dinners, outings, and parties with the big players. Neve was on the front pages and in the front seats. Although all this attention was draining her, she did not shy away from it. You really couldn't when running a major Hollywood studio, but she was always careful to not make the spectacle surrounding her actually be about her. Neve Blackthorne made stories. She never *was* the story.

Now she found herself in the hurricane's eye, and it was wringing her dry. She'd wake up, put on her armor, perform for the crowds and for the sycophants of her court, and at night she'd sequester herself in her suite with a bottle of Lagavulin and a bucket of ice to silence her thoughts and fears in glass after glass of amber liquid.

Amidst the very tumultuous week, her conversation with Danilo Rosilliani had been the least eventful. A lunch in her suite was set up quietly by Barnaby through Danilo's lover—since they were certain that IV&X and Juno had their spies everywhere.

Danilo, while an airhead and generally oblivious to the undercurrents around him—unless they were about underwear models—was very much aware of some of the movements currently shaking and shaping the film world.

"I see you've unleashed some of the top industry people on me. Francis took me aside last night, and Martin made a point of wagging his finger at me, very much like my father used to. Makes me think Italian men fancy themselves the moral compass in all things. I suppose most people who have gone to the trouble of showing me how displeased they are believe your throne is too high for me to climb."

"It is." Neve schooled her features to reveal nothing, even if she silently cursed both directors for their misplaced proactivity, loyal as it was.

Danilo huffed, but his eyes turned shrewd. "I don't think so, but neither am I particularly keen on going to war with the biggest production companies and directors. Juno and Ivor at IV&X believe they can smooth the path for me, throw money, column inches, and awards at most of these big players, but when I agreed to do business with them, I wasn't signing on to be a field general in a guerilla campaign. I also wasn't signing on to actually run a studio, if some of the rumors I hear are to be believed that the deal will not be going through. You do have considerable reach, and I'd rather stay out of the fray, all things considered. Make your offer, Neve. Make it a good one, and IV&X and Buchanan can go to hell for all I care."

By Saturday morning, all her ducks were arranged into straight and narrow rows. Juno was beaten at her own game, with all the entertainment papers announcing the appointment of one Danilo Rosilliani to the brand new Gannon Streaming platform, which was believed to be more extensive than any other on the market, beating IV&X's Flix in every parameter.

Even Allison Summers raised her water glass in Neve's direction when their eyes met over the main course at breakfast on the last day of the festival. So the witch had obviously been in the know about everything that had been going on, and of the danger Neve had just gracefully sidestepped in such a public manner.

The conversation with Juno in her penthouse suite following the breakfast was fraught and unpleasant. At least it was private. *Small victories.*

"What the fuck do you think you're doing? You think poaching Danilo will stop IV&X from purchasing Gannon? It's a done deal. They bought Miramar. Gannon is what they really want, and they will get it. There's no way to stop it."

Pale and visibly shaken, Juno paced back and forth across the luxurious terrace overlooking the Mediterranean. Her high-pitched voice was like nails slicing Neve's skin, loud and abrasive, but she held her tongue. Faced with Neve's silence, Juno was forced to continue.

"I will not stand for this, Neve! We have known each other for over twenty years. I made you. And this deal is going forward. No matter how many of these asshole clowns you throw in my face, pontificating about the purity of art and how money ruins it all, I do not care about it. The deal is unstoppable."

Neve counted to ten in her mind, trying to ground herself in the onslaught of the shouts, but ultimately just willing time to pass quicker so she could get out of there. God, what had happened to her that—faced with the woman who once was her mentor, then her staunch ally, and now seemingly her enemy—she was nothing but bored.

The war wasn't even over yet, and Neve was already eager to leave the battlefield. She was getting more impatient in her middle age, and Juno was getting more and more prone to histrionics as she got older, Neve mused while observing Juno rant and rave about money and power, and other things that suddenly seemed obscene when it came down to it. Films were art. Films were emotion. Films were life. And to quantify all that in dollars? To put a price on a beating heart and a child moved to tears in a movie theater?

She sighed. Yes, she was still just as naive and just as idealistic when it came to her lifeblood. But still, naive or not, Gannon was profitable. Exceedingly so. And she had made that a reality, not Juno, not the Board. Neve had.

It was time for her to end this. A control shot.

"—you cannot stop this, you can either resign, or Ivor and IV&X will fire you. They might have kept you, what with Danilo abandoning ship, but under the circumstances and the stunt you just pulled—"

Neve extended her hand and, as always, her audience fell silent. Good to know some things never changed. She could still command the room.

"I think not, Juno." As Neve spoke, she lowered her voice and Juno squinted at her. Good. She had her attention. "Yes, we've known each other for twenty years. I think I made myself, but you've been a good chairwoman and I don't feel ill will towards you. Much." She gave Juno her trademark sharp smile. The dagger-under-the-ribs one.

"So for the sake of those twenty years, I'm going to tell you that, the day you and the IV&X suits land back in LA, the DOJ Antitrust Division will make it public that they have opened an investigation into the breach of antitrust and monopolies legislation by the Gannon board and IV&X."

The journey Juno's face underwent was almost comical. From pinched and indignant at being interrupted, to wide-eyed and horrified, to utterly slack-jawed and speechless at the announcement.

"I think their press release will state something along the lines of wanting to protect the commitment to the pursuit of economic opportunity and fairness in the entertainment industry through antitrust enforcement. A bit dry, but I only had so much time to prepare. I have to give you credit, Juno. You were *this close* to being successful in pulling a fast one on me. Still, I hold no grudge."

The sound of Juno's mirthless, a touch hysterical laughter did not surprise her. Yes, Juno knew her too well.

Neve's lips tipped up. "Okay, not too big of a grudge. But do stop the IV&X deal. No deal, no investigation. I know you have connections in Washington, but I have to tell you, people high up in the DOJ think this is a career-defining case for them. It's so big and juicy, after all."

"You sicced the Attorney General on me." It didn't sound like a question, so Neve didn't offer an answer. Instead, she walked out with her head held high, leaving Juno to fume and rage. The silence that came with the closed door was more soothing than the taste this victory left in her mouth.

Juno would come for her again, Neve reasoned. She was a powerful woman who hated being made a fool of. Especially in such a masterful and semi-public manner. And so would Ivor Nowak at IV&X. Neve had only met him a handful of times, but he was a slimy sociopath with delusions of grandeur. So Neve would have to take preventive measures regarding Juno and brace herself against Ivor, and soon.

With the events of the week unfolding the way they had, the members of the Gannon McMillan board were slowly becoming aware of what had been thwarted, at least those who still had their wits about them and retained an interest in the business. Juno's cronies had clearly been in the know all along, but they were far from the majority.

Livia Sabran-McMillan, one of the few members of the board under sixty—and one to never miss the Cannes Film Festival—gave Neve a standing ovation after another screening of a Gannon production, applauding with particular vigor. And if the flowers she sent to Neve's suite afterward were a gauge of her opinion of Juno's maneuvering, Neve thought she was way ahead of the curve when it came to securing some of the board members' favor.

At the end of the day, they didn't care about Juno's bruised ego, or her desire for absolute power. They cared about the bottom line, and Neve had been making it rain at Gannon since the day she'd taken over twenty years ago. As golden geese went, she knew she was an absolute blockbuster, mixing her metaphors be damned.

She also knew that she was very tired. Drained to the point of complete apathy. She had just claimed one of the biggest victories of her life, saved herself and her empire from sure demise, yet she had no desire to celebrate.

A couple of important fashion houses were using the opportunity of Neve being in Europe to throw her a sumptuous party at George V in Paris the evening after the festival wrapped up. Being known as a fashion icon herself, as well as extensively featuring couture in her studio's films, Neve was quite beloved in Paris. On any other occasion, she might have enjoyed this crowd, so different yet so similar to her regular Hollywood circles.

But tonight of all nights, all she wanted to do was to sit in the dark and drink her Lagavulin. People exhausted her, and she'd had more than her usual share of them this week.

Still, she always did what she had to do, and standing in front of an enormous mirror in the Plaza Athénée Paris suite,

Neve donned a Saint Laurent suit, one of the last designs of the master himself. Looking at her image, she thought that everything old was new again. She had just been renewed after all, so the symbolism of wearing the design of someone who was eternal of sorts, immortalized by his creativity that had mainstreamed pantsuits for women, wasn't lost on her.

Gustavo, who'd accompanied her to Paris, gushed over her attire as he saw her off to the party.

"It really does send a message about who's wearing the pants in the current power balance at Gannon. It's all sorts of un-PC, bold, and dare I say, just a touch mean, kicking Juno while she's down."

"You're the one who's making it un-PC by attributing my outfit to this type of gender symbolism. And I prefer my pencil skirts. But tonight is different. Plus, I highly doubt Juno would understand this kind of symbolism, anyway." Livia Sabran-McMillan might, but she didn't want to voice her conclusions about the enigmatic board member just yet. "And honestly, I don't want to offend any of the designers attending tonight, so it's a boon. It's a fashion party, and I'm sure half of Paris will be there."

"Most certainly, there will be a lot of fragile egos out there tonight. So many of them would be offended by you singling someone out by wearing their creations. And, you know, Saint Laurent has always been and continues to be the King of Paris anyway, even when he was at his lowest. That is also a symbolism of sorts."

Yes, Neve thought as she winked at Gustavo and took his arm, she was never beaten, and even surrounded by enemies, she still reigned. At whatever cost.

Champagne was plentiful, compliments were flowing, and Neve was on the verge of being done with all these people. Yes, she obliged many of them by being seen with them and being heard talking in some relatively evasive, yet potentially positive tones about whatever it was that interested them.

She was paying her dues to the exulted and adoring crowd. Still, it was fatigue and not elation that consumed her, and the bubbly disposition and bubbly drinks did nothing to wash away the feeling of loneliness. She wondered why it had suddenly taken hold of her.

Tiredness was understandable. She really was on her last legs, but loneliness? Neve had spoken with her son earlier in the day, and Harlan was eagerly waiting for her to come home. She had plans to cancel her Tuesday, excuse him from boarding school, and spend the day together. Plus, she was always alone anyway. True power, after all, was wielded by a single pair of hands and only one head wore the crown.

A gentle tap on her shoulder startled her out of her thoughts, a feeling of discomfort running along her skin at being caught not paying attention to her surroundings. Donatella had monopolized the conversation and tactfully steered it away from her, giving her a chance to collect herself. Yet the hand belonged to none other than Elinor Moncrief, and Neve felt a frisson of a decidedly different quality. These days, Elinor conjured an association with Audrey, and Neve felt her cheeks warm a little.

"Long live the Queen." Elinor's toast rang. Neve smiled and Donatella laughed loudly, starting a chant, with a hundred glasses being raised in her direction.

Neve tilted her head and air kissed the fashion empress' cheeks. It was time to make an exit, and that may have just been her cue. Damn Elinor and her sadistic sense of humor. She of all people knew how much Neve, more often than not, disliked being the center of attention.

"Leaving so soon, Neve? I thought we'd have a chance to catch up, but I see perhaps you are too wiped out for that. Understandable. The feat you pulled off this week must have taken a lot out of you, old girl."

Neve chose to ignore the playful needling. If anyone could get away with that kind of teasing, it was Elinor. Neve just waved her hand and lifted a shoulder in dismissal.

"This was an utterly boring week, even by French standards. Quiet. Quaint."

"Right. Juno will want revenge, dearest. And be careful with Ivor. Watch that exquisite six of yours." Elinor's eyes were shining with concern and amusement.

"I'd tell you you're wrong, but then you'd be wrong about that last remark too, and that's one I can't dispute."

Elinor's laughter was just as attractive as it had always been, and Neve took a moment to appreciate the woman in front of her. She had been careless with her as well. All those years ago, they had in fact been careless with each other, but some things endured, and this friendship of theirs certainly did.

"I'd offer you a ride to Plaza Athénée, but you're wanted elsewhere." Elinor's expression of amusement did not leave her face. Still, there was something lurking in the depths of her eyes. Before Neve had a chance to contradict her and tell her that the only place she really needed to be was her suite—watching the city while drinking her whiskey—Elinor produced a folded piece of paper.

A gentle kiss on her lips and she was gone, leaving Neve to stare at the note in her hand. There, in neat, clear writing, was an address.

Rue Lamarck. Montmartre. The address told her nothing really, but somehow her heart stuttered, and Elinor's words echoed in her mind. *You're wanted elsewhere.*

Amongst throngs of fans and sycophants clamoring for her

attention, for pieces of her, there was truly only one person in Paris who felt that way about her.

As crudely as Audrey had put it when she'd made her wishes known on Tuesday in Cannes—*for old times' sake*—her desire was genuine. Because she wanted Neve even when all the masks of power and influence were off. Perhaps especially then. She wanted Neve with pure, unadulterated lust, even if that lust was tainted with anger and hurt these days.

Paris—unlike New York or even LA—actually slept, although some areas were certainly louder than others. This one, the bohemian part of the city, was a perpetual hive of activity, and it was positively bursting at the seams with parties and people drinking the night away in the avant-garde little bars and cafes strewn along the winding, narrow alleys of the 18th Arrondissement.

There was a time when young Neve, a starving ingenue, had known these streets like the back of her hand. Montmartre had been her stomping ground. Thankfully, her so-called 'paying her dues years' in Paris had not lasted very long, and she'd moved on to bigger and better things in New York.

Even so, that time had served her well, because she landed in New York brimming with hands-on knowledge, not only of French cinema, or camera and lighting work but also of sleepless nights caused by an empty stomach.

She had known hunger, real, palpable hunger, and it set her apart from the crowds of theater and movie wannabes. Running amok in the narrow Paris back alleys, she'd promised herself to never go hungry again, that she'd do anything, be everything it took to succeed. She was grateful to the streets, even if her official biography contained no mention of them or of that time.

So yes, this city had served her well. Like fire and water, it had tempered the steel in her. She'd come to Paris all those years ago to get hurt, but also to grow stronger. Was she back amidst these streets now to get hurt again, in a different, deeper manner?

The town car stopped smoothly at the beginning of Rue Lamarck, allowing her the gorgeous sight of the Paris skyline from Montmartre Hill. The little street was quiet, the view breathtaking, and Neve inhaled the cool spring air, breathing fully perhaps for the first time in almost two weeks.

The door at number 27 opened as a couple exited, and she caught it easily, her muscles humming in anticipation. She felt limber, her fatigue gone without a trace. Excitement was singing in her veins. Neve forewent the dingy little elevator and practically vaulted the stairs to the last floor. She wasn't even winded by the time she knocked on the door of what, from the outside, appeared like a rooftop loft. She was alive.

Neve felt time slow as that door opened, and a sense of wonderful déjà vu filled her. How many times had Audrey opened one for her? Five? Ten? Twenty? Every one of those times, she'd been just as alive. Was it a wonder she was in love with this woman who made her feel like life was saturating her every pore, emotions boiling up, spilling over everything that was Neve Blackthorne? This woman who made her climb five floors in four-inch heels and not feel a thing except anticipation and elation. This woman, who was looking at her first with astonishment and then with not a little self-satisfaction.

"I see Elinor was the perfect messenger. I heard you were successful in defending your throne. Bravo. Masterfully done, though I'll eat my hat if Juno doesn't try to exact some kind of revenge in the near future."

Was that genuine concern in Audrey's voice? For a second, Neve thought she'd give everything for that to be true. But then Audrey just shrugged, stepped aside, and let her into a room that could generously be called an attic. Neve supposed that, even with Audrey's successful career, the location of the loft was quite expensive, and hence she would have had to sacrifice square footage inside the apartment itself. Still, what she could see from the little balcony cut into the sloped roof, the view was very much worth the cramped space in the shoebox Audrey inhabited.

As Neve took a step further inside and Audrey closed the door behind her, they were left standing in the quiet of the candle lit room. It smelled so much like Audrey, Neve wanted to lick her lips. Vanilla and peaches. Candles and wine. God... How lost had she been? And had she finally been found?

Audrey regained her footing first. "Did you come to thank me properly?"

Ah yes, straight to the point. Neve took a deep breath. Into the breach. "We've established that I'm not particularly good at effusive gratitude, Audrey. But you made a not-so-artfully worded offer back in Cannes. I was wondering if it still stands?"

"An offer, Neve?" Audrey's smile turned sharp, feral. Neve trembled.

"'One more time, for old times' sake?'" Not waiting for an answer, she chose her favorite defense and forged ahead, consequences be damned, shrugging out of her suit jacket and remaining in just the tailored slacks and a black, lace bra. Her hands were shaking just a little bit as she reached for the front hook, but she wasn't shy about showing her trepidation.

Here, with Audrey, in this little attic on top of Paris, she felt free and unafraid again—perhaps for the first time in a very long time, even before she and Audrey had gotten tangled up in all these feelings and all this want.

Audrey's eyes followed Neve's movements, scorching her skin, the stare palpable in its suggestiveness, in its carnality.

One of the hooks gave under her fingertips as Audrey took a step forward. Time slowed even further. Audrey's hands covered her own and stopped the quiver. Their gazes locked. Audrey undid the second and third hook, one by one, never once breaking eye contact.

As she pushed the bra down Neve's shoulders, she raised a hand, and Neve closed her eyes, trying to savor the moment, prolonging the anticipation of not knowing where she would feel the touch. As if in a dream, a palm cupped her cheek, then the second one joined in. Her face was being held in those sure, skilled hands, thumbs tracing her cheekbones.

"No, don't close them, Neve. I want you to look at me as I'm fucking you. Look at me."

Audrey's voice was hoarse, betraying both the resentment and the need in her. Neve opened her eyes to face that emotion, that anger, and her insides clenched at the sight, feeling the danger in that look in her very core. She was so wet, throbbing, wanting. *This woman, right now. Do your worst to me.*

It was a blur after that. She knew she was naked in seconds, with Audrey pushing her against the wall and taking her hard and fast, first two fingers, then three, knuckle deep, with the first orgasm hitting her like a slap within what felt like seconds. She did not close her eyes.

She tried to recover, to reach for Audrey's shirt, but she was still too astounded by the sheer force of the climax to even move properly, and Audrey was already taking her hand and ushering her into an alcove off to the side of the room and onto an unmade bed, only to proceed to devour her still pulsating flesh.

Neve barely had enough presence of mind to hold on, to grab at the sheets, to claw at still shirt-clad shoulders, trying to anchor herself to reality, because she felt Audrey spread her lips and suck on her clit, and it was like coming apart at the seams. As she came the third time, she tugged weakly at Audrey's hair, attempting to stop this assault on her senses that was consuming her, overwhelming her, rendering her cries soundless.

Audrey raised her face, covered in Neve's essence, licked her lips, and gave her a smile that did not touch eyes that still burned with unsatisfied emotion. Slowly, she began a leisurely trail up Neve's body, licking and nipping, leaving smears of Neve's juices behind.

She stopped for a longer moment on Neve's breasts, knowing how sensitive they were. There had been times when Audrey had made her come just from playing with them, especially if Neve had been waiting for Audrey's hands and mouth for some time, even more if Audrey was teasing her mercilessly throughout the day with subtle lip bites and breathy sighs.

It seemed Audrey's mind went to exactly the same memories, because Neve could feel a smile blossoming against her nipple before sharp teeth closed around the puckered nub, bringing her unexpectedly and swiftly to the very edge again. Such a simple gesture, just one bite, and she was dying for it again, feeling like she'd burst any second if she didn't come now.

Once more seeking purchase, Neve ran her hands against the hair on the back of the head currently tormenting her breasts. This was new, the short strands pleasantly rough under her fingertips. She had loved the feel of Audrey's long, luxurious mane spread all over her skin, caressing her with as much purpose as the hands or the mouth did. Still, Audrey looked wonderful like this, the short, edgy cut making her appear mature, worldly.

These thoughts somehow cleared her mind of the urgency and the haze that came with it, and she again tugged Audrey's head up. It occurred to her that they had not kissed since that night in the office, when she had broken it off between them. It was time to stop missing the gorgeous red lips, swollen now with the effort of bringing Neve to three astounding orgasms.

It seemed to take them both a second to acknowledge the gravitas of the moment, and then their lips met, blossoming gently in dissonance with their earlier rough exertions. Neve tasted herself on that feather-soft mouth that was so familiar, so treasured, so tender with her now, after taking her so forcefully just minutes earlier, that she thought she could cry. Audrey always could strip away all her defenses and uncover her deepest desires.

The kiss went on forever. They drank each other in, unhurried at first, until Audrey seemed to remember that she still had something to prove. Her tongue invaded Neve's mouth, the tone of the kiss changing, the storm brewing in the depths of those gorgeous eyes hitting landfall again. It was all tongues and teeth and sharp little slices of pain that she knew would leave her bruised tomorrow.

There was significance in those bites. She knew Audrey was marking her, claiming her even if only for this one night, using her as she never had all those months ago, simply because they didn't have the freedom to mark and bruise before. Tonight, that freedom was driving both of them crazy, and Neve lost herself in the hedonism of it.

Peripherally, she felt Audrey get off the bed and heard her rummaging in a drawer somewhere close by. A moment later, Neve was yanked out of her trance by strong hands flipping her on her stomach, and before she knew what was happening, she felt the edge of the strap-on, drawing up and down from clit to slit, like a brush painting her with her own wetness. Neve heard the sound of the bottle of lube opening and closing, but she was sure that was an unnecessary precaution. She was dripping.

They hadn't indulged in this type of sex before. Neve really hadn't been averse. They'd simply not had enough time to really let loose with each other, always wary of getting caught, rarely even taking all their clothes off.

"Tell me to stop, Neve!" Short of breath from anticipation, Audrey rasped in her ear. "Tell me you don't want this." She stroked her clit with the tip of the strap-on, and Neve quivered.

No, there was no way in heaven or hell Neve was going to deny Audrey this. Even if she didn't want it, she would still allow Audrey to exorcize whatever demons were ravaging her and darkening the wondrous eyes.

But Neve did want it. Neve wanted it as much as she wanted to take her next breath.

"You made me listen, Neve. You made me listen to him fucking you in that bathroom. Did you know I heard every grunt, every moan he made? I heard everything. I wanted to kill him for touching you, for taking what was mine. Because you were mine, Neve. I know everything about you. Every moan, every cry, every sigh. I know the cadence of your breathing when you get so close your thighs tremble and your walls start to clench. It took me a while to realize you faked everything. I know what you sound like when you come, and I didn't hear you that evening. I heard nothing at all from you. So I'm going to make you scream now, Neve. Tell me to stop!"

"Don't stop..." She didn't finish her sentence. She couldn't. It felt like she was made of want alone these days, and she wanted this badly.

And then Audrey was pushing into her, inch by agonizing inch, so careful, even in her anger, so tender, even in her staking a claim on Neve.

Neve wanted to tell her that there was no need, that she was hers, all hers. Despite everything that had happened between them, Neve had never been more Audrey's. The shaft was fully inside her, and still she felt Audrey holding back, breathing hard, her anger palpable in the harsh exhalations. All Neve knew was that Audrey needed to erase what ailed her, Neve's own feelings taking a back seat.

"Fuck me like you mean it then, damn you!" she ground through gritted teeth.

She could swear she heard Audrey howl, and then nothing else remained but her own moans and the ringing of her fourth orgasm in her ears. In the midst of it all, she could feel Audrey's own climax hit, her lover slumping on top of her, shirt drenched in sweat, breathing loudly, lips moving soundlessly at first, before Neve could decipher the one word Audrey was repeating over and over.

Mine, mine, mine!

"Yes, dear heart, I am," she heard herself say just before the wave swept her up and the world went gray at the edges of her vision. She was fairly certain Audrey had not heard her.

Neve opened her eyes just before dawn, the twilight playing with shapes and shadows on the wall opposite the disarrayed bed. Audrey was still wearing the strap-on and was half slumped on top of her, making Neve decidedly uncomfortable. But comfort be damned, she'd have gladly stayed bearing Audrey's weight forever if only she could.

As gently as possible, she tried to disengage from the slumbering form. Surprisingly, she was successful, as Audrey did not stir. Their encounter must have taken a lot out of her, physically and emotionally, to have her sleeping so soundly.

Neve stretched, not unlike a cat after a nap in the sun, and took stock. On one hand, she felt amazing, the end of an unwanted year of abstinence bringing much needed relief. On the other hand, she was sore, not entirely pleasantly so, and as she made her ablutions in the small bathroom, she washed small traces of blood off herself.

Neve smiled mirthlessly. She would, of course, live, but at least now she felt like she had atoned somewhat for her cruelty to Audrey, having paid for that sin in blood. Perhaps the debt was finally settled. Dr. Moore would have a field day with this train of thought and with how horribly unhealthy this was.

But it didn't matter. Because Audrey looked peaceful and content now that she had rid herself of this demon that had clearly been eating at her for a year. It was worth a little pain in the end. After all, Neve would have given much more to erase the memory of that bathroom encounter with Dmitriy from Audrey's mind.

The revelation that Audrey knew it was fake didn't really change anything. The pain she had lived through that evening was very much real. So if Neve hurt now, as she had hurt back then when Dmitriy bit her shoulder, it was par for the course for her. One had to pay for everything.

She moved around the room gathering her things, trying to be quiet, although she probably didn't need to be since Audrey was sleeping deeply, her breathing even.

By the door, discarded carelessly on the floor, Neve noticed a phone. She guessed Audrey must have dropped it when they'd gone at each other last night. As she bent to pick it up to place it near the bed for Audrey's convenience, the phone vibrated, a message lighting up the screen.

Freja: *I missed you last night, babe. Too bad you weren't here to fuck me blind. xoxo*

Neve's throat tightened, and she labored to take a deep breath. A sudden hit of nausea only made it more difficult. Well, Neve mused sardonically, as she quietly closed the door behind her, she did come here to get hurt. And hurt she got, in more ways than one.

7

NEVE HOLDS BACK THE RIVER

"You know how many of these sessions of ours start with me asking you, 'so what now?'" Dr. Moore appeared tired. She rarely looked it, but for the second week in a row, Neve felt her therapist was a bit on edge, even off her game.

"Are you asking now?"

"Should I?"

Ah, Dr. Moore was not off her game. She was exasperated and trying to hide it, being the good therapist that she was. Neve secretly, even perversely, relished the fact that the oh-so-by-the-book Helena Moore judged her on some level. It gave her anger and resentment a better target than the only person who was really to blame for her situation. She preferred to go through life not waging open war on herself. Though the past year had been a struggle.

Neve waved her hand in dismissal. "Perhaps it shouldn't have happened. Perhaps it shouldn't have happened the way it did."

"Perhaps? You allowed someone to hurt you to what... Atone?"

"Atonement is underrated, Dr. Moore."

Before her therapist blew her control entirely, Neve raised her hand. For a second, both she and Dr. Moore simply stared at the appendage in question. One gaping at it, the other with a modicum of sheepishness that she'd pretty much signaled her therapist to shut up.

"I understand why you may think I allowed Audrey to punish me. And I am not saying this didn't factor into my reasoning. I hurt her. Deeply. I don't lack comprehension of this issue. The damage I've done is... I dented her self-esteem, her sense of self, and I broke her heart. Should I not atone?"

Dr. Moore actually curled her fingers into fists.

"God, I'm so thankful for some of the deontological rules they drilled into me years ago, Neve. Because the things I want to tell you, the things I do tell you, and the things you provoke in me, are so thoroughly unprofessional, it's unseemly."

"I provoke things in you?" Neve's smile was lethal. But she knew she wasn't getting out of this conversation unscathed.

"You provoke exasperation. At times awe at how deeply wrong a person can be before they break everyone around them and their own heart in the process."

Ah, so Dr. Moore was choosing to play dirty. So be it. After all, Neve had been coming to her willingly week after week after week. She was practically asking for it at his point.

"Look..." She shook her head dismissively, and Dr. Moore settled down. "I wanted everything that happened that night. Everything. Nothing occurred against my will. It was the best experience of this kind in my life. And you know I'm not prone to exaggeration. So when all is said and done, if it serves a dual purpose, I will not bemoan it. I did plenty of that during that night, anyway."

A bark of laughter was her reward for the intended pun.

"You're awful, you know that, don't you?" But Helena Moore was still smiling as she said it. Neve gave her a slight, indulgent grin of her own. Yes, she knew that. Sadly, Audrey knew that too, and she wouldn't be laughing with her anytime soon. Nothing was funny about where the two of them had left it.

Atonement aside, none of her three immovables had been moved. The Bishop, the Knight, and the Rook still surrounded the Queen on *the otherwise mostly empty board. She still had to protect her son, her job, and her reputation or however else she chose to justify the presence of that elusive last piece on the board. Maybe this one figurine seemed trivial to Dr. Moore, maybe under the Paris lights it had seemed so to Neve as well. But years of being* othered *had done their damage. She barely withstood it then, and she knew she wasn't strong enough to withstand it now. Life and her own decisions had chipped away at her once vaunted stamina to tolerate being in pain. Rough sex notwithstanding.*

And while she and Dr. Moore might have broken through a wall of sorts with humor and some acknowledged understanding for one another, Neve knew that where Audrey was concerned, nothing had changed.

Among the multitude of emails and messages awaiting Neve upon her return to New York, one stood out, and not just because it was written in all capital letters.

"HOW DARE YOU NOT TELL ME I WAS HURTING YOU, NEVE?"

Neve rolled her eyes and deleted the email without reading the rest of it. So Audrey had either found the washcloth she'd used to clean herself up after their night together or there were some other clues to Neve's not entirely pleasant morning.

She really didn't understand why Audrey was making such a big deal out of something so inconsequential as a droplet of blood. At the time, with Audrey taking her roughly from behind, she hadn't really felt much aside from the clawing need to come. She'd meant it when she told Dr. Moore that if the orgasm came with a side of atonement, then so be it.

However, knowing Audrey, she had to be swimming in guilt and self-flagellation by now. Neve's personal cell phone was still switched off after spending a perfectly nice day at the zoo with Harlan, and she was in no hurry to turn it back on. Audrey would no doubt be demanding an opportunity to apologize needlessly. Neve wasn't ready to talk to her. She wanted to, craved to hear that voice on the other end of the line, to imagine what Audrey was doing or what she was wearing. She wanted perhaps a bit too much. It was the 'a bit too much' that was giving her pause, because it was just that tiny *bit* that was spinning out of her control.

Her self-preservation was kicking in, steering her away from calming the storms she knew were flaring inside Audrey, as she had done many times before. It was time to save herself first. Now that she had fully realized her feelings for Audrey were indeed something as disconcerting as love, Neve needed to find some measure of defense against the strength of it. She couldn't go on being an exposed nerve around Audrey. It was bound to end terribly for them both.

Still, her chest hurt suspiciously around her heart, and despite how ill-advised she thought it was, Neve turned on her phone and, ignoring the deluge of missed calls and texts, opened a blank message and wrote simply, 'you didn't'. She tuned out the resulting barrage of answers and more incoming calls. She had other pressing matters to attend to.

IV&X predictably pulled out of the Gannon sale. Juno was undoubtedly plotting her revenge even as she sat in her ghastly, cluttered office, sipping her latest scorching, caffeinated concoction. Juno's money and her influence were considerable.

Neve knew that she had to watch her back more carefully than ever, or she'd lose it all. Where Audrey was concerned, sure, she was no longer an employee, so the morals clause in her contract would not apply. But Neve still had other issues to consider. The castle walls of her Rook—like the walls of her closet—the ones protecting her from being 'different' yet again, were firmly shut.

Plus, from the gossip Neve had the misfortune to hear when she'd gotten ready that morning, Audrey was also otherwise occupied. Not that Neve hadn't suspected as much, because Audrey's blog had been conspicuously silent about any new French conquests lately.

The name on her employees' lips, however, hadn't been French at all.

"Freja..." Morag had actually said it with a kind of breathy awe that had made Neve's skin crawl.

"You mean *the* Freja?" Gustavo, the traitor, had sounded impressed. Why was he even at her house so early? Surely not to gossip with Morag. Hadn't he come here with the purpose of discussing last-minute plans before they returned to Europe for yet another series of screenings and festivals?

She'd deal with him later. Because Neve knew only one Freja. Hell, the entire world knew of only one Freja, even if there were undoubtedly many other women with that name on the Scandinavian peninsula and not only.

"Gustavo, amor, she's like Madonna. She goes only by her first name, because it's distinctive enough to set her apart." Morag tugged on Neve's hair a little too roughly, and she winced. If she was honest with herself, her wince wasn't at all because of the pull on her hair.

"Ha, she has plenty of other attributes to distinguish her," Gustavo said and actually snickered.

"Don't be gross!" The low whip in her voice made both her employees turn toward her. She shot Morag a sharp look, and her stylist nodded apologetically before returning to arrange her coif.

Gustavo feigned obliviousness, however. And Neve knew he was feigning it, because it was clear he wanted nothing more than to continue talking about the Scandinavian supermodel-turned-reality-TV-star. So Neve tried to take deep breaths as she sat in her chair and seethed, while Morag teetered about her face, and Gustavo went on and on about Freja. At least he got the message about not being disgusting.

"She's a worthy successor to the generation of supermodels that came before her. An amalgam of Claudia Schiffer, with the long flowing blonde locks, and Cindy Crawford, with the generous curves and pouty lips adorned with a small mole at the very corner."

His pontification did not last, however, as the ever-enamored Sheppard chose that moment to launch an affection-offensive and rolled over his feet, getting as much of his fur as possible on his tailored slacks. Gustavo unsuccessfully tried to disentangle himself from his biggest fan. At his helpless look, Neve snapped her fingers and the dog instantly came to heel, staring at Gustavo from afar with eyes full of love.

But even the small act of getting Sheppard to behave made Neve tired. She wanted to massage her temples. The conversation was giving her a headache. "Are you writing her autobiography? A fashion magazine piece?"

He ignored her and went on.

"You know what I admire about her most? Freja has the fortune of perfect timing. The era of the supermodels is over. Claudia, Cindy, Christie and the rest of the sisterhood were phased out by the skinny, no-name faces of younger girls. And here is Freja, a valkyrie in the era of twigs and indistinctive bodies with no personalities. She is true to her namesake goddess' legacy–larger than life, wild to the point of provocative, and at times downright ribald. She is also more popular than any of her predecessors at their peak, due to her many scandals and affairs."

Neve looked up and caught Morag rolling her eyes before she could school her features. As her hands ran through Neve's hair, she ventured a comment under Neve's watchful gaze.

"You can sing her all the praises, Gustavo, but her mouth has got zero filters. She manages to stay out of trouble because she's gorgeous and thinks fast on her feet. Freja always ends up saying the most outlandish things that would get any other person in a lot of hot water, except she comes out on top, with a brand new endorsement and a huge sack of money after it's all said and done."

Gustavo nodded and suddenly turned to Neve, and she could practically see the dollar signs in his eyes. "Her stints on reality TV have been spectacular. We need to get on that train, Neve. She is not a bad actress. In fact, with some classes and a firm director's hand, she might be somewhat good. And Morag said it best, she's money. We need to show Juno and the Board that we can make fast, easy money."

Normally Neve was quick to jump on any new trendy thing, especially if she hadn't had a hand in setting that trend, because if she hated one thing, it was playing catch-up. Alisson Summers was bosom buddies with the model, after all. Still—her personal feelings about Freja and her very intimate connection with Audrey aside—something about her left Neve a bit unsettled, and Gannon and its more traditional production companies had avoided her, despite other studios clamoring to feature her as their IT girl.

Had it been intuition, Neve wondered, that had stayed her hand several times from calling Freja and setting up a project? They had run into each other in New York during various benefits and shows, with Freja being reasonably polite, if overly showy and completely over-the-top with her entourage.

Her behavior had been borderline vulgar, but then Neve mused that while she personally abhorred anything crass, it had never stopped her from profiting off it. Plus, so far Freja hadn't crossed any lines with Neve herself, since they'd only exchanged the most shallow of greetings between them.

God knew she'd had plenty of boorish people in her movies over the years. If they moved her project forward and were good business, like the seasoned strategist that she was, Neve would use any pawn to further her quest. Within reason, of course. Besides, it was in her job description to tell millions of people what was considered tasteful anyway. Her movies were trendsetting, and she had the final say in what went into them.

Sitting in her cool, quiet office, reminiscing about the events of last week, Neve found it interesting that she hadn't run into Freja in Cannes or Paris. As a massive star and countless brands' ambassador, she should have been front and center at many a premiere or screening, yet it seemed she had not attended any of the parties, certainly not the ones thrown for Neve.

Looking back now, she wondered if it was deliberate. Had Audrey shared the details of their affair with her, and Freja had chosen to stay away from her girlfriend's former lover? Neve didn't want to even contemplate that idea, horrified that someone would have access to a surefire weapon to destroy her career and perhaps her life.

Right on cue, her heart lurched in her chest, and the telltale signs of an impending anxiety attack let themselves be felt. She tried breathing deeply, tried to put Freja out of her mind.

And then Dr. Moore's voice materialized in her head, casually throwing out the visualization technique and reminding Neve how good she must be at envisioning things.

"Damn her, damn that smart bitch, damn her. *Happy place, happy place…*"

Normally she'd think about Harlan, her Malibu mansion, the ocean, the sanctity of her office. Those were the places where she felt most comfortable, safe. But her mind was not about to be quieted. She grasped at mental straws and gasped for breath, the walls closing in on her.

And then she finally closed her eyes and surrendered to the images and the sensations her heart had been craving all along. Her thoughts darted to the smell of Chanel and the long fingers that played with the hair on the nape of her neck while full lips did wonderful things to it. Involuntarily, her hand touched the still lingering marks Audrey had left on her skin Saturday night, the ones Neve had to cover up these past four days. They gave her a thrill of a curious kind. Having never particularly cared for possessiveness, she discovered she quite enjoyed being possessed.

Barnaby's voice in the reception area startled her, and she realized that her impending anxiety attack had passed, not really having had a chance to take hold of her mind. And how could anxiety win when her memories alone were leaving her panting, just reminiscing about Audrey claiming her and murmuring 'mine' with every deep, hard thrust?

The agitation was gone. And so were her worries about Freja and everything else that lay therein. Neve smiled and indulged in one more fantasy. Her last one for today, she promised herself. If Audrey were here with her, she would have quoted something from a movie Neve particularly disliked just to needle her, but she would have also made it a smart, thoughtful quote.

Audrey always picked the most apt ones. Something like, 'what we got here is a failure to communicate,' and Neve would grumble that Cool Hand Luke was not Paul Newman's best work, despite the deep existential subtext. Then they'd banter and spar until one of them would laugh and then they'd kiss...

Yes, the anxiety was gone. Just longing remained. Neve found it ironic that, after accusing Audrey of having no higher ambition than being 'the other woman', she herself inadvertently ended up being one. She had to stay away from Audrey, to save both her heart and her studio.

And stay away she did, delving into work that had accumulated during the two weeks she was fighting her battles in France. The London Movie Festival was only a month away, and while her employees were falling over backwards to set up the logistics for another successful trip for the Gannon delegation, Neve had her hands full with the reshoots and changes she was absolutely convinced needed to be made to the Gannon screenings.

The first day of the London Movie Festival was decidedly better than Cannes. *Unity* came in full force and blew the walls off the place with a reworked version now filled with enormous energy and fresh air, after fixing the issues that had plagued them in France.

Neve felt doubly vindicated because Grace Bishop simply reigned. Three scenes were all it took for the actress to steal the show and cement herself as a legend. *Peter Cross who?* The rumors that accompanied *Unity* for nixing him from the movie were quickly replaced with absolute raves about Grace's performance. Neve smirked all the way through the screening. Grace was amazing. So good that an Academy Award for Best Supporting Actress was almost assured. Dame Judi Dench won hers for all of eight minutes on screen. Grace—with her seven in *Unity*—would set a record. And with the Oscar would come a shield against whatever storms Grace was still weathering.

The feeling of accomplishment didn't leave her until the following day when—during a Miramar production screening that she attended as a pacifying gesture toward IV&X—she spied Audrey staring daggers in her direction. That is when she wasn't smiling angelically at Freja, who flitted from one VIP to the next.

Well, that was that. So much for staying away. Apparently deleting her emails, letting her calls go to voicemail, and telling Barnaby that she had no idea who Audrey Avens was when the assistant sheepishly told her she was on the line for the seventh time, just wasn't enough.

Neve didn't even wonder what Audrey was really doing in London. Freja's guest? Sent to do her job and hunt down some obscure social justice story? Why did it matter anyway? She was here, sullen eyes and pouty lips, and Neve's blood was singing.

Her mind reeled as she dreaded the confrontation that would surely follow some time soon, while her heart trembled in anticipation. She had to have some kind of masochistic streak. This was so out-of-character for her. She was a survivor. She always found ways to walk away from whichever fire unscathed, so why was she looking forward to getting burned this much now?

She completely missed the screening and then proceeded to space out during a Gannon production showing as well. The scowl on her face must have been prominent, because Gustavo elbowed her gently before the director approached them with slumped shoulders, chewing his lips. Neve gave him a tense smile and did not compliment the film. She was just mean enough to revel in his panicked look and tremulous farewells.

Annoyed—and upset at herself for being annoyed—Neve thought perhaps she really shouldn't attend the soirée held by several prominent feminist figures she and Gannon supported. Gustavo seemed to read her thoughts.

"Maybe we should skip it this time? Considering the mood you're in, since you actually hold some respect for those women." She turned on him, almost snarling, and he offered her a sheepish smile. "Well, some of them."

He knew her well enough to not say a word after that until they reached the car. As they settled into the luxurious leather seats, she decided she needed an outlet for her confused emotions. However, before she could round on Gustavo again, he raised his hand and cut her off.

"I had no idea she would be there, Neve. None, zero."

"Like you would have told me, anyway!" She hissed and felt foolish for doing so. This was too much. She closed her eyes and tried to push away the barrage of thoughts and emotions. But dammit, she was thinking too much, feeling too much, and thus reacting so foolishly to the mere presence of a woman she herself had sent away. Neve took a deep breath and tried to regain her composure.

Gustavo, perhaps sensing that calm and cool heads needed to prevail, decided to change the subject.

"I saw Livia Sabran-McMillan in the crowd again today. I don't remember her ever attending both Cannes and London."

Neve took one last cleansing breath and welcomed the distraction. Now that Gustavo mentioned it, she'd never seen Livia attend both events either. It was curious. Livia was a divorced heiress from one of the offshoots of the McMillan clan, numerous enough in itself that Neve more often than not got confused with all the family connections. The Gannons were much fewer and not nearly as involved in any of the business dealings of the entertainment giant.

Out of all the enterprising McMillans, Livia was one of the more savvy and diligent, a steady, reasonable presence on the company board, who took her job seriously and exhibited superlative taste in the projects she supported. She also had a quietly adversarial relationship with Juno, perhaps because of all the aforementioned qualities she possessed, and also because Juno preferred the board members to stay decidedly bored and uninterested.

Deciding to channel her irritation into productivity and a different outlet than poor Gustavo, Neve smiled.

"Maybe I should instruct Barnaby to set up a dinner with Livia. I think it's time to make a friend."

Gustavo's shoulders relaxed, obviously pleased that he'd been successful at avoiding Neve's wrath. "Either here or in New York, and away from Buchanan's beady eyes. Nobody is better at establishing unlikely alliances than you."

"Oh, quit it now with your sucking up, Gustavo." But her eyes crinkled, and he laughed unabashedly at being caught.

"It was a substandard effort, anyway."

The rest of the day passed in a flurry of worse attempts at sycophancy than even Gustavo ever attempted, which—instead of pissing her off—only made her desperately try not to laugh as their eyes met over whomever was doing the sucking up. Audrey's absence smoothed over some of the rough edges of her earlier mood, and Neve could at least be magnanimous to those who deserved her appreciation.

It turned out she didn't need to tell Barnaby to arrange a meeting with Livia Sabran-McMillan. As per their tradition, Gustavo talked her into a glass of something before retiring for the night. The American was such an iconic establishment, the oldest surviving art déco cocktail bar in London, and Neve allowed herself to be persuaded.

The place was busy, which wasn't unusual, but a table was cleared for them in a matter of seconds, which wasn't that unusual either. Just as they were getting their drinks—and Neve could already taste her extra dry martini—a familiar face caught her eye. Sipping what looked like a very convoluted, red cocktail, Livia Sabran-McMillan herself sat gracefully at the bar, doing her best not to stare in the direction of their table. Strange.

"Gustavo, make yourself scarce," Neve murmured without a twinge of sympathy. After all, business was business. He glanced up, discreetly following her gaze, then with an understanding nod slinked away the moment the server brought their drinks.

Neve took a sip of her martini and wanted to moan in satisfaction. She would, in fact, have done just that if Livia wasn't uncoiling herself from her stool in one elegant motion and languidly moving in Neve's direction. Of tall, willowy build, the woman had long, straight, blondish-silver hair flowing down to her shoulders, offsetting a narrow face with sharp cheekbones and a cleft chin. Blue eyes shone on an otherwise pale countenance, finished off by a sculpted mouth. It was a compelling face, full of contradictions that somehow worked perfectly together.

Right now, the vivid eyes were the only spot of color on the woman, the fitted, little, black Dior dress outlining the disciplined lines of a well-trained body.

Livia Sabran-McMillan carried herself with innate poise and an air of something distinctive that could only be called nobility. Some people learned to walk and talk and act like blue blood ran through their veins. Neve surely had, although it had taken her some time to forget her childhood and instead learn the head tilts and voice inflections of the well-born and richly bred. Other people were just given this elusive quality of being set apart from the riffraff of the world.

"Neve." The voice wasn't quite a purr, but there was just enough suggestiveness there to raise Neve's antennae.

With a nod to the chair opposite her, Neve offered her own greeting. It was a little odd; they knew each other professionally, having attended countless board meetings together, but they had never interacted socially. It was even stranger that Livia was in London at all. Cannes was *de rigueur* for Hollywood's high society, but London or the upcoming event in Venice were not as popular. It involved too much travel, with the festivals tending to bleed into each other.

As if reading her mind, Livia smiled and gestured around them with her incandescent red cocktail. "Cannes is great, but The American happens to serve the best Love Potion this side of the Atlantic."

"I'm sure the Saudi Royal family is grateful to you for your patronage of their little shack, as well as for the lengths you go to, to indulge in your love of this cocktail." She realized that her dry humor might not be to everyone's liking, and it wasn't the time to antagonize members of the Gannon McMillan board–especially those with whom she shared a distinct distaste for one Juno Buchanan.

Before she could soften her previous remark, Livia laughed, and Neve couldn't help but smile in return at the melodic, attractive sound.

"I knew I always liked you, Neve Blackthorne. If for nothing else, then for your perspicacious nature. Yes, yes, the Saudi Royal Family would undoubtedly miss my patronage if I didn't show up at the Savoy from time to time. But my reason for being here this week has to do with more than Love Potion cocktails and the revamped Unity screening. Though I have to say, I could see your fingerprints all over the new version."

Livia raised her glass in Neve's direction. "I'm a big fan, and you are a true master of the craft. I was also pleasantly surprised to see Peter Cross no longer features in the production. I'm glad his secret support of anti-LGBT causes has finally been brought to light."

Well, they could certainly talk about homophobic Hollywood outcasts and editing and the latest entertainment trends. Neve was prepared to do it too—feeling like she had to make up for coming close to committing the faux pas of offending Livia—but just as she opened her mouth to get into the familiar role of movie goddess extraordinaire, Livia cut her off.

"I'm sorry, Neve, please don't feel you have to respond. I'm sure after two days of talking about cinema and inside baseball with God knows how many people, you must be tired of it all. Plus, I'm rambling... Dammit."

Livia bit her lip, her face an attractive mix of discomfort and embarrassment, and Neve realized that perhaps Livia's interest wasn't entirely professional. The rambling, the uncharacteristic behavior, the blush now covering her cleavage and neck, the earlier suggestiveness in her voice. Neve decided to tread very carefully.

"Livia, you seem uncomfortable this evening. Are you alright?"

"I am. Guess I'm acting a little strange. I swear this is my first cocktail, so alcohol isn't an excuse either." Her expression turned rueful and self-deprecating.

"Do you need an excuse?" Belatedly, Neve realized her words could be misconstrued as a come-on. She instantly regretted it, but it was too late. Livia was reaching across the table and taking her hand.

"I know that this is entirely inappropriate. You just overcame a pretty considerable foe, and she's waiting in the wings to exact her revenge. I also realize that you will be looking for any and all friends right now. I wanted to say that I can be that friend."

The hand holding hers was warm, perhaps a bit too warm, as the tapered fingertips moved over her knuckles in a tentative caress. It was a pretty hand with the manicure filed short and precise. Under any other circumstance, Neve would find a way to use this opportunity to her advantage. Here was the heiress apparent to the McMillan throne, offering herself on a silver platter.

Neve had her scruples, but the world was what it was, and even though she personally had never had to work for her professional success on her back, she knew plenty of people who'd done just that. She couldn't care less how people had risen to prominence as long as they were competent and talented and brought those qualities to the table. Life was a jungle, after all, take or be taken.

No, ethical reasons were not what was stopping her from turning her hand palm up and meeting Livia's caress. Plus, who was she to talk ethics after she herself had availed herself of the company's assets, so to speak?

The news of her impending divorce had hit the papers while she was still in Paris, which was advantageous for her because the news cycle had managed to move on by the time she'd returned to LA. DMZ was in the throes of another teen movie star scandal, and Neve Blackthorne's divorce was blessedly yesterday's news. Her reasons for not asking an attractive woman up to her room to seal this potentially very satisfying professional and personal alliance were very mundane. Her heart wanted something else, someone else.

Livia was everything she found attractive in a woman, mature, sophisticated, refined and influential. She fit the bill of her previous lovers, male or female, to a T. She also possessed an appropriate degree of reverence for Neve, which should guarantee worship and appreciation in the bedroom. More importantly, this worship would translate into support on the Gannon McMillan board.

Yet all Neve could think of were the now faded marks Audrey had left on her neck and breasts, and how she would like to have them back, have that mouth back, sucking and biting her skin until she couldn't take the sensual overload anymore and she'd beg Audrey to fuck her hard and deep. Damn Audrey and damn her own weakness. Love did make you weak. It was such an inconvenience.

Her face must have shown some of the apprehension, because Livia withdrew her hand slowly. Wasn't it just a shame that this woman who clearly wanted her was also perceptive enough to be able to read her? Such a waste.

"I'm sorry if my offer came at an inopportune time. And I have to apologize if I'm barking up the wrong tree altogether."

Livia gingerly lifted her hand off Neve's. Distracted again, and always by thoughts of Audrey, Neve did not even have the time to hyperventilate about being hit on by a woman. How had Livia known? Had she assumed–?

"I've always liked you. In all the ways." Her smile was cheeky, but Livia then had the tact to turn it sheepish. "I don't think anyone within a mile radius can blame me for trying. You walked in here, and pretty much everyone, man or woman, wanted to sit with you, share a cocktail. Share more afterwards…"

Neve tried to play it cool, tried not to exhale too loudly with the force of the relief that was coursing through her veins. Livia didn't know. Livia was just taking a chance. Livia had no idea.

Oblivious to the tsunami of relief that had Neve reeling, Livia went on. "I see the gears moving in your head. Please do not for a moment think that refusing to see me socially will revoke my support for you with the board. I have my own battles to fight with Buchanan. Her stunt, trying to sell the studio out from under us, thinking that my father and uncles are too old to object and assume they'd only see dollar signs and lessened responsibility for the foreseeable future..."

She shook the silver hair out of her face, the gesture graceful and natural. Several men at the nearby table stared, mesmerized. Neve grinned at Livia utterly ignoring them, as she went on. "Well, she wasn't wrong. But I don't agree, and Juno should really have done her due diligence. There are no circumstances under which I will ever go along with this. I'm sure you and I can team up and strategize on how to proceed from here, even if her cronies on the board outnumber my allies two-to-one right now. I'm of the opinion that if you give an intelligent woman enough time and a fabulous pair of shoes, she can rule the world."

Neve was surprised into a burst of sincere laughter, and her shoulders relaxed further.

"I must say, though," Livia continued, "your shoes are extra fabulous. As are your legs." She took a sip of her cocktail, her tongue following a stray drop of rich, red liquid on her lower lip. "Delicious."

"The cocktail?"

"The legs."

"Touché."

They smiled openly now, easy in each other's company, having established where they stood.

"I will do everything to support your eventual coup against

Juno, Livia. Say the word and more will follow. I'm sure between us, we can garner the support of some of those on the top floor. Gannon McMillan needs a new direction and perhaps a new Board Chairwoman?" Neve half gestured in Livia's direction with her second martini in hand.

"I wouldn't say no to that position. But my priority remains Buchanan's marginalization. I don't even care if she stays on the board. I just want fresh eyes and competent, ego-free hands steering this ship. When I look at how well some of our competitors are doing, what their numbers are, and how they use funds and investments to bring in innovation at every level of their projects, I want to weep."

Neve opened her mouth, determined to explain some of the finer points, but Livia raised a finger and steamrolled ahead. "I'm not saying you're not doing that at Gannon. God knows you milk every cent dry and are always on the cutting edge of whatever new technology there is, but it shouldn't be costing you cuts in other departments. Your ideas should be encouraged and financed properly, and you should be allowed to reign free. The golden goose should be cherished, not accosted at every step."

"This is very much music to my ears, Livia." It seemed she didn't need to explain at all. Her interlocutor understood everything. Only Neve knew the battles she waged with Juno and her CFO over every blessed dollar that went into her studio.

"...Even though I would very much like to accost you myself." Livia's smile turned just a bit dirty. "Because how do you look this fresh and beautiful after a whole day of being drooled over by countless adoring fans? But then you always look beautiful, Neve."

The voice was wistful now, and Neve felt she had to give Livia something by the way of explanation. She had made so many mistakes recently with people who perhaps deserved a little better from her.

"I'm flattered, Livia. The compliments and the support with the board are very much appreciated."

"I do apologize for jumping the gun, Neve. Your husband filed for divorce a couple of weeks ago, and here I am rather aggressively pursuing you–someone who might not be available regardless of the existence of a husband. Honestly, I came to London strictly to engage in a business proposition and not to actually proposition you." Livia smiled at her own joke. "But you look amazing and let's just say I had to take my shot?"

It was flat out embarrassing how relieved Neve felt, but also how propped up in her war with Juno. She had an ally that was both powerful and just very slightly enamored with her. And Neve herself was cynical enough not to spurn those advances completely.

With a suggestive tilt of her head, she bussed Livia's cheeks, the actual touch of lips against skin, not half-hearted air kisses this time, acknowledging both their professional alliance and some tenuous future possibility of reconsidering their personal situation. Just as soon as Neve got her head examined and purged of the ridiculous notion that all she wanted was a green-eyed girl–no, woman–who fucked her so well that she passed out. A green-eyed woman who hated her just a bit these days.

The very woman who was currently slumped against the wall near her penthouse suite, in ghastly Doc Martens and torn, black skinny jeans. The equally black t-shirt did nothing to hide the jutting collarbones and the already hardening nipples. And the suspenders hanging off those lithe shoulders did something illegal to Neve's insides.

Neve swallowed the sudden urge to run and hide. She was exhausted, the emotional roller-coaster of the day taking its toll on her. For the past month, all she had wanted was to see Audrey again, and even earlier today, knowing that she was attending the Miramar screening with Freja, Neve still wanted to just sit there and look at her, drink in the lanky form, the slim arms, and long legs.

Now that the sullen figure glared daggers at her from the doorway of her own suite, she was reconsidering her earlier wishes.

As she opened the door, Audrey irreverently pushed off the wall and into the suite. Neve wanted to protest but found it utterly useless. It wasn't like she didn't know what opening the door would lead to, and if she'd really wanted to keep Audrey out, she would have threatened to call security. The young woman headed straight to the generous mini bar, poured herself a tumbler of vodka, and downed it in one gulp.

Neve could only arch an eyebrow at such a masterful display of drinking prowess. She didn't have much time to do anything else because Audrey was on her in the next second. But the tone of her touch was so different from what Neve had been used to from her. There was no roughness, no urgency. The embrace was strong yet gentle, soothing rather than arousing, and when those still pouting lips touched hers, it was a supplication more than a demand.

Astonished and totally off balance from the newness of this interaction, Neve raised her hands, but instead of pushing Audrey away, she ended up cradling the beloved, troubled face, further gentling the caress of lips and tongues.

The kiss ended, and Audrey rested her forehead against Neve's, still holding her close. Minutes passed as they stood framed by the dark window overlooking the Thames, their embrace silent as they breathed each other's air.

"I'm so angry at you, Neve, all the time, and so tired of being angry, and then you pull a stunt like you did in Paris." Audrey gulped, and Neve was horrified to see such anguish in her eyes.

Still so young, already so tortured. "You let me hurt you. I could swear I wanted you to hurt after everything you did to me a year ago, but not like that. Never like that!" The stormy eyes were earnest, beseeching now, looking into hers for absolution. Such a tender heart.

Neve traced a cheekbone with her thumb and gently kissed the beloved forehead before letting go and stepping out of the embrace.

"I told you already in my message. I wasn't that hurt, and you did nothing wrong. What happened on Rue Lamarck was perfectly consensual and entirely appropriate for the name of the street. Did you know Lamarck was a zoologist? So we went at each other like animals. It was fine, Audrey. It is fine."

Audrey seemed to be completely stymied by the answer, her eyes wide and mouth open. Perhaps it was the random piece of trivia that was somehow so easily at Neve's disposal that surprised her, or maybe she hadn't expected Neve to make light of what had transpired between them.

So while Audrey was silently staring at her, Neve went on and tried to further calm those deep troubled waters of her lover's heart.

"I know you abhor the phrasing, but I enjoyed that night. Let it go."

As she turned away to face the windows and the river, she heard a deep exhale, followed by booted steps. Then Audrey walked up behind her and wrapped her arms around her waist, and Neve felt the movement of lips tickling her temple before she heard the whispered words.

"I can't let go. Of what happened that night or of you, Neve. I tried very hard. Faceless, nameless people. You've said many times that I'm an excellent trier, so I did what I do best. It just doesn't seem to work."

Neve knew she should step away from the gentle arms. This was no longer her place to find comfort. This had never really been her place, no matter how much solace it gave her. Nothing good would come out of her indulging in this weakness. But as Audrey's familiar scent wrapped itself around her and the soft lips wreaked havoc on her skin, she knew she'd lost whatever battle before even stepping on the battlefield.

"Not so faceless, because she does have quite a face, and not entirely nameless, although I understand the impulse to only use a first name, especially when she has such a distinctive one. Will Freja be missing you tonight as she missed you that night in Paris?"

Their position, of Neve looking out the window and Audrey standing behind her, arms still embracing her, was giving Neve a false sense of security. Goddess knew she would probably have never been able to say any of those words to Audrey's face. A year ago, when she'd still been oblivious to her feelings? Sure. Now? Not a chance.

Now Neve wished she could have schooled her tone to be mocking. Instead, it had come out as tired and just a bit sad. Was it the sadness in her voice that made Audrey sigh and hold her just a little bit closer, a little bit stronger?

"Freja and I aren't... Well, we aren't yet. I wish I could say we're friends, but she'd like us to be more. I guess you could say we hang out and like each other's company? It was fun as a casual onetime thing, and I'm not really sure we can be anything else. I can't really do much more than casual onetime things these days. It wouldn't be fair to whomever it is I was with, when all I can think about is how you taste when you come in my mouth."

Even though the tone was matter of fact, almost clinical in delivery, Neve trembled at the words and felt Audrey's smile blossom against the nape of her neck, where a wicked mouth was slowly nibbling and licking her skin, sending more shivers down her spine. God, she was weak.

"You know..." The soothing, quiet whisper of Audrey's voice was weaving magic. "When I left Gannon that evening, when I still knew nothing about the fake bathroom sex, about anything at all... I just wanted to hold you and tell you that you were making this awful mistake. The spell I was under for months was turning to dust in my hands, and you were standing there, absolutely immune to the pain, the sheer devastation you were wreaking."

Sharp teeth nipped at her ear, and Neve shivered. She wanted to say that none of this was true, but Audrey went on, her hands slowly making their way under Neve's shirt.

"It was obvious, even to me, that you were running. Running scared. And I was naive enough to want to stop you, to shield you, to tell you that because I loved you, absolutely nothing could touch you, Neve. And if you had any love for me, it would make me immortal. I wanted to whisper that the universe would move and make space for us, for that love, if you'd only listen or believe me."

Neve shuddered, unable to control her reaction to the words, and Audrey's cheek simply rested against her hair, their breaths coming shallow now, in anticipation, but also—Neve was certain—in recollection of a terrible moment they'd already shared.

"But you kept pushing, kept twisting the knife with each and every sentence you uttered. How does that saying go? 'When people show you who they are, believe them'? I believed your cruelty, Neve. It was so easy. You are very convincing when it comes to that particular emotion. So I never said anything. It was over. It's been over a year now, yet I still think of that night, Neve. And those unsaid words remain in my mind. Maybe to remind me of just how damn naive I was. How you were right about everything when you called me immature. Unsophisticated."

Neve shook her head, unable to utter words when Audrey's

mouth again focused on her shoulder, licking gently, an occasional nip showing her who was in control.

"No? My sweet. I hated you so much, so much, Neve. And I was so confused. Your fear, your desire, your cruelty, all there, like cards in a game of solitaire in front of me. I couldn't make sense of any of it. And I think I just sort of stopped. I am tired of trying to fight with you. And I'm tired of trying to fight you. My bittersweet."

Fingers delved into her hair, caressing before coming together in a strong grip that pulled her head back, exposing her neck and hot lips zeroed in on her pulse point, sucking greedily. She could practically feel the blood rising to the surface, the bruise blossoming like crimson rose petals under her skin.

How could she think that anyone else would do? That anyone else could possibly do this to her? Livia who? She was forgetting the name and the woman as Audrey was slowly turning her into a wanton, needy mess. As if on cue, Audrey reminded her, never stopping the exquisite torment of her neck.

"I saw you with Livia Sabran-McMillan earlier, holding hands. You make a nice couple, though I thought you'd die first before coming out? I get it though. You need all the support with the board that you can get right now."

She didn't know what grated more, that Audrey thought Neve would sleep with Livia to ensure her position—which, granted, she had been contemplating just an hour ago and would have perhaps done under different circumstances—or that Audrey was so sanguine about the whole scenario, just standing there, marking her skin, the fingers of one hand playing lazily with an already hardened and wanting nipple.

Irritating as it was though, Neve had used Audrey's jealousy against her before and had only hurt herself more in the process. They weren't going to do this anymore.

"As nice a couple as Livia and I would make, we aren't. Even if my position was so dire that I would contemplate prostituting myself—no judgment to those who do—to keep it, Livia doesn't have the power to help me right now." It was shocking, really the things she would do for Audrey, explaining herself like a common, lovesick fool. The words she was saying, words she'd normally kept to herself...

Don't tell... Don't tell...

But some of those words she needed to voice, no matter how much the whisper in her mind was insisting differently. Because Audrey deserved better.

"And above all else, I am not interested in Livia."

"That's good," Audrey murmured in that same infuriating, matter-of-fact tone as her other hand joined in. Now both Neve's nipples were being tugged and rolled and tortured just this side of pain. She pushed back into Audrey's groin, and the young woman laughed quietly.

"This is also very good. Mmmm, I love your ass." Audrey did not let go of her breasts, but her hips ground firmly against Neve, making her whimper. Having experienced Audrey's skill with a strap-on, she thought she might just die from the carnality of the gesture and the subtle inference that it carried. "You know, I used to watch you walk around the office all the time and fantasize about all the things I would do if I got my hands on your ass?"

Caught in the web the velvet voice was weaving around her, Neve was startled when the hands playing with her nipples suddenly tore at her blouse, buttons flying everywhere. In the stillness of the room, the sound was like a gunshot, startling and obscene. Audrey did not alter the tone of the encounter, though, still languidly nibbling at her jaw and playing with the now uncovered breasts, after she deftly undid the front clasp of the bra.

Neve thought she could come just like this, in front of the

undraped window overlooking the Thames and brightly lit London. Audrey removed Neve's torn blouse, slowly unzipped her skirt, and slid it down her legs, along with her thong, going down on her knees, kissing the skin just above the thigh highs before proceeding upward to gently lick and bite at the ass cheeks she had apparently lusted for while she'd roamed the halls of Gannon.

Naked, supporting herself against the glass, Neve shut down her brain and allowed Audrey to simply take her wherever she wanted.

It was so different tonight, worshipful caresses and kisses, pleasuring with every touch. Audrey gave her ass one last playful bite before standing up and once again took Neve in her arms. There again was the imbalance of power between them. Audrey fully clothed and Neve naked except for her thigh highs and stilettos.

"I know you said you were okay with what happened that night, but I don't think I am. I don't care if it shows my lack of sophistication or naiveté or whatever. You can say that I don't have to make it up to you, but I want to. Let me?"

Unable to not be able to see Audrey's face anymore, Neve finally turned around, and the light in those green eyes stole her breath. So much love. How on Earth was Neve ever going to resist this hope? This love? Hell, she'd promised herself just last week that it was time to hold back this river of emotion, to shut it off and move the hell on.

She was supposed to be protecting herself and her heart from exactly this situation. The situation that was guiding her away from the windows, her lips hungry yet gentle. This situation that was currently spreading her on the king-size bed and licking tenderly into her, gentle fingers joining in to massage her clit in slow circles. As Audrey's tongue entered her, Neve lost all power to further try to be objective about holding back, her river overflowing.

. . .

She woke up alone the next morning, Barnaby's wake-up call brisk and precise. As she stretched her well-used muscles, she felt no pain, just an invigorating laxness of a satisfied body, pleasured beyond even her lofty expectations.

If her heart ached at the thought of her own impotence to stop this continuous charade, she chose not to dwell on it.

PART II
SOLACE

Solace

part II

8

NEVE AS PREY

"*Venice followed London.*"

"*I feel I will get quite an education in all things film. Or at least film festivals. Is that the actual order? I seem to remember them quite differently.*"

Neve tsked quietly. For once, she actually wanted to share, to get out of her head and her heart the events that had transpired and all these thoughts, but especially the feelings, that were choking her. Yet Dr. Moore seemed anything but interested.

"Everything is arranged differently this year. Cannes in May, London in June. Venice and Berlinale in September, and Toronto was pushed back to October. Things have been in flux after the last couple of years of disarray. That's not really the point, though."

"The point, as you so eloquently put it, is that while you gave her peace and allayed whatever guilt she felt after Paris, for which I have to say, I really am happy—"

"You actually believe I'm heartless."

"What I believe, no, what I know is you're a survivor. First and foremost. And at times only that. The things I'm aware you've survived, and the things I only suspect you've survived…" At Neve's sharp inhale, Dr. Moore raised both hands palm up. A quick nod, and the apology was accepted.

"All I'm saying is that, Harlan aside, it's not in your nature or your nurture—from all I am seeing in you—to allay anyone's fear, anyone's concerns. To comfort and to indulge. And yet, you've comforted and indulged Audrey. To your own detriment. Again. This self-sacrificing streak of yours is perplexing me."

"There is nothing self-sacrificing in pleasure. In taking it."

"Ah, so that's what you're telling yourself?"

"I'm not telling myself anything."

For a second Neve closed her eyes, expecting the hissing voice to be back in her ear, but nothing followed, and she unclenched her jaw, focusing back on Dr. Moore.

A quick shake of the gray-haired head and a disappointed purse of lips, and Neve smiled. She really was getting very close with the acerbic therapist. Good to know that some of her decisions were still golden.

"Be that as it may, Neve. Your uncharacteristic selflessness aside, you two are not talking."

"Audrey calls it a bad romance novel. I think at one point, she told me that miscommunication as a trope is passè. Cliche. Funny that you keep bringing up that other ridiculous romance trope, when Audrey quite literally believes our whole... affair has been one."

"An Ice Queen is not ridiculous in the least. In fact, ridicule is one thing a true Ice Queen cannot stand. I suspect you know that very well."

"I resent the whole comparison to an insipid literary character." Neve watched Helena Moore's lips twitch in what appeared to be an attempt to hold back a smile.

Neve looked around the bright room, the light coming in from the large floor-to-ceiling windows, filling the office with sunshine and a serenity that perhaps was more because of its chief occupant than the sun itself. As she turned to her interlocutor, an uncharacteristic loneliness filled her.

"But you are right, we don't talk."

They had fallen into a pattern of sorts after London. They didn't talk much besides the necessary 'harder', 'oh God', 'three fingers tonight, I think', and 'again'. Those were necessary strings of words because while they didn't talk, they continued to see each other.

Venice was several months removed from London. Audrey didn't show her face at any of the screenings, didn't accompany Freja to any parties, but one night she just showed up at Neve's hotel door and they went at each other like they'd been starving.

The emotionally fraught night in London was forgotten, and so was the tenderness. Audrey brought her best rough game on this trip and Neve screamed, as Audrey sucked her clit in rhythm with the deep thrusts of those long fingers. The rough sex gave them an outlet for all the unsaid things that still stood between them. She also got four fingers into Audrey for the first time and couldn't help a self-satisfied smirk as the younger woman came apart under her hand and mouth, having wondered aloud before if she could really do it.

By morning, they'd been covered in marks and were as satisfied as four orgasms each could make them. They continued not to talk after that.

Berlinale was in early September, and Neve was forced to attend since they were giving her some kind of made-up award, which she suspected was their way of thanking her for Gannon's patronage and money. She'd brought Harlan with her on that trip, to give them more time together, since the Berlinale schedule wasn't strictly work-related and hence less regimented. Neve only attended the ceremony and the dinner party afterwards, and tried to avoid the red carpet and the obligatory pictures as much as possible.

Audrey conveniently had some follow-up on a story about the German government and their social assistance network for migrants, and even more conveniently had a room in Neve's hotel. Sneaking around was coming back to Neve like riding a bike, and she exited the party after 30 minutes and spent the next two hours with Audrey, while Harlan and Barnaby entertained themselves with such pursuits as thoroughly inspecting the Trabi car museum that Neve faintly thought she might have heard about. Before she'd allowed Barnaby to whisk Harlan away, the look she'd given him thoroughly ensured that he was aware losing her child would be tantamount to death. Harlan had a great time.

So did Neve. This encounter fell somewhere in the middle of their sex scale, between London-tender and Venice-frantic. Neve couldn't be covered in bruises in front of her son, but Audrey still managed to leave a couple of marks to remember her by on the insides of Neve's thighs. They remained for several days, marring her skin, and she got distinctly wet every time she crossed her legs and felt them there. She crossed her legs a lot over the next few days.

Neve and Audrey continued not to talk.

―――――

The Toronto International Film Festival wasn't something she normally attended, having deigned to accept the invitation maybe twice in 20 years. Neve felt it was too small for her.

"Didn't you say Toronto was an affront to your sensibilities?"

"I did, and it is." Neve hid her face behind the latest copy of

Variety that had a positive review of Unity. Well, maybe she wouldn't unleash her wrath on them just yet.

"Then why..." Speaking of wrath, one look from her, and Gustavo closed his mouth sharply. Too bad she was as transparent to him as air.

She took Harlan with her again, and he enjoyed the festival and the hustle and bustle of a surprisingly cosmopolitan city.

Neve enjoyed Audrey spread out on the kitchen table of the rented apartment, located very conveniently not far from their hotel.

If Elinor had any qualms about her star reporter being dispatched to do puff pieces from the red carpet at TIFF instead of somewhere where Audrey could really make a difference, the Times' International editor-in-chief didn't say so during the lovely brunch they shared one morning at whatever Michelin star restaurant.

"You look thoroughly displeased. Don't worry, Canadians don't bite, unless you ask them to, though I'm sure someone else has that covered for you. Just like that concealer?" Surely Elinor knew better than to expect Neve to raise her hand to her neck, giving herself and the covered mark away. Instead, Neve just raised an eyebrow and sipped her coffee.

Elinor smirked. "And please don't act like you don't want to be here. As lying goes, you're a master, but we go way back. Some things you could never lie about convincingly. Let me see..." Elinor actually started to count on her fingers. "You are incapable of hiding your displeasure over food. You are horribly transparent when it comes to feeling superior about something, which is pretty much anything because you are. Oh, and you're incapable of faking it with a woman. So, are we hitting a trifecta here?"

At Neve's best withering stare, Elinor just laughed and signaled the server to bring her another cappuccino.

"Now let's see about those standards of yours. The coffee is passable because you have not sent it back, several of your movies are doing amazing—especially the ones you had a hand in yourself, besting Alisson Summers yet again—and Audrey is keeping you thoroughly pleased. How am I doing?"

"Poorly, seeing that you're a journalist and not running a gossip rag, dearest."

Still, despite her denial to Elinor, Neve had little to complain about. Her son was happy, her body was fucked within an inch of her endurance, and Audrey was hobnobbing with the rich and famous, talking to them about their movies and their inspiration.

Neve herself was very inspired when she went down on Audrey in the bathroom while they attended a very select dinner, honoring some actress or other. She felt powerful and desired and just unstoppable as she sucked on Audrey's clit, pumping two fingers inside her.

She felt decidedly more powerful when all it took was less than a three-minute effort, though her arrogance was marred by the fact that she actually did not want to stop licking Audrey, her taste addictive. She refused to think back to the days when she'd called Audrey her drug of choice. So she didn't stop, and Audrey needed both hands to cover her mouth to stop the scream when she came a second time in less than five minutes.

Neve just folded Audrey's ivory silk thong in her purse, allowed her to clean her own juices off Neve's lips with several long deep kisses, and swept out of the bathroom like nothing at all untoward had happened.

She really enjoyed watching Audrey having to step and bend very carefully for the rest of the evening, afraid that her short Gucci dress would reveal that her panties now resided in Neve's purse and not on her body.

When Neve happened to find herself in the same conversational circle with Audrey alongside several actors and designers, and she was asked if she kept up with next year's trends, she arched her eyebrow and said that she couldn't get enough ivory.

The two of them continued not to talk much after that.

———

She hadn't seen her for several months, anticipating the new series of European jaunts soon to come, but she knew Audrey had been signing up for more and more assignments outside of France and wasn't doing the entertainment circuit anymore.

Neve was at times catching her byline, reporting from some godforsaken places on some very boring subjects such as water scarcity and food shortages. The subjects themselves didn't interest Neve much, but as she sipped on her Lauquen Artes, she read every word and would dutifully sign a check to whichever organization Audrey said was doing a good job providing whatever was necessary to help those who were affected.

They still weren't talking, and in her mind it somehow didn't compute at all that Audrey's assignments were evolving into something very different from puff pieces from the Riviera, or even public housing for migrants.

And so Neve was completely blindsided when Gustavo dragged her out of a meeting and to the closest TV that had ZNN on. They were broadcasting live, breaking news from Iraq. It was late morning on December 21. Neve would bear the scar from that moment until the day she died. A bloodied and disheveled Audrey was reporting from a thoroughly dilapidated and war-torn area of Baghdad, while the world was falling apart around her and her cameraperson.

The shooting that could be heard in the background was only interrupted by explosions, and when those stopped, the screams of the wounded and mourners permeated the air. Audrey's face was resolute and professional as she gave voice to the events that were happening around her. She made no accusations or judgments. Instead, she stated the facts and what she observed as she tried to stay out of the line of fire, and out of the way of the first responders and volunteers who were trying to help the victims.

Neve felt that she was watching something from a movie. A set she could have directed herself. It was perfect, really, the realism overwhelming. Her breath had gone shallow and her fingers numb. She could have sworn she could smell gunpowder, dust, concrete. Blood. And above all the fear, so overwhelming that she staggered.

On the screen, that beloved, resolute figure, slim shoulders hunched against the dust that was beginning to settle after the explosions stopped, didn't flinch as more shooting broke out, nor was she running for cover right away, but assessed the situation with a remarkably clear head and calmness even as the camera shook, probably because her cameraperson's hands weren't as steady.

Audrey ended her live feed by retreating to safety and promising that the ZNN crew would return with more information on the attack for the morning news. Neve realized it must be late afternoon in Baghdad. She stared at the screen, speechless, as the news reports moved on to other events of the day. How could anyone move on? She flinched when Gustavo touched her shoulder to pull her into her office and looked at him, eyes wide. Audrey was not a TV reporter. What the hell was she doing there?

Elinor wasn't picking up the phone, and Neve paced the space like a caged animal until Barnaby quietly told her that Audrey had taken a one-month assignment in Baghdad and had been dispatched from Times to ZNN for the duration.

"I read something about it on her blog," Barnaby mumbled, and Neve realized Gustavo was not the only Gannon employee who had figured out some things about their boss.

All those months of not talking had backfired spectacularly.

In their quest to not talk, to not break the spell of the simple physicality, of the sexual connection, and to run away from the conversations they could or should be having, it seemed they had missed some very important things.

Such as the fact that, somehow, Audrey was now a war zone reporter. A war zone reporter who had just witnessed and masterfully reported on a massacre in the capital of Iraq. Yes, her Audrey lived to tell the tale and certainly would make a name for herself in the process, yet in Neve's heart, it was like the boom had been lowered.

Her Audrey was fearless. And Neve's life was consumed by dread.

God knew, fear had been her default companion these past two years, since she'd been caught in this emotional web of sexual haze and complicated feelings for Audrey. How did Dr. Moore put it? 'Her three defenses'? The Knight, the Bishop and the ever-elusive Rook. Fear of losing her son, fear of losing her job, and fear of exposure, of being outed and *othered* yet again.

And while she had learned to live with all three, to allow them to eat at her heart and her mind, she could still stand them. She'd withstood so much, after all. Neve kept telling herself and Dr. Moore again and again that living with them was better than the alternative.

And on December 21, Neve had met with yet another fear, one that was greater than her considerable capacity to overcome. The fear of Audrey's death was slowly choking the life out of her. It was a fear she could not stand.

She's never, ever coming back... Everyone leaves you...

The voice that had been kept at bay by Audrey, by Harlan, by Dr. Moore, the voice from her childhood, the voice that rendered her a numb, trembling mess was back. This time Neve did not push it aside, did not fight it. Back then, she'd cover her ears and close her eyes until her head hurt from the effort. Now she let it wash over her in a prophecy that was both pain and truth. *Everyone leaves.*

Pale, trembling, Neve dismissed Barnaby, canceled her afternoon, and checked in with the boarding school. She didn't need to, but she wanted to know that her baby was okay. Because she felt that she was losing herself, her mind, her heart. And so, after hearing his voice and making sure he'd be home over the weekend, she did something she had not done in over three years.

Neve was going to go to Nevada. Reno, to be exact. She had only really visited the place twice before. The first time had been ten years ago, when she'd moved her mother from a small, cold shack in Harrisburg, Pennsylvania, to the Luxury Reno Assisted Living facility.

The second was when Dmitriy insisted on meeting his new mother-in-law. The meeting had not gone particularly well, with the elderly Rivkah Beloff refusing to come down from her room to visit with her daughter and son-in-law. Neve hadn't insisted, and they'd left, with Dmitryi completely flabbergasted by the whole situation.

Neve herself was fairly flabbergasted now as the private jet took off from the LAX runway.

She knew what was coming when cold sweat drenched her blouse as the plane reached cruising altitude. She could tell she'd break. Her chest was caving in and her ears were ringing. Was this it? Was this how people who have reached their limit felt?

Neve didn't want to know, and so she did the one thing that made any sense. One glance at her phone to make sure it was connected to the cabin Wi-Fi, and she was dialing a number. Irony of ironies, if anyone would have told her eighteen months ago that she'd willingly be reaching out like this, she'd laugh herself silly. Still, if Dr. Moore was surprised, she didn't express it.

"Ziva. That's what they put on my birth certificate. It means bright. So does Neve. I changed it as soon as I left home. I suppose I liked the meaning, but by then I wanted nothing to do with anything they gave me. And the name was a pretty big thing."

She took a couple of deep breaths. Just having Dr. Moore on the other end of the line was calming her frayed nerves. Damn that woman. Neve would bet good money that her therapist felt pretty self-righteous right about now. They'd both known this phone call was coming. And here they were.

"You said earlier you were flabbergasted? Why?" Still, thank God, Helena Moore did not sound jubilant. In fact, she sounded concerned.

"Well, Rivkah—my mother—tends to have that effect on people. God knows she blindsided little Ziva."

Don't tell...

The hiss was back. Weak, almost imperceptible, but there. Neve threaded her fingers into her hair and pulled sharply. The memories were painful, no matter how she tried to dissociate herself from them. Calling herself by the other name, speaking about Ziva in the third person felt like cowardice, and she wanted to be better than that, no matter how much it hurt. *Give me a medal here, Doc.*

She slowly counted to five before straightening in her seat and continuing, "She used to protect me from my father's rages. Which only caused him to rage harder. She'd take his beatings silently. I think maybe even then she knew how his screaming affected me." A sob escaped, and she heard her therapist exhale loudly on the other end of the line. This was embarrassing and humiliating and just as painful as her father's screams.

"Neve, are you okay?" The question, for once, did not sound condescending to her ear. It sounded honest and caring, and Neve wanted to cry harder.

No, she wasn't okay. She hadn't been okay since she was a

little kid hiding in the attic to escape seeing her mother suffer at the hands of her father. She hadn't been okay, and she could no longer stand it. She wiped at her eyes, surprised that tears had not come despite the sobs absolutely wrecking her.

Crybaby... Stop this!

Muscle memory. *No tears, no matter how scared you are.* Seems even when she actually wished tears would come, her body would be too scared to let them fall.

Dr. Moore's steady breathing on the other end of the line made Neve go on. "She'd protect me only to turn around and ground me into dirt with cruelty of another kind. Nobody could humiliate quite like my mother. Cutting little remarks about my pronounced stutter, and offhand assurances that I would never amount to anything, because all the Beloffs were useless and bound to always rummage among the garbage on the streets of Harrisburg."

She felt unmoored, feelings slamming into her in quick succession. Fear, dread, now glee took over. Sucking on her teeth and shaking her head, she found herself laughing, her chest loosening and letting her take deeper breaths for the first time since the plane took off.

"Neve..." Dr. Moore strangely sounded even more concerned than before.

"No, no, I'm fine. It's just so funny, so ironic that I found out quite early that those predictions were wasted on me, since I wasn't really a Beloff, no matter what my birth certificate said."

"Your mother's husband is not your father?"

"*Wasn't*, no. He wasn't. He's dead now. I hope he isn't resting in any kind of peace. It doesn't matter. I learned very early that my mother resented me for being the reason she was married off to a Russian, Oleg Beloff, mostly against her will because she had gotten pregnant, and the father of the baby abandoned her. And no, don't go analyzing my words. Whoever that man was, he wasn't my father. Takes more than sleeping with someone and running away to be a father, doesn't it?"

Neve looked out into the vastness of the clouded skies beneath her and touched her chest. *No, no, this did not hurt, it didn't.*

"It does, Neve." Dr. Moore's voice was hoarse, and Neve was grateful that she wasn't the only one showing all this emotion, not the only one struggling for control.

"Anyway, her parents, wealthy and with some social influence, found Oleg, who, for promises of money and dowry, married Rivkah and pretended that I was his daughter."

Neve stretched her legs and tried to relax her shoulders. To her surprise, the cabin crew did not show up with their usual service, and she made a mental note to thank them for not disturbing her conversation. How strange that she felt certain of their discretion? She needed this more than a glass of whiskey, anyway.

On the other end of the line, Dr. Moore was silent. Her breath was slightly audible, and it was bringing Neve back to the present instead of allowing her to disappear into the pain of her childhood. This she could stand, even if she could not stand said reality at all. Those memories were suffocating her. It had been forty years, and the thought of her father's screaming still left her paralyzed with fear.

"How comfortable are you to tell me more, Neve?"

Neve had to laugh again. And right now, she really wished she had not dismissed that whiskey after all. Whiskey always made things a little bit better. Or, well, numbed the worst of it anyway. It anchored her to the present. She visualized herself reaching for the thread of the voice on the other end of the line, just to pull out of the horror of her past. Drinking was becoming a problem. One she'd take the Scarlett O'Hara approach to and think about it tomorrow. There were more pressing things today.

"Oh, Doc, comfortable is not the word I'd use. But sure, you can have it all. Oleg might've been Russian, but he didn't touch booze. He was an abusive philanderer and a gambler, and Rivkah's dowry and my grandparents' bribe money did not go very far. He was so violent, they cut him and my mother—and by extension me—off and left us to fend for ourselves. My grandparents never received us, never came to visit us, but they paid for my school…"

More memories, more cold sweat. Walking in the rain up the hill to the beautiful building, filled with wonderfully turned out girls, in cute dresses. Little Ziva was drenched and trying to hide a patch on the hem of her skirt. They laughed and pointed. They called her names. She sat alone in the back of the class, the distaste evident even on her teachers' faces.

But this conversation wasn't about any of that, and Neve bit her cheek to try to ground herself.

"Unable to keep a job for more than a few weeks, Oleg dumpster-dived, and Rivkah cleaned the movie theater, among the myriad of other jobs she tried to keep to feed us."

"Ah, a movie theater." There was a smile in the exhalation, and Neve smiled, too. It was coming full circle, after all.

"That's where old Isaac opened my eyes to cinema. In the quiet, airy spaces of that building, amidst rolls and rolls of film, I found myself. I found Neve Blackthorne."

Among all the memories of her childhood, the ones spent at the rickety movie theater were the happiest. It wasn't just a safe space. It gave her a different kind of permanency from her continuous torment and neglect at home. The theater offered a constant sense of security, a sense that there she could relax her shoulders and unclench her jaw. It also served a different role, one she was perhaps even more grateful for. It was an escape into fantasy, into imaginary worlds, so different from her own wretched one.

"Isaac… He'd indulged me ever since my mother had

started to bring me along while she swept the popcorn-covered floors. Perhaps because he was rather lonely, or perhaps later as I grew, it flattered him that I hung on his every word as though he was telling me fairy tales. He may as well have been. He rarely showed any contemporary films. I think he had some contempt for the 'newfangled ways'. But he loved the classics. The old stories, the films that made Tinseltown what it is now. Bogart and Bacall, Cary Grant, Greta Garbo... He'd talk about them and about those tales of Hollywood and Paris and London, of his youth and the old masters who had performed for the kings and queens of Europe and who had created miracles on the stage and big screen. He was a theater buff too, so for him the two, theater and the movies, were very much intertwined."

Neve smiled and noticed her fingers had stopped shaking. She no longer felt that permeating cold. Isaac brought her, as always, to a place of safety.

"He also regaled me with tales of present-day Paris, since he visited his Parisian cousin regularly. And those stories about there being someplace else out there, outside of goddamn Harrisburg, were giving me hope. And Isaac kept that hope alive."

The memory of the scent of old leather, popcorn, the pine floor cleaner Isaac used, and the vinegar from the projection booth, as the old film started to disintegrate, intruded. Neve thought of the countless hours she'd spent there, unseen and unbothered, before ultimately heading home, hoping against hope that her father was either asleep or out with some woman, and he wouldn't notice that she hadn't been home all day. Some days she was lucky, some days not so much.

She must have gotten caught up in her thoughts, because Dr. Moore laughed quietly on the other end of the line, jolting her from her reminiscing.

"He encouraged you to leave Pennsylvania?"

"In his way. He never said it out loud. And he really couldn't. I was a minor, and the community would have crucified him. My father was as good as my master. But Isaac did inspire me. Let's just call it that. The few fashion and movie magazines Isaac would bring from Paris each time he visited were like a breath of fresh air. And that air, it called to me."

She remembered lying in her small bed, trying not to even breathe too deeply because the bed was so old and decrepit that her every move would be accompanied by screeching. And yet, in that very bed, under the covers with a tiny flashlight, she read about all the things that she did not dare even to dream about. They whispered of freedom and of escape from Harrisburg.

"So he gave you a purpose?"

Yes, Neve thought, she had made a wonderful choice a year and a half ago because Helena Moore simply understood her. Maybe it was their long hours spent together during those sessions. Maybe it was Dr. Moore's innate intelligence or her years on the job. But Dr. Moore got her.

"He gave me a mission, a direction that I grabbed and hung onto with both hands, despite the derision and ridicule from my mother and whatever punishments my father chose to deliver."

It was that mission that had made her spend countless hours in front of the mirror at night, practicing her speech, and just as many hours during the day in the public library, reading hundreds and hundreds of books, on etiquette, on style, on history and literature.

And it was that air and that dream that had her watch the same movies with Elizabeth Taylor, Ava Gardner or Katharine Hepburn over and over. After a while, because of her single-minded focus and stubborn resolution, she no longer stuttered, she no longer slumped in a chair as she sat, her walk became measured and graceful, her spine ramrod straight, and she could tell a Bergman from a Kazan just by the editing or the camera work.

"In any case…" Neve cleared her throat and, for some reason, didn't want to say all that out loud. As accomplishments went, they rang hollow in her mind, and they really weren't the point. "The day I turned eighteen, Isaac gave me a letter and a couple of hundred dollars, though I had some stashed from my part-time work at the theater, anyway. Honestly, the money didn't matter as much as the letter. That one piece of paper felt like a golden ticket. He wrote to his cousins in Paris to take me on as an apprentice."

"Your official biography doesn't list any apprenticeships."

"I'm actually flattered you read that piece of fantasy, Doctor Moore."

A chuckle was her prize for the quip. "Well, in that case it was an entertaining fiction. Well written too. Had your fingerprints all over it, you control-freak."

It was Neve's turn to laugh out loud.

"No, I never allowed anyone to know about Paris. Isaac's cousin worked in a very popular costume shop in Montmartre. Old Isaac was more than generous with me. He gave me so much more than money. He gave me a place to land on my feet in Paris. I'll forever be grateful to him for giving me a dream."

Five years later, her talent, her hard work, her ambition and that single-minded focus had transformed her from Ziva Beloff, a young, scrawny-looking girl, working in a small shop on Rue Cortot, into Neve Blackthorne, a ballsy American who had left an impression at some of the most prominent movie studios in France with cunning, guile and her willingness to take risks.

From making props and sewing costumes, to moving on to apprentice under some of the most innovative French directors and cameramen, her vision behind the lense and her knack for direction set her apart.

Leaving Paris, she made her way to New York as a

conquering heroine, getting an invitation to produce and direct a show she had written diligently in her years in France. It started off-off-Broadway and garnered such acclaim as to become somewhat of a cult hit among both critics and audiences alike. A hop to Hollywood was expected, with various studios vying for her to direct their next art features. Except that, after paying her dues and eventually directing two films that both won her Academy Awards, Neve had surprised everyone when she'd taken the job of Vice President and later CEO of the declining Gannon McMillan Studios.

Dr. Moore startled her out of her memories.

"What happened to Isaac?"

"He passed away while I was in Paris. I think he was one of the very few people I genuinely mourned."

"I take it you didn't mourn your father."

"I never returned to Harrisburg and never maintained any contact with him."

"And her?" Dr. Moore was going to be like a dog with a bone with this, Neve could feel it.

"Or her."

"Is there a reason you're talking about the two of them as separate entities somehow?"

Yes, definitely like a dog with a bone.

"There is, but it doesn't matter." She did not sound breezy even to her own ears, but Dr. Moore remained silent. "In any case, I have no idea if either of them kept up with my... let's call them exploits."

"Would you have wanted them to?"

Neve looked ruefully at the therapist. "A million dollar question, Doctor. I don't actually know what my father thought, or if he even ever thought of me at all. I certainly haven't." The lie fell from her lips so easily. It was well-practiced after all. "I didn't hear anything for a long time, and then when I did, I ignored the summons to his funeral some ten years after I returned to the United States."

Neve had been very surprised that Rivkah had found out who she was now and figured out how to contact her. When her assistant at the time told her one morning that a woman claiming to be her mother was on the line, Neve had dumped her coffee all over her desk.

The voice was the same. Decades had passed and nothing had changed. Her mother could still paralyze her with a single word. Except she spoke quietly and was all business, simply stating that Neve's father had passed away, and in case her daughter wanted to attend the funeral, it would be held in two days.

"I declined, and we hadn't spoken for another five years when a stranger called and informed me that my mother had suffered a heart attack and was in intensive care in a Harrisburg hospital. I was also told that her health was in such a precarious state, she was no longer in any condition to care for herself and that, as her daughter, I'd need to do something about it."

"And you did." It wasn't phrased as a question.

Neve *had* done something about it. It was the first time she'd seen her mother in twenty years and the first time she visited her in the facility she'd chosen in Reno. It was far enough to be close, yet not really.

She was told later that Rivkah had been silent and despondent on the flight from Philadelphia to her new home. Upon seeing Neve, she'd smiled bitterly and said: "I've always known you would do well for yourself, if motivated properly."

Neve had wanted to laugh, then she'd wanted to cry and perhaps slap her mother silly. So years of humiliation and cruelty were 'motivation.' She'd either spoken out loud, or her face said as much, because Rivkah had sneered. "Well, it worked. You never succumbed to my fate of giving up every dream you've ever had. It fueled you, and so you got out. You didn't turn out lazy and rotten like him. It molded you into steel, so you had the strength to endure and make something of yourself."

Rivkah was right. Neve had turned on her heels and didn't return until the day Dmitriy wanted to play at being a son-in-law.

"So, why are you flying to Reno now?" Dr. Moore asked.

Ah, if only Neve knew the answer. In fact, it was the question that had caused her fear to almost choke the life out of her. It had also caused her to do the most unthinkable of all things: to call Helena Moore and share with her what she had never entrusted another person with. It had worked, too, since she untwisted her fingers from gripping the armrests until her knuckles had whitened.

"I guess I will find out when I get there." She did not bother saying goodbye, simply taking off her earpiece and switching off her phone. Closing her eyes, she thought of the myriad of things she hadn't allowed herself to even consider for years, chief among them the question Dr. Moore had just posited. Why *was* she going to see her mother? A mother who believed her to be made of steel and who, despite being dirt poor, had too much pride to ever ask anything of her millionaire daughter or to ever thank her for anything.

As she continued to ponder these things in the back of the chauffeured car heading to the assisted living facility, Neve could feel the tendrils of dread crawling up her spine yet again. She was nauseous.

Instead of finally just telling her psychologist everything and not playing this awful twisted game she had been for a year and a half anymore, she was going to see one of her abusers. She laughed bitterly, and the driver of the limo that had picked her up at the airport gave her a startled glance in the rear-view mirror. Yes, she was scaring herself as much as she was scaring her employees.

The lobby was cool, and the faint smell of industrial-strength cleaner was doing its best to counteract the ever-present scent of old age and subtle decay. She thought that not even the luxury of tens of thousands of dollars that she was paying for her mother's care could wipe away that odor.

She was escorted by a pleasant older nurse to the second floor. The woman asked no questions and volunteered just enough for Neve to understand that Rivkah was a model patient, never had any issues, didn't socialize much with the other residents, and preferred to be left alone in her room to read and watch television. The last part was said with a slight smile, and Neve wondered what that was about.

After a brisk knock on a door at the end of the long, beige hallway, the nurse departed. At a faint "yes" from behind the door, Neve entered her mother's room.

She didn't really know what she had expected. Certainly not the clean, sparsely furnished studio without any knickknacks and only one picture, framed and standing on the electric fireplace mantle. A recent magazine-quality picture of Neve, from the Academy Awards red carpet two years ago. Neve recognized the white McQueen gown. She couldn't say what was more shocking to her, the picture or the stack of DVDs on the coffee table. The top two were the movies she had won Best Director Oscars for.

Rivkah was reclining in a comfortable armchair in front of the fireplace that was burning brightly behind the protective glass, despite it being rather warm outside. She was holding last month's issue of Variety that had Neve's interview in it, and her face was quite a sight. Flushed red, eyes wide, and an utterly sheepish twist on those thin lips. Quite a telling reaction at being caught reading her daughter's words.

"Busted," her mother husked and smiled, and Neve snorted.

She couldn't help the noise escaping her mouth, and then she knew she could not help anything at all as she covered her face with her hands as the dam inside her cracked, broke down, and the flood took her over. She started laughing and couldn't stop until her outburst turned hysterical, and suddenly she wasn't laughing anymore. She was crying, sobbing uncontrollably, and sinking to the small sofa, her mind ravaged by stress and fear and loneliness.

After a while, she felt a cool trembling hand on the nape of her neck, and a tissue appeared in her line of vision. Her mother had some difficulty moving closer to her, from her chair to the couch, and was panting slightly.

Neve gave her a concerned look, only to be waved off with such a familiar gesture, it was like looking in the mirror. In fact, Rivkah Beloff was Neve's perfect reflection, a magic one showing what she would look like in her old age. Of course, all the neglect and disease that came with poverty had left their mark on the woman who looked much older than her seventy-five years.

Still, the rail-thin body, the angular sharp-featured face, and the same violet eyes might have been her own. The silver hair was long and tidily braided. Neve suddenly remembered that her mother had turned gray at a very young age. At the time, people had said that it was because they were always going hungry and because she was so overworked. Since Neve's hair had started losing color at 30, she'd done everything to hide the fact that she was fully gray by the age of 35. She guessed it was genetic, after all.

"How are you feeling, mother?" As her sobs subsided, Neve found herself at a loss and was desperately trying to grasp at straws in this terribly uncomfortable silence that was broken only by her mother's shallow, noisy breathing.

Rivkah simply nodded towards the door, the movement both regal and evasive. "If you ask them, they will tell you.

They'll tell you I am not that well. My heart, my lungs..." Rivkah started to get up, but Neve stopped her with a hand on her arm. God, had it been forty years since she'd touched her mother?

"I'm asking *you*, mother."

"I'm fine, Neve."

The name hit her like an uppercut. One punch, and she was down for the count. Her mother had called her by her chosen name. Her mother had a picture of her in her room. Her mother read her interviews and collected her movies. It was impossible. It was horrible. It was something Neve could have sworn she would never, ever see. She wasn't entirely sure she wanted to see it now. It was breaking her heart.

"I'm dying, Neve, and I am not going to have a lung transplant. I told them not to call you or tell you anything. It's my choice. You gave me some very good years in this place. I know you could have me put on the transplant list and get me doctors and work whatever magic you're capable of. And I believe you are capable of a lot of magic when you put your mind to it." The smile that crossed her mother's features was, dare Neve think it, proud.

"I'm old, and I'm ready. These years were plenty long for me. I've seen what I wanted to see in my life. My child made it out and made it big. I'm not sorry, you hear me, Neve?" Her mother's breaths were coming out in harsh noisy rasps now. Neve grabbed the oxygen mask from the chair's armrest and handed it to Rivkah, who took several breaths before continuing.

"I'm not sorry about how it happened. He'd have destroyed you. If not with his fists, since those were reserved for me, then with his sloth and drinking and whoring. I've dreamt of many things in my life, Neve. But once my dreams were all gone, I was left with only one wish, and it came true."

Neve recoiled as if from that blow that her father had never delivered. But Rivkah simply held her hands in an iron grip and spoke as if Neve hadn't moved.

"You got out, and I've never wanted anything else in life. Look at what you have! An empire. You built it yourself. You've made something of yourself, something neither your father nor I ever could. Nobody can take it away from you now. You're strong, a giant. Look what you've *done*! You've created a world for women out there. Remember that. Remember who you are, Neve."

If a heart could be both full and empty at the same time, surely that was Neve's at that moment. She turned away but her mother's hand on her chin made her look back.

"Nobody can take that away from you," Rivkah repeated. " Unless you let them. So don't."

She struggled for breath after that, and Neve helped her put the oxygen mask back on. They sat in silence for a long time, with her mother's breath the only sound in the room. After a little while, the heavy inhalations quieted down, and Rivkah fell asleep, still holding Neve's hand.

As she left the facility and got in the car, Neve felt that she had failed. She'd come all the way to Reno in her moment of need, in her moment of terror, and nothing was resolved. Maybe crying in her mother's arms was why she'd come after all? But it seemed shallow and superficial at best, when the thing choking Neve the most remained unsaid. The questions she wanted answered, the ones she still hid deep down, remained just that, questions.

Perhaps faced with her mother's complete lack of remorse for everything that had transpired between them, Neve was too afraid to hear more truths. And so she had not allowed herself to say what was burning in her chest. She thought maybe she would have another chance. And if she didn't, then so be it. Even having an answer didn't mean she could forgive, forget, and move on. What her mother had done had left a huge imprint on her life, changed its course, and marked her forever. Knowing why would not magically erase it all.

———

On her way back to LA, Neve thought that while she and her mother had found no real resolution or real closure of the wounds that still seeped blood into their lives, at least Rivkah had reminded her of the issue at the heart of her current predicament. She was Neve Blackthorne, and it was time she started acting like it. Audrey, Juno, her first husband… She had let them control her life, her decisions for way too long. It was time to do what she did best. It was time to take back the reins.

She couldn't help but look back and visualize the chessboard in Dr. Moore's office. The Pawn had fallen by the wayside, as her divorce was finalized. She did not want to touch on the Rook. If anything, the memories of humiliation and othering only reinforced her fears. The Rook would stand. And it was time to reinforce some of her other defenses. The Knight, Harlan, was something she'd protect and defend with her life, and it was non-negotiable, but some of her peace where her custody arrangement was concerned was also contingent upon her professional situation. It was time to deal with the Bishop. It was time to take control of her professional environment the only way she knew how. Attack was the best defense.

The next morning, Barnaby was instructed to set up lunch with Livia.

At their rather pleasant lunch, Livia shared that she had been successful at recruiting allies among her own clan and had even roped in some of the Gannons.

"You'll be surprised that many people share your anti-Buchanan invective." Livia gave her a sly smile, which Neve felt compelled to answer with one of her own.

"It's time to get the show on the road."

Their plan was simple. Capitalize on the support from the crew union and the animation guild and the leadership of Gannon McMillan's smaller production firms, with Neve acting as their unofficial representative in front of the board.

They had to line it all up in a rather quiet way and ambush Buchanan and her cronies with the data on neglect, mismanagement, and plain incompetence from certain board members. She would explain how they were not only driving down profits but were also not allowing the studio to reach its full potential because of constant budget cuts and lack of technological advancements and innovation.

Neve felt the excitement of the upcoming battle run down her spine and smirked all the way back to the office.

With Juno taken care of—or soon to be—Neve turned her full attention to Audrey. Or rather, she didn't. Dr. Moore would not be proud of her, for all their progress, for all of Neve's truths, this one was still a Rubicon she was not willing to cross under any circumstances. The revelation that she simply would not be able to overcome it if Audrey died proved that she had been right all along. She couldn't bear this, and so she wouldn't. Simple.

With her new determination to be true to herself and her own interests, Neve continued to not talk to Audrey and had foregone several European premieres for major Gannon productions.

Instead, she sent a very small note. Remembering their conversation in London about Audrey letting go of their affair and trying to forget Neve, she simply wrote: "Try harder. N."

Her cellphone got the brunt of the subsequent abuse that Audrey unleashed on her in the form of numerous messages and calls. Those went straight to voicemail. Neve pretended not to notice that, only seconds after her phone would go quiet, it was Gustavo's that would vibrate, and he would give her an already well-practiced exasperated look before excusing himself to take it. Neve ignored him as well.

After a while, she received a message that just read: "So be it. I'm trying harder. A."

She continued to ignore thoughts of Audrey until Academy Awards Week arrived, and then she couldn't do so any longer, because Audrey was virtually everywhere. The heroic war zone reporter and a celebrity in her own right in LA, Audrey attended every party, every afterparty, and was seen with more glitteratti than ever before. Neve avoided her like the plague.

Audrey's, 'right place, right time' courageous report from Baghdad had made her a favored nominee for the Pulitzer Prize for International Reporting, and Neve wasn't at all surprised.

In the meantime, Audrey's relationship with Freja which had only been rumored before, was confirmed with widespread fanfare and dubbed 'the new celesbian Brangelina'. The media branded them 'Fredrey'. Neve sniffed at the ridiculousness of the portmanteau. She heard Barnaby and Gustavo joke it was way too close to 'Fraudrey' and allowed herself a second of schadenfreude.

They looked good together, though. Both tall and slender, a brunette and a blonde. An acclaimed journalist and a world-renowned supermodel bad girl making inroads into the movie industry, they were definitely an interesting and captivating couple. Audrey was growing her hair, and it was starting to reach the middle of her long neck, giving her a slightly tousled appearance, as if a lover had just run rough fingers through the mahogany silk, disheveling it.

Los Angeles was gobbling it up, with every paparazzo on

their tail. All the yellow rags were brimming with stories of their romance, extravagant dates, wild escapades, and grand gestures. Freja wouldn't stop gushing about their relationship, and her every public appearance was even more of a spectacle than the previous one.

Neve avoided seeing Audrey, talking to Audrey, and even thinking about Audrey. She lied to herself that she was entirely successful at all three, with the very small exception of the nights when the memory of blood on Audrey's face and bombs going off right next to her would assault her consciousness.

Those twenty minutes of watching her love speak in calm and measured tones from the heart of a terrorist attack had been the longest, darkest minutes of her life. And so she felt validated in her decision to let Audrey go, and in turn, to enable her to try to let go of Neve as well.

Her reason was rather simple. All she cared about was that there was no amount of strength in her that would enable her to see Audrey die and continue as if her heart did not die as well.

The amount of damage that anything happening to Audrey would do to Neve was inconceivable in all its enormity. It would destroy her. Simple as that. And if her conversation with her mother served anything, it was as a reminder that she'd suffered and sacrificed too much to be destroyed by her own weakness. She couldn't do this. She couldn't live like an exposed nerve, so vulnerable, so defenseless to the world, with virtually all her life out of her control.

And so Neve didn't regret her message to Audrey and the end it put to their relationship. She did not regret that Audrey had moved on rather quickly with Freja, since Neve knew the reality TV star had been waiting in the wings for quite a while, showing real staying power considering the flighty and frivolous reputation she had garnered.

Neve continued to speak with Dr. Moore and threw herself into work with renewed focus and zeal.

When she felt strong enough, she dispatched Gustavo to put feelers out to Freja's people. It was time to stop wasting opportunities because of petty jealousy and give the Gannon Board what they were asking for. Freja would be a part of a Gannon production, making Neve a lot of money in the process. Let Audrey read into it whatever she wanted.

Freja's people were amenable to Gannon's proposal to feature the superstar in an episode on one of their most popular TV shows, and the planned appearance was coming along nicely, if Neve said so herself.

The showrunners were brilliant, creating a rich, sumptuous concept that would feature Freja in her best light. The set would brim with luxury, and the gold accents would complement her nicely. This would be a role that would really do Freja justice and, without a doubt, firmly establish her as the hottest commodity in their realm.

Then, suddenly, the whole thing hit an almighty snag. The appearance was supposed to be accompanied by a rather extravagant media tour, which wasn't at all unusual since having Freja feature in a Gannon production was a massive deal. Gustavo and his people arranged for Freja to do a circuit of the Morning TV shows and feature in high end magazines, capitalizing on her popularity and bankability.

Out of nowhere, and to the surprise of absolutely everyone involved, Freja rejected the proposed media schedule, and particularly the interview with the Editor-in-Chief of Poise.

Neve was quite startled, and so was poor Benedict Stanley. Aside from being a huge name in the fashion industry and recently finding renewed relevance for the magazine with Vivian DeVor, the biggest artist of their generation, by his side, he was also one of Neve and Gustavo's oldest friends from New York.

"He's stupefied, Neve." Her second-in-command was pacing all over her office and wringing his hands.

"Is he offended? I would be." What was that willful harpy playing at? Neve wanted to chastise herself for thinking badly about Freja, but she couldn't. She and Audrey were being photographed all over LA and Paris and Rome in all sorts of compromising positions, all grabby hands and sucking faces, and Neve's jealousy was overflowing.

"Bene is... Let's just say he's perplexed. Freja has never been on the cover of Poise, and that is in itself an oversight of theirs. They were looking forward to Freja doing the show and then going guns blazing with a full-court press, cover, and the interview. D&B even has a whole collection planned around her that she would wear during her guest appearance with us that Poise was also going to feature. It's all very strange."

"Bene?"

Gustavo darted his eyes towards hers too quickly, as if caught, and then a sheepish smile spread on his face. Neve raised an eyebrow, and he sighed deeply, but not unhappily.

"You know, we had a thing twenty-or-so years ago. And then we had a bunch of drinks that night in London when you were chatting with Livia, and we maybe reconnected?"

"*Maybe reconnected?*"

Gustavo was being cautious, but his eyes were shining, and his face was alight and Neve felt happy for her friend.

"Let's just say we're taking it very slow. Turtle slow. Snail slow. And I'm not in New York as often these days anyway—"

His phone rang, disturbing the positively congenial atmosphere in her office, and he picked it up right away, raising a finger. After less than thirty seconds, he hung up without a word.

"Freja will only grace the pages of Poise and do the TV

show appearance if Neve Blackthorne herself interviews her, otherwise the whole thing is off. She wants the concept to be 'an artist and the muse' type of thing. You, being one of the greatest directors of our time, making two of the most acclaimed movies elevating the feminist cause, and Freja being the one to inspire countless others, blah blah blah…"

They were both silent for a good minute, stunned by the outlandish demand.

Gustavo tugged on his tie before continuing, "Well, now Bene is pretty offended and by far not the only one who's perplexed."

Neve got up from her chair and walked out onto the balcony overlooking her domain. She disliked this town. Hollywood was a dirty and cruel place. It ruined lives; it ground people into dirt and turned careers and dreams to smoke. In fact, that was one thing Los Angeles was full of. On days like today, when the smoggy air was oppressive, she could taste the overheated dirt on her tongue.

Still, the views were killer. This one, the hills in the distance splayed in front of her, or the one of the ocean on her beach in Malibu. You win some, and you lose some, after all. Especially in Tinseltown. But just as she could always taste the dust and smog in the air, she could always taste a trap. And this one, the mysterious switcheroo that Freja was trying to pull off? Neve could tell a game was afoot, and she was being played for a fool.

It wasn't exactly a rare thing. Celebrities interviewed celebrities all the time. Variety had a whole series where famous pairs of film or music stars interviewed each other. It could be fun or fall flat, but it always sold well.

Still, this one request was particularly odd. Gustavo seemed just as surprised by Freja's demands as Neve, especially when the model's management sent the list of questions that Freja insisted be included in the interview.

The questions seemed innocuous at first glance and to a

lesser observer probably did not hold anything in any way objectionable; Freja's influences, her idols, her inspiration, the source of her happiness these days, her plans for the future, in both her personal and professional life, and her role as a D&B brand ambassador.

However, Neve wasn't a lesser observer. It was clear as day that all the questions were leading to one thing and one thing alone. Freja wanted to talk about Audrey. And she wanted to talk about Audrey with Neve. Well, as unexpected as such a request was, it also solidified Neve's belief that Freja knew about her affair with the young journalist.

"I don't want to presume that this is indicative of certain things becoming known to certain people, Neve, but even I can see that something's rotten in this Dutch kingdom. Or Norwegian kingdom?" Gustavo echoed her thoughts and tugged at his tie, giving her a cautious look.

"You think, Gustavo? And don't mangle the Bard too much. Hamlet is set in Denmark, not Holland." Neve sipped her coffee, and Gustavo relaxed in his chair, visibly relieved that she hadn't taken his head off for broaching the subject of Audrey.

"Freja's ego is rumored to be the size of Jupiter, and she is notoriously provocative. Still, I don't see why she would pick a fight with you."

"Neither do I. But I think it's time I found out. She stayed away from me in Cannes, London and Venice last year. I don't believe in coincidences of those proportions."

"You noticed, huh? I thought it was strange since every household name was falling all over themselves to get your attention, particularly in London after Gannon survived the IV&X takeover attempt. I looked up one of Freja's recent interviews on the subject of her rumored hop to Hollywood. She was asked specifically if she plans to star or feature in any Gannon productions, since we lead the awards predictions for next season and are clearly raking in the most money and have the highest audience numbers on any platform. She said that all her future projects were near and dear to her heart, pointedly sidestepped Gannon's name, and remained non-committal throughout the interview."

"When was this?" Neve was getting more and more intrigued by the situation. She also realized she needed more information.

"About a month ago. You think she has something else on the hook? Or is she planning some sort of subterfuge?"

"I do. You don't refuse an opportunity to flaunt yourself on the cover of Poise, unless you have something else on the immediate line. Send Morag to see that friend of hers at Laurner Studios. Let her do what she normally does when we need discreet information about what Summers is up to."

"So you think she's got Laurner and is laying all these roadblocks in front of us to delay or sabotage her TV debut? The request for you to interview her is outrageous, though. If she doesn't know this herself, surely her people must realize you'll refuse outright. Even when you were still directing and producing movies, you never vied for that kind of attention."

Neve just tilted her head and raised her eyebrows, and Gustavo smacked himself on the forehead.

"She's actually hoping you will refuse! Hence the questions about her happiness and her newfound inspiration. She knows that even if you accept, you will surely not want to talk about Audrey, and the whole thing is bound to be canceled. She will tell everyone Neve Blackthorne is stuck-up and too arrogant to lower herself to interview a reality TV star and accept Freja's presence on her TV show."

Gustavo gesticulated wildly, clearly getting extremely worked up. "In the meantime, she makes a huge splash with Summers, if that is her play, showing up Gannon and letting the world know that it's time to declare a new studio *en vogue*.

Alisson Summers would be forever indebted to her for hyping Laurner to the detriment of Gannon and embarrassing you in the process. Damn, Freja can't lose."

"Except she can." Neve gave him a look and he stared back at her, his features turning blank before a wide grin spread on his face.

"We don't know for certain if it's Summers and Laurner, but I don't see Freja settling for anything less. MGN is too small for her to throw over Gannon, and no other studio can do for her what either we or Laurner can. So it has to be Summers' dump of a studio. Send Morag on that reconnaissance mission, Gustavo. And tell Barnaby to set up a lunch for me and Freja. Very public, very visible, but perhaps with bad acoustics. I want to be seen with her. I don't want to be heard. Oh, and be so kind and discreetly let D&B and perhaps some of her other sponsors know that you think I disliked their new ideas and might not feature their products in whatever major projects we have planned."

Gustavo went still and his eyes widened, then his expression morphed into pure, delighted glee.

"It seems that with my other preoccupations, people have forgotten what I'm capable of, Gustavo. It's time to remind them."

As he scurried out to execute her orders, Neve again turned around and looked outside at the city spread before her. Yes, some people had definitely forgotten their place in this very world. They'd forgotten they were indeed beneath her, and that the Wicked Queen still ruled the fires of hell if need be.

She felt the adrenaline course through her veins in anticipation of a hunt. Her mother was right, she was Neve Blackthorne; she was nobody's prey, and it was time to remind them of that.

9

NEVE AS HUNTER

"*I* appreciate you not returning to the subject of my mother and why I went to see her." The words had been stuck in Neve's throat the entire session as Dr. Moore studiously ignored anything that happened during the fateful breakdown on Neve's flight to Reno.

"I've decided to give you space. You've been crowded for some time now. No less by your own anguish and fears. I think you've found a semblance of solace in those fears, in that anguish. It has become, if not comfortable, at least familiar."

Patronizing witch! Of course, the detente between them had been too good to last. Neve bared her teeth and Dr. Moore inclined her head in a go-ahead motion. Either she was done spouting her moralizing bullshit, or she was allowing Neve to dig a deeper hole for herself.

Neve ran a hand on the edge of the band of her shirt collar. Had it gotten tighter in the last five minutes?

"There are no fears and certainly no anguish. There is simply a great deal of me being busy."

"Ah, someone is vying for your throne."

"I wouldn't call it that. But she has disrespected me, and that is not something that will be allowed to stand."

"I've heard about a few people and what happened to them when they didn't really slight you directly, but were still punished rather swiftly."

At Neve's raised eyebrow, Dr. Moore continued. "Peter Cross. Those two male actors on whatever that TV show of yours is called..."

"Ah, Cross. He was mediocre at best." Neve waved her hand, dismissing the issue. "The fools who told the enthusiastic fans the pairing they wanted to see on the show would never happen because it was two women and then were unwise enough to taunt them? That's just bad for business."

"Oh, I'm sure it is. No doubt. Bad for business. So bad that neither of them has been able to find any work on stage, TV or in film for a year now. Not even voice work. Bad for business indeed."

Sarcasm dripping off her tone, Dr. Moore simply smiled. Neve acknowledged that Gustavo and his people had done the blacklisting well. Her lips twitched at the fact that it had become known in certain circles exactly why they were fired and why they couldn't get work anywhere. Good.

Dr. Moore allowed her a moment to preen and then motioned with her hand. "And now there's Freja. And her relationship with Audrey complicates your dealings with her."

Neve sniffed and allowed herself to finally relax in the chair.

"Or maybe it simplifies them."

―――――

It had to happen in New York. Freja, ever the astute reader of a room, had chosen to not meet in LA, Neve's playground, and to make herself available only in the Big Apple. Neve acquiesced. She had business in Manhattan anyway, but the graciousness cost her. It was a concession. Still, she could be agreeable on occasion. When it suited her.

Seated at a white-clothed table on the second level at Per Se, Neve felt both on display and yet entirely secluded in the privacy of the balcony. Barnaby had outdone himself. Neither of her favorite restaurants, Marea, Batard, or Le Bernardin, would have suited her current purpose–to be seen but not heard while dining with the *star du jour*.

And so everything was perfectly arranged, her Lauquen Artes, her utensils, and even her swordfish that would arrive in ten minutes. Except her dinner companion had yet to bless Neve with her presence, despite it being five minutes after the hour, and in Neve's world, that was twenty minutes late.

She was absolutely sure Freja had scouted the place in advance and figured out that the game was to be visible, and so she was making Neve Blackthorne wait in an obvious manner and in a highly public place. After all, the whole movie industry knew of the Gannon CEO's idiosyncrasies, and tardiness was akin to a mortal sin.

Still, Freja was very much alive and flamboyantly unrepentant as she entered the restaurant seven minutes later in a shower of oohs and aahs from patrons, a cacophony of paparazzi, and her entourage dispersing either outside or to the various still open tables on the lower level of the establishment. Well, Neve mused, that was one way to make an entrance.

As the model strolled up the stairs to the upper level, Neve had some time to observe her quarry. Freja's tall, blonde, and fashionably rumpled figure exuded an air of indifference and superiority, as if she had just rolled out of bed after an afternoon quickie and was bestowing some of her much treasured time on a mere mortal whose company the superstar simply tolerated.

Definitely an afternoon romp, if Neve was to judge by a very pronounced, very fresh-looking hickey on Freja's long, graceful neck. Bile rose in her throat and Neve's fingers twitched, wanting to break and claw and clench themselves into fists, but she made a deliberate move to place her hands palm down on the tablecloth. Now wasn't the time.

And you did this to yourself…

With anyone else, Neve would have been out of her chair and out of the restaurant before her companion had reached the table. Hell, Neve would have left five minutes after she arrived, because she never waited for anyone. But she wanted to see this one through. A game was being played, and even if she suspected what it was and had told Gustavo as much, there were clearly facets to this that still eluded her.

Chiefly, Neve wondered about the motivation behind such blatant disrespect as was evident in Freja's behavior. So she quieted her fury at being kept waiting and suppressed her anger at being treated like a commoner beseeching a queen for an audience. She could lower herself to playing games with Freja, if only to ensure that nobody ever dared repeat the mistake of insulting her ever again.

Freja reached her in a cloud of perfume and derision.

"Neve," she offered by way of a greeting and plopped herself down in the chair opposite with a lazy, catlike move. She raised her hands to her face and then deliberately caressed her neck in an obvious attempt to focus Neve's attention on the red mark on her skin.

Neve just gave her a tight-lipped smile and signaled for the server who appeared at her elbow.

After Freja had ordered the octopus, joking that one could never have too much *octo-pussy* in one afternoon, the red-faced boy scurried away, and Neve finally understood what this whole charade was about. Freja was rubbing her nascent relationship with Audrey in her face. Very calculated and very blatant. Well, as staking a claim went, it was a strong, if vulgar, attempt but as a career-defining moment, it was suicide.

Neve wondered if Freja's manager and agent knew of her tardiness, the overall affront, and her clear provocation, and were so bad at their jobs that they'd sanctioned her behavior, or if Freja was independent enough of her handlers to overrule them. It seemed altogether unlikely that D&B, Lucci, and a myriad of other brands who were associating their names with Freja, would condone this type of comportment from their ambassador. Nobody humiliated Neve Blackthorne and lived to tell the tale.

"It's nice to finally meet you properly, Freja." Neve decided it was time to get some answers. Hence, she plastered on her most spurious smile and started the conversation while their drinks were being served.

"Oh, I know all about you, Neve. I have for a while now." The leer sent Neve's way was downright obscene. "I'd like to say I'm a big fan, but all things considered, it would be quite hypocritical of me, ya know?" Freja reached for a celery stick, devoting her full attention to the vegetable.

"Be that as it may, we are here to discuss your appearance on *The Empress* and the Poise interview you wanted to arrange before the episode airs." Neve's tone was bland, affecting just a touch of disinterest, and Freja's head shot up in surprise.

"We're still doing it? I thought you were here to let me down gently." She laughed and chewed on her celery, her expression alight with actual humor and something akin to victorious despondency. "So you're going to interview me then? And do what I tell you to do?"

It took Neve superhuman effort to not react the way she wanted. Nobody dared talk to her this way. Not Juno Buchanan. Not even the almighty board. Yet this girl fancied herself powerful enough to dare.

"Domenico from D&B tried to tell me to mind myself, but I informed him it wasn't a secret that you don't have the backing at Gannon McMillan you once had, and if not for the old fossils like Martin and Francis rallying around you in Cannes, you'd be out. I let him know that's why you're so desperate to bag me for your little TV show. After all, Alisson has already signed me for two!"

Well, this was news, but it also confirmed Neve's suspicion that Freja had inked a deal with Laurner recently and hence was pitting that against a Gannon production.

With an exaggerated flourish, Freja pulled a glossy magazine out of her oversized bag and threw it on the table with a resounding thunk. There, in beautiful pink hues, were Audrey and Freja in an intimate embrace, their lithe limbs naked and intertwined, with a silk cloth strategically covering parts of their torsos. In a rather gauche typeface, if Neve was to judge, the cover proclaimed "Fredrey ENGAGED". If there was any doubt, the massive square-cut diamond on Audrey's left hand confirmed as much.

Neve chose not to react to the sharp pain that lanced her heart. She chose not to shrink away from the rending of said organ, a rending so loud, it surely could be heard by everyone in this restaurant. Distantly, she wondered how her heart continued to function? Four months. All it had taken Audrey was four months to move on from her. Well, the young woman was a trier, after all, and a known overachiever. She must have tried really hard this time.

"Congratulations." She marveled at how the word didn't simply stick in her throat, how it had flown so deliberately out of her mouth, her tone devoid of any inflection other than boredom. Somebody ought to erect a statue to the vaunted Blackthorne endurance. Maybe she'd instruct Barnaby to do just that as soon as she got out of this torture chamber.

Freja had the look of a cat that had eaten the canary, self-satisfied and languid in every move.

"Why thank you, Neve. Honestly, I don't know how you are so magnanimous about this whole thing. After all, Audrey is magnificent." She licked her lips and wiggled her eyebrows, and Neve thought she could vomit.

"Audrey was a wonderful spokesperson and my recommendation to her next employer after Gannon said as much. However," Neve pressed on as Freja smacked her lips and leered some more, "since your manager has sent the questions you'd like to be asked during the interview, I think we have some logistics to iron out, don't you agree?"

"My, my, Neve, your position must be as desperate as they say it is if you have such a hard-on to get me to appear on your show. Didn't they tell me it was actually doing well? Must not be true." She threw her long hair over her shoulder with an exaggeratedly practiced motion. "Fine, you can handle the logistics with my team. I will let Lars and Angela know we'll be doing the Poise cover, and you will interview me instead of that boring Benedict Stanley. I mean DeVor certainly could, she is so very fine after all, but I'm not here for that, so maybe another time... Can't be next month though since this baby right here is going to be front and center on all the shelves and I'll be shooting for Alisson." Freja caressed the cover with a long-fingered hand.

Neve wanted to count to ten. She wanted to grab the knife off the table and throw it at Freja. Even more so, she wanted to wipe that arrogant, insulting smirk off that arrogant, insulting face. Instead, Neve simply visualized her goal and schooled her features.

"We'll see that your projects and schedule don't overlap. Since you have outlined the questions for the interview, I think it is only fair that you trust me and my team to direct the episodes you will appear on?"

"You'll direct? Ooh-la-la. Sure. One thing I can tell about you...you have talent. I watched your movies, and my, I can see why they gave you the Oscars, even if it was back in the Stone

Ages." Freja laughed again, the sound like nails on a chalkboard to Neve's ears.

They didn't linger over their food, and Neve swore to never dine at Per Se ever again. Despite the late hour, she instructed her driver to take her to Gannon's New York Headquarters and was greeted in her office by Gustavo, with Barnaby hurrying in on her heels with four venti cups of black coffee. Morag walked in briskly after everyone was settled, her features determined. The Laurner Studios mission must have been informative.

"By the look on your face, Neve, I take it you were right about Laurner?" Gustavo ventured. "Nothing puts thunder in your eyes quite like Alisson."

"Yes, it's them alright. But I don't think Alisson is fully aware of what's at play here. What have you found out?" Neve turned her head to Morag.

"Well, the two TV appearances were a major surprise to everyone over at Laurner. They had Salma lined up and ready to shoot when Freja's people got in the mix and everything literally happened within a couple of hours. Contract signed, new scripts being written–the works. My friend...," Morag stumbled sheepishly over the word and Barnaby snickered, "she doesn't know which role, since clearly Freja and Salma are quite different in pretty much everything. Salma is a sweetheart and talented. Freja is, well... And they're all saying there's so much buzz surrounding her right now."

Neve flicked a piece of lint off her sleeve. "I've seen some of that so-called buzz. She doesn't just have the Laurner contract. She flaunted an unpublished cover in my face. More like threw it at me. I guess that's why she was hesitant to go with Poise, because she chose Benedict's main competition. All in all, the cover is more of a tabloid type of ordeal, and is utterly beneath even that gaudy publication, but it will make them a lot of money and will sell like hotcakes."

"Freja looks good on it then?" Gustavo asked incredulously.

"She does, but it is the announcement of her engagement that will drive up the sales, because I'm sure the interview is full of salacious details."

She saw Gustavo's jaw drop, but decided to ignore it for now. "I understand that a decent production team is hard to come by these days and good covers are difficult to produce, but this one is just reaching for the stars in terms of tastelessness."

Neve chose not to dwell on the continuous tearing of her heart. Since she'd laid eyes on the cover, she'd had a distinct feeling she was functioning on autopilot. It was fortunate her vocal intonations and facial expressions were so practiced, since this provided her with a level of inscrutability and therefore security. Because it would be the ultimate humiliation to show her employees how much she was being cut into pieces.

There would be a time and place to fall apart - later when she was alone. Right now, she had plans to make.

"Engagement? What bloody engagement? That Norwegian cow is dating our Aud…" Barnaby's outburst drew her attention back to the present and to the foul mood she nursed, and then the words died in his throat as he belatedly caught the murderous look on Neve's face.

Neve knew her palpable outrage was coming through loud and clear. Gustavo was one thing, but for all of them to be acting with such familiarity was unacceptable. She watched Barnaby close his mouth and take a large gulp of hot coffee, noticeably burning his tongue. Served him right, Neve thought.

"What are we going to do about *The Empress* episode and the Poise interview?" Gustavo was all business in a clear rush to move past the tense moment.

Neve tapped her fingers against her coffee mug. "We will proceed as normal while scheduling a regular guest appearance, Gustavo. As for Poise? I'll ask her the questions she wants me to ask her."

"You will interview her?" Now it was Gustavo's turn to lose the last remnants of his cool.

"I will. She is hellbent on gloating. She also thinks I'm finished in this industry and it is only a matter of time before Buchanan replaces me." Now Neve actually smiled when she spoke.

All three of her associates had their jaws hanging open. After a second they seemed to shake off their stupor, with Morag cautiously inquiring, "And she walked out of there on her own two legs?"

Neve's laughter was sincere for a change. "They are gorgeous legs. It would have been a shame to break them right then and there, when Gannon is about to feature them on quite an unprecedented TV episode."

Yes, she smirked, it was good to have a plan.

"An unprecedented episode?" Gustavo gave voice to their intrigue, as three pairs of eyes watched her intently.

"A very special, once-in-a-Gannon-history spectacle. Because it will make quite a splash, believe me, and the reverberations from this will be felt far and wide in our kingdom, Gustavo. Trust me, this nonsense Freja is spewing about me being propped by the industry's old guard—one leg in my grave? It's not insular. More people either already think so or they will once she gets her message across that Neve Blackthorne needs Freja to keep herself relevant." Neve's smile turned feral.

"We have work to do now. Gustavo, get Michael and the showrunners to work overtime and get me an estimate for the most luxurious scenario for Freja's appearance on *The Empress*. I want absolute decadence, a no-expense-is-too-high kind of budget."

She took a second to consider her option. "Actually, tell

them to give me several of them. Expensive, more expensive, and insanely expensive. Every single idea they've always wanted to incorporate into a TV show but could never afford, let them throw it into this one. Get me the numbers by tomorrow morning."

Gustavo was biting his lip while his eyes were gleaming, his face a mixture of apprehension and possibility.

Neve turned toward her assistant. "And Barnaby, get me on Juno's calendar first thing when we get back to LA. She has been very bureaucratic lately about me having to justify budget overruns with her. It's against my contract and against the outlined responsibilities of my office, but this one time I will gladly do it. It's time to beg our esteemed leader for the funding for a once-in-a-lifetime TV episode."

As Morag and Barnaby left, closing the door behind them, Gustavo stood up and walked closer to her.

"Neve..." he clearly was going to broach the subject of Audrey, and she knew she would shatter like glass if he continued because even her discipline and strength could only take so much abuse.

"It will all work out, Gustavo. Have some faith in me." He nodded, and she was once again alone.

On her way down to Juno's office at 7:15, holding a neat folder with three varying budget proposals for Freja's episode of *The Empress*, Neve did not feel tired, even though she hadn't slept a wink in three days. Returning to her Malibu mansion, she'd brooded on the beach, digging her toes into the sand, Sheppard snoozing next to her, just close enough for her to absentmindedly scratch behind his ears. When she'd stopped, lost in thought, he gave her a derisive snort and trotted into the house with the huff of a thoroughly disgruntled spoiled pup.

When night set in, she'd gone to Harlan's room since he was back from school for the long weekend and observed the disarray and her son sleeping askew half under the covers, Sheppard now curled alongside him on fresh sheets. Her heart squeezed painfully. Harlan's feet were dangling off the bed, he was getting so big. Neve kissed his cheek and covered him fully, deciding to ignore her own decree that the dog was not allowed on beds under her roof. Just this once, she told herself and closed the door behind herself.

That fateful day when she stood paralyzed in fear in front of the TV, watching Audrey bloodied and bruised, she'd made a decision, one she knew would haunt her one way or another. If it happened to be much sooner than she hoped it would, well, that was the price she'd have to pay for her actions.

Married to Freja, Audrey was sure to be safe and sound and far, far away from bombs and bullets. That was good enough for Neve, even if she drank way too much Lagavulin to try to numb the pain and loss she was feeling.

Neve had work to do. Work that was sending shivers of anticipation and, dare she say, excitement down her spine. When was the last time she'd actually been champing at the bit to speak to Juno? Probably never, but this meeting was instrumental to her plan, and she wanted to play her role to perfection.

In the end, it proved to be even easier than Neve had expected. Juno took one look at the budget estimates and blanched, refusing her on the spot in a tone that brooked no argument.

"You're insane! You've actually gone over the bend. Look, you are a disloyal shrew, a traitor for sabotaging the IV&X deal, but I could overlook all of that. This? Do you actually *want* Gannon to go bankrupt? What the hell are you thinking?"

Juno turned ruddy, her nostrils flaring and her mouth agape at Neve's extravagant proposals.

"This is an outrageous amount of money. I don't care if Princess Allegra of Savoy herself dances the tarantella on *The Empress*. This is some model, some god-awful reality TV star. What the hell is even happening here?"

Neve did not recoil at the shouting since she knew it would please Juno to see her overt reaction, but it was a close call. Instead, she focused on choosing her words carefully. "She's not just some model, neither is she just a reality TV star, Juno. She is golden. Freja's the new... I don't even know. The *IT girl*. She's the goose that lays eggs made of pure Benjamins. Surely you see that securing her, first as a guest on our best-performing show and then perhaps offering her a recurring character or even making her a regular, would make us a ton of money?"

"I don't care if she is the fucking center of the universe. There is absolutely no way we are spending this much money on one episode. That is out of the question, Blackthorne!"

"Laurner will give her this and more!"

Juno's sneer was downright grotesque.

"Last I checked, Neve..." There it was again, the mangling of her name, the drawing it out until it sounded like two pieces of Styrofoam rubbed together. The gleam in Juno's eyes told Neve that she was very much doing it on purpose. "It was your job to ensure that Gannon is the most prestigious and well-performing studio in Hollywood. Do not come running to me if Summers outsmarts you. Do your job! If you feel you can't do that anymore without making scandalous demands like this pathetic stunt you are trying to pull, you know where the door is."

Affecting an air of disgruntlement, Neve left with a parting grumble that she hoped Juno's poker game would suffer tonight.

"Not likely. I'm feeling lucky," Juno crowed. "After all, it's not every day I get to gloat that I've successfully overridden you, because you're losing it, Blackthorne. And if you think I will not let absolutely everyone know how ridiculous you've become, you're mistaken."

Neve kept her head down and her expression stormy until she reached the elevator, making sure everyone on the executive level who had heard the shouting would witness her defeat. She only broke into a satisfied grin as she rode in solitude up to her floor. Exiting the elevator and schooling her features once again to reflect her displeasure, Neve stalked back to her office.

She summoned Gustavo, and once the door closed behind him, Neve smiled enigmatically at him.

"So that beautiful, expensive concept is not going to be funded, my friend. We shall have to make do with something very cheap. Too bad, so sad."

"Wait." Gustavo gaped at her. "You're actually happy about this? And *happy*? My God, you're delighted! What's happening here, Neve?"

"What's *happening here* will continue until I am satisfied and my objectives are reached. I will direct the episode myself. Tell Barnaby to call those worthless handlers of Freja's and schedule the filming on the same day as the interview. I don't care if she is fully booked for that afternoon already. She did give me the freedom to do what I pleased with the direction, and so I'm doing just that."

"But what about the logistics of it all? What is your concept?"

"My concept, Gustavo, is to do the cheapest, crappiest TV episode in the history of Gannon. So get me that useless man I fired from *The Road To Nothing* years ago. He certainly must be around, and he'll be dirt cheap. His camera work was atrocious. Tell Thoman he can take the day off from *The Empress*. Also, let Morag know I will need her, and she had better bring her A-game. The amount of dramatically bad makeup I'll have her do..."

As she continued to enumerate her requirements, each more ridiculous than the one preceding it, Gustavo's face was getting even more worried and aggrieved.

"Neve, I understand that this has been remarkably difficult time for you, with Audrey getting engaged–" He did not get to finish his thought as Neve whirled on him.

"Gustavo, none of this has anything to do with Audrey! It's about me. About my lifeblood, my studio and the idea that people dared, for even a second, to believe that they can tell me what to do. Or prohibit me from doing everything possible to deliver absolute quality and maximize the profit and standing of this studio. Nobody, you hear me, *nobody* tells me what to do in regard to my art, to my movies." She'd lowered her voice even more than her usual volume, but she might as well have screamed because Gustavo flinched.

"People are assuming I'm finished because Juno dared to negotiate with Danilo and IV&X behind my back, and only a last-ditch effort by my staunch supporters kept me alive. And this rumor is currently being propagated by one of the biggest names in social- and traditional media. Moreover, Freja's entire behavior towards me speaks much louder than any words she could ever utter. It's high time to prove her and everybody else wrong. And it's time to show Juno her place too. She overstayed her welcome a long time ago and has been nothing but a thorn in my side since the IV&X fiasco, forcing me to have her approve every single expenditure."

Unable to keep a proper reign on her emotions, Neve turned away from Gustavo and walked to the massive bank of windows overlooking the studio and the Hollywood Hills. The view calmed her, reminding her of who she was and what she could do. What she was indeed doing.

"I helped Juno rise to her position back when she was CEO

and I was Vice-President, but it seems she's forgotten something very important. Today, this is my world, Gustavo. They are simply allowed to live in it, as long as they are useful to me."

The absolute silence behind her told Neve she had revealed far more than she had intended. Perhaps she was much angrier than even she knew.

She heard Gustavo finally draw a deep breath, perhaps getting his gumption up to speak, but she was so tired. Words had exhausted her, and she'd heard enough for one day. "It's fine, my friend. Let's move past this. It will all pass one way or another, even if it passes like a kidney stone. Now tell me, what did Domenico say regarding my so-called concerns about their products being placed in Gannon productions?"

As Gustavo started to haltingly share Domenico's understandable panic at Neve's sudden disapproval of D&B, Neve smirked.

"Let it be whispered—quietly for now and without much corroboration from our people yet—that it isn't D&B that I have an issue with, but a certain blonde Norwegian model who is beginning to have ideas above her station. It is my understanding that Domenico tried to caution Freja that she might be messing with the wrong person when she took me on, but she didn't heed his very astute warning. So he at least knows that she's playing with fire. D&B should be better at choosing who represents their precious brand."

Her gaze fell on her own bespoke purse, and it reminded her of Freja's. Yes, what she was about to do was petty. She didn't care. "Also, let Lucci know their line of oversized bags will not be featured. We'll be choosing whomever their main competitor is in that market instead. Work your magic, Gustavo, and leave the rest to me."

"So you're going after Freja?"

"Play stupid games, win stupid prizes. She's in the big leagues now."

As he exited with a remarkably fearful expression on his face, Neve mused that, despite the total wreckage that was taking place in her heart, she still had her touch when it came to scaring people. That was something, at least.

"Barnaby, schedule lunches for tomorrow and the day after tomorrow with Amanda at Writt Productions and Nicholas at Remote. Do not disturb me in the next thirty minutes and tell the driver to be ready when I need him."

She dialed Livia from her cellphone and was gratified when her call was answered right away.

"How's the alliance-building going, Livia?" As she listened to the other woman recount her successful recruitment expeditions among various McMillan clan members, she could almost taste the sweet anticipation of victory. The stars were aligning, and soon it would be her turn to step on the stage.

Her lunches with the heads of two of the biggest production companies Gannon worked with went as she predicted. Both had seen Juno tightening her fists more after the IV&X fiasco as a sign to jump ship soon and to start working with studios that didn't haggle over budgets quite so obsessively.

They were very open about how Gannon was losing ground to their competition, and not just the other major contenders. Neve commiserated and chose to share some of her plans. Both Amanda and Nicholas were delighted, and Neve left the meetings in buoyant spirits. Her plan was coming together nicely.

Her interview with Freja, that preceded the filming of the supermodel's three scenes on *The Empress*, went about as well as she had expected. Freja was full of all sorts of sordid details about her relationship with Audrey, decidedly rubbing it in Neve's face. She was still wary of Freja having direct corroboration—and perhaps even details—of their affair, so while she felt extremely pressured to behave, she walked a thin line between insulting Freja and pulling her punches. Still, if anyone could straddle that line, it was Neve Blackthorne.

The filming was a total disaster–which they pulled off masterfully. Freja wasn't interested in the end result much, still ecstatic at such an easy victory over Gannon's Wicked Queen.

Once the dailies of the episode were done, Gustavo brought them to her office with a visible tremble in his hands.

"Neve, they are awful. From the composition to the technique, to the acting. And the light, the scenes, the clothes... I don't even know where to start!"

"Oh, yes, these are positively grotesque, aren't they?" Her voice rose slightly with giddy mischievousness, and she could tell Gustavo again wondered what was happening. But Neve kept her own counsel and simply locked the dailies away safely. With the board meeting scheduled for tomorrow, she had work to do.

In the end, when the hammer fell on Juno Buchanan, it fell loudly and from out of nowhere. At a routine board meeting—one Neve knew with absolute certainty Juno hadn't even bothered to review the agenda for—she was ambushed by a vote of no confidence spearheaded by Livia Sabran-McMillan, with the biggest partnering production companies backing her all the way. All the recent budget cuts were exposed, all the innovations that the competitors were introducing and Gannon

McMillan's productions had been refused, were brought to light.

Per their plan, Neve herself delivered the kill shot. She had produced the most grotesque, cheap episode of a TV show the Board had ever seen. Freja looked decidedly ugly in this gray monstrosity. The board members were told in calm, measured tones that Neve both directed the episode herself to raise its profile, and had even interviewed the star personally in an attempt to drum up more interest and somehow save the project.

Livia called it 'quite a momentous endeavor on Ms. Blackthorne's part, a last-ditch effort to save Gannon's reputation as innovators and trendsetters'. Neve recounted her strained meeting with Ms. Buchanan and how she had debased herself to beg Juno for funds for a completely different episode. She even presented the board with the proposals for the luxurious scenarios that would have made Freja look like an angel and would surely have been a brilliant feature for the show.

"Except, despite all of my honest efforts, I was completely unsuccessful, met by a wall of derision and ridicule from the Chairwoman." Neve sighed theatrically. If she was overplaying her hand, she didn't care anymore. She knew when an audience was lapping it out of her hands.

Suddenly, some of the board members who were also Juno's poker partners recalled how she'd bragged and gloated about overruling Ms. Blackthorne on an exorbitant budget for an episode of *The Empress* just weeks ago, and how she'd told them Neve was losing it and would be gone in a matter of months.

They were all appalled that Juno's shortsightedness would be costing them a lot of money. What had been a joke at the poker table suddenly wasn't funny anymore when the real damage was exposed.

The pieces were falling one by one, and within an hour Juno Buchanan was voted out and Livia Sabran-McMillan was the new Chairwoman of Gannon McMillan's board. The press release was sent to the media before the meeting had fully concluded, with Juno slinking away in a cloud of shame.

By the time the champagne was finished and the new chairwoman was fully feted in her new capacity, Neve was decidedly tired. The endorphin- and adrenaline rush of the fight and subsequent victory was wearing off.

She went up to her office and found Gustavo waiting for her there, the TV on DMZ, which was running interviews with the major players. Livia and some of the board members, as well as the crew union leader and production company directors, were all remarkably gracious in their victory and in thanking Ms. Buchanan for her years of service to Gannon McMillan and the filmmaking industry.

"I guess I don't have to wait to see if you gave an interview." Gustavo's face was devoid of worry lines for the first time in months, perhaps even since that night in Cannes.

"I could never be that gracious or complimentary to the outgoing chairwoman. She was a pain in the ass and I did all the tongue-biting I could during that spectacle."

"You know, it took me a while to figure out what game you were playing. I have to tell you, as the results today have shown, it was pretty brilliant. To use your predicament with Freja against Juno like that? Stroke of genius. My only concern was that you would go a bit too far and actually stream that episode."

"I still might, Gustavo, don't tempt me. I'm done with Buchanan, but Freja still needs to be shown her place. Juno was the chairwoman of the Gannon McMillan Board, so one might say she was entitled to some leeway from me. Freja, on the other hand, doesn't have any such privilege. Send her the tape of the episode. I want her to see it. And make sure Lucci drops her. I'm not particularly interested in how they manage that."

"Barnaby tells me that Domenico already called to try to get on your calendar. And that was before everyone found out that Livia is the new chairwoman, and your position is stronger than ever. So that is well on its way." He gave her a cautious look before continuing. "Neve, not to tell you what to do, but don't you think that if Freja knows as much as she does about you and Audrey, she might expose you?"

"With Juno gone, not much can touch me here at Gannon. The role I played in bringing her down will be known very quickly. If no one else, the unions and the production companies present at the board meeting will make sure of it. So what can Freja do? Spew some gossip? I have full faith that Audrey will never go on the record, and without Audrey's corroboration, it remains just that–gossip."

And with that, it hit home that the Bishop on Dr. Moore's chessboard was off to join the Pawn on the sideline. Her Queen stood covered by only two more lines of defense, the Knight and the Rook, and those were the last things standing between her and Audrey, the two reasons Neve kept pushing her away.

Toppling the Bishop had been vital, and she understood that. Nobody could threaten her job, her lifeblood, her professional security. She got up and walked away from her desk to the windows, looking out. She felt like crying and didn't know why. Shouldn't she be celebrating, her future secured, instead of feeling defeated?

She turned around to catch Gustavo looking at her with his mouth wide open. His expression was so incredulous it was almost comical. She replayed in her mind what she'd just said. *Faith.* She had full faith in Audrey. Understandable that Gustavo would be thunderstruck. Neve Blackthorne and trust were more often than not incompatible.

"Yes, Gustavo, it's rather unbelievable that I have faith in something. I do though. Some things are just that–absolute. This is one of them. You are another." She returned to her desk and pulled a folder out of a neat pile. "With Juno gone, it's time to clean house. Danilo knows this, so he chose to jump before he was pushed. He just told me he will be moving on to pastures new. Gannon's streaming services need a CEO, my friend. See if it catches your interest."

When he just stared at her, she stood up and left the folder next to him on the sofa. "I don't need an answer for another couple of weeks. I thought you'd like to have the option. And I figured you would enjoy spending more time in New York, now that you and Benedict are close again. I would miss you, but since you've allowed yourself to meddle in my personal life, I'll, in turn, allow myself to say that you let him slip away once. Maybe it's time to try for real?" And with that, she left him to his thoughts.

Just before she was out of his earshot she heard Gustavo whisper, "Will she ever stop confounding me? Perhaps that is a good thing, the very best thing." His tone was reverential. "I do so love New York in the spring."

10

NEVE RUNS WILD

"So you won?" Dr. Moore often voiced her questions with a finality that brooked no argument and, Neve thought, needed no answer. So she remained silent, her eyes reverting to what was now their habit of watching the waves. God, this city, this job, this coast took more from her than they gave her. But the ocean... The ocean made it all worth it. At least half the time.

"How does it feel to have vanquished a magnificent foe? Two of them actually, since I keep reading about a certain Norwegian supermodel losing all her meaningful sponsorships and endorsement contracts."

Without any concerns for pretenses or appearances, Dr. Moore took the Bishop off the board. However, unlike the Pawn, whom she'd simply toppled, she quietly set the Bishop down to the side. Neve didn't roll her eyes, but she wanted to. Yes, yes, just two figures left and her Queen would stand defenseless and alone. Dr. Moore really would not have made it in the movie industry with this insouciance for the subtle.

"Feels like business as usual." Neve looked at her nails, then the view of the Pacific beckoned yet again.

"And Audrey?"

That got her attention, and the waves became inconsequential.

"Audrey has never been a foe. A cage, a sentence, a punishment, but never a foe. And either of those things was only true in the beginning. Since you and I both know none of them were real. Except Audrey was. Real. Aside from Harlan, maybe the only real thing ever in my life. A benediction, an absolution. And she's gone, in any case."

"You do know that, despite you opening up and telling me some of what is really eating at you, I'm still not treating you."

Neve smiled then, her lips stretching into an awkward grimace. It seemed she hadn't smiled in a while, and the gesture felt rusty. Still, it was honest.

"I know. I also know you're here if I need you. Ready and able to treat me. Appreciate it." She looked at the board, where one Queen had unleashed such devastation. "I'm not easy to love."

"You tend to grow on a person after prolonged exposure." The gray head inclined, hiding an answering smile before the astute gaze met Neve's head-on. "Love is violent, Neve. Yours in particular. We go back to that 'Icarus and the sun' metaphor."

Your violet, violent eyes, my sweet, my bittersweet... Neve lowered her face to her palms for a moment, as the memory of Audrey caressing her cheekbones intruded.

"You should write poetry, Dr. Moore. And when did I start enjoying this patronizing and romanticizing of my own life by my own therapist?"

"I'm also not romanticizing your life. I may call you an Ice Queen and agree with how perfectly you fit the archetype, but the difference between Neve Blackthorne, the CEO who walked into my office years ago and declared that she's fucking her underling and would like to stop, and the Neve Blackthorne sitting in my office now is light-years. Light-years filled with pain. With violence inflicted by her own hand and mouth. The violence that is eating at her, and is taking away her ability to consider herself worthy of help, of love, of compassion."

"I'm sitting right here. There's no need to separate the imaginary me from the real one, Doctor. But if we are doing this, let's do it well."

Neve raised her eyes. "That woman? In fact, either of the women you seem to separate me into so neatly? Neither one of them was worthy of much if you consider how easily Audrey gave up. And not just Audrey."

She realized belatedly what she'd said and how much she'd revealed. She expected Dr. Moore to pounce on this new piece of information. To push her to say more. Instead, there was nothing. The therapist looked away, her shoulders taut.

At Neve's sharp inhalation, Dr. Moore turned back, got up, and walked up to her. When a hand reached her shoulder and squeezed it gently, Neve thought she'd shatter.

"You're worthy, Neve." She could feel the warmth of the fingers through her shirt. "Whether you're being unfair to Audrey is debatable, you feel the way you feel. But I'll tell you this: Let someone in. The Ice Queen is meant to melt, but in your case, I fear the worst. Let someone in before the moment when you break instead. The aftermath of this particular Ice Queen breaking will not be a walk in the park in your Louboutins, dear. And we are approaching that fateful 80% mark of your story."

It took a couple of days for the details of the operation behind the ousting of Juno Buchanan and the people responsible for the successful coup to make the rounds. Neve's calendar was busier than ever, with Barnaby fielding calls, emails, and flower bouquets from everyone. The office looked like a hothouse, with all the white orchids and baby pink roses.

The same couple of days also brought a decidedly subdued Domenico from D&B to her office, and the conversation that followed was mostly one-sided, with the designer apologizing profusely. If Neve wished, he assured her, D&B would drop Freja in a second. They had been telling her that she was playing with fire, they at no point endorsed the disrespect or the type of behavior she'd exhibited. He and Neve were old friends who went way back, and he was surprised by how far his brand ambassador had gone. Neve should just say the word, and it would all be done.

As satisfying as all that might be, Neve had no taste for it now. So she spent a pleasant hour with Domenico, sharing gossip and discussing his marriage that was putting a decidedly pink hue on his cheeks, and sent him on his way. It really wasn't his fault. And as the winner, Neve could be magnanimous.

No, she did not want Freja dropped. Lucci had already done so. The girl was young, and perhaps her minders needed a firmer hand. Domenico gave her a hug and cheek kiss, and she waved him away and told Barnaby to cancel her afternoon.

She was tired of all the attention, all the sycophants, and all the groveling. She took advantage of Harlan being home for the holidays and spent the afternoon with him at the zoo and made all sorts of sacrifices to her personal taste by deciding to take him to an evening at Chuck E. Cheese.

"Mom?"

Something in her son's voice made her do a double-take. He was being careful with her again.

"Arcades are great and all, but are we really doing this?"

She had to laugh at that. Yes, Harlan was very much her child.

"You think you're too cool for an arcade?"

"My name is Harlan Melgren Blackthorne, mom. I think being *too cool* is not a choice. Otherwise, I'm just a brat with a pretentious name."

"Is that what you think?" Neve raised an eyebrow, only to be met with a mirror gesture from her son. She smiled, and he smiled back. The tender moment stretched, and she felt comforted despite herself. Even if everything else was gone, even if they took it all away, some things no one could deprive her of. Her son was a constant. No matter how tormented she was, he was her Northern Star, her Polaris.

And then her Polaris shocked her.

"I mean, it's not really an original thought. You know, about my name. And you said not to lie no matter what..." He broke eye contact and chewed on his lower lip. When his fingers dove into his disheveled mop of hair, an anxious gesture she herself had been prone to once-upon-a-time before she'd taught herself that her anxiety should never be manifested because she viewed it as a sign of weakness, Neve knew he was about to drop a bombshell on her.

"Audrey told me. You know, about my name."

Feeling as if she had been hit in the solar plexus, Neve desperately reached for something to say. She didn't need to bother, because Harlan wasn't even looking at her, clearly wrestling with whatever secret had been tormenting him.

"I mean, she never dissed it or anything. She just said that I should really, you know, be as cool as the name is." He chewed on his lip some more, and Neve held her breath for whatever would come next. "We talked, sometimes. I mean, she was at the house so often. You know, back then."

He finally raised his eyes back to hers, and Neve was afraid she wouldn't be able to speak around the lump in her throat.

"Yes, she was."

Wasn't it a wonder that the one woman who haunted Neve's dreams and waking hours had made such an impact on her son? Harlan, who had known Audrey for all of twelve months and interacted with her sporadically at best during that time, apparently still carried a torch two years after. Maybe it was genetic or something, Neve mused.

"So she would talk to me. Sometimes. She knew what names meant. And she had, like, theories and stuff. I liked her. Did you know that blackthorn and avens are types of plants from the same botanical family?" Neve shook her head, utterly speechless.

Harlan's eyes lit up as he went on about a subject he'd clearly given a lot of thought. "Blackthorn and avens are both members of the Rosaceae family. Like roses. I thought it was kinda cool that she knew stuff like that. She got me a book on plants, right before she left for her other job."

Neve had seen the book, but in her grief and her self-absorption, she'd paid it no mind. Armand, for all his faults, was a diligent and attentive father, who kept a steady stream of literature coming Harlan's way. She felt a pang of failure.

"I didn't realize you and Audrey were that close." The words came out even more quietly than usual.

"I wanted to be. I follow her on her work Instagram. Dad checks it regularly, so he okayed it. He said her blog was a little too adult for me though. "

"But you don't follow her on Twitter." Neve didn't phrase it as a question because she knew the answer to that all too well.

Harlan hung his head. "No, because you are in charge of Twitter, and I didn't want to make you sad. Sadder." His reasoning and his correction damn near broke her heart. He was eleven years old, and he already saw things so clearly.

"You wouldn't make me sad, sweetheart. And I'm sure if things were different, Audrey would have been a good friend to you. She can definitely be a very good friend."

Mother and son shared a long look, and Harlan's lips lifted hopefully.

"Someday?"

"Someday, baby, someday…" No, she never lied to Harlan. But she felt like she was deceiving none other than herself. And in that case, what was another lie in the big scheme of things?

"Now, how about that Charles E. Emmentaler?" As she predicted, her joke made him giggle. Not so grownup just yet, she thought, running her fingers through his unruly hair. God, not just yet. "Charles E. Roquefort, maybe?" He giggled louder and her heart lifted. "Fine, fine, Charles E. Brie it is." She joined him in silly laughter, and if there were tears in her eyes as the car stopped at the arcade, she hoped he'd think them happy tears.

They managed to have fun. Unsurprisingly, there was no Chuck E. Cheese in Malibu. But at the one in Burbank, she stuck out like a sore thumb. Still, despite Harlan's eye-roll at her choice of attire, she'd never be caught dead in something that would have made her less visible or less of an attraction. Because, even in an Old Navy shirt, she'd still be Neve Blackthorne and would still be accosted by fans.

After signing a considerable number of autographs and even posing for pictures, Neve simply stepped away, and the crowd parted in front of her. At Harlan's raised eyebrow at her magnanimous attitude towards people she'd normally shun, she just ruffled his hair again. Harlan, despite his earlier claim that he was too cool for an arcade, had the time of his life, and Neve could tolerate the gaudy monstrosity for one evening every once in a while.

Getting home, she tucked Harlan in, kissing him goodnight, and leaned against the doorway for the longest time, just watching him sleep. His young face relaxed, a small smile playing happily in the corner of his mouth. He was too smart for his own good. Too smart by far, and she suspected he understood more about Audrey than he let on. But she wanted to just look at him for a bit and maybe pretend at least something in her life was safe and stress-free.

As she retired to her ground floor office, knowing Sheppard would keep Harlan company and steal half his bed despite her very stern edict that he was to sleep in his crate, she poured herself a glass of whiskey, the ring from her front gate reminded her that only part of her life was actually settled. Looking at the familiar shape on the small screen, she mused that it was like Harlan speaking about Audrey had conjured her out of thin air.

Putting her glass down, Neve considered doing nothing, to just sit here and sip her whiskey. She wasn't a coward, but neither did she seek out danger or volunteer for drama. Audrey, however, had surprised her plenty in recent times, and she didn't know anymore whether her former employee and lover was above raising hell and waking up her son. Lately, Neve felt like she really didn't know Audrey at all. Taking a large swallow, she pressed the gate button, deciding it was time to be brave once again.

Audrey burst across the threshold the moment Neve cracked the door open. All anger and blazing eyes, she stalked into the small office and crossed her arms as her chest noticeably vibrated with what could only be rage. Neve just sighed and followed her inside, closing the door quietly but firmly behind herself. She had a feeling this might get loud.

The moment she crossed to her desk, Audrey whirled on her with fury.

"You blacklisted Freja? How petty are you? You got Lucci to drop her, and Domenico at D&B just finished taking her apart limb by limb like she's some high school kid. Nobody will tell me, but I know you did this. Freja is not complaining and is being entirely too noble about this whole thing, but I know you did this because of me."

Eyes alight with anger, Audrey looked beyond beautiful. Even though it pained Neve to see her love distraught, she wished for a camera to capture the stunning effect heightened emotion was having on the beautiful face, on the gorgeous, expressive eyes. She was fury in motion, a sight to see. Neve couldn't look away, even if she tried. She hadn't seen Audrey in so long, her eyes simply feasted.

Something in regard to what Dr. Moore had said about Icarus long ago sounded in her mind, like vestiges of a thought that she couldn't quite grasp. It felt important, but everything was happening around her too quickly.

Unaware of her effect on Neve, Audrey continued her monologue, getting more animated by the minute. "You left me! Worse, you discarded me. You decided we had no future, yet you went after my girlfriend?"

"Fiancé."

All it took was one word spoken in a very calm, almost whispered cadence. And just like a pinprick to a balloon, with those three syllables, Neve seemed to deflate the rage behind Audrey's eyes, leaving them with only hurt.

Hands trembling, Audrey picked up Neve's glass and finished the drink. Wordlessly, Neve filled two more tumblers and sat in the chair behind her desk, gesturing for Audrey to take a seat in front of her. The stage was set for the possibility of a civil discussion, if not a particularly cordial one. She could really never quite do cordial with her exes. Perhaps she wasn't all that perfect after all.

"I won't explain myself, Audrey. I never do, in case you've forgotten. As for things people did or said, I might ask you to consider the beam in your eye before observing the speck in mine," she suggested, her voice filled with disdain.

"What are you talking about, Neve? You and I do movie quotes, not the Bible."

The lack of understanding in Audrey's eyes was genuine, and Neve toned her derision down a notch.

"Our *arrangement* was a mistake. It ended, and I do not regret my decision, Audrey." Neve almost managed to keep her voice steady as she uttered the words, both lies, and truth. "I had my reasons. You were always a smart girl–"

"Don't patronize me, Neve!" The steel in the beloved voice was so achingly raw, Neve's chest was cracked open again. But she couldn't allow it to show. She *wouldn't* allow it. For Audrey's sake as much as for her own. So she waved the remark away and went on.

"Perhaps you've figured out some of them, or you should have. I won't apologize for anything. I don't think you had any such presumptions about me anyway. But *I* had some expectations of privacy from you. I understand the need to find a shoulder, but to out me and to arm your fiancé with ammunition against me? To help Freja strengthen her position to get a better deal? I honestly hoped for more from you. I guess at the end of the day, having hope is simply inviting disappointment. And I am very disappointed."

She thought she could have knocked Audrey over with a feather just then. Wide-eyed, mouth opening and closing, Audrey's shock was so believable, so honest, Neve stopped in her tracks. Was she wrong? Freja clearly had some knowledge about the true nature of their relationship, but the look on Audrey's face was earnest and heartrendingly surprised. Neve really didn't know what to think anymore.

To her credit, though, Audrey recovered quickly, shaking off the accusation, reaching again for her anger.

"I have no idea what you're talking about, but your usual deflection and manipulation won't work here. I never told a soul about us. Not my therapist, not my priest, and certainly not Freja. It's really despicable that you'd try to shift the blame for you ruining her career onto Freja and me. She's entirely innocent here. She knows nothing about us. And for you to accuse her like this? Victim-blaming now? This is a new low, even for you, Neve!"

"I don't know what you're talking about when you say 'a new low', Audrey."

"A minute ago, you told me I was a mistake. That our relationship was a mistake."

Neve wanted to turn away, to shield herself from all the guilelessness and all the honesty on Audrey's face. She couldn't sit anymore. Not that her unsteady knees were any help, but she took a deep breath, got up, and made herself stand taller.

"I said no such thing. I said our arrangement was a mistake. You and I never really had a relationship–"

"Bullshit." The harsh word was said with such a calm, reasonable inflection, and then Audrey followed it with a smile. A smile that was victorious, brilliant, sincere. A smile Neve could not afford to look at these days.

"My sweet..." Audrey's voice was like velvet. "You'd forget how to breathe when you looked at me. No, no, you can lie to yourself. Maybe it makes you sleep better at night. Certainly helps you avoid my calls and my messages. Helps you make decisions for both of us. Helps you throw this love away. But I know, my bittersweet, I know." The usual cadence of appellations was both pleasure and pain. "But let's leave this little 'mistake', as you call it, aside. Freja deserves better."

A slap would have hurt less. Neve actually wanted to raise her hand because her cheeks felt scalded. Well, she really had no one to blame but herself. Still, it hurt. It hurt like hell.

"Well, it's gratifying to see that at least some people in your life have your full loyalty, Audrey. I already told you, I will not explain myself. If you want to know what transpired and find out why things happened the way they did, I advise you to speak to your fiancé."

"Stop saying that word with that tone of yours. Just stop this!" Audrey hurled herself from the chair and started pacing the small room. Neve looked at the door. The concern must have been etched so clearly on her face that Audrey raised her hands up in apologetic surrender and stopped her erratic movements.

"Why does it bother you so much? I thought the ring was rather nice, no? Where is it, by the way? Too large of a stone for you? I mean, it is on the flashy side, but I guess Freja needed it to be seen from the moon, or at least on the cover of that magazine…"

Audrey gave her a mirthless smile and tugged on a chain around her neck. In the dim light of the office lamps, Neve caught the glint of the diamond dangling from it.

"It needs resizing and I snag it on everything, the cut being square like it is. But the ring doesn't bother me. None of it bothers me." Audrey sounded petulant, and those gorgeous, full lips turned into a slight pout. Neve thought tiredly that, in spite of everything, Audrey was still so young, so painfully naive.

"It doesn't, and don't tilt your head at me like that. I'm not a moron, I know what that gesture means. You're forgetting I can still read everything about you like nobody else can, Neve." The pout and the immaturity were gone from the beautiful face, leaving such a profound expression of longing that it was Neve's turn to be completely surprised.

"Be that as may, Audrey. Perhaps it's me then, who has lost all ability to read you."

"You mean Freja, don't you? The disgust in your voice every time you say *fiancé* is obvious."

Neve did not respond, using the same tilt of her head to get Audrey to continue.

"She wanted me, Neve. Simple as that. She's wanted me for a very long time when nobody else did. You yanked my chain for years, but you didn't want me, not enough. Your job, your studio was more important, and you gave me up easily enough. Freja never did. Despite my heart never being really into it, she was always there. So that's that. If you think I'm pathetic, if you think I'm pitiful, I really don't care."

Audrey rubbed at her eyes and Neve's own almost watered. "I care that you're destroying Freja's career. I'm asking you to stop it. I saw a tape of the episode. It's a mockery and we both know it. Freja is terrified you will stream it. I'm asking you not to."

The pain and loneliness in those tired eyes were palpable. Neve couldn't help thinking that the things they did to each other, the amount of hurt and suffering and torture they still inflicted on one another, were staggering. Was there really no end in sight to any of it? Even as she thought it, Neve knew she was being unfair to Audrey, because all Neve's pain was self-inflicted in this scenario.

Audrey's strangled voice, full of unshed tears, interrupted Neve's introspection. "I never asked you for anything before. Just this once, give me something. Please."

The one word rocked Neve to the core. Audrey never begged. In their escapades it was Neve who usually ended up begging, being made to utter 'please' over and over again until Audrey gave her everything she wanted and needed to be fulfilled. Audrey had never, not at any time, been in a position to have to ask, simply because Neve usually satisfied her every need without as much as a whisper—as hungry and as greedy as she always was for her. To hear Audrey beg now, and doing it for Freja's sake, tore a very painful strip off Neve's heart.

They sat in silence after that, time stretching between them like a thread. The same thread that connected them, the one that they kept twisting and pulling at, now lay at their feet, just a tangle of red silk. Audrey's face regained some composure and as her now steady fingers touched just below her collarbone, Neve imagined them tugging at the knotted silk, fancifully feeling the answering pull in her own chest.

In the quiet of the room, the massive clock measured their

silence. When Audrey's voice sounded, Neve felt the moment break like ice under her fingertips.

"I'm leaving the US again tomorrow, following the 82nd Airborne on their deployment to Afghanistan before the US troops are fully pulled out of the country. Elinor is returning me to newspaper reporting and writing features. It'll also give me the opportunity to bring my Nikon along. It's been a while, I guess. I hope this assignment will not only help me clear my head but also remove me from the scene long enough that you'll recover some of your famous cool and calm, and sanity will prevail. Don't ruin Freja. It was never a competition between you two and it's way too late, anyway. We've both made our decisions and our choices. It's time to lie in the beds we've made. So please... For me."

Audrey took a long sip from her glass, Neve mesmerized by the muscles of the smooth throat working before she spoke again. "You know, there was one other time in our history when I should have asked you to do something for me. Years ago in your office, when you were kicking me to the curb. I should have asked you to have courage. For me."

She could have hit Neve at that moment, and the action would have done less damage because one word, *courage*, undid Neve. God, would this woman stop seeing right through her, stop being the one to really know her?

"It took me a little while to understand what you were doing. You were scared, running, saving yourself. And I was too hurt to realize how afraid you were. Acting like a total bitch, pushing me away. Pressing all my buttons to enrage and hurt me with surgical precision. And yet, simply running scared—"

"Audrey, this is nonsense—"

"Sure it is." And the look in those green eyes was anything but naive. "But it doesn't matter anymore. I regret many things, Neve. But my love for you was honest. Selfless. Stupidly so. I'd have done anything for you. I'd have waited ages for you. Ages.

And I'm done wondering what you would have done for me. Because it's clear that it's not all that much. We've hurt each other ten times over and over and over again. Don't ruin Freja. Whatever we shared has nothing to do with her. Us tearing each other open for sport has nothing at all to do with Freja. She's collateral damage. So please, for me. Just this once. I know you can do anything."

Neve could have told her all the things that Freja had done, that she had willfully disrespected her, that she'd used the information she somehow possessed to subtly blackmail and humiliate Neve. That the model was absolutely not the person Audrey thought she was, and was ultimately utterly unworthy of the beautiful soul that was Audrey.

The last sentence evoked a memory Neve cherished in particular. A long time ago, after an especially bad day at the office, which had resulted in Neve losing the bids for several projects she had been particularly excited about, she had somehow found herself at Audrey's apartment. Small, clean, a little avant-garde, the place felt cozy and lived-in. Her fears of being unwelcome had been unfounded. Audrey's face radiated pure joy at Neve being in her space.

They ate and drank wine, and Neve let go of some of her troubles as Audrey massaged her shoulders, desire humming in Neve's veins as those wonderful hands slid lower and lower to her ass. But then Audrey leaned in and murmured right in her ear. "You can do anything, Neve. There's magic in you at times like these. It's a sight to see. You will turn this one around too. And you will have everything. Everything you want. I believe in you." It was ridiculous how hot it had made Neve, how ravenous. Audrey's words had always done things that both amazed and frightened her.

This time, the speech Audrey had just given her—about being wanted, being cared for when no one else was there for her—cut Neve open and made her feel like she was bleeding out. There was nothing left for her. And although Audrey might be settling for the Norwegian, there was enough devotion and loyalty between them to somehow at least partially redeem Freja in Neve's eyes.

Neve sighed, her shoulders tense and her muscles aching. "You're right. I can do anything. And thus you can have anything. Everything really."

Audrey furrowed her eyebrows and then closed her eyes. Yes, she remembered as well. But Neve wasn't done. Evoking memories for memories' sake wasn't what she had intended.

"This one thing, it's small indeed, since Freja is inconsequential to me, when all is said and done. And you've never asked me for anything, even when I'd have perhaps wanted you to."

Audrey scoffed, although Neve could see her eyes fill with tears.

"You play games, Neve. You push me away. And you surrender to me when it's convenient for you. So you don't get to play the victim here."

Neve actually smiled then. Such a beautiful, beautiful young woman. Was it a wonder she had filled Neve to the brim for years now? Audrey was so bright, so completely captivating, from her brilliant mind to her beautiful face. And her heart? Unencumbered by the harsh realities of Neve's youth, she was pristine, except for the scars Neve herself had left on her. Neve hated herself just a little then, which in turn triggered a self-defense mechanism in her. When in doubt, attack…

She chose her words with great deliberation rather than say what was on the forefront of her mind and felt righteous. Still, even the most careful of those words were inherently unkind. The whiskey was warming her blood and making her reckless. It was also making her honest, so she let the words fly.

"I don't know, dear heart. Is it selfish to have wanted you to fight harder? And before you explode with your moral indignation about me playing games and pushing you away... You're right, nothing could have changed my decision. Yet, I still would have wanted you to try. You are a trier, after all. And you've proclaimed your love for me often enough, only to surrender it all too easily. Didn't you just say you'd have waited forever? You let go of that forever quite quickly."

"You wanted me to!" Audrey was in motion in a second, stalking closer, pushing into her personal space.

It was all pain, everything, everywhere, and chief among it was the ache of this woman that Neve could not let go of even when she did. "Ah yes, I'm a selfish bitch though, Audrey, and the heart wants what the heart wants, even though the mind knows it's impossible."

You'd ruin me, you already have, she wanted to say. And how could she say that her own conscience, her own mind, were rebelling against her heart's utmost desire and were the root cause of much of the anxiety attacks that had plagued her over and over, until she'd given Audrey up and the fear subsided?

So why was she wishing for Audrey to have perhaps shown more permanence in her feelings and not run to Freja mere minutes after Neve had set her free? She had no answer; she had no succor; and she knew she was being completely unreasonable about the whole thing.

But she still yearned, and despite all her fear, Neve still wanted Audrey and her devotion. Too bad Audrey was giving all of that to Freja these days.

Foregoing more introspection for when she was alone with her Lagavulin, Neve sidestepped Audrey slowly, intent on walking her out. But Audrey did not follow her, continuing to stand in the middle of the small office.

As Neve turned back towards her to inquire if there was something else she wanted, her fingers were grasped in a soft hold. The touch was so familiar, Neve almost whimpered. God, how was it even possible to still feel so much for someone who had clearly moved on? Especially when she herself was so determined to do so as well?

Nobody had ever affected her like this. Not even when fully naked and caressed in the most intimate ways by other people, had she ever felt as much as when Audrey's fingers were loosely, gently holding hers. Her sins in previous lives must have been awful to be punished quite like this in this one. To have found the one person whom she loved like she had never loved before, whom she wanted more than she had wanted anyone else, and to never be able to claim her as her own. It was the ultimate penance indeed.

The tender, unassuming touch was unhurried, and Audrey did not seem to be taking it anywhere, simply looking down at their intertwined fingers as her thumb gently caressed Neve's knuckles.

So it was Neve who broke the spell by taking a step forward, by sliding her fingers into the still rather short tresses at Audrey's neck and tugging the beloved face close to her own, demanding, yet giving Audrey plenty of opportunity to break free from the embrace.

When Audrey just met her gaze with a tormented one of her own, reflecting the storm and her own longing right back at Neve, it was like something snapped. Their mouths met with force, none of the gentleness of the previous caress present anymore. Tongues clashed, teeth nipped, it was more than a kiss; it was a battle of wills, and Neve almost felt like she was winning this war, soon to be proclaimed the conqueror, only to remember in the last second that this particular castle belonged to someone else. She was simply a trespasser, no matter how much she wanted to reside in this embrace forever, in this kiss, with this taste on her lips.

She wrenched herself away from Audrey and they both looked at each other with weariness, with finality, breathing heavily.

"God, I loved you so much. So much." The past tense in Audrey's words felt like another slap, sharp and punishing. Neve raised her chin just a fraction on pure instinct, and when their eyes met, she knew that whatever Audrey saw in hers wasn't nearly what she really wanted to find.

"Damn you, Neve." With those parting words, Audrey was gone, and Neve was left feeling guilty and ashamed, and so dirty that no amount of whiskey was going to wash her soul clean.

11

NEVE'S SCARS

"*I* think it was bound to happen." She was fighting her tears with everything she had, the final indignity of falling apart now. "The first time I went to see my mother, I bit my tongue. She even helped me find my equilibrium when the world was closing in on me. And I thought that I could do it again. See her again. Allow myself to need her again..."

She heard her own words as if from a distance, tasting bile on her tongue. Deep breaths, deep breaths. Dr. Moore's face held such tenderness, Neve's tears spilled reflexively. She wiped them away on the same instinct.

Nobody can see, nobody can see you cry...

Don't tell...

Neve blinked at the hiss that was appearing less and less often these days, but she soldiered on.

"I don't know why I went back to visit her. Years and years and years I told myself she would get nothing from me, that she was even worse than him, and then I still do this. And don't you dare tell me she's my mother!"

The blunt fingernails were biting into the skin of her palms. In another instant, she'd be drawing blood.

"I wasn't, Neve. It doesn't matter that she's your mother."

"Doesn't it?" Her own shout seemed to abrade her skin, the sound piercing her mind, almost blackening her vision. She covered her own ears with her fists, the noise cutting her to ribbons.

She moaned in pain, and Dr. Moore was on her feet in a second, reaching for a glass of water. Neve closed her eyes, wishing herself anywhere but there, anywhere where there were no soft footsteps and no gentle hands slowly unclenching her fist.

A tsking sound and a harsh inhalation of breath told her she must have drawn blood after all. When she opened her eyes, finally getting enough strength to look at the aftermath of her weakness, Dr. Moore was carefully holding out a wet wipe to her.

"I always suspected you have a physical aversion to noises. Loud ones and those that aren't even that at all, sometimes just strange, unexpected noises. The times you are due in my office, the music in the reception is off."

"I haven't noticed..." Neve watched as the cloth was being saturated with her blood, crimson overtaking the pristine white.

"But I think I underestimated just how much this... let's stick with calling it 'aversion' for now, is triggered by memories, how this condition is something that is caused by your trauma."

"You'll tell me it's PTSD or something just as boring. Other people get PTSD, Dr. Moore. Neve Blackthorne does not. Neve Blackthorne is not someone who cannot get over the fact that her father was an abusive motherfucker who beat the crap out of her mother. Beat her all the time, no matter what she did or didn't do."

"Did he—"

"No, he never touched me. He didn't give a damn about me. I wasn't his daughter, so I wasn't his problem. She was his wife, however, and he was obsessed with her."

Through the cotton that was clouding her ears, she could hear her own breath coming in ragged bursts. She was safe, she wasn't there anymore... One, two, three... Peripherally, she sensed more than heard the slow tapping of a Montblanc against a palm and met Dr. Moore's gaze.

The pale gray eyes looked at her own violet ones, and Neve could tell that the therapist was deliberately helping her breathe. Helping to center her on that rhythmic drumming of the pen, instead of the shards of glass in her ribcage.

A small gesture that meant the world. A little act that spoke volumes. Because although Dr. Moore had not uttered a single word about her diagnosis, she certainly knew how to treat it.

For the next twenty minutes, they sat in the silence of counted breaths and taps. Neve simply let her tears fall.

Since the gate opened automatically to allow the late night visitor, the knock on the front door was very much a courtesy. He'd lived in this house for years, after all. Yet even back then, he'd knocked. Neve wondered if that was an indication that Armand never felt comfortable in the space they had both called home for a few short years. With her heart in her throat, she almost leaped to answer.

"This is not about Harlan."

The raspy voice and the small smile that followed undid the steel bindings that held her chest. Neve knew he hated her. If she were still capable of rousing enough energy, she would say she had never forgiven him, but her heart was no longer in their feud. She would never let go of what had happened between them. She simply wasn't capable of moving past certain things, but she did appreciate that he knew her well enough to try to abate her anxiety as soon as he could.

She opened the door wider, and he crossed the threshold in a sure, long stride. Letting him in was such a practiced gesture. How they danced around each other, with restraint but little respect. They were social animals, well-versed in the art of showing off to the crowds. They had done it for most of their marriage. And even when they were alone like this, they performed just the same.

Handing him his preferred brandy, Neve stood by the windows overlooking the back deck and the ocean that she knew was waiting for her in the dark. She allowed Armand a few minutes of silence, and when she turned back to face him, she caught him appraising her, his eyes full of something she couldn't read.

"I think you will laugh at me, Neve." His words finally broke the silence, and his eyes lost their unreadable expression. Now he shrugged, crossed his arms, and she felt more at ease at once. She could deal with him when he was upset. It was when he was calm that Neve was expecting a blow.

"It's almost midnight. You drove all the way here…"

"God, woman, would you let me try to gather some courage before I tell you that you were right? About everything. About marriage, about cheating, about children. Especially about children."

Armand took a long breath and reached for his breast pocket. He gave her a questioning look, and she crossed over to him, taking a cigarette out of his silver case. He lit hers first, in another well-practiced gesture between them.

As she inhaled and the smoke filled her lungs, she felt time turn back, just for a second. When she was young, when she was reckless.

"How is it that twenty years went by and you are still the same, Neve?" Armand smiled at her, and she found herself smiling back. They'd broken each other twice over, yet here they were.

"Not the same, not the same at all."

"Still victorious then. I remember when you came to LA all those years ago. Like a conqueror. One battle after another, everything you wanted was yours. The studio, actors, movies, me." His smile turned into a grimace of self-deprecation. "I never felt worthy of you, and it killed me. I had the money, the connections, the family name. But you had the drive, the talent. I couldn't touch you. No matter how I tried."

Neve turned away from him. The steps back to the windows and then onto the back deck calmed her racing heart. Well, it had only taken eight years to hear what she wanted from him.

His heavy steps echoed behind her, and she felt him stand next to her, his body heat and the smoke from his cigarette touching her like fingertips.

"So you hurt me, humiliated me, and threw me aside because you felt what? That I was out of your league? That's some ego soothing technique you have there, Melgren."

"I am sorry. It took me years to wrap my mind around everything. By that time, you were out of reach. But then you always were–"

"Armand—"

"Don't, please don't, Neve. I've done enough therapy and introspection to know that I was the biggest cad in this, but you were never there. You were my wife and unlike me, you made a commitment and you'd have never betrayed me, and you gave me Harlan. But you were never there, Neve."

She could have denied it. After all, he was the one who'd ended it. But he was also right. Still, he seemed to be at some kind of crossroads where he was admitting fault and taking responsibility. Neve, not particularly a fan of self-flagellation, just looked on.

Armand sighed, the sound familiar yet heavy. "Roxanne is divorcing me. And demanding sole custody of our children."

Ah, well, that explained much of it. Armand's second marriage seemed happy, and his twin toddlers were the apple of his eye. Harlan spent a lot of time with the boys and loved them dearly. Neve had caught herself several times grudgingly admiring Armand as a very good father in juggling a marriage, three children, and several successful business ventures. Apparently, she had been somewhat wrong about the success of it all.

"I think it's some sort of karma for what I tried to do to you." His throat worked, and he sucked greedily on his cigarette. Neve all but forgot about the one in her hand. "I was trying to get some kind of sick revenge on you, even though I was the one to divorce you and I…"

When tears glimmered in his eyes, Neve felt rooted to the spot. "Sorry, I can't bear to lose them. Just thinking that this is how I made you feel all those years ago when I was fighting for sole custody over Harlan… I'm sorry, Neve. I'm so sorry."

She went to him then, the fingers of her free hand carding his hair. It was thinning on top, they were not getting any younger. Maybe it was time to forgive and let go of some things?

"Shhh." His tears fell in earnest. She could feel them soaking her shoulder, permeating her blouse. His chest shook against hers as she held him. "She can't take the boys. You have first-hand knowledge of how difficult the custody process is."

She leaned back and gave him a stern look. "Get yourself together, Melgren. Get your lawyers. Unless you did more than cheat this time, there's no way to deny you your parental rights, although those babies are way too adorable… Are you sure they're yours?"

As expected, the joke made him grin, and again time reverted to years ago when they were happy. He stole the dying cigarette from her hand and finished it off in one drag.

"God, I'm such an ass. Thank you. And as far as Harlan is concerned–"

"I will ruin your life if you ever try to take him away from me, Armand."

He looked around, obviously wanting to flick the two cigarettes he was holding away into the white sand before noticing her narrowing eyes and grinning at her sheepishly. He stubbed them out and carefully placed them in the pocket of his thousand dollar suit. Then he sobered and nodded.

"I wouldn't. And he would kick my ass before you could anyway. Thanks for tonight, Neve. I guess I needed a shoulder." He gestured to the wet patch on her blouse and had the decency to wince at the damage he'd done.

"Funny how you always cost me, Melgren. Always. A favorite silk Marc Jacobs blouse this time."

He did not touch her as he left, and she was grateful. He knew she hated it, and the fact that he respected her wishes for once was gratifying.

In the morning, a silk Marc Jacobs blouse was delivered along with a bouquet of white tulips. Neve magnanimously accepted the apology.

During her next session with Dr. Moore, Neve herself removed the Knight from the board, setting the figurine reverently to the side.

―――――

Life went on. Gannon prospered with the expanded budgets at her disposal. Neve was on track to have one of the most exciting years of her life. She thrived in her professional security and in her wonderful relationship with her son, who was growing by leaps and bounds, turning into a smart, funny kid, coming into his own.

She missed none of Audrey Avens' wonderfully crafted features from the front lines, beautiful and heartbreaking stories about soldiers and local people struggling to survive and, at times, simply make it from one day to another. Audrey had found her voice again, clear and enticing. Her eye seemed to be back as well, with heart-wrenching images of Afghani children and American soldiers alike, hit by the misery of war.

Someone should suggest she release a book. All the articles from the front lines would make a poignant story, accompanied by the vibrant pictures. It was something worth immortalizing in more than newspaper pages.

She wanted to suggest as much to Elinor, but it was time to remove herself from this vicious cycle. Neve had no right to remind Audrey of her existence, and so she kept her counsel.

She did no more to disadvantage Freja's career, and Freja bounced back somewhat. However, with Neve's new protegee, Giselle, a former supermodel-turned-successful-TV-star taking the industry by storm, Freja was largely left with the scraps. Still, a promise was a promise, even if Neve had not actually made it, but rather Audrey had asked and she'd relented.

Neve still didn't know what to believe about Audrey's claims that she had never told Freja about their relationship, and sometimes, during the later parts of those less-than-sober nights, Neve pondered if Audrey was truly sincere in her assurances.

Occasionally, she'd convince herself that Audrey had lied to her, using Neve's feelings to save Freja, but those times were rare. And much more often, all Neve could think about was the agonizing longing in Audrey's eyes and the unabashed lust in their last kiss.

One could fake many things, but Neve knew passion, especially when it was mirrored in herself. Despite being engaged and believing Neve was purposely destroying her fiancé, and even though it was absolutely true that Neve had abandoned her to her own fate and devices several times, Audrey had still wanted Neve.

And despite all the love and all the lust, Neve was still afraid. When she thought about the myriad of things that scared her, she usually started with some of her most innocuous fears, perhaps in an endeavor to avoid the one that she dared not speak about and the one that broke her again and again when she did.

She'd start with the most obvious fear. Was it grounded in internalized homophobia? Was it an ingrained childhood trauma of being different, of being separate from the rest and thus ridiculed for it? She'd often remember the feeling of being looked at with derision and disgust as a child, for being poor, for being scrawny, and for stuttering. For a host of other reasons that she'd had no control over, such as having a proud, unpleasant mother and a violent father.

The memories of being laughed at in school over her old dresses or over her faltering speech still felt raw and so fresh, it was like being back in Harrisburg and trying not to gag as her father lowered her into one of the big dumpsters—overflowing with garbage that was rotting in the summer heat—making her scour for food.

The smells, the sounds, the sensation of being worthless, different from her pressed and polished classmates, had never really left her. Were these memories responsible for her abject fear of being outed? An innate desire to not be *othered* anymore? Had she given up her chance at happiness because her fear of being out and free and her fear of losing everything were too all-consuming and thus unconquerable even for Neve Blackthorne?

She didn't have any answers, and neither did the Lagavulin. Dr. Moore perhaps might be able to enlighten her, but Neve's ability to share was at best intermittent.

The incident that Neve looked back on as the catalyst that broke most of her windows and kicked down some of her doors started absolutely innocently. Peaceful even. Copacetic. And then it simply destroyed Neve, prompting a humiliating but inevitable breakdown of sorts in Dr. Moore's office.

It started with her getting the absolutely foolish idea to visit her mother. Again. The first time had been fine. She'd escaped unscathed. Why did she think that she'd be able to do it again?

She spent the afternoon telling Rivkah about some of her new projects, exciting new movies, and working with Gustavo across the continent to establish Gannon Streaming. Her mother seemed weaker than she was the last time Neve had seen her.

But Rivkah was visibly pleased to see her daughter and very interested in listening to the anecdotes Neve shared. But her breathing was labored, and she couldn't participate in the discussion a lot. Despite everything that had transpired between them, despite her mother's absolute faith and belief that she had only acted in her daughter's best interest when she'd subjected little Ziva to incessant bullying and abuse, Neve's treacherous heart was filled with concern for her.

As she was getting up to leave, Rivkah touched her fingers, and Neve had a flashback to Audrey taking her by the hand just six months ago, in her office before shipping out. Neve's aversion to being touched was notorious, but suddenly a childlike desire to be comforted by her own mother surfaced, a desire Neve was certain had been dead for years. She grasped the old, frail wrist and held on as Rivkah struggled to either find the words or the breath necessary to say what she wanted to say.

"You come to me... when you are hurt... always done so... no matter what I did to you... Who hurt you... now?"

Neve smiled mirthlessly at her mother's astuteness and at the few good memories from her childhood, of being cuddled when she'd desperately needed it.

"I'm not hurt. I'm restless, I guess. And I worry about you." She sat back down by her mother's chair.

"Don't worry... about me... I've still got some time left in me... you have other things... I can see... you are troubled, Neve." It was still such a jolt to hear her mother use her chosen name.

As she struggled to come up with an answer, Rivkah haltingly continued.

"Don't know who hurt you... but you are hurt... I see it... should ask for help. I regret not giving you that... taking that away from you... ask for help, Neve. You came to me... twice now... means you need help."

And then her mother shocked her again, with something neither of them had dared touch upon for years.

"I lied... Said I don't regret anything... I do, Neve... Regret leaving you with him... One regret... Abandoning you... I had to go, couldn't stand being there... You know all about being able to stand something and reaching your limit... I couldn't anymore... You were so young... And he was vicious, and I couldn't handle the pain anymore."

As if from afar, her own reply came to her. If she didn't know she was the one speaking, she wouldn't have recognized her own voice. The desperation in it; for answers, for the truth, but also the fear. The very fear of the answers, of that truth.

"And you chose to run away and leave an eight-year-old with a monster?"

Her mother's sharp inhalation was followed by a coughing fit, but Rivkah did not drop Neve's hand, and Neve did not move from her chair.

"You don't know... you don't know what I went through... with him."

Neve could sit no more. She also felt like she might break the fragile bones under her fingertips if she kept holding her mother's hand. It was all too much, too loud. She paced almost frantically before turning back towards Rivkah.

"I know exactly what you went through! I was right there.

Everything happened in front of me. And after every beating, you took it out on me."

Neve felt the walls closing in on her. Memories were slamming into her mind, first one by one and then like an avalanche all at once. A sob from Rivkah made her recoil.

"And still, I would have given my life for you to have taken me with you. You left me. You left me with him. How could you?"

"*Neshama sheli–*"

"*Your soul?* How dare you? You had no business calling me that when I was little, and you have absolutely no right to call me that now. *Neshama?* How was I your soul when you left me with the man who tormented you, and who made it his mission in life to ruin me after you left?"

Tears were falling down Rivkah's face in a continuous flood now, a tissue not at all a match to the sheer power of obvious regret.

"I couldn't take you with me... Neve..." Rivkah had to stop to draw in a ragged breath. "I simply couldn't... He'd have found the two of us together... And alone, I could hide from him."

Neve's laughter was brittle to her own ears.

"Ah, so we are back to how selfish you were."

"I'm so sorry, Neve... The one thing I am sorry..." Rivkah coughed, her body shaking under the strength of it. "For leaving you..."

But then the steel was back behind the watery eyes and the trembling hands firmed into fists. "But not for forging you... That helped you survive... Helped you stand up to him..." The frail voice rose up to a shrill scream for a second, and Neve gasped, her own hands lifting to her ears, but it was impossible to stop the words from coming. "Look at you!"

In the eerie silence that followed the outburst, Neve lowered her hands and turned around, utterly disgusted by the twisted logic.

"You hurt me so that his torment would not do as much damage? God, listen to yourself." Neve took a breath. The flow of air did nothing to calm her down. On the contrary, the more her mother spoke, the more Neve felt she had to escape, to run. "You talk about damage. Fuck the damage he has done, mother!" Rivkah started at the curse word and Neve took perverse pleasure in the ability to perturb her.

"What about the damage you've done? Do you know I cannot connect with anyone because I am so afraid they will leave me? Like you did. Do you know that every relationship that I start comes with a countdown? A ticking clock for how long I will allow it to live before I destroy it? Otherwise, it might destroy me, they might abandon me, and I can't allow that to ever happen. Nobody I ever truly loved can leave me. I cannot survive watching anyone I love walk away again."

And now both of them were crying, sobs wrecking them, echoing off the bare walls of her mother's sparse apartment.

"And through everything, you always whispered that I was not to tell. I still hear you hissing at me, and I can't stand it!"

"Neve... Neve... I simply didn't want... you to be even more ostracized..." The ragged breathing was loud, and Neve felt each inhalation like sandpaper against her skin.

"No, mother, you didn't want the family to be shamed! And you know what? Who gives a damn anymore?" Neve closed her eyes and finally reached for the root of it all, pulling at it and feeling her own skin flaying open along with it. "I stood there and watched you go. He was away, and you came home from the hospital after his latest beating, took your things and that was that. I remember it was raining, and I stood behind the window and watched you simply walk away. The window fogged up with my breath as I cried and called for you. I screamed myself hoarse until it was all too much and I passed out from the sound. I woke up in the dark, and the only thing that was still there was the window with the streaks my hands and my tears had left on it. And you didn't come back. I waited for you. Every day, for years! You never did... How could you?"

Rivkah did not recoil, nor did her face change. The tears were flowing still, and Neve had a feeling her mother no longer felt them. When she spoke, her voice was very quiet, as if atoning for Neve's earlier revelation.

"I couldn't, *neshama sheli*, I couldn't... I was so hurt... I was just so tired of being broken all the time..." Rivkah's hands rubbed against her arms, and Neve could see the bruises that had once marred that pale skin in her mind's eye. The quiet voice was breathless now, the sound no more than a whisper. "And everybody just looked away... 'A family matter, you're his property, they'd say'... And I knew... I knew he didn't care about you, you aren't his daughter and he'd not raise his hand to you, he never did before..."

Neve realized this, had known it for years in fact, had rejoiced many times that she mattered so little to her father that he never expended much energy on her. So why did the words feel like barbed wire? Cut, release, cut, release, cut, release, the sharp-edged string being dragged against her skin.

"There are so many ways to hurt a child without raising a hand, mother..." But Neve was struggling to hold on to the pain, to the hate. Opening these floodgates was like opening a vein.

She felt weak, tired, powerless. She wanted silence. She wanted her beach. And she wanted Audrey, as perverse as that was. She wanted Audrey to hold her, to play with her hair as she had done so often, to just run her fingers through it and massage her scalp. In silence. She wanted nothing else.

No, having a child herself, Neve did not understand how her mother could have simply discarded her. But she understood survival, and some of Rivkah's words, some of those wretched explanations, had reached her. Her mother was a victim, and she had faced impossible choices. To save herself and abandon her daughter.

Neve knew she'd never forgive Rivkah, but with the black bird no longer trapped behind her ribcage, she felt she could breathe. So she allowed herself to simply sit down again, say nothing, and offer her mother another tissue.

Rivkah ignored the offering, instead reaching for Neve's hand again, and when it wasn't jerked away, she held it tight and muttered things Neve didn't care to decipher. Forty years too late, her mother was holding on to her like she genuinely cared, like she was sorry, and wasn't that a kick in the gut?

Rivkah's grip on her fingers had been painful, but Neve hadn't minded it, her mother's tears washing the sting of the hold away as she'd bent her head over their joined hands.

"I should have asked for help... Instead, I left... I will always regret, Neve... *Neshama sheli*, forgive me... I see you in pain... I see you troubled... Don't do what I did... Neve... Ask for help, child, ask for help."

Neve thought that if nothing else, Dr. Moore was proud of her progress, of the things she had let go and the things she managed to save. And if Audrey knew, Neve thought she'd be proud too. Both of them had wanted her to ask for help.

Some things Neve was not ready to process just yet, but the visit to her mother had opened her eyes to her own feeble attempts to cope in her own completely dysfunctional way. Perhaps allowing Dr. Moore to treat her wouldn't be such a bad thing. Perhaps, Neve thought, she was ready.

12

NEVE'S FULL AND UNRESERVED SURRENDER

"*What is happiness to you, Neve?*"

The question jerked her out of her reverie. The previous session, right on the heels of her episode with her mother—as she'd decided to call it—was still fresh in her mind. Yet this one, despite starting with Neve finally acquiescing to actual therapy, was not going according to plan.

For one, Dr. Moore hadn't said much about the treatment itself. And for all the rest, she seemed determined to ask questions Neve had no answers to.

"I... ah... I never actually thought about this, Dr. Moore."

"Well, that's as honest as you've ever been with me. Think about it now. Please."

The 'please' made her raise an eyebrow, but her therapist just gave her a small smile and nodded.

"I'm not sure. It's not something I've actively sought. I don't think I am really capable, as such. I mean, look at my life. Several times, I thought I had all the necessary pieces to assemble that happiness puzzle. I had a husband, a child, a dog, my job... Oscars, recognition, fame, certainly fortune. All the things I thought I needed seemed to be there. I just never knew how to put them together. And I think I either kept positioning them wrong, or didn't even try to at all."

Neve waved a dismissive hand. "And this answer is neither here nor there, but perhaps it'll give you plenty of material to analyze."

"You think after almost three years, I don't have enough material?"

"Is that even a professional question?" Her tone was imperious, but Neve gave Dr. Moore a smile of her own. "Fine, fine. To your question, no, I am not sure what happiness is and honestly, I don't think that was something I set out to achieve. I had other priorities, shall we call them that? How does one even define happiness, and if I can't define it, how can I actively pursue it?"

She looked at the board, the beautiful set never too far from her sight when she was in this office. Her Queen and the Rook stood solemn and still. Just as Neve and her fear remained alone.

"I've had many happy moments. Harlan's birth, his first steps, his first word. His constant presence in my life, his love for me. My professional success. My ability to choose my own projects and creative avenues. All those brought great joy. Does that count?"

Dr. Moore reached for her teacup. "I'm not the one to say what happiness is for you, Neve. Only you can."

Damn her, always so wily. Happiness?

For some reason, the rain-streaked window, the one she'd forbidden herself to think about for decades, flashed in her memory. But it wasn't the window of the hovel they'd inhabited in Pennsylvania when she was a child. It was one in her mansion in Malibu, and she was overlooking the ocean, its vastness foaming in the distance. And among the high stormy waves was a figure. Except the person was walking towards the house, not away from it. And the hands on the glass weren't those of a child, but those of a 48-year-old woman.

Between the rivulets of rain on the window, Neve could tell that, in slow motion almost, Audrey was making her way to her. And the emotion that filled her chest, the unfettered joy, spilled from her, her breath fogging the glass, this time not with despair but with elation. Was that happiness? She didn't know, but the moment she shook her head to dispel the fantasy, the joy left her and loneliness filled its space.

"Where did you just go, Neve?"

The fact that she immediately opened her mouth to share, to answer, startled her, and she paused to draw a breath and marvel for just a moment at how things had changed.

"It started out as a fantasy. Audrey was walking towards me. But I realize now it was a memory as much as my imagination, because Audrey has walked up that path from the beach to the house, and I've watched for her. So I must have lived it. I had it. This happiness, or whatever you want to call it. But at the time, I felt only fear and panic, even if there was nobody there to catch us."

"What were you afraid of?"

"Of her walking away instead. Of her never coming back."

"And then what you feared happened." Dr. Moore's voice was muted, and Neve was grateful for that. "So what is happiness, Neve?"

"The solace of her returning. The whisper of her voice, telling me she's back." She spoke the words without putting any deliberate effort into them, but they rang so true, so sweet. She felt her hands curling into fists. *To have, to hold, oh, to hold…*

The wondrous Los Angeles rain pelted the office window in steady streams. Neve could hear the seagulls and the roar of the stormy ocean in the distance. Rain was so rare here. When it arrived, Neve reveled in it, from the water in the palm of her hand, to the petrichor afterwards. She missed it constantly, despite rain having been an accomplice in the most tragic moment of her life to date. Now she knew it had also witnessed one of her happiest ones.

When she finally tore her eyes off the glass, Dr. Moore looked at her with steady, kind eyes.

"Now, let's begin our session, Neve. I want you to meet someone. I'm not ambushing you. They're not here in person, but let me tell you about a specialist I think you and I should include in your treatment schedule. Their name is Lane Brady, and they are an expert in PTSD and sensory processing disorders caused by abandonment, abuse, and trauma. Do you think we could do that?"

"I..." Neve opened her mouth, to refuse, to draw back, to close whatever door she'd just opened by uttering those ridiculous words. Solace? God, how pathetic. But the vision of Audrey coming towards her... Or Harlan running behind her, catching up to her and Audrey swinging him around. Of herself simply looking through the rainy window and not recoiling from her breath leaving vapor marks on the glass, beckoned by the vision in the sand.

So therapy it was, even if it would not bring Audrey back. She wanted to write her name on the wet glass, she wanted the solace of rain falling all around her without the shard of panic lodged in her chest.

"Yes. Therapy. Specialist. Yes."

Still, when her worst nightmare came to life, she felt utterly unprepared, and no therapist or specialist would have been able to help her. When your cell phone rings at four in the morning, it is never good news. Her first thought was her mother, and that she wasn't quite ready to hear that she no longer had any time to sit next to Rivkah in silence while avoiding talking about what had broken them years ago. And wasn't that a shock, that after forty years of hating her mother, she really wasn't ready to let her go? They still had unfinished business. So much of it, in fact.

But the number displayed was French, and she thought it must be Gustavo, who was taking a month-long vacation with Benedict in Europe and had been quietly ecstatic in his effusive emails and phone calls with her these past couple of weeks. Maybe he had forgotten the time difference?

Yet the voice on the line was Elinor's, and Neve could have sworn her heart stopped beating entirely before the Times Editor finished her apologies for calling this late–or early. Somehow Neve knew what would follow. She stood up, took a couple of steps and then simply sank to the floor with the phone at her ear, her mind refusing to process what Elinor was haltingly trying to relate to her.

"Some ambush or something, Neve. I don't know, I don't know anything." Elinor seemed both shocked and angry, the seasoned reporter in her clearly upset at the lack of information. "Someone from the Department of State got in touch with me since I'm her employer, to inform me that Audrey, along with several military personnel and the accompanying interpreter, are missing." To Neve's disbelief, Elinor's voice broke at the last word.

"They are fairly certain they've been kidnapped. They've begun a recovery operation, but they don't know much. The official I spoke to said they were visiting a construction site, a bridge in Asadabad, one of those big US government projects to improve the area, an absolutely routine outing, when they were ambushed. Two soldiers from the 25th Infantry Division were killed and the rest of them taken. I asked if he was certain. I asked. He said there were no additional bodies, Neve."

It was Neve's name that finally broke Elinor, who clearly had been fighting hard to keep her cool. A deep, shaky breath, once, twice, and then a sob reached Neve, and all she could do was hold on, shutting her eyes, bearing the high-pitched wail.

Amidst the sensory overload, Neve peripherally wondered how it was possible that her heart didn't seem to be beating at all. Surely the laws of biology simply did not work that way.

"I can't find her mother. The people at the State Department couldn't either. Some mix-up with addresses or numbers or some such thing, dearest. I feel helpless. I broke my leg a week ago, I'm still bedridden. I didn't know who to call, but I had to tell you... Because she's gone and it's very bad. And you would know what to do, Neve."

Out of the litany of words, only two syntagms were actually registering beyond 'she's gone' and 'very bad'. How could Audrey be 'gone' when she had just published a beautiful article about a local women's program set up to safeguard them against domestic violence?

The pictures and the stories were so poignant, so sad, Audrey's words bleeding life and compassion from the page. How could Audrey have been kidnapped? How could it be so 'very bad' that the normally even-tempered Elinor seemed beside herself?

None of this could be happening, and she shook her head in an attempt to deny, to refuse. Maybe if she tried hard enough she would wake up?

Yet nothing helped, and she slowly started to realize that her personal hell wasn't a dream after all. It was time to take charge then, because Neve Blackthorne never bent to the world, she made the world bend to her.

As if acknowledging the challenge, she could feel her heart pump all the harder again. She worked her best when backed into a corner with seemingly no way out. It's when she saw clearest of all.

"Get me all the information you can, Ely. I'll figure it out. Audrey must have left some kind of record years ago with HR."

"God, dearest, you haven't called me that in twenty-five years..." More sobbing could be heard on the other end of the line, and Neve thought with some disdain that Elinor needed to get it together.

"If she dies, Neve, if she dies, I will never forgive myself! You hear me? Never. She begged me to give her that assignment. I thought she would want the transfer to New York, since she and Freja... Jesus, Freja, I have to call her. Neve, she didn't want to stay in New York or LA, she didn't want to return to Paris, she was so adamant that she needed to get away. How was I supposed to know she was on this foolish, self-destructive mission? I will never forgive myself."

"Hush now, Ely. I have to go. I will let you know how things progress. Get me addresses and names. You're the Times Editor, put your people to work for crying out loud, and stop the tears. This isn't helping, dammit. I need everything you already have, and whatever your sources can get me as soon as possible, so I can start pressuring people on my own end."

She hung up on the still crying Elinor and took a deep breath. First things first. She had to find a way to get a hold of Audrey's mother and bring her to wherever she needed to be. She had to call her lawyers. They'd be the best-positioned to know whom to contact and what buttons to push with the authorities.

Neve, for all her experience, became acutely aware that nothing had prepared her for a situation like this. She knew nothing about what went into recoveries of American citizens abducted abroad. Why on Earth hadn't she looked into this when Audrey had shipped out before? Did she assume that somehow, by being with some infantry division or another, Audrey would be bulletproof? Or safe from everything that military and civilian personnel were subjected to in a war zone?

She only knew, from the bits and pieces of information she had learned throughout the years, that time was of the essence in abductions, and if any moves were to be made, they needed to be made now. Immediately.

Armand would take Harlan, who was home for his summer break. The myriad of details connected with the studio would just have to wait. Her mind worked in overdrive, trying to determine her course of action amidst the pain and fear that were threatening to consume her.

She remembered Audrey telling her how they had a thread

between their chests, attached to their ribs, and how they pushed and pulled and twisted it to hurt each other. This time, that connection was tearing her open, being strung across the miles and miles that separated them. But she felt it, the pull of that thread, no matter how painful, how devastating it was. It was there, and it meant that Audrey was still alive. Surely, Neve thought, she'd feel it if Audrey was no longer...

Neve could not finish that thought. And so she stilled herself for a full minute and did something she'd thought she would never do again. Was it Neve Blackthorne or was it Ziva Beloff who started reciting a prayer in a language she'd told herself she had long forgotten?

It had been thirty years since she'd last prayed. She wasn't sure why she was doing it now. She'd never really believed in any deity, not even as a child, considering that if one existed, it would never allow so many injustices to befall those who worshiped their god with such fervor. Still she prayed, the Tefillah falling from her lips in a familiar cadence.

Over and over, one after another, she recited the prayers, so well-remembered, so despised in her childhood. Yet she clung to them now, her shoulders shaking with suppressed sobs, held inside because her mind was so focused on the sacred words she couldn't contemplate stopping. With the sun peeking its first rays through the heavy curtains of her bedroom, she recited the Sabbath blessing.

Baruch atah Adonai, Eloheinu melech ha-olam...

She did not have a sense of how long she'd lost herself in prayer. When she surfaced, her face was dry, and her body was reinvigorated by the familiar words and ritual.

Her call to Barnaby was short. "Cancel all meetings. Audrey has been taken." When Barnaby yelped and then quietly asked if he should contact people on her behalf, the list of powerful names he recited and his resourcefulness left Neve awed and speechless.

She heard a series of squeaks and more sobs on the other end of the line. "I care about that stupid jerk. Last time I talked to her, I told her to get lost because she was hooking up with that horrible piece of... with Freja. So she can't die on me. I still need to rip her a new one for being such a complete fool. So you get her back and tell her that, Neve!'"

Leaving everything in Barnaby's capable hands, Neve quickly packed a small bag for Harlan. She let him sleep, aware that, until his father got to Malibu from Santa Monica, there was no reason to disturb him. Her phone was a non-stop vibration of text messages both from Barnaby about trying to find Audrey's mother, and from Elinor with snippets of information about the situation, and speculation, and more decrying her recklessness in sending Audrey to that accursed place that would surely kill her. Neve closed her eyes, willing the images of this very event to dissipate. She'd fall apart later, if the time came.

Things went into overdrive from there. With the sun rising in Washington, Neve and her attorneys were making phone calls. State Department, Department of Defense, the insurance company that had issued Audrey her Kidnapping and Ransom Policy. God, she hadn't even been aware there was such a thing as *Kidnapping and Ransom Insurance*, yet here she was on an intercontinental call, with who knows how many people, discussing the fine points of Audrey's coverage, the intermediaries, and the inability to predict the devolving situation.

And it was devolving rather fast. In something approaching ten hours, Neve finally managed to get some answers from the European Command. The military operation to recover the hostages was failing. They didn't say it quite like that, but it was obvious that all the resources thrown at the operation, including the proverbial kitchen sink, had been unsuccessful.

"The assumption we are operating under right now is that the kidnappers have crossed into Pakistan, ma'am." The voice on the other end of the line was calm, collected, and utterly emotionless. Her attorney, the one in an ugly blue suit, raised his eyes at her and then shrugged in defeat, and Neve vowed that he'd be fired the second they were done here.

Unaware of how close to his dismissal he was, the blue suit straightened his tie and, looking around the room, spoke dismissively. "Well, if you don't have anything else–"

Neve would have none of it.

"What does that mean, Colonel?"

Silence reigned, and Neve wasn't sure if that was because they all knew the answer, or because there was no satisfactory answer to give.

"Um…" The long pause after that utterance told her it was likely the second option. "Ma'am, with the terrorist cell crossing into Pakistan, it is out of our hands."

"*Out of your hands*?" Another one of her attorneys—wearing a somewhat nicer black suit—winced at her tone, and she shot him a dirty look. This was not the time to be polite or measured. If she sounded murderous, it was because she was. Because it had now been twelve hours, and neither the State Department nor DOD had any answers for anything other than some acronym-soup and gibberish.

"Well, Pakistan being a sovereign state, we can't just attack—"

"Something so trivial as another country's sovereignty has never stopped the United States of America from retrieving its citizens before, Colonel."

"Ma'am…" Now he sounded tired, the kind of tired that screamed, 'I'm done dealing with the hysterical woman on the line.'

Neve closed her eyes and vowed to ruin him. Later. Along with her fool of an attorney. The blue suit. Not the black one. Maybe both since they kept sitting there looking like dolts. Even if that meant she had to keep doing everything herself. So she would ruin all of them. Just as soon as she got answers.

"The US Ambassador to Pakistan will activate the PRWG—"

"Speak English!" She didn't bother to try to hide her visceral reaction to her outburst, flinching and breaking out in a cold sweat at her own raised voice. The room was eerily quiet again.

"Personnel Recovery Working Group, ma'am. It consists of representatives from the State Department, the Department of Defense, the Central Intelligence Agency, and the Federal Bureau of Investigation on the ground." That he spelled out even the well-known acronyms told her he was kowtowing now. No, she wasn't a major political donor, a fact she now sorely regretted, but something told her he was scared of her. Darkly, it would please her any other time if she had the energy for it. But she didn't in that moment.

"What will this PRWG do? What can they do?"

"They'll try to determine the location of the hostages, and whether a recovery is at all possible. I'd contact State if I were you, ma'am. It really is out of our hands now."

She pressed the *end call* button with particular force. Black Suit was already dialing on his cell phone. So maybe him she would keep.

An hour later, they were in the hellish hellhole of holding for some medium-level consular bureaucrat, and Neve was at the end of her tether.

"Tea? I made some herbal concoction." Neve turned sharply at the sound of Gustavo's voice. When did he get here?

"No... I... No. Thank you."

He sat down next to Neve and cradled the mug he'd just offered her in his hands. "The waiting is doing me in. I swear. I looked at every name in my fucking contact book, and I got no one in Washington. I just avoided that cursed place full of ill-shaped suits and bland ties like the plague. Yet, here we are, fucking needing their help."

Something tugged at the edges of Neve's mind, like a tiny memory that was too tangled, but still there. Despite her earlier refusal, she reached out for the mug in Gustavo's hands, and when she took a sip, the convoluted mixture exploded on her tongue with flavors that had no business being blended together. Juno drank ridiculous drinks like this all the time.

Juno... Juno Buchanan, whose nephew was Assistant Secretary of State. Juno Buchanan, one of the biggest Democratic donors, who was in DC every month for luncheons with the First Lady and the representatives of the Women's Democratic Caucus... Juno Buchanan, who hated Neve's guts.

Gustavo must have sensed something in her, because he reached out immediately and snatched the mug that was about to shatter from her trembling hands.

"Barnaby! Get the plane ready. I need to get to New York right now!"

Six hours later, surrounded by the always noisy and never quite dark Manhattan late evening, she was standing in front of Juno's brownstone.

Taking a deep breath, she carefully set her Louboutin-shod foot onto the granite steps leading up to a massive black entrance. As she pondered the symbolism, Neve was surprised when the heavy door was suddenly flung in her face, and there was Juno looking at her with an almost sadistic expression in her eyes.

"Colin called earlier. He is a careerist airhead and absolutely not my favorite nephew, but he is a wonderful snitch.

And he told me a very curious thing, Neve. Very curious indeed. He said that *Neve Blackthorne* is terrorizing State Department employees on both sides of the Atlantic, demanding all sorts of things. Whichever. And all because a Times journalist was kidnapped. Do I have the facts right, darling?"

Neve chose not to sigh, or roll her eyes, or even acknowledge the veiled insult in the smooth-as-silk *darling* thrown her way.

"Says the woman whose demands were always legendary."

Surprisingly, Juno cackled and opened the door wider, motioning for Neve to come in.

Unsurprisingly, the massive townhouse, despite all of its enormous windows, looked like a cavern. Books and clutter were strewn on every surface. Neve's latent claustrophobia reared its head. Juno brushed past her and waltzed into the kitchen, where it looked like someone had tried to bake something and kept abandoning the task, distracted by either one of the million Times crosswords that covered the counters, or by the multitude of empty or half-filled wine glasses.

Something must have flickered on Neve's face, some form of disgust at her surroundings because Juno narrowed her eyes and when she spoke, her voice was barbed-wire-sharp.

"Don't judge me, Blackthorne. You, of all people, with your functional alcoholic vibes, should absolutely not even dare to go there. Especially since you came here to beg me to pull all the impressive strings that I can for that girl of yours."

Juno did not bother to keep her voice quiet. In fact, since Neve had crossed the threshold, Juno had made a whole lot of noise. Slamming the door, dragging her feet, pushing various things out of her way. Now she drummed her long nails on a piece of aluminum foil, and Neve felt her skin crawl. She bit the inside of her cheek, the metal taste of her own blood giving her a semblance of feeling grounded.

"Well..." Juno reached for the glass nearest to her and threw back its contents. Then she simply extended her hand and gestured impatiently towards Neve. "Beg!"

The counter under Neve's fingers felt unclean, the floor under her shoes even more so and just as sticky. She was wearing a brand new pencil skirt, and she was halfway to her knees when Juno actually jumped to catch her.

"Oh, for fuck's sake, Blackthorne! What the hell is wrong with you? A simple *please* would have killed you? Kneeling? Way to make me feel like a complete witch. Jesus. Dramatic much?"

Neve's head spun as she was pushed into a remarkably comfortable chair, with Juno handing her a glass of her own. She wanted to refuse, considering the state of pretty much everything around her, but she just scrunched her nose, closed her eyes and drank. The wine was tart, but went down smoothly. Juno watched her drink like a hawk before refilling her glass. Then she took the chair opposite her and they sat in silence for what seemed like forever. A black cat came in, gave Juno a wide berth and unceremoniously plopped itself onto Neve's lap.

"Damn traitor."

"I assume you mean the cat?" Neve decided to sip her second glass instead of tossing it back again. She hadn't eaten in 24 hours, and this wasn't the company to lose her presence of mind in.

"Both of you." Juno didn't appear to have any of Neve's sobriety scruples as she emptied her glass and poured herself some more. "The cat at least knows that she depends on me for food. You? Whatever you thought you were doing by aligning yourself with Livia Sabran-McMillan, I have no idea. I wasn't so bad..."

The last sentence came out as almost petulant, and Neve just raised her eyebrow.

"Yeah, yeah, the IV&X deal was perhaps too hasty on my part, and I should've brought you in on it instead of trying to sell the studio out from under you."

Neve looked around incredulously. Juno admitting to being in the wrong?

"God, I hope it doesn't snow in July, Buchanan. I am rather fond of these shoes."

"Oh, quit it. I never understood this Wicked Queen Of Hollywood appeal of yours. All sarcasm and cutting remarks. All low, husky tones and perfectly cut skirts."

"Well, you're about ten inches shorter, Juno. You'd have to stand on a footstool to make a skirt like this work for you." At Juno's furious expression, Neve simply raised her hand and turned away apologetically.

"Fuck you too, Blackthorne. *Fuck you too.* I'm trying to tell you that I don't hate your guts quite as I did half a year ago, and you can't even accept that much from me. I didn't trash a whole damn house for months on end to do little to no reflection. I also did a lot of digging around... Mostly in your dirty laundry."

Juno stood up and left the kitchen. The cat purred in Neve's lap, and the entire sequence of events that had transpired since she had come up the granite steps and through the black door seemed absolutely surreal.

She traced one black ear with her fingertip, and the purring intensified. As distracted as she was by the creature who was studiously ignoring her while quietly demanding more pets, Neve missed Juno's return and only raised her head when a stack of pictures was laid in front of her on the table.

Before she could speak or even reach out to leaf through them, Juno spoke up.

"Now, don't look at me like I committed some kind of cardinal sin. I've done worse than asking some very shrewd people to look into your life, and we both know it. I have to say,

I vetted you extensively when I hired you. I didn't want any scandals, and there seemed to be none around you, but boy, was I wrong or what?" Juno actually wagged her eyebrows.

"You can totally try to stare me down with that infamous glare of yours the way you do, since you never raise your voice, but I don't care. This was a fascinating journey, digging through your private stuff, Blackthorne. *Fascinating.*"

Neve didn't bother to reach for the pictures, so Juno pushed the stack closer. The top one was of her and Audrey locked in an embrace in her ground-floor study, taken with a long-range lens. Did the photographer shoot it from a boat, since logistically, Neve didn't see how else it would have been possible?

The shard of broken glass in her chest twisted. It was a picture of their last kiss. No, they weren't together, no they weren't each other's and neither of them knew what was coming, but Neve could still taste that kiss, feel those beloved hands on her face, holding her still, Audrey's mouth taking its fill.

She bit her cheek again, the wound fresh enough to give her more of that coppery taste, but this time, the blood did nothing to stem the tide of emotion. She knew her eyes would betray her—tears would spill any second—but she still raised them, looking at Juno head-on.

"Well, if kneeling wasn't dramatic enough, then surely whatever this is definitely qualifies. My, my, the great Neve Blackthorne loopily in love with a girl eighteen years her junior."

"Nineteen. Almost twenty." She was afraid to move, the pain like a rent in a seam, ruthless, unstoppable.

Juno tsked and collected the pictures.

"I don't understand you. You love her. Yet you throw her away, by all accounts. Then you want her back, and then you ruin her girlfriend. You let her go to Afghanistan, of all fucking places, because you can't make up your mind about whatever it is that made you toss her aside in the first place. And now here you are, prepared to kneel in front of me and beg for what, exactly?"

Neve tugged at her starched shirtsleeve, straightening an imaginary crease, and then lifted her eyes to meet Juno's. "Help me get her back. State is bullshitting me and dragging their feet, and the insurance company that issued her Kidnapping and Ransom policy is telling me they're in the way of the intermediaries the company normally uses on the ground to find people. Your contacts on the Hill, not to mention in the Cabinet, are what they are–"

"I've already talked to Colin. They're running rings around both you and the insurance company because nobody actually knows anything, and so they're stalling. It's quite embarrassing for everyone involved. An operation of this scale—to capture this many Americans and to do it right under everyone's noses —took guts, but it also means a considerable amount of balls were dropped."

Juno barreled on as Neve looked on in astonishment.

"What? I knew you were coming. I had to have the facts, and Colin is afraid of me. So he gave me some information. Then I made some more calls. Believe it or not, my money still opens a lot of doors. The senators still adore me."

Juno came closer and tried to scratch the peaceably purring cat in Neve's lap, only to jerk her hand back as the furball turned claw-monster on a dime. Juno hissed and clutched her injured appendage and the cat went back to purring. Neve felt like she was a spectator in a comedy of errors played by amateurs.

Juno stuck her hand under the faucet and went on as if nothing had happened. "Well, I don't have much good news. The official US government line is and always was the same. 'We don't negotiate with terrorists.' And after that whole affair in 2016, when they tried to pay to get back that soldier, a lot of egg remains on a lot of faces. In any case, they won't pay—"

"I will pay." Neve's words seemed to surprise Juno, who blinked up at her.

"Neve..." Her name was spoken almost gently. "It's tens of millions of dollars..."

"I'm a very wealthy woman. You know this. And if I can't secure all this money right now, I will find ways. I will borrow. People owe me more than money. I won't have difficulty getting my hands on whatever the amount is. Tell me who to pay, Juno. Just tell me."

Juno shook her head as if Neve was disturbed and left again.

Neve could hear her voice in the room next door, speaking on the phone. There was a lot of cursing, followed by more cursing. Neve stroked the silky ears of the now sleeping cat and tried to tune Juno out.

What seemed like hours later, Juno returned and plopped down in her chair with a disgruntled expression on her face.

"As I said, State will do nothing. The Ambassador to Pakistan is total chickenshit. Fucking career paper pusher. Doesn't want to make any waves. So here's what we are going to do. Call the insurance company. Colin agreed to give them everything State has. And there are some people on the ground who will help too. They will need to be compensated."

She handed Neve a piece of paper. "Here's a number. It's a private company. They call themselves something very genteel these days, but make no mistake, they know everything that is happening over there. If it's a ransom that's required, they will know whom to pay. They coordinate with the insurance guys who have their own people on the ground, and when all the proverbial ducks are in a row, they all do their jobs, and State closes their eyes and prays the local government doesn't find out until after either the payment or the wet work is finalized. Here's how much it will cost you."

Juno pushed another piece of torn paper her way, with six zeros on it. "And the rest should be covered by the insurance policy Times took out for the girl."

"Audrey. Her name is Audrey." The cat under Neve's hand was breathing deeply, the little chest moving up and down in her sleep.

"Damn, Blackthorne. 'Loopy' may have been too tame a word to describe how smitten you are. Get a hold of yourself, woman. Audrey, Aubrey, whatever—"

"Audrey Clare Avens."

"For all intents and purposes, you kneeled in front of me. You didn't blink when I showed you proof of how easily I can ruin you. And this is where you draw your line in the sand? At her name?"

"Yes." They looked at each other then, the moment stretching, and finally Juno gave her a slight nod, lowering her head.

"Audrey then. Give me your lawyer's details, and I will take it from there. You sit here, complete lunatic that you are, while you pet that traitor of a cat and wait. I'll be back. There's food in the fridge, though I don't know if it's fresh. I've been living on takeout mostly, or made sure I was seen in all the swanky restaurants to prove I'm neither dead nor disgraced, so I'm not really sure what's in there."

With that appetizing last remark, Juno was gone, leaving Neve in the dirty, cluttered kitchen with a sleeping cat in her lap and a lot to think about.

Hours later, it was almost twilight when Juno came in and simply gave her the phone. The voice on the other end was cultured and accented, something German or Dutch. Neve tried not to focus on that and to instead listen to the words because those were devastating.

Hostages freed... No casualties... Audrey C. Avens wounded in the ambush... Unconscious and losing blood since capture... Being evacuated to Landstuhl... Unresponsive...

Neve did not hear the phone clattering to the marble floor although it must have made a sound, nor did she see the cat running out of the room, no doubt scared by the sudden commotion, as she crumpled in the middle of Juno's kitchen.

13

NEVE MOVES MOUNTAINS

"*D*o you know there's no state law dedicated to minors' emancipation in Pennsylvania? In that godforsaken place, children under 18 can't legally get free of their parents unless they meet a number of criteria. You can't petition the court for the procedure that is pretty standard in many other states."

She looked at her hands, absently noticing that the knuckles were white and that the fingers were gripping the armrest so tight it should be hurting her, but she felt nothing.

"I didn't know anything. Obviously, I didn't have access to legal advice. I was so scared to tell anyone what was happening. So I went to the library and read about emancipation. I have no idea where I'd even heard the word. I was 16, and those evenings reading about freedom filled my heart with so much hope."

"Neve..." Dr. Moore seemed incapable of saying anything other than her name. Her eyes were gentle and for once, it didn't scrape Neve raw.

"I went to the courthouse. And some clerk told me they couldn't do anything for me. Since there was no law, it was a highly individualized, case-by-case examination of each petition. And that it almost never happened, since, if my father was proven to be abusive, they wouldn't emancipate me, they'd just put me in a group home until I turned 18. That my only chance at emancipation was to prove myself to have independent means, or to graduate high school early, and the conditions were just so complicated. Plus, they said that the investigation into abuse allegations would be invasive. And the thought of a group home scared me so much. Much more than the pain of his screams."

"Neve..." Her name again, her chosen name, the one she'd painstakingly decided upon after months of reading and researching the meaning of various appellations.

"You know, it feels like a theme in my life."

"What, Neve?" Every time Dr. Moore said her name, she felt comforted, and it did not escape her that the therapist was doing it on purpose.

"This pattern that I have. Of reaching for comfort in the well-known pain because the fear of change is greater." She knew her smile did not reach her eyes, but Dr. Moore just nodded.

"Leidensdruck. It's the Leidensdruck concept." At Neve's blank stare, Dr. Moore sat deeper in her chair and relaxed her shoulders. "It's a German word and a psychological term. The literal translation is 'the pressure of suffering', but as with all things German, nothing is quite that easy about understanding the phenomenon. What the concept suggests is that the suffering inherent in not acting must exceed the suffering one expects to experience if one acts. That the 'Leidensdruck', the pressure has to be high enough to become the impetus for moving forward, for change."

"Basically, the known pain has to be much greater than the anticipated pain and the fear of the unknown to motivate the person to finally confront their fear? Apt." Neve crossed her legs, one heel dangling precariously from her toes. She felt disheveled, even though she knew her coif was pristine, arranged just an hour ago by the ever-diligent Morag. But the dangling shoe spoke volumes to her. A small detail, but as she raised her eyes, she saw Dr. Moore watching her with furrowed brows.

Neve never relaxed, never allowed herself to show even the slightest of imperfections in anyone's presence. As she looked away from her therapist's sympathetic and all-seeing eyes and into the early morning storm whipping up the darkening Pacific outside, she felt like she didn't care if anyone saw her fall apart.

"Well, Leidensdruck then. My teenage self did learn to find solace in that pain. I was too scared to move on from it. So I stayed, and the day after I turned 18, I simply ran. And the rest is history."

Dr. Moore sat motionless, and Neve felt her chest contract painfully.

"So, no, I am not angry with my mother for leaving him."

"What are you angry about, Neve?" There it was again, her name. A touchstone. The lighthouse amidst the waves she kept watching.

"I'm angry because she left me!" Tears she did not realize she'd been holding back spilled over then.

"She left me, and then Armand left me, and Elinor and Dmitriy, and I couldn't give a fuck about any of them, but Audrey would have eventually left me too, and it was the one thing I could not stand. I couldn't..."

On the long plane journey across the Atlantic, to the Landstuhl military hospital, Neve's mind did not allow her to settle. She couldn't sit down, so she spent a considerable amount of time pacing the spacious cabin, not giving a minute of peace to the crew, who—while familiar with her demanding nature—found it absolutely disconcerting that she hadn't even asked for a glass of water, yet didn't sit down either. She could tell by their darting glances, whispered conversations. They checked on her periodically, but she would just wave them off every time.

"You know..." Dr. Moore's breathing was steady on the other end of the phone, and Neve had a déjà vu of talking to her therapist from her private jet. "The one thought running through my mind over and over is that all this pain, all this foolishness, has been in vain, has been totally wasted."

She rubbed the bridge of her nose as tears threatened again.

"All my issues aside, I tried my best with Harlan. He is his own person and I love him. I never doubted our ability to have and maintain a relationship. At least there, with him, I did something right."

"It's a very healthy approach to parenting. And you did many things right, Neve."

Neve wanted to laugh. Then cry. "I denied myself happiness, denied myself love and passion and devotion, out of fear of losing. Out of fear of being abandoned again. And yet here I am on the very verge of losing the one person I've ever..." She couldn't say the word out loud. She felt it would be the ultimate betrayal to say it out loud to anyone but Audrey, and yet she knew she may never have the chance to do that.

"I've never cared for anyone, neither Armand, nor Dmitriy, nor scores of men and women in between them."

"You've never been so afraid of any of them either," Dr. Moore said, no intonation or emotion coloring her early morning rasp.

"I didn't lose myself in any of them, or pushed as hard to get free from the emotion and the fear as I did with Audrey. And I've never lived through as much pain as with the amount I both dispensed and experienced with her."

Neither had she experienced as much elation or as much happiness with anyone else. *Safe, loved, treasured.* She was beloved in those lanky arms.

No amount of fear erased her love for Audrey. No amount of lies she'd told herself, that sending Audrey away would stop Neve from loving her, would end her fears and anxiety. None of it worked. Neve loved her. Neve loved her, and her heart was telling her she might not survive if her beloved did not make it through this.

No, Audrey wasn't hers. She belonged to someone else and probably hated Neve more now than she had at any other time. But none of it mattered. Neve's whole being was resolute. Running away hadn't worked. Letting Audrey go hadn't worked. The bloody woman had gone and gotten herself ambushed and kidnapped and shot and was probably dead because of Neve. She wasn't deluding herself. Elinor's words had confirmed as much. Audrey had run away to Afghanistan, run away from the constant torture that her feelings for Neve entailed.

"Would it have been so terrible if I'd allowed myself to simply love, simply accept that I might be very powerful, yet still helpless to stop my need for someone half my age? My need to be loved by someone who completed me in every way? Throw in that this particular someone is also quite extraordinary in her own, Pulitzer Prize-winning way? One of the nicest and most genuine people in American journalism? Would it have been so bad to make the covers of the gossip rags for being in love? What did I care? *Why* did I care?"

"I can't answer that, Neve."

She wanted to hit her head against the bulkhead. She wanted to push the plane to fly faster. Her mind was spinning from worry, resignation, and from fear for Audrey's life and for her own sanity if something were to happen.

God, let her live, let her live and be with whomever she wants to be with, just let her live. Baruch atah Adonai... The silent prayer never left her lips, but in her mind, it was on repeat.

―――――

By the time Neve landed in Frankfurt, Elinor and Barnaby had compiled the information and cleared her access to Landstuhl Regional Medical Center, where Audrey had been evacuated.

The ride to Ramstein Air Base and its adjacent hospital facility at Wilson Barracks took another agonizing hour and a half that Neve spent in constant worry. Once she finally reached her destination, Neve simply ran.

Four-inch heels be damned, Neve rushed through the long, quiet corridors, panic pushing her to go faster, to disregard all the incredulous looks thrown her way by medical personnel and patients alike. Distantly, she thought she had never run as much as she did from and for Audrey, and certainly not in high heels. The things that woman made her do.

The nurse on duty took one look at her and stuttered to a faltering explanation that Ms. Avens had indeed been brought in earlier, but they were not allowed to release any information until next of kin was notified.

Rocked to her core, Neve stumbled and barely managed to brace herself against the wall to avoid falling. This could not be happening. Audrey had been alive not more than 30 minutes ago, according to Elinor's message and the information Juno was sharing from the State Department. Yet, the nurse was telling her they were still trying to notify the next of kin? Since they'd dispensed information to Elinor before without hesitation, this could only mean one thing. Her Audrey was dead. Her purse fell out of her limp hand, and she leaned heavily against the wall, eyes closed, tears running down her cheeks in a constant stream.

I love you and so nothing can touch you, Neve. And if you love me, it makes me immortal. The universe will move and make space for us, for this love, believe me.

The words came back to her then. The romantic, fanciful words that Audrey had whispered to her in London. She remembered the green eyes, so alive, so vibrant, filling with tears as she spoke them. Where the hell was this universe now? Where was that immortality? Where was that space for their love?

Her prayers had been in vain. Just like in her childhood, when she'd prayed for her father not to scream at her again. Just like she'd begged that her mother would return to her. God never heard her, anyway. And why was she focusing on such absurd thoughts when her mind was crying with despair?

"If I didn't already know that you loved her, this would be all the confirmation I'd need." Freja's voice jolted her out of her stupor. As Neve turned to her, Freja went on.

"She's alive. The nurse was right, they do need to notify her mother. Neither you nor I are her registered next-of-kin or have medical power-of-attorney, if that's what that piece of paper is actually called. She'll require significant life-saving procedures, and she's a registered donor. Even though she doesn't have a DNR provision, they still need to bring her mother on board with everything. They've proceeded with the urgent measures anyway, both in Bagram, where they stabilized her after extracting her from Pakistan, and here, so last I heard, she is critical, but she's here and they're helping her."

"And how do you know any of this?" The relief was making Neve lightheaded.

"Colonel Martin from European Central Command is a fan of mine. He's not as discreet as the hospital staff here." Freja smirked and turned to leave, Neve's hand on her forearm jerking her back and stopping her movements.

"What is being done? Tell me!" Neve couldn't keep the impatience from her voice. Now that she knew Audrey was alive, she needed details, needed more information.

"Now who's forgetting herself?" Freja's laughter was bitter. "Now you need me? You fucking ruined me, and now you want answers from me?"

"You ruined yourself, Freja." Her tone resolute, Neve stood her ground.

A second, a heartbeat, then two, and Freja's shoulders drooped. Shaking off Neve's hand, she crossed her arms in front of her chest, leaning slightly against the wall. Her long bangs shielded her eyes, but Neve could tell most of the fight had been drained out of her by that one statement.

"Yeah, I figured as much. I didn't quite understand the situation with the comings and goings at Gannon McMillan, and Alisson was so sure you were toast. I guess I believed her and Laurner Studios a bit too much. Or wanted to, since I really needed you out of the picture, both on a personal and a professional basis. I learned a lesson. I hated you just a bit too much to open my eyes and see what was happening."

"Hated me? We'd barely spoken before that dinner at Per Se." Neve was mystified.

"Oh, I hated you for a very long time. You had something I wanted above all. Audrey loved you. I wanted all that love for myself."

Neve knew her poker face was failing her, but she was past caring. Everything made sense now. And Audrey hadn't lied. Just one more thing Neve had to beg forgiveness for. *God, please allow her that much.*

She must have made a noise, inhaled too sharply perhaps, because Freja blew at her bangs and gave her a poisonous glare.

"Don't look at me like that. She didn't need to tell me anything. I saw how she couldn't avert her eyes. How you looked at her. That week in London, I could have fallen on stage and Audrey wouldn't have broken her gaze away from you. What confirmation did I need? You might be better at hiding your feelings—after all, you did send her away—but I saw myself in you. I know that look, that emotion. I wanted her just as much as you did. I'm not stupid, so I recognized it right away."

As Neve was still reeling from the revelations Freja was throwing her way, the Norwegian kept landing punches.

"You thought you were fooling people? You weren't. You

didn't fool me for one second. You're the fool here, Blackthorne! You let her go, and she's mine now. And I don't want you here. I told you how she is, and that's all the thanks you'll get."

At Neve's questioning head tilt, Freja tsked.

"People talk. But I don't care that you organized this whole thing, that you pushed Juno Buchanan and the US State Department and whomever else. You think because you were laying down all those millions of dollars to ransom Audrey and the rest of those poor boys she was with, you suddenly can buy your way in here? The insurance company rescued her after the government stepped aside. I spoke with their CEO, also a fan of my body of work, so to speak..." Freja patted her cleavage with an exaggerated gesture.

"In the end, Audrey didn't need you. Nobody needed you. And I sure as hell don't need you here. As soon as her mother arrives, I'm telling her to throw you out. She has no warm feelings towards you, anyway. So you better leave while you still have some of your dignity intact."

Giving her one last hateful look, Freja walked away, and Neve watched the provocative gait of long legs as they moved down the corridor and disappeared through a doorway. Well, now she knew Audrey had never betrayed her, and that her judgment of Freja as an immature airhead might have been slightly premature.

But none of it really mattered, because she also knew that Audrey was alive, and while her condition was critical, she was getting help. That was enough for now.

Furthermore, nobody told Neve Blackthorne what to do. She sat down in front of the duty station and prepared to wait for Audrey's mother. She wasn't leaving this corridor, this hospital, this country, until she saw Audrey for herself. She'd move mountains if need be.

Well, she'd move more of those damn mountains, since she'd already hurdled some insurmountable obstacles to get

Audrey and herself here. What were a few more? Nothing, when you considered that Neve Blackthorne was an unstoppable force, and so far in her fifty years, she'd only encountered only one immovable object, her own heart that loved Audrey Avens.

And so she tipped her head back and closed her eyes. She was ready to beg Kate Avens, bribe the nurses and doctors, and get anyone within the US government involved to ensure she had access to Audrey. And so she sat in the long, empty hallway at Landstuhl Regional Medical Center in Germany and waited.

14

NEVE'S CITY OF BAYS

"This has been a journey, Doctor."

"Is that what you call it?" Helena Moore raised her mug and gestured with it between them.

"I have no idea what you call any of this, since you weren't really treating—"

"Oh, I was treating you, Neve. Maybe not from day one, because no matter what I say regarding your shock and awe strategy being ineffective, it kind of was." Dr. Moore's smile invited a grin from Neve.

"You waltzed in here in those amazing shoes and ordered me to heal you as if you had a common cold. And when I sat there stupefied, you actually tapped your foot impatiently. I have to say, that testicular fortitude of yours isn't legendary for nothing. Or should it be ovarian fortitude?"

Neve sighed and looked back at their rocky beginnings, at their verbal sparring, at their—at times—open hostility. And then she looked at how, for these past three years, she had been propped up by this woman, who'd unobtrusively stood by her.

"You must have thought I was pathetic..."

"I thought you needed help. And I was very happy that, if for all the wrong reasons, you ended up in my office. And while I'm sorry that you've gone through so much, it is gratifying that you're here and that both Lane and I are able to offer that help. And that you're willingly accepting it."

"I don't think there is any particular willingness about any of this, Doc, no offense. But the past three years have been rather revealing in surprising ways. I am not alone, it seems."

When she did not elaborate, Dr. Moore simply allowed her to gather her thoughts.

"When I first came to you, if you'd have asked me, I would have told you I had no friends. Now, it seems that I do."

"It seems?" Dr. Moore's expression was amused.

"There's a meme, Harlan showed it to me. Something about how some people are simply adopted by others, and they're friends now and there's nothing to be done about that. I think this is what happened with my life. Gustavo, and by extension Benedict, Elinor, Morag..."

"I may need some time to process the fact that The Wicked Queen of Tinseltown is familiar with the concept of memes." The therapist took a long sip from the steaming coffee and offered her a bland smile. "I'd say that those people were always your friends, but you were too stubborn to let them in. But we both know that's who you are. Stubborn to a fault."

"I heard that's part of my dubious charm..."

"Nothing dubious about your charm, Neve. Moreover, you know it. That's one thing about you. You are insecure about a plethora of things, but not this. You know you are fascinating and interesting, and that people clamor for your attention, not just because of what you can give them, but also because of who you are. The Ice Queen with a timeless allure and appeal in spades. But I do agree with you, when all the smoke and mirrors of you being in my office were gone, I knew you were feeling very much alone."

Neve had so many dismissive words ready to spill from the tip of her tongue. Not so much to the compliments. Those were due her. But the overall sentiment just sounded like too much. Still, Dr. Moore just kept looking at her with those patient, kind eyes, and she relented.

"Thank you, Helena."

As the first name left her lips, Dr. Moore stilled and after a second simply inclined her head towards Neve. No, she wasn't making a big deal about this. And neither would Neve. She had finally let the esteemed doctor in, all the way in.

"Now tell me, this journey you've mentioned..."

Neve reclined her head, resting it on the armchair's high back, the ceiling smooth and overrun with sunlight too bright for her eyes. How apt, she thought before speaking.

"Icarus. Sun. One of our very first sessions, you mentioned the myth of Icarus and how I burned Audrey's wings."

In the eerie quiet of the office, the waves from the outside kept time better than a metronome.

"You weren't wrong about many things in those three years, but you were mistaken about this one. She *is* the sun. She *was* the sun all along, and I was, and still am, the one who gets her wings burned when I get close to her. You had it all wrong. I had it all wrong. Moth to the flame. I can't live with her, and I cannot live without her. So simple, so ignorant, so goddamn foolish. I am Icarus, Helena, I am."

When her interlocutor said nothing, Neve raised her head. The gaze was still compassionate, understanding.

"The sun simply did what it was supposed to do, Neve. Icarus was reckless and paid the price for his own actions. There's no comparison here."

"Oh, there very much is. Don't go backing out of your own metaphors now, Moore. She might have burned me all along, with me being older, meaner, so much more focused on my work. She would have dumped me one day anyway—"

Her own voice was rising, and she desperately scrambled to control the cadence. But it was Dr. Moore who interrupted her in a lower tonality—obviously sensing her distress and bringing everything down a notch—both decreasing the volume and returning some reason to the conversation.

"Hypotheticals, Neve? Please. Boring. Stop the pity party. Miranda Priestly wouldn't be having one."

"You're on your Ice Queen horse again…"

"I don't think there's a grander dame in all of Ice Queendom than Madam Priestly. But in your stubbornness, your arrogance, and your veneer of untouchability, I think you have every chance to be up there in that Parthenon of cold, detached, remarkably obtuse characters."

"Well, I guess I can just call it a day then, having reached such a benchmark."

———

In the end, it was Gustavo who was the key to the resolution of Neve's conundrum.

After sitting and waiting in the hospital's hallway for hours while Freja barred her access to Audrey, and the hospital staff staying far away from the two feuding women, he swept in, harried and distraught, with Audrey's mother on his arm. Neve had actually never met Kate Avens, but the resemblance between mother and daughter was uncanny. Her heart squeezed painfully in her chest.

So this was what Audrey would look like in 30 years? Same wide, honest, green eyes, same generous lips, and a slight graying at the temples that only added character to the flowing mahogany mane.

As Neve sprung to her feet and Freja miraculously appeared in the hallway as if to ensure that Audrey's mother served as an arbiter in this conflict of theirs, Kate just waved her hand at them.

"I want to see my daughter, and I don't want to hear from either of you. Gustavo, somebody, find a doctor or anyone who can tell me what has been done, what needs to be done, and what will be done!"

As the older Avens stormed past them, both Neve and Freja eyed each other with malice and stepped aside.

Some undetermined amount of time later, when Neve's phone battery died and she was simply reclining her head against the cold wall of the hallway, she felt a presence at her side. Thinking it must be Gustavo, her lips unwittingly curled into a mirthless smile, and the words left her mouth without her opening her tired eyes.

"God, Gustavo, I hope you're here to tell me I dreamt the whole thing. That it's yesterday, that I'm in LA, you're in Paris with Benedict, and the woman is safe on some godforsaken military base in Afghanistan, writing her beautiful pieces, trying to save the world. And then you need to tell me what I have to do to make sure she stays safe to continue to pen her articles, and I go and do it and bring her home. I don't even care who she lives happily ever after with, as long as she lives. Tell me? Please?"

"She lives. Barely. The doctors here are competent and have assured me of that much." At a low female voice, Neve's eyes opened quickly, only to be faced with Kate Avens' steady, thoughtful gaze.

"As for what you can do? I want you to bring her back to the US. Now. They tell me that normally patients recover here until they can walk out, and their rehab takes place in the States. Audrey is in an induced coma now. With her not being a neuro patient, transfer is not discouraged. Considering there's no hazard involved in her flying, I would like her home. Or at least on American soil. I think you agree with me on that…"

The weighty pause stretched for what seemed like hours before Neve nodded.

Kate leaned against the wall next to Neve and let out a tired sigh. "I spoke to the boys who were held with her. You know, the soldiers, so young... How are they all so young? From what I understand, she has been out since the ambush happened. Doctors said initially it was the impact of the injury that made her lose consciousness, then perhaps the blood loss. Maybe that's for the best, and she is spared memories of their 24 hours in captivity."

Kate closed her eyes, and Neve could see the shudder running through her. She stood up and extended her hand, then dropped it, not knowing how to comfort. Before she could decide, Kate spoke again.

"It doesn't matter... It's over now. But what does matter is this: the whole medevac process is complex. Some legalese that I'm simply too tired to comprehend. The insurance, the costs, the transportation. I don't understand any of it. I know Times must have set up a lot of measures for her safety and security before she left, but the red tape it's all encompassed in at the moment is... Not something I can deal with. Not that I'd know how. But I have some inkling of what you are capable of. I know who you are, and I know what you've already done for Audrey. All the work to get people to cooperate. And all that money. I have no idea how I could ever repay you. While Freja is throwing her territorial tantrums, I want you to bring Audrey home. Can you do that?"

"Yes." Neve's voice was firm, and her eyes held Kate's gaze. "May I see her? Have they completed the surgical procedures? What has been done for her?"

Kate's eyes flashed with something Neve didn't have the energy to decipher. If it was hatred, if it was disgust, she would bear it. Her desire to see Audrey was too great to give up now.

"You may see her, as long as you're not wearing anything flammable, because I think Freja's eyes will be shooting flames." Kate smirked, then her face returned to its previous stony expression. "When Gustavo hired Audrey, I thought she'd found her place. He was a great boss, and she was certainly learning a lot. But amongst all that, she was just so full of things to say about you. Never anything good at the beginning. I always thought there was more to the initial vitriol Audrey would spew about you. It was just too much, and despite it being thoroughly unpleasant, it was still the only thing she wanted to talk about. You. Neve this, Neve that. Absolutely appalling things."

Neve was no blushing girl, and she would never apologize for her exigence of excellence. Still, faced with the open judgment in Kate's eyes, she averted her own.

"Gradually, the appalling things turned into interesting things, and when the stories Audrey would tell me became amazing and beautiful and educational and fascinating, the transformation was complete. She was such a changed person, learning, growing, as a woman, as a professional. I guess I should've seen it. She was still all about you, but the tone was decidedly different."

Neve's hands trembled, and she regretted not having pockets to hide her reaction to Kate's words. She knew what was coming and had no wish to hear it. Did she really need reminders about her own perfidy? About how callously she had treated Audrey, even when she was deeply in love with her? *Selfish, selfish.* Trying to save herself and only damaging both of them further.

"Then, suddenly, she stopped talking about you. Just stopped. So abruptly, as if you had never existed, and the grief in her eyes was so deep, so heartbreakingly plain for all to see. I had my suspicions then, but Audrey waved me off, and I let her go. To Paris and to wherever her reporting took her. Then to Freja and to this nonsensical engagement after being together for such a short time."

Kate paused for a second and Neve thought she'd glance over her shoulder, but she just pursed her lips, resolution evident on her face, and went on, "I did not like it. I still don't.

Freja has been nothing short of wonderful to Audrey, and her love for my daughter is so apparent, and yet, Audrey never talks about her. Not even when she accepted that completely over-the-top proposal. She still watches every Gannon production and wears the Chanel that she'd gotten used to wearing while walking those hallowed hallways, I imagine, and then rebels by wearing skinny black jeans and beanies, only to go back to slim fitting skirts and blazers. Your employees are well known for their fashion-forward style."

Neve felt like a deer in the headlights, overwhelmed by the information, by the emotion in this older version of Audrey's eyes.

"And the first person I see in the hospital, sitting here guarding the door to my daughter's room, is you. Sure, Freja's there and so is Gustavo. But their presence is easily explained, her fiancée, her friend. You? Why are you here? Why was it your assistant who found me? Why was it the indubitably formidable Barnaby who got me into a limo and on a private plane to Germany? And it's been hours and hours, yet you're still here, begging to see my Audrey? The woman who owns a world of her own, sitting in a plastic chair, with dark circles under tired eyes. Eyes that dare me to hate you. I wish I could because I have a pretty good idea what my wayward, misguided daughter kept running from. But why are *you* here?"

"Because I did this." One had only so much strength, and Neve's had run its course. She could no longer hold the steady gaze of the mother of the woman she loved and had ruined.

"I did this. She left Paris because we ended our... association." Her voice stumbled at the word, so foreign, so uncomfortable. *Association*? What they shared was so much more. It was everything, yet she couldn't give it any other name.

"I sent her to Europe, to Elinor, to save myself from her. To end what neither of us had the strength to end, the madness, the insanity. My reasons were excuses, really, to stave off my own insecurities and issues. So I sent her away, but she didn't *stay* away, and so I made her leave again. And here we are. I did this. I am responsible."

"A guilty conscience is keeping the Wicked Queen of Tinseltown awake for probably 48 hours straight, in crumpled clothes, beseeching a stranger to see a former lover?" Kate's voice was scornful.

And Neve could dissemble no more. Her chickens were finally coming home to roost. Looking into the exact same shade of the adored green eyes, Neve Blackthorne simply put her guard down and came clean.

"I am here for her."

Before Kate spoke, Neve raised her hands and belatedly realized how the gesture looked pleading.

"And in light of everything, in light of how much pain I already caused her, Kate, she can't know about any of what has transpired. My involvement is inconsequential. It doesn't matter at all. Please, don't put another burden on her shoulders. She owes me nothing and I owe her everything. I didn't do all that much."

The older Avens' stare did not change or turn away in disgust. She tsked and shook her head, then tsked again, and it was so thoroughly reminiscent of her daughter that Neve's heart broke all over the brightly lit corridor in the middle of nowhere in Germany, and tears stung her eyes.

"I don't have the energy to deal with any of this right now. Honestly, how did two smart women make such a mess of something not too terribly complicated? Fools. Both of you. Just…" Kate seemed to search for words, then simply gave up. "Just follow me."

The first thing Neve noticed in the wide, white room were the complicated machines that beeped and breathed and did things that she did not understand but knew were nonetheless essential for the life and well-being of the person lying in the middle of all the cacophony.

Freja had all but climbed in bed on the other side of Audrey, holding on to the pale, still arm and periodically kissing the limp fingertips. Kate entered right on Neve's heels and seemed to ignore her future daughter-in-law, simply pushing Neve towards the bed.

Her vision narrowed, encompassing one thing only. The battered and bruised body lying motionless in front of her. The rest of the room—the machines, Freja, Kate—all melted away, and her legs somehow took her closer, until she was standing directly above Audrey, who was covered in nicks and scrapes and bruises turning purple.

The face was peaceful in its stillness. Neve couldn't see the full extent of the injuries under the covers except for the bandaged chest and the shoulder nearest to her. Her hands reached out of their own volition, and she traced the edges of the gauze carefully, not disturbing the cloth nor touching the skin, translucent in its fragility.

She had no idea how long she stood there, just her fingertips caressing the dressing, when she heard Freja's disgruntled, pointed cough. Neve raised her eyes to meet her angry, possessive stare. Right, well, that told her. No matter what Audrey's mother thought, whether she approved or not, Audrey was engaged, and it was time to return to that reality.

Plus, Kate had asked for Neve's help, and that needed her direct attention, anyway. She had to move, to leave this bedside, while her legs still could, while her emotions were still reeling in shock, while she still functioned.

She bent her head, and damn Freja and everyone else who might have any objections, but she gently touched her lips to the bandaged shoulder as if kissing it might heal Audrey, yet that absolutely childish conviction did not allow her to leave without this silly gesture. Love did silly things to you, after all.

Love also made you do amazing things, Neve marveled as she marshaled all the considerable logistical forces available to her, involving medical professionals on both sides of the Atlantic to determine the best possible avenue for Audrey's further treatment and recuperation. Throwing money at things always helped, but throwing your personal attention and effort at a problem made everything go smoother and speedier. If she did all this to help as much as to forget herself and the guilt, nobody needed to know.

Yet all her efforts were rewarded when, two days later, Audrey was securely transported via private plane to the New York Hospital for Special Surgery, where the best thoracic surgeons the State of New York could provide operated on her again. If the hospital was located on 70th Street on the Upper East Side, well, Neve didn't gloat. The situation was fraught as it was, and she didn't need to antagonize Freja too much by letting the horrid woman know that Neve's penthouse in Manhattan was just a block away.

Still, she offered Kate that she could stay there. It was spacious enough, and Neve was barely ever home, to begin with. When they'd discussed this on the plane, sitting by Audrey's sleeping form, Neve could see Kate consider it and then reluctantly refuse.

Freja was making her own way to New York, and she was bound to raise hell about it. Neve could tell that preserving the peace was starting to wear on Audrey's mother, so she chose not to press the issue. Especially when she had another favor to ask from the senior Avens.

A favor Kate granted with raised eyebrows and a slightly agape mouth. Yes, Neve thought, she surprised herself too. Wanting to spend nights by Audrey's bedside, simply watching her sleep, was very much out of character for her.

Having received the blessing she needed, Neve walked the block to the hospital every night and spent several hours reading to Audrey. Hour after hour, book after book, coffee mug after coffee mug. Neve still had some standards left, refusing to drink the hospital swill, and the coffee shop across the street became quite familiar during her nightly vigils.

She wasn't aware whether Kate had spread the word that she was not to be disturbed, or perhaps Neve's notoriety extended itself to the East Coast as well, but the nurses, the on-call doctors, and the other personnel had never once bothered her in the ten days she'd been there from midnight until dawn.

Freja mostly visited during daytime hours, having finally arrived in New York with her entire prerequisite entourage, and so Neve had the nights all to herself.

She sat in the dark and in the quiet, holding the still bandaged but already healing hand of one Audrey Avens, who'd received the New York Defense of Liberty Medal for her heroism under fire in Afghanistan.

Neve had had no influence on Audrey receiving the medal, though she was sure Elinor—who was recovering but still somewhat hobbling—may have raised some ruckus in Albany for that recognition to find the deserving reporter. There would be a ceremony, the medal would be pinned to Audrey's chest, and people would applaud. It would be crowded, judging by the wall full of get-well cards and the constant stream of flowers being sent from all over the world.

But Neve would not be there, would not wince at the loud cheers nor roll her eyes at politicians giving vacuous speeches and trying to bask in the light of Audrey's achievements. In Audrey's light. Neve was content to sit here and read, with the hospital being a perfect backdrop, never quite silent, reminding her of a sleeping bees' nest, the buzz of it dulled by slumber but still there.

Sometime during the second week after surgery, Audrey was awoken from the medically induced coma. Kate called Neve herself to relay the good news. She even extended the invitation for Neve to finally make her appearance during daytime hours, since Audrey was now fully conscious. But Neve dared not come during the light. The guilt suffocated her.

It was a horrible thing to know that Audrey had gone to such awful lengths to go to Afghanistan, of all the unsafe places in the world, only with one true purpose - to escape her yo-yo relationship with Neve. The thought was so distressing to Neve, she couldn't forgive herself. How many things would she not be able to do when it came to Audrey? Forgive herself, let go, move on... So much she seemed incapable of these days.

Sitting on a decidedly uncomfortable hospital chair, sipping a marginally better coffee, Pride and Prejudice in her lap, fingers holding the page where she'd stopped her reading, Neve couldn't help but study the motionless, adored profile and wonder about all the damage she'd done to this woman. She was so innocent still, despite all the depravity the world and Neve had subjected her to.

Putting the book down, her eyes feasted on Audrey's now somewhat longish and disarrayed locks. She still couldn't decide if she liked the hair longer or shorter. The sun in Afghanistan had bleached it somewhat, and the tips were burnished gold in contrast to the vivid mahogany. She couldn't touch Audrey, she could do nothing but hold her hand gently. Anything else felt invasive, and she knew she had no right to even be here.

It was like a curse and a benediction at the same time,

because she always found her salvation in this silken skin, her peace but also her anguish, one always coming on the heels of the other. She'd never been able to just touch Audrey. It had always turned into more and they'd inevitably ended up entwined in each other, fingers and mouths fitting like pieces of a puzzle. Simply perfect.

So all Neve could do now was allow her eyes to trace the god-awful hospital gown that was so oversized, it looked like it just swallowed the still sickly thin and frail Audrey whole. Even as she shook her head over the ghastly attire, Neve continued to gently caress the bony knuckles of the long-fingered hand. In moments like this, her chest felt so full it physically hurt.

The duality of her own situation did not escape her. Doomed if she did and doomed if she didn't. Damned either way. The dreaded catch-22. She had wanted Audrey but was so scared that Audrey would leave her one day, frightened by all the things Neve held hidden. So she'd pushed Audrey away, only to realize what a fool she had been.

God, how could a heart hold this much love? This much emotion? Where did it all fit?

She could viscerally feel her body overflowing with tenderness. The fact that her eyes were filled with tears seemed just a natural reaction to being overcome with this feeling.

She loved so much, and she had no right to be here, to touch or to be crying over Audrey. No right at all. Freja made sure that the ring that normally hung around the graceful neck was now adorning the left hand ring finger. Neve had heard one of the nurses complain about it, but apparently the model made quite a fuss with the hospital staff, and some strings had been pulled. Freja was possessive to a fault.

Well, Neve couldn't blame her. If Audrey was hers, these days she'd probably take out a billboard on 5th Avenue to announce it.

My, my, how the tables had turned. And it had taken

Audrey almost dying for Neve to realize that her fear, her anxiety, her issues were nothing really in comparison to the all-encompassing cataclysm of not having this woman simply exist somewhere in the world. So she was Freja's. So she was getting married. As long as she lived, then perhaps that would be enough.

In the light of the small lamp, shadows played over their joined hands, following the comings and goings of the people in the hallway. Light followed by the dark, then it was gone, the light resuming its reign. Neve lowered her forehead to the bed and tried to relax the aching muscles of the neck twisted in an uncomfortable position, and recalled a conversation she'd had with Dr. Moore on her flight back.

"When is that moment when the pain becomes unbearable and the fear of change less terrifying as a result? When do you stop finding solace in your pain, in your fears, and break through?" Neve heard her own voice as if in a dream.

"When you lose what matters most. Then both pain and fear are all-encompassing, because there's nothing else left. In your childhood, you had your dream to leave, to make something of yourself, to be free. And you've never lost that. It made the pain and fear worth it. And therefore you could stand both. Now? You lost her who matters most, first almost to death and then certainly to another woman. And because it is all gone, the pain is unbearable and the fear is insignificant. No more solace in either. And there's nothing you can do. Nothing but move on."

That conversation had done nothing to dispel her despair. And she hadn't yet been ready to admit to her therapist that there was no moving on. Nothing to move on to. And she didn't have any desire to do so anyway.

Now that she'd opened herself to therapy, she was sure they'd get to this subject eventually. Now that her wounds were pouring out all the trauma and spreading all the blood of her childhood all over Lane Brady's pristine ivory carpets, Neve knew it was only a matter of time. But for now, she was hiding this particular snake at her chest, letting it silently tear at her flesh. Just a little longer.

And she allowed herself the guilty pleasures of these nights, of these clandestine visits to Audrey's bedside, where she indulged in watching her beloved's long lashes flutter in her medicated sleep, and in knowing that she wouldn't wake up and catch Neve laying her head on the edge of the pillow simply to be able to inhale the familiar scent that was now slightly diluted by the inescapable hospital smells.

Neve knew that her visitations would soon come to an end since Audrey was making good progress, and they were only keeping her medicated at night due to her trouble sleeping. In a week or two, she would be transferred to an outpatient facility, and then the plan was for her to move in with Freja, thus cutting the current thread of connection with Neve–a thread that Audrey was completely unaware of.

Gustavo had returned to New York from his extended European vacation the day before, and while they enjoyed a rather pleasant brunch, he shared with her that, when he'd visited Audrey earlier that morning, she'd told him of a curious recurring dream she kept having due to the medication she was receiving–or so she believed.

"She said she keeps seeing you in her dreams, that you come to her every night and read her books, or tell her about something amusing that's happening at Gannon, or about Harlan."

Neve took a long sip of her coffee, keeping her eyes steady on her friend.

Gustavo's lips twitched before he continued. "And you know

what I find most amusing—and she laughed at that too—is that, in those dreams, you read her Jane Austen. I still remember that scathing speech you gave about how, despite their importance to romantic literature, you wouldn't be caught dead picking up any of those books. I think it was that little factoid that convinced Audrey that these nightly visions were indeed just dreams. After all, here you are, very much alive, and obviously you wouldn't have touched the esteemed author's creations."

He took a cigar out of his breast pocket, running the length of it through his manicured fingers. At Neve's disgusted look, he smiled.

"I'm quitting. I'm making Benedict quit too. And we're trying to qualify for the marathon next year. This thing between us... Neve, it's amazing and fragile. *Delicate.* You know, I went to see DeVor's exhibition—now that she's finally shown herself and her art in such an uncompromising way. And that was the one word I could think of while wandering the Archibald-Avant Gallery... How *delicate* love is. Because that whole exhibit is love. Pure, fragile, delicate love. And how we should cherish it. If we are ever lucky enough to find it."

Gustavo gave Neve a pointed look, but did not pursue the subject further.

They sat in silence, her turning her tall latte glass in her chilled fingers, and him smiling serenely at their surroundings, averting his eyes, pretending not to notice the tears in hers. And she, in turn, pretended that her stomach didn't tighten with both trepidation and some kind of twisted pleasure that Audrey sensed her, that despite the sleeping aides, despite everything that continued to separate them, Audrey could feel her presence.

Wasn't that the purpose of her late nights? How was Neve going to give this up?

Before telling her goodbye, her friend held her tight for just a second too long.

"Audrey is making progress in leaps and bounds, her chest wound is healing nicely and they'll soon be able to treat her shoulder outside the hospital for the foreseeable future. Jane Austen is running out of time, Neve."

———

But as Neve made the now-familiar trek down 70th Street and onto the elevator to the 5th floor of the hospital, she did not expect that one of her last nights of allowing herself to be in the sleeping Audrey's company would be cruelly yanked away from her.

The room wasn't dark, and through the slightly ajar door, she could see that Audrey was awake and struggling valiantly not to fall asleep while Freja was talking a mile a minute, detailing some sort of plan.

"... and then I had to throw away those ugly flowers. Man, I have no idea what she was thinking! Babe, your mother is driving me crazy with the muted colors and the ivory and all that. I won't be able to take much more of her these next three months until the wedding. Can't she understand I want fuchsia and purple? Oh, oh, oh, and you have to see the dresses I got Lhuillier to send us. Next week, when you're out of here, we can try them all. Those people, I always forget the brand, the one you really love, sent some gowns as well, but I don't like the cut, it's just too simple, and I want to shine, like a princess at the ball..."

And just like that, it was over. Not with a bang, but with a whimper. Neve took one step away from the door, then another, and then another. She had no idea how she made it to the end of the corridor. Some kind of autopilot must have activated inside her.

Just as she stopped by the elevator, observing in surprise her own hand convulsively pressing the button again and again, a nurse ran up to her.

"Ma'am, we tried to warn you. My colleagues asked me to keep watch for your arrival, but I had an emergency and didn't see you come in. The fiancée has been here all evening, and we keep telling her that Audrey needs her rest. It must be taking her some superhuman effort to stay awake at this point with all the meds, but that loudmouth just doesn't get it."

The high-pitched tone would normally make Neve flinch, but the pronounced Brooklyn accent soothed her nerves and made her give the nurse a tight-lipped smile. Life had been simpler when she'd lived here.

Belatedly, she looked down to see her own hand holding the coffee tray with the usual four to-go-cups trembling. Dammit, she'd forgotten she'd brought coffee for the nurses on duty, and almost spilled the whole damn thing all over the scrubbed floors.

"I'm sorry, here. I almost left with your coffee." The nurse, Shanna—Neve had to search for a name for a moment—took the tray, extricated a cup, then tried to pass the rest back to her. Neve stopped her with a jerky shake of her head, the hair obscuring her vision for a second. Or were those tears?

"Thank you, Shanna. It's quite alright. I remembered that I have somewhere else to be." Trying to preserve her dignity at all cost, Neve gave the nurse a nod and entered the waiting elevator, head held high. She did need to be somewhere else, anywhere, as long as it meant she was away from Audrey. A very much engaged-to-be-married Audrey.

It must have shown on her face, all the anguish she was desperate to hide because the last thing she saw before the elevator doors closed was the look of utter pity on Shanna's face. Great, people pitied her now. How pathetic was she?

Yes, she felt totally and completely pitiable as she exited the hospital into the ever-noisy and never quite dark New York night and made her way along the still busy streets. This city had once been hers and was the one she still mourned, even sitting in the glorious privacy of her own beach at sunset. Walt Whitman had it right in his exaltation of this *City of Bays*, rare smart man that he was.

And like a giant that never slept, it was watching over her now, keeping her company as she walked with no particular direction, having nowhere to be anymore. The penthouse, with its abundance of quiet and whiskey, did not appeal at all.

And so Neve continued to walk, four-inch-heels and tight pencil skirt be damned. Not a bang, but a whimper indeed. Three months. Audrey would be married in three months.

Tears pricked at her eyes, but she willed them away. Was it not supposed to be a joyous occasion? She shouldn't cry. Audrey had made her choice and was going to be happy. Was happy already, Neve corrected herself. She was with the woman she loved and who loved her and, more importantly, chose her every day, despite Freja's childish disposition and tantrums over ivory lace.

Suddenly Neve remembered something Gustavo had said to her this morning, something about choices they made and how they dictated the life they lived. Neve had scolded him again for always mangling Shakespeare, but the line had stayed with her. So had Gustavo's benevolent gaze, urging her to reconsider, to take a different path. How was Neve to tell him that her choices were all made and were all wrong? That she had thrown it all away, and it was too late.

Neve was in Audrey's past. Her destructive fear, cruelty, and selfishness could no longer touch that precious, darling heart, whose rhythms Neve had learned to distinguish like no other. She knew how it beat when Audrey slept peacefully. She knew how it soared when Audrey was in the throes of a climax at

Neve's hands, when Neve's fingers stroked her to a unique rhythm that never failed to bring her to the very brink, while the thumb teasingly flicked the clit, alternating gentle teasing touches with firm pressure. Neve's lips would be fused to the pulse point on that long, graceful neck, counting the thumps of the strong heart pounding its way to orgasm.

She knew how that pulse stumbled just before the velvet walls would start to contract and clench around her thrusting fingers. She also knew the beating of that heart when Neve would rest her own head between Audrey's breasts as she made her way up from between long lithe legs, her mouth still wet and tasting of her essence, her tongue pleasantly tingling from the effort and the pleasure of having Audrey come against it.

So not a bang, but a whimper. And Neve couldn't help but whimper quietly herself. Why couldn't she have quietly divorced Dmitriy, just as quietly as she had deposed Juno–and then loudly married Audrey? What did she care? What did she care when Audrey loved her then, loved her so much she was willing to do anything, give up anything for Neve, only to be pushed away so cruelly, so callously? God, what had she done?

Audrey was the one. Her one. Her only. And now Neve had to live with the knowledge of someone else learning the beating patterns of her beloved heart. Making it soar and quiet down.

Regret and anger were tearing her apart, and she growled aloud, scaring a street vendor who hastily retreated away from her path. She pulled a handful of twenty-dollar bills from her purse and handed them to him with a somewhat apologetic expression.

"Shouldn't walk around here at night, lady. Might be dangerous, but with that scowl, guess ya' ain't afraid."

She just gave him a bitter smile and raised her arm for a cab. She had no idea how she'd gotten to this part of Manhattan, and she belatedly realized that she'd perhaps walked the whole length of the island, her feet certainly feeling the exertion of miles in heels. It was time to go home. It was time for the rest of her life. Alone.

15

NEVE IN THE PATH OF THE HURRICANE

"You're not going to ask me 'what now', Helena?" If Dr. Moore heard the note of resignation in her voice, she didn't show it, and Neve turned away. The coffee shop was utterly empty in the early afternoon hour, and she sat there in the sun, looking at the ocean, peaceful, the waves calm yet steady, like a heartbeat.

Since Neve had started her specialized treatment with the PTSD expert, Helena changed things around for their session and liked to surprise her now. She would change up the location of their meetings, from a nice walk on the beach to a quiet, empty cafe, just like this one. Neve wondered if it was a kind of treat, and then she'd scoff at being rewarded for good behavior. Helena would only laugh.

Still, as strange as it was, this unpredictable nature of their sessions was something Neve actually looked forward to these days. And maybe that was indeed the point.

"It's been years, Neve. I know better now. The first year, it was just a complete nightmare trying to get you to say anything. I had to ask, and you'd get irritated that I even made a sound. I had this defeatist thought all the time that you'd simply come by to sit in my *presence and brood. I was wondering why you even bothered. You would say less than ten sentences to me."*

Neve felt the corners of her mouth tip up.

"Times have changed."

"You have changed. And so have I. You taught me something."

As Neve's eyebrow rose, Helena's smile grew wider.

"You know a psychologist, like a lawyer or a doctor, is not at all obligated to like their patient or client. A therapist simply must do their job. Do no harm, endeavor to make better..."

"Is this your way of telling me you hated me on the spot?"

"No, this is my way of telling you that for years, I have not allowed myself to care about my patients outside of my office walls. I'd always do my best. I'd give them all of me. And they'd either need more and come back, or get enough and get better, and I'd never see them again."

The now familiar cadence of fingers tapping on the rim of the coffee mug slowed down and Neve met the watery gray eyes.

"I was not making you better. And I was forced to watch you get progressively worse, day by day, week by week, month by month. You were not allowing me to give you anything. And I had so much to give."

"Are you drawing parallels, Doctor?" Helena simply waved away the old appellation.

"You inevitably attract people, Neve. Your blessing and your curse, I guess. And you've never ever allowed them to get close enough for you to need them. And then slowly, very slowly, a crack appeared."

"When I went to Reno."

"No, right before Paris. You stopped lying to me then. You weren't telling the truth, but you stopped lying to me, and you stopped lying to yourself. I think that was the day I knew that my agony of not being able to help you was over. After that, it was a matter of time to wait you out."

"I thought you were ridiculous. Honestly, with this version of me as some kind of romance novel Ice Queen—"

"Oh, that was neither romanticized nor ridiculous. In the years we've spent locked in our conversations, you've undergone the full Ice Queen journey. From lying, scheming, downright cruel and at times just awful, to kind and strong and utterly lovable. Despite what you yourself seem to think."

Neve scrunched her nose at the words. She'd never been uncomfortable with compliments, but she'd also never known Helena to dispense platitudes easily. She herself had delivered the good news from her trauma specialist just as they'd sat down, that she was progressing well, and this was the pat on the head she got? Mortified at her own discomfort at the praise, she decided to change the subject.

"So this is it, I'm... cured?" She meant it to come out as a joke, lighthearted and funny, but her voice betrayed her, breaking on the last word, and she tried to cover it with a cough.

Dr. Moore slowly turned the mug in her hands. "Therapy is a process, Neve. And it's not a panacea. Plus, there's one more figure on your board. And while the Pawn, the Knight and the Bishop were something that we both understood—since they were concrete people or concepts—it's the Rook that has always been a sort of enigma to me."

"You know about my childhood, about being different. I went through years of horrifying bullying for being who I was and the way I was. Tiny, skinny, stuttering, poor, hungry. I couldn't stand it—"

"Neve, you are none of those things anymore. In fact, you could buy and sell any of your detractors several times over. Are you afraid of how Harlan will take it? Armand? Your mother? Who or what are you afraid of?"

Neve remembered the loud baritone screaming obscenities into her ear at the top of his lungs as she huddled in a corner. No, in her lifetime she had been afraid only of one man and he was long dead.

"The idea of everyone in the world knowing. The idea of everyone in the world seeing... looking... judging. I can't stand it. I'm not afraid of one man. I'm afraid of all of them."

"So the Rook—the castle, the wall, the closet—stands. And we have work to do still."

To stop this particular line of conversation from continuing, Neve tried to rewind to something that had sparked her curiosity earlier.

"You said I lied to you?"

"The very first day. I asked you what you call Audrey. And you said you don't call her anything at all."

Neve felt the hairs on her arms stand. The feeling of returning to that moment in time, to that choking sensation, of being cornered, of being trapped... Yes, she had made progress through the years, but had she really achieved anything? It was time to find out.

"Ask me again. Please."

Helena shook her head indulgently, but her voice was sad when she asked.

"What do you call Audrey, Neve?"

Neve closed her eyes and murmured the truth.

"My everything."

"Mom, mom, you're missing it!" Her son's voice jerked her from her stupor over her early morning coffee. The time difference between LA and New York always gave her a weird sensation in the morning of being allowed a do-over, since it was still night in LA, and she had all the time in the world.

Except she really didn't. Harlan had been talking about the 'event of the century' for days, and she knew she was running out of time. She'd been meaning to speak to him, for once to tell the absolute truth or at least some half-palatable version of it, even took him to New York on this trip with her. No, she made a point of never lying to her son, but she still had no idea how to talk about this. About Audrey. And least of all, about today being her wedding day.

Harlan was making a valiant effort to eat his cereal while not taking his eyes off his tablet, and Neve finally succumbed and rose from her chair at the kitchen table, swallowing the last of her coffee to stand behind him.

If she'd had any illusions as to exactly what was happening right now not so very far from her corner of the Upper East Side, then seeing Audrey in a wedding dress dispelled any and all of those. Neve knew nothing. In fact, Neve thought she may never know anything else ever again because Audrey looked so beautiful.

Her gown was a startling white, no ivory for her and Freja, just as Neve had overheard Freja decree all those months ago, back at the hospital.

"Shame about the dress," she mused, and Harlan twisted around to look at her.

"The word on the street was that she would wear the Elies Saab, whatever that means."

Neve smiled at her son's attempt to appear mature and sophisticated, even as he mangled the designer's name slightly. When had he grown up on her? Where had the time gone? And where was it going now?

"It's Elie Saab, darling." She corrected Harlan gently. "And yes, ivory would have been better with her skin."

Ever the masochist when it came to Audrey, Neve had made a point of looking up the dresses that 'word on the street' had indeed ascribed to the wedding of the *Goddess of Reality TV*. So she knew in advance what either of the brides would be wearing. Freja had made sure every little speck of information leading up to the event was readily available online.

Finding Freja, the gauche and vulgar TV show that she had begun to star in right after announcing her engagement, was to stream the whole affair live. The *Wedding of the Century* would be on all day long. And Harlan was enthralled. Mercy.

Thankfully, she had a couple of meetings at the brand new Gannon Streaming offices and hoped she'd be able to escape the torture of Audrey's wedding happening just a couple of blocks away from her.

She watched in a sort of trance as Gustavo and Audrey's mother fussed with her hair and dress, despite the fact that the makeup artist had just instructed both of them not to touch anything. Audrey was standing in front of a large mirror and fiddling with the lace on the bodice that covered her injured shoulder.

"...don't smudge anything, darling." Gustavo gently swatted her hand away, but not before she'd tugged on the probably uncomfortable half-sleeve.

"The scars are fading." Audrey's voice was almost dream-like, as though she wasn't aware she was speaking, and Neve stood motionless, drinking in every word, every sight, every sound. "They weren't a big deal anyway, don't you think, mom? And do people really care how they photograph?"

The still-so-young face showed signs of self-consciousness, and Neve's heart beat painfully in her chest. Damn Freja, damn her to hell and back.

And speaking of Freja and her manipulative endeavors, on the screen a familiar figure banged on the door. Photographer Robert O'Donovan made a grand entrance, the second camera clearly positioned strategically to capture his arrival. This was a live event, Neve thought, but it was also somewhat scripted. Nobody in the room showed any sign of being surprised at the sudden arrival. Nobody except Audrey.

"Audrey! Congratulations. Lovely to see you and on such an occasion. Sorry, it took me a bit longer than anticipated. Freja was being a diva. Which is to say, your bride-to-be was being her usual charming, supermodel self about how I photograph her."

His laughter boomed, and Audrey flinched and gaped at him, clearly not comprehending what was happening. Neve got a strange premonition.

Shortly after Audrey had gotten out of the hospital, Neve had extended an olive branch. Freja accepted with as much graciousness as she could, which was to say practically none. Neve gritted her teeth and bore it. If not for her own sake, then for Audrey's. Letting go was like flaying herself, but it had to be done, and if honoring her promise to not ruin Freja was the last thing Audrey ever asked of her, then so be it.

After Freja and she had buried the hatchet as it were, Neve had offered a rather extravagant wedding present. The one and only Robert O'Donovan, a photographer who was more in demand than Annie Leibovitz, and who was more famous and more revered than Peter Lindbergh, was to be that gift. He shot royalty and had a years-long waiting list for his services. Neve had arranged for him to suddenly be very much available for Freja and Audrey on their special day.

She knew that Freja and her people had turned the wedding into a publicity fest, with professional photographers and paparazzi swarming the event. She also knew that they were going to sell the pictures to the highest bidder and make a huge splash on the cover of something or another.

Neve remembered Audrey speaking of O'Donovan in such reverent terms all those years ago when he'd worked on a Gannon project, and so picking up the phone and asking for a favor from an old friend had been a no-brainer. She could give Audrey next to nothing at this point. But she could give her this. And so she had.

However, judging by Audrey's face, either she had made a terrible mistake, or Audrey had no idea what was happening.

. . .

"Mom?" Harlan's voice and his astute look made her finally surrender her high ground behind his shoulder and sit next to him at the table.

She could see her hands tremble as she poured more coffee into her dirty mug. As Harlan extended his own, smaller hand and took the now empty carafe from her, setting it aside, she did not resist. He opened his mouth and closed it again, and Neve braced for his question, but the events on the screen drew both of them back into the elaborate spectacle that was playing out for millions of people, with the stream jumping back and forth between the two dressing rooms.

In one of them Freja twirled and drank Champagne and issued orders left and right, and in the other, Audrey smiled at Robert and looked plainly uncomfortable with the attention.

Robert, ever the efficient and competent photographer, had taken charge of the situation, placing Gustavo—as the best man—and Kate into the shots, while the older Avens adjusted Audrey's sleeve and swept a stray lock of hair behind her ear.

Still, Audrey looked utterly befuddled and finally, as Robert stepped back to adjust the lighting, she voiced her confusion out loud.

"Mr. O'Donovan, I'm honored that you're shooting the wedding, truly, and I really don't want to sound rude, but what on Earth are you doing here?"

Neve knew exactly where the bewilderment was coming from. Freja had told someone that her people tried to get O'Donovan to shoot the wedding and had been turned down in a rather definitive manner. Neve's sources, chief of them Morag, were always on the money, and had also told her O'Donovan did not enjoy working with the supermodel.

"What do you mean, Audrey? Your first observation was right on the money. I'm shooting your wedding."

The 'duh' in his tone was so obvious, so funny, that Neve almost laughed out loud. But Audrey's now even more confused and slightly panicked expression stopped her mirth. Whoever was filming was a very good cameraperson. Neve made a mental note to look into their services.

The way they framed the faces, and the amount of patience they took with their subjects and their emotions, waiting to catch them in the most interesting moment, was captivating. So far, they had captured the myriad of reactions on Audrey's face, and all of them were overwhelmingly telling.

"For some reason, he thinks she should have known about something, but she didn't. Mom, did you send O'Donovan to Audrey? Is that why he had dinner at the house a month ago?" Harlan's expression was pensive.

"It's Mr. O'Donovan to you, darling. And I did not *send* him. I merely wanted Freja and Audrey to have beautiful shots from their wedding."

"Pfft." The derision in her son's voice was so pronounced, the sass so funny, Neve did allow a smile to bloom.

On screen, Gustavo seemed to sense Audrey's rising discomfort and quietly stepped in, sending Robert on his way with some elaborate arm waving and shushing. It was like pantomime theater, and Neve might have enjoyed it, if she hadn't known what would probably come next.

Finally, Robert emitted what Neve could only describe as a squeak, exclaimed, "Oh my God! No way!" and hurried out of the room. Audrey's face showed her continued bewilderment, her eyebrows squeezing together.

"Gustavo?" At this point, even Kate was giving her a concerned look, and Neve observed Audrey do a double-take in the mirror at her white gown that was way too bright for her pale skin. Still, nothing seemed wrong with it other than its pallor. Her makeup was still intact. Audrey was clearly trying to figure out what she was missing.

Meanwhile, to Neve's pronounced 'tsk', Gustavo seemed to have found the courage to speak about what was happening, and she desperately wished he'd let this one go. He didn't.

"Ugh, Audrey. Did Freja talk to you about Robert?" At her head shake, Gustavo gulped and looked like he was gathering himself for a long discussion.

"Freja accepted Robert's services as a congratulatory—and I imagine a conciliatory—gift from Gannon…"

Neve felt like she'd been struck in the solar plexus. She was expecting it, but once the words were out, she knew all hell was about to break loose. Harlan stiffened next to her, indicating that her intuition was spot on.

"Gannon?" It was like watching something happen in slow-motion, a gradual rising of a wave bubbling up, and Audrey's voice crested right with it. Her whole posture straightened. Her face was pale no more. And then the slow-motion became a fast reel, and the film snapped, the projector rolling in blank. She looked dead into the camera and then simply dismissed it, as if her earlier self-consciousness and clear trepidation didn't matter anymore. *Snapped indeed.*

Neve swallowed hard.

"I feel like I've been missing quite a lot of things. Wallowing in my own misery and self-pity, running away to Afghanistan and getting injured, and then lying in convalescence and wallowing some more like a total fool. I've definitely been passed by the events. Because nothing really happens at Gannon without—"

"Well, ahem, *her,* obviously…" Gustavo raised his eyebrows expressively, giving Audrey a wide-eyed stare full of significance, even as he'd shrunk a bit from Audrey's raised tone. But she was like a full-on hurricane now. The quiet misery in her had clearly found an outlet, and the storm in her was gaining speed and power. Neve knew that there was no stopping her now. If Audrey, who was so excruciatingly private, stopped caring about the whole world watching...

"*Her?* What the hell does *she* have to do with my wedding, Gustavo?"

"Well, really, there's no need for such language, darling..." At Audrey's glare, her mother went silent.

"Listen, Audrey..." Gustavo did give a rather forceful glare of his own to the cameraperson, but they certainly knew a million-dollar scene when they saw one and didn't stop rolling.

In Harlan's hands, the iPad shook a little.

Neve was once again struck by how much she'd been lacking decisiveness. Yes, she had thought about talking to Harlan, had even tried to do so repeatedly. They'd forged such a strong bond in the past months, spent all of their time together when Neve had been free, and she'd come very close to telling him. Both about her sexuality and Audrey.

But despite hours of therapy and her own obvious progress, something had stopped her. She often wondered if telling him would be the absolute final act of surrender, because no matter how she phrased it to Harlan, she'd have to tell the truth, a truth that was still painful and raw and so very deep.

So she'd kept her silence and it had backfired, because if the conversation on the screen continued to progress the way it seemed to, he—and a whole slew of other people, if not the entire world—would soon be introduced to all the reasons why Neve Blackthorne had done a great many things for some seemingly random reporter.

Those who knew her, be they few and far between, would

absolutely understand that nothing she had done had been out of altruism or the goodness of her heart. Certain conclusions would follow and things about her would become exceedingly obvious to them, and her closet, nay her castle—the one that had protected her throughout her adult life from the scorn and from the *othering* she had endured as a child—would crumble under public scrutiny.

The Rook next to the Queen shook.

In the meantime, Gustavo paced under Audrey's tumultuous stare, raised and lowered his hands and picked at his tie, before finally stopping in the middle of the room, seemingly having come to a decision.

"She felt like some conciliatory measures were needed, so she and Freja agreed that perhaps Robert could shoot the wedding. As a gift. And you know how Freja needs the publicity." Neve knew Gustavo well enough to understand he was making light of the situation, acting like things were totally fine and not a big deal at all. His features showed forced mirth, but one look at Audrey's high color must have told him she wasn't done, so he valiantly swallowed his nervous giggle.

"And nobody deemed it important enough to tell me? That my girlfriend is buddying up to...to... to my... screw this, Gustavo! She... she... she ruined me, and now she is offering to resurrect Freja's career after she destroyed that too?"

Despite the concern of her closet walls being blown away in front of Harlan, Neve still found it telling that months of engagement had not transformed Freja into a fiancée or a bride-to-be in Audrey's eyes. It would have been gratifying under different circumstances. Neve did not realize that she was holding her breath, but despite anger, despite outrage, Audrey was wording her outbursts somewhat carefully.

Harlan gave Neve a long look, and she wanted to cry. She was sure he could hear the tears in her voice as she spoke.

"I give her that first part, but the second?"

To her surprise, her son gently took her hand, and that warm feeling of having him firmly in her corner, no matter what, reached something inside her.

So many emotions were running through Neve. She went from being afraid that she'd be outed in front of the whole world, to elated that Audrey obviously cared very much about her privacy, to being thoroughly heartbroken by how little Audrey seemed to care about her own.

Audrey was breathing heavily. Even through the iPad, Neve could almost see the thunderclouds gathering above her head and lightning shooting out of her hands. Underneath that anger, Audrey was so visibly hurt that Neve could sympathize with why the fact that Gustavo and her mother were looking at her with such pity, such understanding, only seemed to infuriate Audrey more.

How many times during their fights had Neve wanted to just take a bite out of that slender neck, feel the pulsing of the vein right under her tongue? How many times had she actually done so? Enough to know exactly the rhythm Audrey's heart was beating out at the moment. Goosebumps erupted on her arms and a shiver ran down her spine.

Gustavo cleared his throat, pulling Neve out of her reverie.

"Audrey, *she* just wanted to extend an olive branch. Freja wanted the best photographer and she couldn't get him. *She* could. And so she did. And she didn't ruin anybody's career, either. It's complicated. Look... she... damn, she's been really good. After the whole State Department thing and then the hospital thing... She was staying away, I swear. She's in town, but she's minding her own business. Also, ahem, can we have this conversation off-camera?"

"We can't stop rolling." The voice behind the camera broke the illusion of a cozy family affair... "I'm not in charge here, obviously, but the director told me that no matter what, the cameras stay on."

"Gustavo, I... State Department thing? Hospital thing? What is going on? I can't wait for explanations. I need to know. I feel like I'm a spectator in this show that is my life, and not actually the main character." Audrey's voice was almost a whisper. "Tell me."

Harlan's hand squeezed Neve's again. Either in support or in reflex, but Neve had had enough. Obviously, Gustavo had talked himself into a corner, and he'd have to tell the truth. Neve wasn't sure she wanted to listen anymore. The hits just kept coming.

"Harlan, how about you and I get going to Gannon HQ? I have meetings, and it's time to get on with them."

He nodded absently, adjusting his sweater. Her boy was growing up.

More emotion, more tears scalded the backs of her eyes as she turned to put on her Jimmy Choos. Audrey would learn the truth, she would have anyway, but Neve could do nothing about any of it at this point. So be it, the show must go on.

She could viscerally feel the walls around her tremble. Maybe not everyone would jump to the conclusion that Neve Blackthorne did everything she had done for Audrey Avens out of sheer love, but a considerable amount of people would. And then one or two diligent reporters would tug on that thread and unravel her whole life. Was this the price she had to pay?

Without answers, Neve chose to tune out most of what was

happening on Harlan's screen, as the boy continued to be enraptured.

Through their short walk outdoors to the waiting car, she could hear the argument brewing like a storm, the spring getting twisted tighter and tighter. What would happen when either Gustavo or Kate said the wrong thing?

As the driver closed the door behind her, she also noticed that the stream solely focused on Audrey's suite now and they weren't cutting to Freja anymore, the director no doubt seeing the advantage and the ratings ballooning from the showdown happening in Audrey's dressing room right now.

"State Department thing? Hospital thing?"

Audrey's voice coming from a distance while Neve sat on the long backseat of the town car, seemed to narrow down her world. She knew that any second now, her tunnel vision would take over, just like it obviously had for Audrey, who had now zeroed in on Gustavo with the precision of a shark, as if this one little detail had become the only thing that mattered.

Still, despite her earlier decision to tune out the livestream, she couldn't help herself and peered at the screen. Gustavo seemed to understand that he'd said too much, and with a glance at Kate, who just sighed and nodded, sat down heavily.

"When you were taken, she pushed and pushed and pushed, with senators, the Secretaries of State and Defense, the Bureau, the Agency, to get you out of captivity. She asked me not to tell you, but since we've gotten to this point... She was ready to lay down the ransom money, but in the end, the insurance company came through and rescued you."

Neve winced as her actions were laid out loud in the cold light of day.

"Then, when you were injured, she was there. She got you out of Landstuhl and into the hospital here in Manhattan. She pulled a lot of strings, strings I wasn't even aware she could pull, to get you transferred. Probably got God himself involved. Astonishing, really. She did everything to make sure you were safe and got the best care. Since you're not military, the cost would have been prohibitive..."

"Mom, you're trending on Twitter! I mean along with other names, but they're speculating who the 'she' that they're all talking about is, and with Gustavo saying Gannon earlier, Twitter is in overdrive that it might be you!" Harlan's excitement was now uncontainable as he tore her attention away from the screen. His hands trembled with emotion as he held up both the iPad with the livestream and his phone with what looked like the Twitter page opened in a browser. Neve raised an eyebrow. His expression soured somewhat. "I don't have an account, mom. This is dad's. He logged in and then forgot to log out the other day..."

"The other day?" Neve tried to keep her voice measured because her anger was mostly with herself. She'd failed her son. She should have told him months ago. Instead, here he was, being sneaky and devious to get the information she should have offered him herself.

"Well, a few days?" His tone rose slightly, questioningly at the end, and Neve simply watched him squirm. "A few months? He didn't close the tab after he checked his account and I wasn't gonna keep it open. Honestly. But then Audrey's engagement happened and I just..." He dropped his chin and peeped at her for a second from beneath his messy bangs.

"I kinda, sorta might've seen you kissing Audrey? But like ages ago? I was still little back then... But I like her and she made you really happy, not even dad made you that happy. I guess I just wanted you that happy again?"

Neve swallowed around the lump in her throat, and this time when tears burned her eyelids, she let one fall. She hugged Harlan close, and he hugged back. It was awkward since he was still holding the gadgets, but she didn't care.

"I'm sorry. I... I wanted to tell you..."

"It's okay, mom." His voice sounded muffled, and Neve smiled as she let go of him and he extricated himself from her jacket. "It really is okay. Well, not really. But you know... Talking is not your strong suit."

His eyes got huge, and Neve realized that he had not meant to say what he did, and so for a second they just watched each other, both equally shocked. And then she—honest to god—let out a peal of laughter and Harlan's small shoulders relaxed as he followed her outburst with a giggle of his own.

They laughed until her sides ached, and when she tried to calm herself by giving him another hug, he nuzzled into her.

"I love you, darling. But after today, you're grounded with no electronics. Two days." Neve ruffled his hair, ready for an argument, but he just nodded.

"Fine, fine, I knew the stakes. But did you hear what I said? You're trending! I mean, you've been since Gustavo started blabbing, but look. It's thousands of tweets now. Freja's official account is running a transcript of what's being said on the stream. I mean it's obviously run by her PR people, but they're tweeting every word now, and Juno Buchanan just QRT'ed the tweet about the strings you pulled and how you got to even God himself and she said '*I AM THAT GOD*,' and now people are all over the place with what that means."

His voice rose exponentially with every single word he uttered, and Neve's stomach sank lower.

Yes, Audrey would not out her, and it was clear by the way Kate and Gustavo kept her name out of it that they wouldn't either, but Juno seemed to have zero qualms about doing just that and so much more. Paybacks were a bitch indeed. Now, perhaps not just those close to her would start asking questions about why exactly Neve Blackthorne had been so involved with this whole rescuing business.

Employing one of her techniques to distract herself from the anxiety that was starting to creep in on her, Neve tried taking in her surroundings. As the car smoothly drove through the bustling streets of Manhattan, Neve thought that, if not for her strip of ocean, she'd return to this city. Her years on Broadway had been kind to her. Much kinder than LA. New York never allowed her to feel lonely. She was at her worst when lonely, after all.

In the background, she could hear Kate's patient voice explaining, placating, clearly trying to stop the spectacle that was unfolding for the whole world to see.

"... millions of dollars?" Audrey's voice was now filled with hysteria.

"Honey, you honestly think I give a damn who paid how much to have you returned to me? You honestly believe that I'd have been too proud and stupid enough to reject it for one second? She didn't ask me. She was holding those negotiations, and good for her. I was a lost cause, as scared and anguished as I was. I am not sorry she took over, Audrey. And when you know everything, I don't think you'll be either. It's done now. You're home, you're safe and while she was extremely generous, her money wasn't needed anyway."

Kate seemed to finally return to her assertive persona, perhaps overcoming her obvious skittishness in front of cameras.

"When I have all the information? There is more? And no, don't look at the camera. You and Gustavo and Freja and everyone else seem to know everything about this, and you allowed me to stand here in front of the entire world, exposed. Too late now. Tell me. Please, mom."

Neve couldn't see Kate's expression, but she knew if her

own child ever asked her for anything in that tone—the broken and distraught voice of someone who's hanging by a thread—she'd never be able to say no.

Kate couldn't either, since Neve could hear a long-suffering sigh just before she heard Audrey's mother speak again.

"The hospital... Baby, she... well, that wonderful boy, her assistant, actually found me, and then she sent her plane for me, to bring me to Landstuhl. When I found out about the extent of your injuries, how long treatment and recovery would take, and that you'd need rehab, I was so overwhelmed, and she was just standing there in the hallway, because Freja..."

Kate obviously realized she'd said too much. "Well, you know how those two don't get along at all. Everyone knows. So Freja wouldn't let her in to see you, and I... I saw her and I couldn't *not* ask for her help. Well, I pretty much ordered her to bring you home. And she did, like magic. She pulled all the strings she needed to pull, and a couple of days later, you were on the plane that took you to the best orthopedic hospital in the nation. And here you are three months later with barely any lingering effects. You can't blame me for appealing to her for help any more than you can blame her for helping. I'd have appealed to the devil if it would have saved you!"

Harlan stifled a giggle, and at Neve's questioning look, he simply turned his phone to face her. Right under Juno's, *"I AM THAT GOD"*, tweet was a brand new one.

@TheJuno: *"NEVE WISHES SHE WAS THE DEVIL."*

So Juno had paid her back. With everyone else tiptoeing around her name, the witch had no such qualms. In fact, Neve was fairly certain she'd done that on purpose. So that was that, putting this particular genie back in the bottle would be some undertaking–if she were to choose to go that route.

Harlan picked that moment to look up at her and his eyes

were filled with so much emotion, she set her own anxiety aside. Surely the universe would grant her some time to fall apart later.

With her heart heavy and Harlan still holding her hand with concern etched on his face, she chose to go with levity. Neve rolled her eyes demonstratively.

"God, does she feel that shouting is really necessary?"

"Mom, at this point, Juno is pretty much Cher, who gives everyone catchy quotes but only tweets in all caps." Harlan's nose was back in his iPad.

"Son, please tell me that Cher is so much more to you than her quirky Twitter persona? Because I can't believe I've done so wrong by you..."

"Oh, if you could turn back time?" Harlan's face remained impassive only for a second before both of them smiled at each other.

"Hey, look, Grace Bishop chimed in too. Isn't she filming somewhere in Europe? The Kingdom of Savoy or something? Anyway, here's her two cents. I knew she was cool. But she's kinda my hero now."

On the phone screen, under the *Trending* section, Neve could see a number of tweets that mentioned her name in replies to Juno's. Grace's was the one getting by far the most likes and retweets.

@GraceBishop *"Bow to the Absolute Queen. None of us are worthy. Long may she reign."*

Well, this was nice. Harlan nodded at her, and both of them returned their attention to the iPad. There, the shouting was intensifying, and Neve wished the car would move quicker. Maybe in the sanctity of the Gannon offices, she'd have a good excuse not to follow the live streaming of her own evisceration.

. . .

Audrey's raised voice interrupted Neve's musings. "Mom, and you Gustavo, especially you, since you damn well knew about everything that happened... I can and I will blame you. And don't get me started on how many things I will blame her for. In fact, I will blame her for any freaking thing I want."

Neve closed her eyes. Her chest felt heavy. Audrey, in full anger, was a sight to see, but she arduously wished for all of this to stop. She could almost sense Gustavo shrinking away. Harlan interrupted her musings.

"Mom, is Audrey losing her mind? It sounds like she doesn't really care that everyone can see."

"Harlan, sometimes... Sometimes I wish I could lose my mind exactly like this. And say what I want to say and damn the torpedoes. She's been through a lot, darling. I think the world owes her a bit of latitude. Don't you? It's her wedding day."

Even as she was speaking, desperately trying to keep her voice calm and her words reasonable, the thunder in her mind was deafening, and her vision was blurry. It was Audrey's wedding day, after all.

"She never once cared about what happened to me."

Gustavo's sigh was almost theatrical. "Audrey, c'mon now, she always cared. Always cared too bloody much, if you ask me. I was there. She called Elinor herself..."

Yeah, the hits just kept coming. With Juno effectively naming her, Neve was absolutely certain more and more people were starting to figure out just how deep Neve Blackthorne's involvement with Audrey Avens went. She could practically sense the walls of the Rook crumbling.

On the screen, Gustavo was sheet white. The magnitude of his revelation was so much bigger, so much more all-encompassing, that Neve felt the world tilt. For herself, for Gustavo and his big mouth, and especially for Audrey. In perfect symmetry to her feeling, Audrey swayed, her hand grabbing for something as her mother steadied her.

"Audrey, baby. Please."

"No, I need to hear him finish this. Tell me, Gustavo. Did she organize a career for me then? Why? To assuage her guilt? Why Gustavo?"

"Oh, no, please, I'm sorry. It's not like that." He reached for her hand, and she shrugged him off.

The green eyes were filled with tears, and Neve could tell the enormous strength it took Audrey to keep them from falling.

Dear heart, my brave one.

"Tell me! Because up until this morning I may not have had much. My choices were suspect, and my personal life was encompassed in a white dress that is much too bright for my skin tone, but at least there was one thing I still had. My career and my accomplishments were my own."

"They are! She never... I don't know how to explain, and I'm not that clear on the details. She never does share, you know, but you are one of the best journalists I know, and I know many. You are your own woman. Times is lucky to have you, the work you did in..."

Harlan giggled again, his attention clearly not on the drama unfolding on the iPad screen. Neve had an inkling why, and did her best to smile at him.

"Juno again, I assume?"

@TheJuno *"SHE NEVER DOES SHARE ;)"*

He didn't bother showing her the screen this time. "All caps, but there's a winking emoji to go along with it."

"Someone should totally take her phone away."

"Aww, mom, you are no fun. And shhh, this is about to get good. Audrey just went all offended, 'spare me the plaudits since I don't deserve them,' on Gustavo. Man, next time he comes by, I gotta tell him that keeping silent is the absolute best strategy with women."

Neve wanted to thank the heavens for her son and the little reprieve he was giving her from the torture that this drive was turning into. He was sensitive and kind, but she was very grateful that he was young enough to not fully grasp the seriousness of the situation. And by being an eager spectator to the drama unfolding, was forcing Neve to put on a brave face. Who knows how she'd be reacting otherwise?

The car finally turned to pull up in front of the skyscraper housing the Gannon offices, while she could hear Audrey listing all the troubles that had befallen Freja.

"... I know Lucci dropped her and D&B marginalized Freja so much, she might as well not work for them anymore!"

Like clockwork, because apparently nothing was sacred anymore, Gustavo, ever the loyal soldier, stood up to defend his queen.

"Except Freja did that to herself. Nobody insults and humiliates her and walks away whistling. She gave that girl every chance to get it right, extended her hand plenty, only to have Freja bite that very hand and spit in her latte. She disrespected the Queen. In public!"

Neve just sighed at the moniker Gustavo chose to hide her name behind. Why did he bother anymore? Of course, she was trending on Twitter and neither of the three protagonists on screen knew that she had been named. Seeing them struggle to still preserve her privacy was painful. Was it too late to pray or to ask the ground to swallow her whole?

As they boarded the elevator, Harlan now simply extended his hand to show her Juno's latest public mockery. Except this one didn't read quite as barbed. And the caps weren't present this time. It was just three words, but they rocked Neve, rocked her, and amused her, she was sure as the old broad intended them too.

@TheJuno: *"I should know."*

"Is this her saying she's sorry, mom?"

"I think despite totally throwing me under the bus just minutes ago, and despite making me go through hell to get her to help me, Juno has finally lost the last vestiges of her sanity and is actually telling me to hang in there, Harlan. Now I have a meeting. Will you be fine with Barnaby in the reception area, or do you want me to ask him to take you out somewhere?"

"No, I'll sit tight. I gotta see what happens next. How will you know what's going on though? Will you watch, mom?"

Neve shook her head and gently ran her fingers through the silky, a bit too long strands of his hair.

"No, baby. I think I've seen enough."

16

NEVE IN THE EYE OF THE STORM

"*If* I didn't watch it all happen, I don't think I'd have believed it, Neve. It's movie-like." Dr. Moore's eyes were alight.

"Well, I'm glad my life continues to fascinate you now that I, as you have repeatedly told me, have melted. Isn't that the moment when Ice Queens become boring?" Neve faked a yawn, but her look held no malice. It had been quite a day.

"I was actually very worried for you." Helena leaned in and patted Neve's hand somewhat awkwardly, tentatively. Neve sighed and turned her palm up, squeezing the doctor's fingers in a gesture of gratitude. If what had happened had shown her anything, it was that there were plenty of people in her corner.

"I don't think I really understood what was about to happen, and once it started devolving, it was unstoppable. Like a crash. You can't do anything, and you cannot look away. The way the revelations kept coming one after another, you know, like the defenses of a citadel, they were taken down one by one. The moat, the drawbridge, the outer castle walls..."

Neve looked at the chessboard in front of her, the Queen tall and proud, and there was the Rook—her castle, her closet, her prison—as her last loyal companion. After all, her fear had kept her company forever. "I could see every single thing coming to light, into quite a public light. And there was nothing I, of all people, could do to stop it."

Dr. Moore tapped her pen quietly and Neve, after numerous sessions of working with Lane on her PTSD, confirmed her suspicions that her erstwhile therapist was employing a variation of a treatment technique, quietly grounding her in a rhythm and a sound to allay her anxieties. And she had been doing it since their first session. Honestly, Neve had no idea how she could ever repay the universe for guiding her hand in choosing Helena Moore.

"So, yes, I felt powerless. I don't often feel that way. And it's quite a full circle from where I am standing. I was in control of everything when it started. And I had none of that control when it was all ending."

"Was it ending, Neve?"

"Well, all things are bound to end, Doctor. That's what epilogues are for."

As she turned away to walk in the direction of the conference room where she could see Barnaby flitting around with stacks of reports and a guilty expression, Harlan took two steps to catch up to her, and suddenly she found her arms full of boy.

"I love you, mom. And... I guess I'm sorry." He raised his eyes, the blue in them shining so brightly now in the sunlight streaming through the massive windows.

"I love you too, darling. I love you too. And there's nothing you can do, so don't be sorry. I'll be fine."

With one last glance at the screen where Audrey looked so sad and confused that it tore at Neve's heart, she turned around and strolled into the meeting.

The faces around the table were impassive, some doing a

much better job of hiding their obvious knowledge, and perhaps even their enjoyment at Neve being raked over the coals from pretty much every side—her former boss, her former employee, a world-renowned supermodel—in a very public manner. She could see the assistants in the reception area sneak glances at their phones and then at her, obviously watching the livestream. And she could swear one of the production directors had just turned off the TV in the conference room a second before she'd walked in.

"If any of you have anything to say that I need to hear..." She let her words trail off and turned her hand palm up, gesturing for them to go ahead. Nobody dared move, let alone speak. "Then I suggest you forget about your phones and the spectacle on Twitter and on the livestream, so we can proceed."

Things continued smoothly after that. She had some of her dignity left, and she was still Neve Blackthorne, dammit. They continued to fear and respect her, no matter what amount of dirt was being flung at her out there. She tried not to worry too much about what reaction the Gannon board might have. Livia's presence there was reassuring, but business was still business, and Neve was being dragged through the mud with no possibility to stop and control the narrative.

About an hour into the discussion on trends and targets and indicators, with her mind reeling from figures and projections, Neve was adrift, forcing herself not to think about Audrey being married by now. Surely, it wouldn't take all that much time, and how long was the drive from the hotel to City Hall, anyway? Mere blocks, even with Manhattan traffic?

A sudden commotion outside brought both Barnaby and Harlan into focus as they burst through the glass doors with varying degrees of excitement, urgency, and trepidation.

"Mom, mom, mom, you gotta see this." Harlan was waving his iPad like a flag.

"Neve, turn on the TV, now!" If Barnaby was afraid of her, at this moment he was clearly prepared to take his life into his own hands, because Neve had never seen him quite like this. Within a second, her usually reverential assistant almost jumped over her Development Department Head in order to reach the remote control for the immense screen hanging on the wall behind her.

"Harlan, Barnaby!" Her raised voice stopped them both dead, but Barnaby simply pressed the power button before handing her the remote.

"Watch now and fire me later, Neve. Audrey is confronting Freja about everything."

Her fingers clenched over the device, the plastic cool in her grip. *Oh, God, breathe, breathe.* The screen blinked and came to life to a scene unfolding in what looked like the inside of City Hall, if Neve's memory served her right.

"You lied to me about her going after you, didn't you?" Audrey's face was shot from the side, with the cameraperson clearly scrambling to keep up with the two leggy women.

"What?" Freja stopped mid-stride, mouth half-open. Except she couldn't hold a candle to Neve's acting prowess when it came to fooling Audrey.

"Don't lie to me now. How did you figure out that... How did you figure out what to blackmail her with?" Audrey had halted in the middle of her sentence, obviously still attempting not to out Neve.

She wanted to laugh. Juno was single-handedly keeping her name trending on Twitter, and had thrown enough gasoline on the fire of Neve's very public burning at the stake. The speculation alone was pretty damning at the moment. Still, it was making her heart break all over again to see Audrey try so hard to sound ambiguous and protect her.

Freja raised her eyebrows subtly in the direction of the

camera, but Audrey was having none of it. Hurricane Audrey indeed.

"What? Now you care about all of this being filmed? I begged you not to livestream the wedding. I begged you not to make fools out of both of us with this gaudy monstrosity. I begged you…" Audrey's voice rose and then fell to a startling broken whisper, and Neve could see a shadow of contrition on Freja's face.

"Babe… I don't know what you want me to say. I have no idea who you're talking about." But if the contrition had seemed honest, the last line wasn't even close, and Audrey's eyes shone with anger again and not with sadness. Perhaps the gloves were truly off.

"You know well enough who… She's a viper when cornered, I give you that. She'd eat you alive to set an example as well. But how did you know what buttons to push with her?"

Like someone yelling 'cut' on a movie set and all masks falling off, the veil lifted off Freja's face. The contrition was gone, the dishonesty was gone. Arrogance and dismissal took their place. To Neve's and the on-screen Audrey's apparent great astonishment, Freja just rolled her eyes as if Audrey was a recalcitrant and not particularly bright child.

"Because I knew! I watched you and your expression every time you looked at her, or when someone talked about her, or her *sacred name* was even mentioned, and I saw myself. I loved you. I wanted you, and all you wanted was her. I did everything, and she kept fucking with your head and throwing you over, and you still didn't want me. I thought after our night together things would change, but you came to London and only had eyes for her."

Clearly, Freja had no such compulsion in terms of keeping even the modicum of anyone's privacy. Well, it wasn't like she'd had any left to begin with.

Neve sighed and felt Harlan's smaller hand slip into hers for the second time this morning.

Audrey seemed to have similar thoughts on screen.

"Dammit, Freja!"

"Don't *dammit Freja* me! And she wasn't much better than you back then, and she certainly isn't now. You are mine, and she still wants what's mine. So I pushed some of her buttons to show her she can't bully me. I let her know that I knew everything. So fucking what?"

Audrey actually shook, the tremble clearly visible. Out of rage or impotence, Neve didn't know, but Audrey's face showed an array of emotions Neve could no longer decipher.

Then Audrey threw her hands up and actually growled.

"*So fucking what?* Are you insane? No wonder she stomped all over you. You don't know what she's capable of!"

If this were a movie and Neve was directing it, she'd insert some kind of comic relief at this point. It was clear that things were coming to a head, but the high level of drama was draining. Not just on her, she was strung out by it all to the point that she had no idea how much more she could take before breaking. But also for the audience. *Give everyone a breather.*

Because, while Neve's privacy was being trampled on with every new scene unfolding on screen, it was actually Audrey's truth that was being dismantled with every new word. And the gravitas of those two obliterations was crushing.

So something was needed, to just be able to draw one breath, one second of respite. Neve turned to Harlan as he scrolled through his Twitter feed, perhaps reading her thoughts. Juno did not disappoint.

@TheJuno: "*Ha. Freja doesn't know what wrath she has awoken? DAMN STRAIGHT. Or something like that.*"

Barnaby's hiccuping squeak returned their attention to the big screen.

"Well, Alisson at Laurner Studios said she was finished... Yeah, maybe I got burned 'cause she's like that cat who has nine freaking lives or something, because she bounced right back, but I don't regret it. I did what I did. You're mine!"

Neve thought she could hear the ticking clock on the time bomb. Freja had not yet uttered her name. How come they were dragging this public humiliation out for hours on end and still leaving it all up in the air to be this ambiguous? Sure, she was trending on Twitter, but so far nobody on screen had said her name out loud. It was all conjecture and still spinnable. If she wished it to be.

Neve had a reckless thought that she actually wished one of them would finally say it. Get it over with. The devil-may-care moment was predictably followed by her breathing getting shallow and her mouth going dry. Still, that one-second thought had felt freeing.

At this point, Audrey's breath was coming out more as a wheeze. "Freja..."

"No. Audrey, don't you dare. The whole world is watching. You can't do this!"

And yes, Audrey was still shockingly bad at poker, because her face showed exactly what she was about to do, and Neve was afraid to even blink in order to not miss what was coming next.

"Are you concerned that the world is watching, or that I'm

calling off the wedding?" The beloved voice was very calm, despite the high color on her still-too-thin cheekbones.

Freja halted her pacing and the wringing of her hands, and her face was an almost comical blend of exasperation and embarrassment. She took a deep breath and smiled, regret evident on her face, the cameraperson catching the glint of a diamond in her canine.

"You know, Audrey, I'm not really sure which."

And that, as they say, was that. The *Wedding of the Century* was no more, and the shard in Neve's chest that had twisted every time she'd thought of Audrey and Freja together in the past months was pulled out. It lay bleeding in her hands, still sharp enough to cut if handled wrongly. But it was done, and as tears threatened once again, Harlan tucked his face into her shoulder, gently holding her.

On screen, Audrey was looking at Freja with a mix of affection and disappointment.

"Thank you for the truth, then. I'm sure you can blame me for this whole thing and come out on top. I know you can do it."

Neve thought that the entire world could see the wheels turning in Freja's head and her vivid blue eyes narrow with all the possibilities.

"Ha, by the time this is all over, Freja will be the long-suffering, innocent victim, utterly beautiful in her heartbreak, getting even more publicity than if the wedding had gone forward."

Barnaby's analysis was spot on, even if she could have done without him gushing about Freja's beauty. Her raised eyebrow must have told him as much, but he just guffawed.

"You can be magnanimous now, Neve. She lost." At her glare, he quickly closed his mouth and turned back to the TV.

. . .

"I need to get out of here though, before the journalists and the guests cotton on to what is happening." Audrey was saying on screen.

"You are going to run to that woman, aren't you?" Freja sniffed, and her distaste was palpable.

"Well, I do have some unfinished business there. Plus, think about it this way–by the end of the day, I will probably be prosecuted for murder, because I will absolutely kill her the moment I can reach her neck and wring it."

Freja's smile was rueful, and she gently laid a hand on Audrey's face.

"If only you'd shown half the passion for me as you're showing in your anger for her." Freja got closer and placed a tender kiss on her cheek. "Claim she drove you to it. Maybe you can plead it down to manslaughter. I will always love you, even though you are such a fool for not loving me back, Audrey. "

They hugged, and as Audrey made her way to a side door, the screen split, and the cameras followed both her on the left and Freja on the right.

In the silence of the conference room, Barnaby's whispered, "Lesbians, now watch them stay besties forever after having the most dramatic breakup in the history of breakups," sounded particularly loud.

Neve was about to dismiss everyone from the room, trying to process the information from the last couple of minutes, but her jaw dropped as she saw Audrey stop at the curb right in front of City Hall, throw up her hand to stop a cab, then pat down her wedding dress, obviously remembering that she didn't have a wallet. Neve actually gulped at what happened next. Audrey flung her heels off and headed in the direction of Uptown at a run.

Surely not... And yet Gustavo's earlier on-screen words about Neve being in New York rang in her ears.

The whole room watched in awe as the cameraperson tried to keep up with Audrey as she sprinted up Broadway and 5th Avenue, hurdling over bushes in Bryant Park on her way to 6th. Surely, there was only one destination for her... Gannon McMillan lay exactly in that direction..

Neve could see the gawking onlookers and tourists trying to capture pictures of Audrey, who looked magnificent in her full stride. After all, how often does one see a literal runaway bride? And one making good time at that.

After about a mile it was clear that the cameraperson was rapidly losing ground to Audrey, and the split screen disappeared to be overtaken by Freja giving ridiculous and over-the-top statements to assembled reporters, seemingly taking the whole thing on the chin. Surprisingly. Something about how life went on. She would rise again, she would love again...

Neve pressed the off button and turned to face the room that was deathly silent. Even Harlan wasn't staring at his gadgets. She looked at every face, every pair of eyes trained on her, and then she simply took her seat and waved them all away. They filed out like soldiers, with Harlan breaking ranks to give her a hug and a quick cuddle. Just as he was about to let her go, she murmured, "I love you," so quietly, she thought he wouldn't hear her, but he did and whispered it back to her as he closed the door.

She lowered her head and struggled to return her breath to some semblance of normal. She knew what was coming, after all. Or rather who was coming.

But before she could do anything to prepare herself, say her goodbyes or maybe write a will, her proverbial clock struck midnight. This time, it wasn't Barnaby or Harlan bursting into the conference room, but a disheveled, out-of-breath Audrey. In a torn dress, covered in dirt and assorted street debris, she was a sight to see. Was that blood on her feet?

Neve could hear a scuffle going on behind the closed doors, with Barnaby cursing a blue streak and Harlan shouting and pushing away security guards, and then, unexpectedly, both of them shoved Audrey all the way into the room, the doors banging open on the wall loudly enough to make Neve involuntarily raise her hands to cover her ears.

And as she did so, for just one moment, before she lowered them again, Audrey's face was gentleness itself.

Why had Neve thought, even for a moment, that she'd successfully hidden all this from her lover all these years? And why was she so consumed by the fear of being rejected that she hadn't simply shared? It was obvious now that Audrey would have helped her. Would have made all of this so much easier. Neve felt like a fool.

Time stood still for what seemed like an eternity, with the two of them simply standing there, a massive conference room table between them. And Neve again felt that if she was directing this particular movie, she'd never resort to such blatant cliches. But here they both were and time did lay between them, suspended in the air as they drank each other in.

Then suddenly Neve remembered they were far from alone, with a number of guards spilling into the room after Audrey, gawking at them. And while none of them mattered, what with the whole world now being privy to pretty much her entire life, some things required privacy. One nod from her and they all fled.

And then they were finally alone. Alone for the first time in months, alone with both of them unattached, and Neve could see her own longing reflected in Audrey's eyes. Then those eyes narrowed, and Audrey broke the silence.

"You know, it's not even funny, but I had all these things I needed to tell you, to throw at you, to completely decimate you with, after all these years and all these miles and all these tears. And I run here, all five, dirty miles, barefoot through Manhattan, and the first thing I see is you literally commanding a dozen people with a mere nod, and this kind of display of raw power renders me totally weak."

Audrey shook her head with something that was a cross of irritation and astonishment before continuing.

"Those eyes, the violent, violet eyes, that laser focus of yours. Be it work or play, you would always find this state of complete and utter concentration, and when you turned it towards me, I always knew I was in for it, that I would end up in a sweaty, mumbling, exhausted heap on either a floor, a desk, a couch, or a bed. You do great work no matter the surface. Amazing work really, phenomenal."

Neve didn't know what to say, how to answer any of this, and so she just stood there, her knuckles white, gripping the table for support, for reason, for succor.

Yet Audrey just went on. "I keep forgetting how you command meetings like a general running a deadly campaign. I've seen both now, Neve. I can attest to the fact that it looks exactly the same. One word from you—and sometimes not even that—and the world moves. And you fuck like life itself depends on it. Nobody else has ever done this to me, nobody ever could. Damn you, Neve, damn us both to hell."

Audrey took a step, another, and then she was halfway across the room, and Neve was still standing there, paralyzed by what was happening.

As if echoing Neve's earlier thoughts, Audrey mused, "You'd have a better eye for this scene, if you were to film it, but it's a perfect juxtaposition, don't you think, Neve? You—flawless in every way—and me in a state that is so far from said flawlessness, it is rather laughable."

She sighed and simply sat down, folded really, into one of the chairs that were spread around the table, wiping her face with one hand and leaving two small trails of blood where her fingers had brushed her skin. Neve started at the sight, realizing that Audrey was bleeding and dragging that blood all across her cheek and dress.

Staring at her own, ruined hands, Audrey chuckled mirthlessly. "Huh, I must've fallen on my way here... I don't remember falling."

The murmur was matter-of-fact and almost inaudible, fitting perfectly into the state of numbness permeating the room. Distantly, Neve wondered if this was the calm before another storm.

Seemingly in a trance herself, she turned to the side panel and, with a first aid kit, sat next to Audrey, taking her hands and tending to them with a wet wipe, gently cleaning the blood and the gore.

Her actions must have awoken something in Audrey then, because by the time Neve moved to carefully tend to her feet, which had taken the brunt of the run through the glass and garbage of the New York City streets, Audrey's tears simply spilled over her cheeks, like a faucet opening, probably knowing she was powerless to stop them.

"Don't, Neve. Please, stop!" Audrey tried to wrench her foot out of Neve's gentle hold, and was unsuccessful because Neve held her gently but firmly.

"You have a deep cut here. I don't think stitches will be needed, but I should at least clean it."

"You're so calm, this tone of yours is so irritatingly familiar. I want to howl. I am so angry with you right now, Neve, so angry."

Neve could see the same rage from the livestream and from the few moments they'd glared at each other in front of all the people earlier returning as Audrey balled her hands into fists and tried but failed to will it all back, her eyes still shooting daggers.

"I see hurricane Audrey is gathering speed and power." Neve knew her words were mocking, but her tone was remarkably devoid of any malice, just a teasing lilt to it that made Audrey smile despite her anger. Neve smiled back, pleased that she still knew how to defuse Audrey's wrath. Once upon a time, she'd known how to allay every hurt too, and she pressed a kiss to the side of Audrey's instep, where she had just run a sterilizing wipe.

"Hurricane Audrey is about to make landfall, so I'd be a bit more careful if I were you. I just told Freja that I couldn't marry her because I would certainly end up in jail by this evening on charges for the murder of one Neve Blackthorne, and that she really didn't need to be tied down to a felon."

At the confirmation of what everyone pretty much had seen on the reality show minutes ago, Neve's heart soared. At Audrey's exasperated smile, Neve decided to keep up the teasing.

"You could plead extenuating circumstances. Temporary insanity, perhaps? Though you really can't call it temporary. You and I both know I always, always drove you crazy. So perhaps a crime of passion? We had that in spades, darling."

Neve dragged her fingers up from the ankle, then crept higher and higher, and paused at her garter, making Audrey hold her breath and bite her lip. Then Audrey simply laid her own hand on top of Neve's, effectively stopping her.

"No, don't take the wind out of my sails just yet, Neve. I have things to say, and it's time I say them. I feel like I'm a character in a bad drama, where the main theme is a total lack of communication, and with this being one of the last chapters, we already had our 80% conflict point, and the readers deserve to see the leads finally talk their shit out, don't you think?"

"I feel like people around me all read and watch too much

romantic drivel," Neve murmured but just inclined her head, as her fingers—prohibited from delving higher—gently traced the garter.

Every advantage she could, she would take now. Ever the apex predator, she knew what she was doing to Audrey's resolve and her composure. But Audrey shook her head and pursed her lips, and Neve sighed. No, she wasn't getting out of this one so easily.

"I know I'm being flippant. I'm not sure if I mean to be, or if I'm simply too afraid of what will happen if I stop..."

Audrey's hand on her own, still over the garter, squeezed firmly.

"I ran here, and all I could think about was how much you've hidden from me. The potential ransom, the hospital, the nightly reading–which felt like a dream, a very sweet dream that I cherished—only to have it turn out to be an impossible reality, the constant back and forth, and yanking me around by my feelings and by my clit... No, don't you dare laugh!"

The hand clutching hers lifted, and fingers that were surprisingly strong despite their injuries gripped Neve's chin and held it. Audrey firmly looked her in the eyes and forced Neve to face her fully. *So much for the advantage then.*

"The hospital?" Neve desperately tried to stall, at least for a little bit, to gather her scattered thoughts. It was indeed time to come clean, and she needed her composure. But all she could feel was Audrey's grip on her face and her own fingers on Audrey's thigh, and she kept losing herself in this dream. Surely it could not be her reality. She wasn't worthy of it.

"In the limo, on our way to city hall, mom spilled the beans on that too. Which I'm very happy she did not do in front of the cameras. Because I am not sure how the demons of Hollywood would have reacted to the Wicked Queen sitting at my bedside night after night, reading Jane Austen and holding my hand. Sappy much, Your Majesty?"

Neve tried to lower her gaze, but the fingers on her chin were bruising in their insistence.

"And she said you went to beg Juno? You actually went to that old hag and asked for her help after everything that happened between you two? God, I can't believe you sometimes. You are legitimately the worst, and I wish I could express to you how absolutely enraged you make me. For meddling, for ruining me, for leaving me, and for never really leaving me at all."

The fingers on her chin gentled, and a palm cupped her cheek, thumb caressing her cheekbone with familiar motions. But Audrey wasn't done.

"None of those things are important, though. Because I have so much rage and so much lust, and I swear, I will either kill you or fuck you right here with all those people in the hallway, pretending not to watch us right now."

At Neve's pronounced shiver, Audrey smirked, and yeah, two could play this game. Neve thought that Audrey had learned plenty from her, since Neve was sure she would use anything to get answers right here and now. And then the green eyes sobered and Neve felt the moment infuse with gravity.

"Is my career my own? And why the fuck did you do whatever it is you did? And don't flinch at the curse word. I don't care how unladylike you find it when it's not used as a verb related to my exact actions of fucking you 'till you scream. Tell me, Neve!"

Out of all the things that Audrey could have demanded answers for, this one surprised Neve the least. Of course, Audrey would need additional reassurance about her professional success, since it was something to be rightfully proud of. After all, her career accomplishments were legion and to tarnish them all with even a drop of nepotism would be unbearable. Still, as thoughts crowded Neve's mind, her face betrayed her, and she could see Audrey's shoulders droop.

"So you did meddle. You did get me the job and the promotions and fucking hell, I can't, I can't..."

Audrey wrenched her hand from Neve's face and was about to stand up.

"I'm nothing, and nothing is mine. It's all you and all yours."

"No! Audrey, no, darling, stop." Neve could hear the anguish in her own voice, and suddenly she knew it was that emotion that held Audrey in place much better than the force of Neve's hands cradling her face.

"I swear. Yes, I talked to Elinor, to make her see you, notice you, to take you away from LA because I was too close, I wanted you too much, and I couldn't stay away from you if you continued at The Tribune. But there was nothing else. She didn't hire you because I told her to, I swear, ask her! You were good. You are so good. She wanted you for your talent. Paying me back for whatever favor she owed me was inconsequential. It simply doesn't work that way. And certainly, if you weren't gifted you'd have never advanced. You are your own person, Audrey. You made yourself. Please, if nothing else, believe this. I beg of you."

"Neve Blackthorne doesn't beg."

"She does if it means giving you this, Audrey. I want you to be happy, and I want you to have peace. You're much too troubled for someone so young, and it's all my fault."

And just like that, Neve felt their storms collide, that unstoppable force meeting that immovable object, the classic paradox stymieing both of them. She gentled her hands on Audrey's cheeks and finally dared to look her in the eyes, her own barely holding back tears now.

"How much more pain are we going to cause each other?" Audrey shook her head, carefully placed her hands over Neve's, nodding once, then again, seemingly coming to some sort of decision.

"This is my line in the sand. The demarcation. Things have to be resolved here, one way or another. You always make the wrong decisions anyway, pushing me away and screwing with my brain, and then martyring yourself by groveling to Juno. I can't even imagine what that old crow made you do to agree to help you. And after everything, you sent Robert O'Donovan to shoot my freaking wedding. Clearly, you can't be trusted to make the grown-up decisions in this relationship anymore."

Audrey's bandaged fingers held Neve's hands firmly in her lap, anchoring both herself and Neve to the certain realities that she proceeded to state.

"Look. You were a total bitch to me. Back when you made me listen to you pretending to fuck your husband, when you were yanking my chain, sleeping with me, yet never really talking to me."

They both sighed, and Neve looked away for a second, unable to hold the steady gaze piercing her.

"When you sacrificed yourself for some stupid reason and didn't tell me about Freja being a complete asshole to you, and again when you kept coming to my hospital room like a total creep to read me books. And don't get me started on you meddling with my career. That stops now."

Neve just kept looking at her, and suddenly Audrey's pale cheeks pinked, and then so did the tips of her ears.

"Okay, I have no idea how you manage to look guilty and contrite while also looking entirely edible, but you have to knock it off, because my priorities are starting to get confused."

Audrey trembled, but straightened herself and soldiered on, although she sounded very disgruntled. Neve had to smile.

"No, no, none of that! Because I know you, and my body knows yours, and you smell the same and it's just… Please, don't, because I have things I need to say. Because we are honest-to-god adult women, yet we behave like bad romance heroines. All of that ends now. Today, you hear me?"

"And this" Audrey motioned with their joined hands between them. "This ends today as well."

Five words and the tears that Neve had been holding back valiantly since Audrey had started leveling accusations against her fell from her lashes. She didn't care that her cheeks were wet, that her makeup was getting ruined, as she simply stared at Audrey with as much longing and as much love as she had, trying to convey without words that she understood and accepted her punishment.

But Audrey wasn't finished, and after a moment she took mercy on her, lifting her chin up once again, even as her thumb caressed Neve's lower lip.

"Not like that, Neve. This silly game we've been playing for years now, this torture that we put each other through. Well, you put me through. Whatever I did was obviously in retaliation and self-defense and thus clearly deserved."

Audrey smirked again, and Neve gave her a watery version of her own smile back. She despised cliches and avoided them at all cost in her movies, but she was flooded with relief, staggered by it, and the thought made her smile even wider.

"Clearly." She knew she must look so pitiful, so sad, and yet suddenly also hopeful.

Quite close-by, Neve could hear the sounds of a helicopter, and as she turned away to wipe her tears, she could see a TV crew filming through the massive windows of the conference room. The producers had clearly decided to continue pursuing Audrey's story. She could have gotten up and closed the blinds with a press of a button, but even that was too much and too far, especially when Audrey's tone was so playful.

"Neve Blackthorne, you look so cute." Audrey reached up and wiped a tear from under Neve's eye.

 "Surely you must be wrong, because nobody, absolutely nobody, has ever said out loud that Neve Blackthorne was cute." She tried to imbue her tone with as much hauteur as she could. She knew she'd failed miserably, because Audrey just smiled at her.

"But you are. Washing my feet, teary-eyed and your nose red from crying, clutching my hands like they're your only lifeline, Neve Blackthorne is immeasurably cute. What am I to do with you? You are my heart and my life, and you are beautiful and selfish and spoiled rotten and can be the biggest bitch I've ever met, yet you also drop everything for me and part the seas to bring me home? You are so very real in this world, where everything is absolutely fake. Where the tinsel is nothing but cheap plastic. You alone are real. With flaws, with impossibly high maintenance demands and crazy-ass standards, but I'm just competitive enough to look forward to a lifetime of satisfying those demands and rising to those standards. I love you beyond words, beyond reason."

And just like that, whatever was left of Neve's Rook, along with her fear and desire to keep hiding, crumbled down. Years with Dr. Moore, therapy, and all the progress she had made had prepared her for this moment. Allowed her to take it all in and accept it. What was fear when it was faced with all this love and all this devotion? What was terror of humiliation when here was her one and only person watching her with adoration?

Those cliches just kept coming up in her mind. Come hell or high water, she'd handle it. She'd work through fear, through her own history, and through whatever else life threw their way, as long as Audrey never stopped looking at her like this.

So Neve did what Neve always did. She took charge. If she was to be irrevocably, unquestionably, irrefutably outed, she'd do it on her own terms. Or at least bend those terms to her will as much as she could. She slid off the chair and knelt next to Audrey, who gasped and tried to pull her up.

"Neve, don't! What are you doing?"

"What is it with everyone trying to keep me from kneeling

these days? Is it so hard to believe that I would actually do this?"

Audrey actually laughed. "Yes, it really is. You're... I mean, you're you! You're Neve Blackthorne. The whole world knows you don't do this sort of thing."

"Well then, I guess I will just have to prove you and the whole world wrong." Neve steadied the light tremble of her fingers and grasped Audrey's hands, careful of her cuts.

"I think through the entirety of our story, you were the fearless one, and I was choked by terror. I think it's time I do what a true leading lady is meant to do. Become something I wasn't when it all began. It's high time I was fearless too. Character development moment, dear heart."

After that, what else was there to do but kiss Audrey with the cameras rolling, crushing the last remnants of her closet under the gaze of millions?

And so Neve did just that, and Audrey met her demanding mouth with force and passion, and just enough bite to punish her for all the months and years, and all the pain and games.

She licked and bit at Neve's already swollen lips, making Neve's breath catch. Their tongues met, and here, too, Neve submitted, allowing herself to be taken, to be cared for, to be devoured by Audrey's sheer, raw need. She gave as good as she got, even in submission she was never passive, and Audrey's insolent mouth suddenly smiled under Neve's lips, gentling her caress only for a second to let out a jubilant laugh, before grabbing Neve's hair and pulling her back into the bruising kiss.

As their lips parted, the kiss tasting of tears and regret and maybe, just maybe, finally of forgiveness, Audrey laughed and looked over Neve's head at the circling helicopter. It was much closer now, and obviously must have gotten the whole thing on camera. But Neve didn't care, and when Audrey returned a questioning look, she simply shrugged and kissed her again.

That earlier thought that she'd considered reckless at the

time, the one about getting this whole coming out over with, was sweet instead. She felt free. She felt happy. It was exhilarating.

If this was going to backfire, Neve would survive that too. She had survived plenty. Her life was survival hoisted upon her by her parents, by her peers and ultimately by her own hand. Why did it matter to her so much, being *othered*? She wasn't so very different in her desire to love and be free. It was a simple fact, and it didn't matter anymore. Nothing mattered. Audrey was kissing her back, and it was glorious.

She felt very foolish, for the time, the loss, the mistakes she had made. But also very lucky that all that foolishness had brought her back here. To this moment.

And so Neve decided that doing silly things had worked so far, and what was one more? Because in this situation, only a truly over-the-top gesture would do. They'd thought they were being so smart when they had tried to stay away from each other and had all those bright ideas of seeing other people and sacrificing themselves for one another. So Neve, for once trying to tackle problems head-on, simply said that one foolish thing that was left.

"Marry me?"

Audrey just looked at her, those brilliant, viridescent eyes clear and thoughtful. Something sparkled in their corners, and it got Neve distracted. So distracted, in fact, that she almost missed the quiet answer.

"No."

17

NEVE'S BATTLES AND WAR

"I hope you didn't faint."

Neve gave Dr. Moore an imperious glare.

"I did nothing of the sort." No need to tell the good doctor that it was a very near thing. Hearing Audrey refuse her proposal was... not easy.

The slight curve of her therapist's lips told her that Neve wasn't fooling her in the least. They stared at each other for a moment before Neve jerked a shoulder and looked out the window.

"She thinks that to jump headfirst into marriage after everything either of us has been through would be... unhealthy." Neve drew the word out, infusing it with as much derision as she could.

"She is right." Dr. Moore wasn't even trying to hide her glee. "I'm so pleased."

"I knew you'd react like this." Neve grumbled, moving her gaze to the chessboard that stood symbolically empty between them. "Needs must, Doctor. I will do everything I need to in order to make her happy. And to keep her so. For as long as she will let me."

Dr. Moore followed Neve's eyes and sighed. "You honestly think this is a battle?"

"Of course it is. Everything is, and I may have lost this one." Neve *picked up the Queen from the satchel holding the marble-carved pieces. She carefully placed the lone figure on the board and finally smiled. This time, it touched her eyes. The Queen stood proud.* "But I won the war."

Their first date was to be a movie premiere. Audrey had decreed that they needed to do everything by the book. Make a grand entrance, followed by a massive splash in the media, and give everyone what they were desperately hungry for after the social media storm that had followed her failed wedding to Freja. Then they could just be. Enjoy each other and enjoy their relationship in peace once everyone had had their fill. Neve had to give it to her, her lover did know the rules of Tinseltown well.

Still, Neve had grumbled and moaned about the whole ordeal, but she acquiesced. Her initial reaction to being refused marriage had been one of shock, disbelief and sudden grief. She'd wanted to flee, to hide, but she remained on her knees, and for one heartbeat, it felt like the rest of her life played out in front of her. It was not a happy film.

But the heartbeat passed and when the next one came, she was told in no uncertain terms that, "We can't get married just like this! What kind of woman do you think I am? And what kind of woman do you think I think *you* are? Courting is the word of the day." Audrey kissed her lightly on the lips and then simply cradled Neve's face in her hands. "Plus, we have three years of talking and making up to do. Well, and making out. It's the healthy way to move forward."

Neve did not argue. She knew to pick the hills she'd choose to die on. This wasn't one of them. As long as she had this, she'd be more than fine. And then she'd probably press her advantage and claim this hill sometime later. So she kissed Audrey instead. Slowly, savoring her, gently deepening the kiss, until she slipped her tongue in Audrey's mouth... Only to be not-so-gently pushed away.

"And no, none of this will be happening. You're dangerous!" Audrey laughed, but her eyes were uncertain. And aroused. Neve wanted to smile. Instead, she bit her lip, Audrey's taste lingering.

"No, no, no! Stop that! No sexy lip biting." Neve gave her a longer look, and Audrey actually sat farther away from her. "No lip biting, yours or mine. You're gonna make me spell out the rules. I knew it. I'll make you a list."

"How about I make you a list of all the things I want to do to you? And all the things I want you to do to me?" Neve ran her fingertip over the inside of Audrey's wrist and was rewarded with a shudder and a deep inhalation.

"You're a menace." Audrey caught her wandering hand and held it between her own. "You make that list, and I will make mine. I mean it. You and I horizontal—or vertical, for that matter—is a recipe for disaster. A hot, sexy, incredibly satisfying disaster, but a disaster nonetheless."

She raised Neve's hand to her lips and lightly bit a fingertip. Then another. It was Neve's turn to tremble.

"Audrey... Must we?" She could hear the whine in her own voice.

Audrey dropped Neve's hand and exhaled loudly.

"We must. Despite all the years and all the sex and all the drama, I want to do this right. And right means communication, honesty, and none of this sexiness. It's distracting."

Neve had wanted to argue, but she didn't have to dig very deep to know that Audrey was right. Maybe not regarding sex, because god, why would they deny themselves something that was so intrinsic to who they both were? Sexual creatures who had been apart for too long.

Still, Audrey had a point about the need to talk. Three

years' worth of conversations. Of communication. Wasn't that what happened in good romances? Characters talked.

Neve had almost shaken her head to deny, to hide away. And yet, she felt she owed Audrey all the truth. Not snippets and half-spoken memories. Everything.

———

And so they went to the damn premiere. The earth did not open to swallow Neve whole, and she didn't get drenched in a cold sweat. In fact, Audrey's hand in hers was warm, the fingers twitching periodically, returning Neve to the present and steering her away from her own musings and regrets.

And muse she did. Regret too. In fact, she did a lot of the latter throughout their entire first date. As they got out of the limo, the cameras flashing and the photographers screaming at them to look their way, Audrey's fingers squeezed hers gently, steadying her, allaying the effect of the noise.

Neve straightened her shoulders, took a deep breath, and then took her first step. The skies did not open up to smite her. She reigned supreme. A head tilt, a shoulder shrug, a rare smile here and there, and without answering any of the dozens of questions hurled at them by the reporters, they made their way into the venue.

"You're amazing." Audrey's words in her ear both calmed her and aroused her, the hot breath caressing the shell sending a thrill down her spine. She turned her head and their eyes met, their lips inches apart. Neve couldn't help herself. She slipped her hand free from Audrey's fingers and traced the line of her jaw with a fingertip.

"It's you who is the belle of the ball, dear heart."

"Aww, you two are adorable!" Gustavo's gushing exclamation made Neve close her eyes and count to five. Of all the times, he'd picked this one to come back from New York. She glared at him and he laughed at her. Then, just to make sure she hadn't lost her touch, she glowered at some glitterati or another who dared to try to approach their group. They scattered. Next to her, Audrey shivered, observing the display. Neve just raised her chin and gave Gustavo a look down her nose.

"Now Gustavo, behave..." By his side, Neve recognized a rather scandalized Benedict Stanley. "Good evening, Ms. Blackthorne, Ms. Avens."

"Do not *now Gustavo* me, Bene. I've waited years, years! I rooted for these two. It's my moment of celebration." He actually twirled on a tiptoe.

Audrey laughed, and suddenly Neve wanted to do the same. And so she did, a sincere, joyful laugh of relief and happiness. Audrey was alive, Audrey was here, with Neve, and her proverbial cup was overflowing. She could see, among her outburst of mirth, that people were staring, heads turning in their direction, especially when both Gustavo and Benedict joined in their hilarity. And yet, she didn't have the heart to care. Not even a little. When her happiness was uncontainable, nothing else mattered.

And so she allowed herself this moment—but unlike the last time she'd done so in her mother's room in Reno—when the tears came, they were happy ones, and she gently dabbed them away before taking Audrey's hand and pulling her towards the mingling crowds.

———

Their second date wasn't a date per se, yet Neve firmly marked it down in that column. She was the one keeping score, after all, and how she managed that was her own business. Still, it was a complete change of pace and happened spontaneously. The plan had been for Audrey to take Harlan to a baseball game. A feat that only Audrey could accomplish, since Neve's son was absolutely disinterested in all things athletic. And yet here he was getting ready, even putting on a baseball cap that Audrey had gotten him. Neve all but gaped. Harlan refused to wear hats of any kind. They were 'seriously uncool'.

Audrey just smiled at her wide-eyed expression and fist-bumped Harlan. Then she gave Neve a kiss on the cheek that was just a little bit too close to the corner of her mouth for it to be unintentional.

Neve spent the evening by herself with a glass of wine and a script she was surprisingly taken with.

When Audrey and Harlan returned four hours later, and Neve got the play-by-play from the duo, she felt something blooming in her heart, something that had taken root there a long time ago, and was now magnificent in its splendor and taking up all the space. Taking up everything she had, everything she could give.

"I never loved anyone the way I love you, Audrey Avens."

She hadn't realized she had spoken aloud. The words just left her lips, like breath, like air. Except it was too thick, too heavy, and Neve felt her fingers go numb and her chest constrict. Surely at any moment gravity would do its job, and the confession would inevitably shatter on the marble of her kitchen.

But Audrey simply stepped closer and lifted her chin, gently laying her lips over Neve's, catching the words, catching them before Neve could fall into the all-familiar pattern of retreating into herself.

"Neither have I, Neve Blackthorne." Audrey's palms cupped her cheeks, thumbs tracing the cheekbones. "That night when I left, when you pushed me too far, I knew you were scared then. I knew you were running. I loved you anyway. And I know you're afraid now. I know, because you're standing here, in the middle of your home, and your heart is beating a staccato. I can see the pulse fluttering in your neck. But you're here. And you've said the words out loud. Keep saying them. Always tell them to me."

They turned to the sound of a camera shutter from the doorway to see Harlan standing there, a mischievous grin on his face and his phone in his hand.

"I think I fundraised for my new XBOX, just by taking this picture." He darted away and giggled as Neve made a grab for him, only to be caught in Audrey's agile arms and relieved of his phone in a second.

"With that kind of shot? If I were you, kiddo, I'd be rich by now! Instead, you want a console?" Audrey taunted and held the phone out of his reach before handing it over to Neve.

"I am a trust fund baby, Aud. I don't need to embarrass my parents for money." He and Audrey play-wrestled while Neve looked at the screen in her hand. Yes, love was definitely thicker than air, because it was difficult to breathe, but who needed to anyway?

The image showed them holding each other's face, and the look in their eyes, their expressions... It was love. She sent the photo to herself immediately. Her thumb hovered over the delete button, but then she glanced at Harlan, absolutely enraptured by Audrey, while he stepped closer to Neve and gave her a half hug. And so she allowed him to keep the picture on his phone.

After he had gone to bed, they stayed up, Neve relaxed in her chair on her beach, while Audrey sat at her feet in the sand, throwing a hunk of rope to the ever-agreeable Sheppard, until he, too, tired out and laid by them, gnawing happily on his toy.

"I saw you reading when we came back earlier. You had the most peculiar look on your face." Audrey reclined against her knees and Neve allowed her fingers to dive into Audrey's hair. Burnished mahogany in complete disarray. Her favorite state.

"What kind of look?" It was getting late, and she knew Audrey would leave very soon to drive back to her place in

Silver Lake, the one she'd somehow held on to through all these years. So asking her questions was a sure way to delay her just a couple of minutes more. And Neve cherished every single one of them.

"Like you were meeting an old friend?" Audrey sighed and allowed her head to fall back under Neve's ministrations.

"It's because I think I was?" Neve's fingertips massaged Audrey's scalp, and she could feel tension leaving both of them. "It's a script by an unknown writer. It made its way to me by chance and... I feel as if I wrote it. Or like it was written about me. In any case, it has these strange metaphors about chess and Greek mythology, and it made me *feel*. A sort of serendipity, since my therapist keeps bringing up both chess pieces and Icarus."

Audrey turned her face halfway to her, and Neve saw her smile.

"Is it about a gorgeous, sex-on-heels, corporate executive in front of whom bows the whole of Hollywood? And who is smitten with her utterly graceful former spokesperson?"

They both laughed, and Neve leaned in to kiss Audrey's temple before settling back in her chair, her eyes on the ocean and her hands back in the dark silk of Audrey's hair.

"It's about a woman losing herself." She felt Audrey stiffen under her hands and hurried to quell that fear. "I was lost, dear heart. I'd been lost since I was eight years old, and I was not willing to be found. Until somehow, against all odds, in came you, and you pulled at me and pushed me, until I opened up enough to let you in. I had to fight my demons to do that, and there were dark times in between, but there was no looking back for me. Once you were in my heart, I was found."

Neve could hear Audrey's breath catch, but neither of them said anything for a while, their silence interrupted only by the thrum of the ocean and Shep's snoring.

"You said the script made you feel?" Audrey's voice was still cautious. Neve hated herself a little for that. She leaned over and pressed her cheek to Audrey's head before holding her close, arms wrapped around her shoulders.

"It made me feel seen. But it also made me feel like doing something I haven't done in fifteen years." It was exhilarating just thinking about it. It was freeing.

Audrey's quick turn almost caused their faces to collide, and Neve frowned, only to see the expression of relief in the eyes looking at her. "You're going to direct again?" The pure awe and joy in that beloved voice were everything.

"I just might, darling... I just might."

Their third date was a dinner. Neve didn't care about the place or the cuisine or anything else. She'd spent a week in Europe, missing Audrey like a limb, despite talking to her every day and seeing her face.

True to her word, she didn't attempt any kind of phone- or video hanky-panky. Although, she'd been seriously tempted, with Audrey answering her call one evening wearing nothing but a pair of boxer shorts and a white men's dress shirt that was more unbuttoned than not. Still, Neve had endured stoically. She'd promised Audrey she'd behave, and behaving she had been.

Until they were seated, and Audrey licked her lips and appeared to be paying absolutely no attention to what Neve was saying. Suddenly she had a thought that perhaps she wasn't the one who should have been told to behave. And that perhaps Audrey's choices of attire had been on purpose. And just maybe, she wasn't the only one who was reconsidering this whole 'no sex' charade.

"Not having the paparazzi follow me everywhere in Europe was a nice change of pace..." She let the end of the sentence dangle, waiting for Audrey to say something. Neve knew for a fact that the press only went nuts when the two of them stepped out together and mostly left Audrey alone when she was by herself.

"Hmmm," was the only response she received.

"And I think Grace Bishop would be perfect for my directorial return. *A Whisper Of Solace*, I may have settled on the title. I have to say, changing it forty times was exhausting for both myself and the screenplay writer. You know how I love having the details reflected in the story itself, hence the title, and even the posters have to be perfect and everything finds its home in the narrative…"

Neve narrowed her eyes at her companion. Audrey looked at her, but appeared to be miles away.

"And then I took my clothes off and touched myself."

"What?" Audrey's voice was high-pitched, and her pupils were enormous, almost covering the entirety of that brilliant green. "Sorry, I must've heard you wrong. I need a minute… Bathroom…" she muttered as she dried her mouth with her napkin, despite not having taken a bite of her salad.

Neve allowed her a couple of minutes before settling the check. She had a hunch this dinner was not going to progress past appetizers anyway. Texting her driver to be ready, she followed Audrey to the bathroom. The moment the door closed behind her, two strong hands and a pair of lips were on her. She froze—even expecting this, she still found the force behind it quite shocking—then surrendered entirely to the hot, demanding mouth.

"It's been weeks." Audrey moaned between kisses. "Months." She bit Neve's lower lip. "And I missed you. And you're just so… God, I can't get enough of you."

The kiss turned into something more, something hungry and just a little bit dangerous. Neve whimpered. How she'd missed this. But no matter how much she wanted this, no matter how wet she was, a public bathroom wasn't the place, and she needed one question answered before she could proceed.

"Home... Let's go home." She lifted her head and stared into the almost delirious eyes looking back at her. A breath, another, and one more, and Audrey nodded, gave her another hard, bruising kiss and brushed the collar of her blouse, tsking at some damage she must have inflicted on it.

"It's just a blouse." Neve waved one hand dismissively, the other on Audrey's back as she guided her out of the restaurant and into the waiting car.

"It's not. You look amazing in it." Neve wanted to smile at Audrey's pout. Then Audrey brightened, and her words shot tendrils of desire that had long been dormant everywhere. "Well, I am partial to it, and you look amazing in it, but it would look so much better on the floor."

Neve laughed, and Audrey took her hand as they walked into the house, empty now that Harlan was spending the weekend with Armand.

But instead of taking Audrey upstairs, as she had clearly expected, Neve pulled her towards the back deck and the beach. She shrugged off her shoes as soon as they met the sand and continued walking and tugging on Audrey's hand until they reached the ocean's edge.

Audrey's face was an expression of confusion as Neve looked at her, and she opened her mouth, no doubt to ask what was going on, except Neve had things to say. It felt like she might burst if she didn't share them.

"You could have taken me in the bathroom. You could have taken me in the car. The divider was up, and I pay my driver an exorbitant amount to keep his mouth shut anyway." Audrey gulped audibly at Neve's words. "But you asked me a couple of weeks ago not to distract you, to court you."

Neve looked around. She did not need the weighty pause,

but she felt like the lump in her throat had suddenly gotten too big to talk around.

"You *are* courting me, Neve. And you are amazing at it. But then you are pretty much amazing at everything. Though a bouquet of roses a day is a bit much, don't you think?" Audrey finally smiled, and Neve felt herself smiling back.

"I absolutely do not think so."

"Blue flower, red thorn…" Audrey whispered and bit her lip, her shoulder shaking with rather obvious suppressed laughter.

"You did not just quote that green ogre to me!" Neve actually gasped.

"Ah, but it was the donkey who said that." Audrey allowed herself to laugh freely now, and Neve just watched her and marveled at how beautiful she was, how very much alive. Safe. Hers.

"You are a nerd, Audrey Avens. But you did ask something of me, and it was a little more than to abstain from seducing you which, believe me, I have had a very difficult time doing. But you asked, and I would give you the world if I could."

"I asked?" Audrey seemed confused.

"You asked me to earn your trust. To keep my promises. To not distract you with things we do so very well. To talk. You asked me to be honest with you. Maybe not in so many words, but ask me all those things you did." Neve raised Audrey's hands and kissed her knuckles.

Then she got down on one knee.

"So here is where I tell you that I am absolutely honest with you. And that three dates are where I've reached my absolute limit. You seem to have too. But now is also the time to tell you that I am afraid and I am tired and I made you wait three years, and it is simply unacceptable that either of us wait any longer." She took the ring out of her pocket. The simple band with a row of embedded diamonds in the middle.

"Marry me, Audrey Avens. Share my life. And please make

love to me, because I love you, but sometimes you have the strangest of ideas, dear heart–" She did not finish the sentence with Audrey pulling her to her feet and picking her up and twirling her.

"Yes, yes, you absolutely insufferable, totally infuriating, perfectly imperfect creature that you are! I'll marry you, and I will make love to you 'till you scream, 'till you beg me to stop."

Neve shivered and Audrey laughed. "This 'no sex' thing wasn't a very bright idea, anyway."

And as Audrey laughed yet again, her face alight with happiness, Neve thought not for the very first time, that Dr. Moore was wrong, and that the brightest of all suns was her Audrey, and Neve was the Icarus, and for a glimpse of this warmth, this pure unadulterated exultation, she was ready to burn. In fact, Neve hoped she would never, ever stop.

18

NEVE AND SPACES NO LONGER EMPTY

*T*hings had a tendency of coming full circle. She almost laughed at the pun. Coming... yes, she was very close. And if Audrey's fingers would only circle her a touch harder, just a breath closer to where she needed her most, Neve absolutely would.

"More... God, please... more... harder..."

"Mhmmm... I love it when you beg, Neve."

She felt suspended in this state between her second and third orgasms, one so far away already, the other just within her reach, if only Audrey would roll her hips a little faster and give her those blessed last inches. Instead, the maddening woman was torturing her, playing with her, prolonging this beyond her capabilities to endure. God, she wanted to come more than she wanted to breathe, and she wanted Audrey to make that happen now, right now, damn her. And if she had to beg for it, well, needs must.

"Audrey, please, now!"

The thrust of Audrey's hips did not alter even by a millimeter, the strap-on penetrating her only halfway and at the wrong angle, by far not even close to hitting her in that sweet spot. Audrey's fingers were playing with her as well, but that only complemented the utterly insufficient thrusts, as the fingertips circled around her clit, not touching it, not providing anything close to the relief she was so desperate for. Neve was ready to sob or scream from frustration.

And speaking of those circles she'd started with. Yes, they'd been making love and yes, it was magnificent, but deep down Neve knew Audrey had also still been atoning. Just a little. Just a touch.

After the much-publicized, and now deemed 'legendary,' reconciliation scene at the Gannon Offices, Audrey had been careful. Gentle. Yes, she'd talked a good game and teased mercilessly, but when it came to sex, she'd been tender. The strap had not made an appearance once. Neve had a feeling that after Paris, and then whatever it was they were doing to each other all over the globe, Audrey still felt apprehensive about using it. Despite Neve's assurances that she not only welcomed the damned appendage but relished it and the versatility it allowed them, Audrey never opened the drawer that contained it or any of their other toys.

And so, months later, vanilla had still ruled the day. She had no issues with vanilla. Just being close to Audrey was heaven. Neve didn't lack for anything. She was satisfied and loved within an inch of her life. Often, passionately, yet oh-so-tenderly. As if she was family heirloom china. Not that her family ever had any such crockery to begin with, but that was beside the point.

As time went by, Neve had gotten progressively closer to the end of her tether. In her newfound endeavor to engage in 'healthy communication,' she had attacked the problem head-on. To her great surprise, instead of opening up, Audrey had turned cagey. Well, Neve was having none of that. And neither was Audrey. All those 'immovable object' and 'unstoppable force' metaphors that had haunted them throughout their relationship came roaring back in Neve's mind. They argued.

"Are you saying our sex life has been lacking?" Audrey's eyes narrowed, and she folded her arms in front of herself.

Defensive, dammit. That wasn't where Neve wanted to take this evening at all.

"I am saying you've treated me like I'm some kind of piece of marble on my mother's mantle."

"Marble is actually quite sturdy, and your mother doesn't have any on her mantle. In fact, her whole place is so sparse, I am tempted to bring her all sorts of gaudy tchotchkes, just to see her reaction."

Neve rolled her eyes. Audrey's narrowed even more. "I have no idea what you're talking about."

Well, this would not do at all. Not just defensive, but avoidance to boot. They did not do this anymore.

"I am not fragile, Audrey."

At Neve's gentler tone, Audrey hugged herself tighter and sighed.

"I hurt you back then. You said a lot of things, but I did hurt you, and now that you're mine and we're together, I just don't want to hurt you ever again."

Neve's chest tightened, and she tried to speak around the lump in her throat.

"Darling, if you don't ever want to use any toys, that's fine. I only want you. But if you're hesitating because of misplaced guilt, please don't. I love you, I love us together and I am telling you, again and again, I have wanted everything you've ever given me, every time we were together, making love or straight up—no pun intended—fucking, I loved it. I reveled in it. You make me sexy, you make me invincible, you make me beautiful."

Audrey came closer and laid a hand on her cheek, searching her face, and Neve poured everything she had into that moment, hoping her love, her sincerity, would show and Audrey would see it and find some comfort in it.

Something flickered in those brilliant eyes, and Neve held her breath, waiting. Audrey licked her lips, and the hold on Neve's face firmed. They were inches apart, her own mouth open, ready to be taken, she could feel arousal burning low in her belly. Audrey leaned in... The door to the mansion banged open, and Harlan ran in along with Sheppard, and Armand—carrying their various shopping bags—concluded the procession. Neve had closed her eyes and gnashed her teeth.

Audrey had given her a small peck on the lips and whispered, "Later, love," before going to meet the rowdy gang.

They had tried again the next evening with even less success, as Gustavo and Benedict decided it was a good idea to drop by with a wonderful bottle of Clicquot to celebrate their engagement. Neve was happy for her friend, but she was just about ready to howl.

It was time to change tack. She'd planned like a fiend. Armand took Harlan and had orders so strict, he'd wiggled his eyebrows at her when he picked up the boy earlier that evening. Barnaby's instructions were equally rigid–absolutely nobody was to disturb her. Unlike her ex-husband, her assistant knew better than to show he had any inkling of what Neve had in mind.

She donned a burgundy set of Agent Provocateur, complete with stockings and garters, covered herself with the skimpiest black silk robe, and stepped into a pair of mile-high Manolos she'd bought that very morning, then sprayed a little perfume on her pulse points. She unpacked the brand-new strap-on, its leather harness shining in the low light of the room.

Audrey's eyes almost glazed over when she came into the

bedroom about an hour later, still talking about her day and the interviews she'd conducted for her upcoming piece on women in the military–a collaboration with the acclaimed investigative reporter Jameson Walker. Audrey made a low, deep sound that went right to Neve's core. A shiver ran up her spine and her toes curled.

But Audrey's face still showed hesitation when she turned to her, and Neve simply undid the sash on the robe, letting it fall to the carpet. The hesitation was gone, any trace of guilt was gone, pure unadulterated lust took over. Audrey actually growled and Neve's knees buckled.

They shared a look, and Neve knew that this time, she had gotten through, because she finally saw the veil of the remnants of guilt and doubt lift, and when a sly, slow smile stretched those full lips, Neve knew she was in for it. And it would be glorious.

Audrey took her on the bed on all fours, and Neve felt like she could cry. It was freeing, and it was unbelievable. Rough and passionate and perfect.

Afterwards, as they'd lain in a sweaty heap, caressing each other everywhere they could reach, Neve had turned in Audrey's arms, took hold of the shaft and guided it into herself again and this time, it was face-to-face and slow, and the heady rhythm of long strokes had driven them both out of their minds.

She couldn't quite remember how they'd found themselves in the office on the ground floor hours later. But here they were. And Audrey was driving into her from behind again, with an indolence that Neve found maddening. And it seemed that, despite Neve's entreaties, Audrey was not at all swayed to give her what she wanted.

"Hmmmm, I feel that wasn't so much begging as it was ordering, was it, Neve? Do you still feel you can just snap your fingers and you will get everything you want?"

And God, that voice was doing more things to her than the strap or the fingers or anything else in the world. Low, husky, and entirely too cocky—pun intended—it was sending chills down her spine. Neve knew what usually followed that husky tone. She'd get everything. And she was going to love every single moment of this small death.

Indeed, the maddening hips snapped once, twice, and the silicone was all the way inside her, hitting her exactly where she wanted it, stretching her, giving her everything she craved, making her see stars. The blessed voice didn't stop either, whispering more filth into her ear as Audrey roughly bent her over the desk.

"You do this on purpose, don't you, Neve? Try to order me around so I will inevitably have to punish you by fucking you into whatever piece of furniture is close by..."

God, she loved this game they played with each other, where she'd push Audrey to the limit, tease her or test the edges of her control, until it would snap, and Neve would lose count of the amount of times she'd come and have trouble walking the next day. She also loved being taken just like that, with the absolute illusion that she had no agency and no say, as she relinquished all control, and she loved this woman who gave her everything, every dirty, filthy fantasy she'd ever craved.

She loved Audrey, and while she adored it when they made love, she'd missed being fucked by her. And she was so engrossed in her upcoming climax, it didn't even occur to her that—of all the things to worry about—getting caught should probably have been higher on her list.

And yet, here they were, Audrey bare below the waist with a leather harness around her hips, currently hilt deep in Neve, while Neve herself was spread on the desk with a pile of new screenplays lying right beneath her. She might actually need to burn the damn things, since she'd surely smeared herself all over them.

No doubt Audrey would be so damn smug about how wet she got her and how utterly impatient Neve had become in her arousal that she couldn't wait even a second to throw whatever was on her desk on the floor, instead of coming all over the papers.

What a picture they must have made when the door suddenly opened. Neve just closed her eyes, letting her forehead drop to the surface of the desk with a loud thump. How many times had she obsessed about just this scenario? Hadn't this very thought of being sure they'd get caught started this whole insanity to begin with?

Later, she'd appreciate that as tropes went, beginning and ending the story with the same thought by the protagonist was perhaps not the worst idea. But at the moment, she cared nothing about tropes or protagonists. All she could think was that they were indeed caught. God, why hadn't they been more careful? Why hadn't they locked the door?

"Sheppard, boy! Not now, baby. I'm a bit too busy to play with you right now." The laughter in Audrey's voice was downright insulting. The dog gave an indignant snort and left the room, his claws clacking on the wooden surface.

Just as Neve was ready to breathe a sigh of relief at it just being the dog, horror of horrors, Audrey dissolved into actual laughter, pulling out and sliding to the carpet. The fit of giggles was unstoppable it seemed, and Neve watched in utter disgust as it continued to escalate until Audrey was all but prostrated on the carpet, clutching her abdomen, the glistening dildo standing proudly at attention from her groin. Neve wanted to groan. Or snarl. Maybe Sheppard would understand.

"Are you finished with the hilarity, Audrey?" Neve couldn't quite infuse her own voice with sufficient disappointment. The situation was utterly ridiculous. And somewhat funny. Okay, maybe more than somewhat. If not for her throbbing clit and a ruined orgasm, Neve might have laughed too.

She tried to straighten her bustier, but Audrey just pulled her down to the floor, still laughing, tears now streaming down her face, and Neve smiled, instinctively reaching to wipe the smooth cheeks.

Sometimes it hit her how much she loved this woman, how much emotion was evoked in her when simply watching Audrey do anything at all. Was it a blessing or a curse to be this vulnerable to another? Neve didn't know and frankly didn't care, and so she sat there, touching Audrey's face while the younger woman recovered from the fit of hilarity.

"I'm sorry... sorry... but you have to admit, it's funny. Of all the times we could have gotten caught? In your office? In the limo? At Gustavo's Christmas party? Yet, it's Shep who finally busted us."

Neve just looked at the beloved features, so alive now in mirth and happiness, the bright eyes shining with love and tenderness, the wide glistening mouth, most certainly still tasting of Neve herself, the long skilled fingers that loved her so well.

How had she gotten so lucky? How did she deserve this after everything? She shook her head, dismissing that last thought. She may not have deserved this, but she had signed on the dotted line, and so had Audrey–to have and to hold.

And Neve both had and held, and she was never letting go. Audrey was hers and she would have what was hers just as soon as she crated Sheppard in Harlan's room for the night. With the weekend ahead of them, Neve planned to have and hold for two days, and she didn't really care who knew about it.

Even though their wedding had been a completely intimate affair with just Harlan, both their mothers, and Gustavo serving as best man, they'd still published the announcement in The Post, and to Neve's great surprise the sky didn't fall down.

Everyone knew they were together, especially after their much-publicized series of dates to premieres and benefits and galas.

Between all the publicity and the runaway bride stunt Audrey had pulled, they were gossip fodder for months, and Neve had worked long and hard with her new therapist and with Dr. Moore to stem the tide of panic and anxiety. She felt stronger, better, like she could take on the world. There was something to therapy, she thought. She would never share this with Helena, or she'd be even more insufferable than ever.

And just as absolutely everyone around her had predicted, Tinseltown, in all its splendid, tainted glory, had moved on to the next juicy bit of gossip, and she and Audrey became yesterday's news. Particularly because a year later, they were still going strong, and no salacious gossip was tied to either of their names.

Neve directed A Whisper Of Solace and was steadily working on a connected feature film, A Fragment of Longing–a twisty tale of a Hollywood powerhouse in her late 40s and an exotic dancer who was not at all what she seemed.

With Livia firmly in her corner, loosening the purse strings and green-lighting every single one of Neve's projects, Gannon prospered.

Audrey wrote about her time in Afghanistan, focusing specifically on the impact of the war on American soldiers and the lives of the locals. The book became critically acclaimed, and her newest endeavor with Jameson Walker would absolutely be even more so.

So they lived in Malibu, in the house on the ocean shore, and raised Harlan who was over the moon about the whole deal, because Audrey was surprisingly good at all sorts of video games and baseball and was one of the cool moms at his school, unlike Neve herself who did not fit any of the above bills. Neve counted her blessings.

And she knew that her blessings were about to multiply,

just by observing Audrey's speculative look at Neve's naked thighs, generously marked by her wife's earlier attention, with the bites slowly turning red. Audrey licked her lips and pushed Neve to the carpet, possessively spreading her legs and taking a first long lick. Neve's breath caught on a long moan.

Oh yes, blessings indeed.

ACKNOWLEDGMENTS

The first words of this story were written in February 2020 and were, in fact, the first ones I have ever put on paper.

The idea blossomed and found form in a fanfiction story published in those early days of the pandemic. Despite wrapping it up in a matter of months, the story stayed with me. It felt unfinished, it felt like it could do and say so much more. And so 50,000 words of the original turned into 115,000 words of A Whisper Of Solace just so Neve Blackthorne could find her true voice.

I was very fortunate to have my hand held throughout this journey. And I have many thanks to give.

To Diana Kane. She is the one who walked with me through my fledgling attempts to put this story on paper. She encouraged, she cajoled, she pushed, and she praised in that no-nonsense style of hers, that made "yeah, it's okay," feel like the highest of accolades. For putting me on this path, DK, I will always be grateful. Thank you.

To Em. You know that neither The Headmistress nor A Whisper Of Solace would've been written without you being with me. At times being there instead of me, when I was struggling. There aren't many words that I haven't said to you, said often and maybe not as eloquently as you deserve. Thank you.

To Jo. For being the steadfast presence on whom I can always count for last minute encouragement, a pair of eyes, a kind word, an email full of praise and support. I may not be as responsive as you deserve, especially when I'm in the weeds, but I know you're there for me and I appreciate you. Thank you.

To you, the reader. I have an enormous amount of gratitude to everyone who has ever picked up any of my books. Whether you read and liked them, or closed them and shook your head, I appreciate you taking a chance on me and my work. It means the world. Thank you.

Where does the road take us from here?

Well, several characters from A Whisper of Solace demand to have their own story told and my idea book is overflowing. The 80s among the bohemian narrow Parisian streets? A return to Tainted Tinseltown? A couture and heartbreak drama in Italy? Or a visit to a kingdom and a princess that don't even exist?

Watch this space...

ABOUT THE AUTHOR

Milena McKay is a Lambda Literary and Golden Crown Literary Society award-winning author.

Milena is a wlw romance fanatic, currently splitting her time between trying to write a novel and succumbing to the temptation of reading another fanfic story.

When not engrossed in either writing or reading, she runs and occasionally practices human rights law.

She is a cat whisperer who wears four-inch heels for work while secretly dreaming of her extensive Converse collection. Milena would live on blueberries and lattes if she could. She can recite whole episodes of The West Wing by heart and quote Telanu's "Truth and Measure" in her sleep.

Her love for Cate Blanchett knows no bounds.

www.milenamckay.com

ALSO BY MILENA MCKAY

The Delicate Things We Make

The Perfect Match: A Valentine's Day Novella

The Headmistress

Printed in Dunstable, United Kingdom